True Thomas

Nigel Tranter

CORONET BOOKS
Hodder and Stoughton

British Library C.I.P.

Tranter, Nigel
  True Thomas.
  I. Title
  823'.912[F]   PR6070.R34

ISBN 0 340 32815 0

Printed and bound in Great Britain for Hodder and Stoughton Paperbacks, a division of Hodder and Stoughton Ltd., Mill Road, Dunton Green, Sevenoaks, Kent TN13 2YA (Editorial Office: 47 Bedford Square, London WC1B 3DP) by Clays Ltd., St Ives plc.

TRUE THOMAS

"My lord—why? What folly is this?" the newcomer demanded.

Alexander Stewart turned. "Ah, Learmonth—you," he said. "That is the fourth. The fourth coble to go. Two going, two returning. Only one has won back safely. It is damnable . . .!"

"But—what, my lord? What are they at? It is madness. Small boats in that sea . . .!"

"That large vessel, Learmouth, the merchanter, carries all the spoil, the treasure, gathered by Hakon on this entire venture. All the gold and siller and gear, stolen from a hundred churches and halls and towns. That is what," the Steward declared.

"Treasure! Gold! Is that what now concerns you? Is that what those men are dying for? The realm in direst danger, and siller your concern! We believed you to be in battle with the Norwegians, not, not . . ."

"So we were, man—so we were. They have retired now, yonder—we drove them off." Stewart pointed over to Cumbrae island. "A pity to let notable treasure sink to the bottom."

"Pity that men should die before your eyes for it!" Thomas returned strongly.

Principal Characters

In Order of Appearance

THOMAS LEARMONTH OF ERCILDOUNE: Vassal and esquire of the Earl of Dunbar. Poet and predictor, known as Thomas the Rhymer.

ALEXANDER THE THIRD: King of Scots.

HENRY THE THIRD: King of England.

PATRICK, 7th EARL OF DUNBAR: Great Scots noble, kinsman of the King.

EDWARD PLANTAGENET, EARL OF CHESTER: Elder son of Henry, later Edward the First.

MARGARET PLANTAGENET: Queen of Alexander.

CHRISTIAN BRUCE, COUNTESS OF DUNBAR: Patrick's wife and sister of Robert Bruce of Annandale.

LADY BETHOC: Eldest daughter of Dunbar.

ALAN DURWARD, EARL OF ATHOLL: Great Scots noble. High Justiciar and Hereditary Door-Ward.

SIR DAVID LINDSAY OF LUFFNESS AND BYRES: Former Regent of Scotland.

SIR JOHN COMYN, LORD OF BADENOCH AND LOCHABER: Head of the house of Comyn.

BISHOP GAMELIN OF ST. ANDREWS: Primate and Chancellor.

SIR ROBERT BRUCE, LORD OF ANNANDALE: Great noble, later known as The Competitor.

ALEXANDER COMYN, EARL OF BUCHAN: High Constable. Half-brother of John Comyn.

LORD PATRICK (PATE): Eldest son of Dunbar.

LADY GELIS: Second daughter of Dunbar.

LORD ALEXANDER: Third son of Dunbar.

LORD JOHN: Second son of Dunbar.

EWAN MACDOUGALL, LORD OF LORN: Highland chief, sometimes styled King of the South Isles.

MARJORY, COUNTESS OF CARRICK: Countess in her own right, married to Adam MacDuff of Kilconquhar.

ALEXANDER fitz ALAN or STEWART: The High Steward.

MAGNUS OLAFSSON, KING OF MAN: Son of Olaf the Morsel.

ALEXANDER, PRINCE OF STRATHCLYDE: Heir to the Scots throne.

CARDINAL-DEACON OTTOBUONI OF FIESCI: Papal Legate.

PRIOR NICHOLAS OF FAILL: Trinitarian friar.

SIR REGINALD LE CHIEN OF INVERUGIE: Thane of Formartine and Sheriff of Banff.

LORD FERGUS COMYN OF LOCHINDORB: Brother to the Earl of Buchan.

SIR MICHAEL SCOTT OF BALWEARIE: Famous philosopher and scientist. Known as The Wizard.

CANON BAIAMUNDO DE VICCI: Papal envoy, usually called Bagimond.

PRINCESS MARGARET OF SCOTLAND : Daughter of Alexander, later Queen of Norway.

MASTER THOMAS CHARTERIS: Chancellor of Scotland.

ROBERT BRUCE, YOUNGER OF ANNANDALE: Second husband of Countess of Carrick, and father of Robert Bruce, later King.

YOLANDE DE DREUX, DUCHESS OF BRITTANY: Daughter of the Count de Dreux and widow of Duke of Brittany.

Historical Note

This is a novel about Alexander the Third, King of Scots, last of the old Celtic line, and Thomas Learmonth of Ercildoune, known as Thomas the Rhymer or True Thomas, set in the second half of the thirteenth century. Alexander's story is straightforward enough, however dramatic; but True Thomas is a very different kettle-of-fish, taxing the writer's imaginative abilities as well as the usual diligence in research. For Thomas Learmonth although a genuine historical figure, renowned far outwith Scotland, and indeed probably that nation's first major poet, is no easy character to delineate, with great gaps in the record, legend ever accruing and the supernatural inevitably liable to take over. So I have had to guess and invent frequently, but with, I hope, informed and reasonable invention — the prophecies at least I have not had to improvise; and my researches in Aberdeenshire and the north-east, for other books, have produced useful by-products in this respect.

I have always made a point of keeping my historical novels as factual as possible. In this instance I crave the reader's patient forbearance.

N.T.

Part One

1

When the Lion of Alba trips a measure,
The foxes watching take their pleasure:
But when the Lion makes man's estate,
Then let those watchers watch their gait!

Thomas Learmonth of Ercildoune dipped his quill into the little silver inkhorn he always carried at his belt, beside the dirk, examined the table-top to ensure that there was no spilt wine, spread his paper on a dry patch, and scratching out the word foxes, wrote jackals above it.

The young English esquire sitting on his right, leaned over to peer. "What are you?" he demanded. "A clerk apeing the honest man? Or an honest man smitten with a clerkly sickness?"

"What ails you at clerks, friend?" the Scot asked. "Because *you* cannot read nor write, it does not mean that those who can are inferior beings!" He had to raise his normally quiet voice to be heard above the din, the clash of cymbals and loud music, the thud of feet, the shouts and the skirled laughter.

"I make my mark with sword and lance and spur, lame man!" the other asserted loftily. "Not with a goose's feather! But then, to be sure, *I* am no cripple!"

Thomas Learmonth's grey eyes lifted from his paper to stare levelly at his neighbour at the esquires' table — and something in that strangely piercing steady glare from one so seemingly inoffensive, caused the speaker to draw back involuntarily.

"I will meet you tomorrow with sword and lance, wherever you say, Englishman — and make *you* the cripple, 'fore God!" he said, his soft voice as even as his glance. "Name you but the place and time."

"Lord — not so hot, man!" the other esquire jerked. "I meant you no hurt."

"Then guard your fool tongue better, sirrah!"

"I would meet you tomorrow with pleasure, Scot, and teach you your lesson. But my lord of Surrey, and the King's Grace also, would not allow it, you Scots being guests here." The young man ostentatiously turned his shoulder to Learmonth, to talk to his less prickly neighbour on the other side.

Thomas smiled gently. He went back to his paper, crossed out the word take and substituted grasp, in his rhyme.

When he raised his eyes again, it was automatically to fix them on the big young man, perhaps a couple of years younger than himself, who was flinging himself with such enthusiasm into the dance, there in the centre of the great hall of London Tower, leaping and skipping with a super-abundance of verve and energy, yet with remarkable grace considering his height and build, to the breathless alarm and disarray of his flushed and all but collapsing partner. She had been lively enough at the start but now had a glazed look about her eyes, had her feet whirled off the floor much of the time, her skirts flying immodestly. Her low-cut gown was unfit for the strain, so that one full and shapely, pink-tipped breast had escaped, to flounce about spiritedly, whilst the other looked ready to join it at any moment. The Lady Alicia de Warenne had not quite realised what she was taking on when she had agreed to partner Alexander mac Alexander mac William, King of Scots, Thomas Learmonth's Lion of Alba. It was a Scots dance, of course, of typical vigour; and Alexander was, as it were, showing the Lion flag.

By no means for the first time that evening, Learmonth turned his glance up towards the dais-table at the head of the hall, where the lofty ones sat, wine-cups in hand — such as were not fallen in drunken sleep over the spilled contents. There were a number of gaps at that long table, mainly where Queen Eleanor and the more modest ladies had retired. Few of the English great ones thought to risk or demean themselves with dancing, especially Scots dancing. In the central chair, Henry Plantagenet, third of his name and style, was certainly not asleep. He was watching his son-in-law's cavortings set-faced — and although not a strong face, when set it could look not so much formidable as dangerous. Most clearly he was not amused. But then, to be sure, Queen Margaret of Scotland, his daughter, lay upstairs, brought to bed belatedly the day before of a daughter, a first child; and this banquet was to celebrate the event — that, and to mark the proud father's departure, the day following, for the Scotland from which, as he had made it abundantly evident to all, he had been absent for too long.

The lame esquire applied pen to paper again:

> *Henry of Aquitaine has leopards three,*
> *Let Scots keep all in sight:*
> *While two in front their smile you see,*
> *The one to the rear can fight.*

He shook his head over the word fight, and changed it to bite.

A hand clapped his bent shoulder. "Rhyming again, Thomas? I vow you never weary of it. What are you scratching this time?"

The young man looked up to see his own lord standing behind him, Patrick, seventh Earl of Dunbar and March. "Better scratching than being scratched, my lord! When there are claws all around." He pointed with his quill towards their dancing monarch. "You could tell *him* so!"

"My royal cousin might not thank me, I think. What ails you at him, man? I would say that we should bless him for providing such bonnie sight of the Lady Alicia to gladden our eyes!"

"He has a wife and new-born babe upstair — and a glowering goodsire at yonder table, my lord."

"Aye — well, there is maybe something in that. But, see you, a man wed to a mouse deserves a loosened rein now and again!" Undoubtedly the Earl Patrick would not have spoken so, even in mixed metaphor, had he not been just somewhat drink-taken — like so many another present. Margaret Plantagenet, Henry the Third's daughter, was scarcely an exciting personality. She had been married for ten years and this was the first child — but most of those years she had been forbidden to cohabit with Alexander, on her father's stern orders. They had been wed, admittedly at only the age of ten.

The wild music tailed off and the dance ended. Alexander led his dizzy, gasping partner back to her place, helpfully assisting her to tuck her heaving, overflowing bosom back approximately into its covers. Then, seeing Earl Patrick, he came strolling over, laughing cheerfully and waving to plaudits right and left. He was a good-looking young man, of features rather too squared and rugged to be handsome, with curling fair hair, very blue eyes, a short straight nose and strong jawline — not notably regal-looking to be the representative of the oldest royal line in Christendom, besides which the Plantagenets were as jumped-up-yesterday men.

Thomas Learmonth rose to his feet.

"You were not dancing, Pate," the King cried. "Shame on you to leave it all to me! Or are you too drunk, man?"

"Not so, Sire. Only sparing my strength and agility for later. I can think of better places to jig a woman up and down than in front of half England — and your royal goodsire!"

"Ha! Have you someone in mind, Cousin? Who? You, see you, are situated otherwise than am I. *Your* wife is four hundred miles away!"

"And her father not sitting frowning yonder!"

Alexander looked towards the dais-table and grinned. "Henry frowns even in his sleep, I swear! Perhaps because he grows old and fat and cannot dance any more. If ever he did! His frowns will not hurt me." The King glanced down. "And what are *you* at, Thomas Rhymer? Ever with that pen in your hand." He reached out to take the paper, and read it. "Ha, the Lion of Alba trips a measure, does he! You mock your liege lord, sir! And . . . makes man's estate? Aye — some might be wise to watch their gait, indeed! Some even who sit and watch and pen treason rhymes, eh?" But he punched the lame esquire affectionately on the shoulder. "Sit, man — sit. Lord — I need wine after all that skipping! Come, Pate."

Somewhat apprehensively the Earl Patrick followed his royal kinsman up to the dais, towards Alexander's seat on his father-in-law's right hand.

"Thirsty work, dancing," the young monarch observed, reaching for his half-full goblet. "Our Scots ones call for a deal of wine!"

"Better less wine and more discretion, Alexander," Henry said thinly. "That was . . . unedifying."

"I edified Alicia de Warenne, at least!" his son-in-law gave back, smiling. He looked along the table to where the lady's father, the Earl of Surrey, sprawled asleep. "If men danced more, Sire, they might plot less!" And his glance switched to the other side of Henry, to the left, where at a remove of three seats, two of them vacant, a notably handsome and very tall man sat, young also but stern of expression, mouth downturning, as he toyed with his wine-cup. "Eh, Edward? *You* should dance, man. Forbye, it is good for the liver and spleen!"

The man addressed inclined his noble-seeming head. Edward, by-named Longshanks because of his height, Earl of Chester, was Henry's elder son and heir to the throne, Lord of Gascony and known as the First Knight of Christendom. Aged but twenty-three despite his appearance and reputation, he did not get on with his father, strong man versus weak — indeed he had only recently been accepted back at Court, after leading a revolt against Henry's rule. Alexander of Scotland found his brother-in-law arrogant in the extreme, and was not the man to swallow it.

"Should you not go see your wife?" Henry suggested, ignoring the reference to his son. "Lest she weary."

"She will be asleep by this." Alexander shrugged. "But I will go . . ."

He moved over to the dais door, and out, followed by the Earl Patrick. And seeing them go, Thomas Learmonth rose and limped after them — for it was not acceptable that kings and great ones should go around unattended. He was the Earl's esquire, not one of the King's; but Alexander de

Lindsay was involved with a young woman at the bottom of the hall, with eyes for none other meantime, and the only Scots royal page present had been asleep for an hour and more. It was that sort of banquet.

Up two flights of the winding tower-stairs the trio came to a firelit bedchamber. A lady-in-waiting rose from the fireside, to curtsy to Alexander. Putting finger to lips she nodded towards the great bed and then to the little cot beside it, and tiptoed from the room. Thomas stood aside to let her pass, but remained within the doorway, the Earl Patrick moving only a little further into the chamber.

Alexander went to look down at his queen. And, as often happened, his heart went out to her in a brief surge of emotion. It was nothing so fine as love or devotion; more pity than anything else, and a sort of rueful affection, for one who, like himself, had been caught in a trap early on, but who *unlike* himself had never managed to get out of it — and never would. She lay there now, plain-faced, lumpish — although admittedly less lumpish than she had been for months — hair sticking to her moist brow, lips parted and snoring just a little, her arms outside the bedclothes with fingers curling like a child's. In fact she looked childlike altogether; but then, she always did, a rather bewildered, frightened and not very attractive child — Margaret Plantagenet, Queen of Scotland since the age of ten, now plunged into alarming motherhood.

Shaking his head helplessly, Alexander moved round to the cot, to peer down at the tiny creature therein. It was almost with a shock that he realised that the eyes were open wide and looking up at him in an unblinking stare, as though questioning. Equally questioning, the man stared back at this strange object, his own offspring. And Margaret's, of course. Eyes, round, dark, utterly unabashed, a new person, one day old and somehow part of himself, a mystery — much more interesting indeed than the woman who in pain and dread had given birth to it. Was that unkind? A princess of Scotland. The pity that it was not a son, to be sure. But there was probably time enough for that.

The child gave a choking cough, and a white flood of milk came smoothly out of the diminutive mouth in the most casual fashion, whilst the stare continued wide, unconcerned.

The man drew back in distaste and alarm, prepared to call for the lady-in-waiting, the nurse, anybody in this emergency. But the choking sound had awakened the Queen, who sat up, blinking.

"Sick!" the King cried. "Ill! Spewing all over. What to do? What to do?"

"It is nothing, nothing," Margaret said, and actually smiled, she who was no smiler. Perhaps for once she felt herself to be the sure one, the assured, not at a loss or inadequate. "Babes do that. She will be well enough." She sank back on her pillow, and the more normal anxious note of questioning came back into her voice, as her glance darted from her husband to the two men near the door. "Is, is aught amiss? What brings you? All is well, Alex . . .?"

"Yes, yes. I but came to see how you fared. Nothing is wrong. I did not mean to wake you. It grows late. I will be for my own couch soon now. For I have decided to ride tomorrow . . ."

"Tomorrow! But . . . you were not to go until the following day. You said so." That was all but a wail.

"Aye — but I had better be gone. Every day counts, see you. I have been away too long, as it is, God knows! So much awaits me in Scotland."

"But one day will make no difference, Alex. You said the day following."

"It is better so. Each day I come nearer to blows with Edward and his arrogant crew. I have had enough of them, of all here. And, and . . ." He swallowed the rest of that. "Besides, what difference does it make? You are well enough here, in your father's house. Your mother near. They dote on you. And you will come north when you are fully well, and the child can travel. It is best so. I shall ensure with King Henry that you come within forty days."

She bit a trembling lower lip and turned her head away.

Seeing it, he shook his fair head, frowning, then leaned forward. "See you, lass, it will not be grievous. We do not know what I shall be going back to, in Scotland. There could well be trouble. Indeed, I intend that there shall be! I have scores to settle! No place for you and the bairn meantime. Later will be time enough."

She gulped back a sob.

"We shall start as early as we may, in the morning. But sun-up will not be before nine hours. I shall see you before we go. Sleep again, Margaret."

"I . . . I shall not sleep now, I think."

Lips tight, he was turning away when, on impulse, he stepped back, to stoop and briefly kiss her moist brow, before striding for the door. "A plague!" he jerked, as he passed the other two — but he did not amplify that as he headed for the stairway.

At the turnpike he paused. "Go back to the hall if you wish," he said. "I shall not. Lest . . . I fall further from grace! I go up to my own chamber. Enough is sufficient! We eat early in the morning, mind. Rise betimes. See that all know it and are ready. A goodnight to you. Both."

Bowing, the other two eyed the royal feet taking the turnpike steps two at a time. Then the earl turned to the esquire.

"Many to be warned of this early start tomorrow, Thomas," he said. "I have a little matter to attend to. Elsewhere. See you to it. And — tell that fool page of mine to go to his bed. Sleep well."

Thomas Learmonth watched his lord hurry off cheerfully downstairs — whilst he would have to spend the next hour and more finding, rousing and spoiling the sport of all the Scots party, to inform them of the King's decision — to no increase of his own popularity, undoubtedly. One day he would pen a rhyme on the facility of the great ones to make uncomfortable decisions and then pass on the carrying-out to others.

*　　　*　　　*

Like penned greyhounds released, the Scots raced northwards after the weeks of cramping inaction in London whilst they had awaited the birth of the monarch's first child. Seventy superbly mounted men, they pounded the wet and slippery roads and tracks of an English February in a splatter of mud and clods and the splash of surface-water, the quaking of mires and the spray of fords, lashing and spurring their beasts on and on. Alexander aimed to cover fifty miles a day throughout — no mean target for even the finest horse-flesh and the toughest riders, in winter conditions.

Thomas Learmonth at least held none back. Spurred on by his lameness he had made himself one of the best horsemen in the kingdom. He rode with the other personal esquires immediately behind the King and the great lords and before the knights, pages and men-at-arms.

They went by the easterly route, by Cambridge and skirting the fen country, so that they could pass at least two of the nights in the far-flung domains of the great Honour of Huntingdon, so much larger than the mere shire of that name, lands spreading indeed over no less than eleven counties, the rich English earldom which the Scottish crown had inherited through the marriage of David the First, Alexander's great-great-grandsire, with Matilda, Countess of Huntingdon in her own right, a goodly heritage although productive of much discord between the two kingdoms.

In these southern, level lands, mud and marsh and forest were the principal sources of delay; but the further north they went the more hilly grew the terrain, with river fords becoming ever the greater problem and major detours frequently necessary. Moorland often made for better riding than did woodland and cultivated land; but winter torrents were the bane of travellers, even spirited ones.

As they neared Scotland something of the high spirits and feelings of carefree release gradually faded. However anxious they were to reach home none, even the least informed could not fail to realise that this homecoming might prove less than joyful in some respects, fraught with tension. Alexander was bold, eager, but the forces he would be challenging were strong and had long been predominant.

The King's father and predecessor, Alexander the Second, had gained no heir from his first marriage and by his second had left only the boy of seven to fill the throne. And Scotland then, as always, required a strong hand at the helm. In the subsequent power vacuum two great parties had developed, hating each other and each seeking to control the child monarch and so the realm. It was personalities rather than policies which dominated these factions, although one became known as the English party, not because it in any way favoured English domination, but because it more frequently tended to call in English Norman help to aid it. It might have been expected to represent the Norman families in the Scottish nobility and ruling class, as against the native Celtic, for many Normans had been introduced by that great reforming king, David the First, four reigns before. But this was not so, the Normans having almost without exception adopted their new nationality entirely, inter-marrying with the old race, so that they looked upon themselves almost as thoroughly Scots as anyone else; and there were just as many Celtic lords in the 'English' faction as in their opponents. But the English party *had* approved of the marriage of their child liege-lord with Henry the Third's daughter, and having been in power at the time, had been able to see it through. Anyhow, between these two sections of the land's powerful ones, the boy-King had suffered a grim childhood and youth, always the prisoner and chattel of one side or the other, the real rule being wielded by the ascendant faction, who appointed the Regent. On his eighteenth birthday, Alexander had become rather more than a mere cipher, able to assume a theoretical but severely limited authority. But now he was come to within a month or so of his full age — and he intended to demonstrate who now ruled in Scotland.

The hard-riding cavalcade dropped down from the Northumberland moors by Redesdale and Carter Fell to cross into Scotland down Jed Water and so to the Teviot. Where Teviot joined Tweed, on the evening of the seventh day out, they came to the royal castle of Roxburgh, where Alexander decided to spend a day or two sending out summonses to all the lords and chiefs and officers of his kingdom to assemble before him at Dunfermline in Fothrif in two weeks' time for a Great Council, under pain of sternest royal displeasure, fast couriers to be sent out far and near. The Earl Patrick of Dunbar and March elected to ride on the seventeen miles further to his castle at the Earlstoun of

Ercildoune, where was his wife and family. Thomas Learmonth, naturally, went with him.

Thomas in fact had his own little stone tower on the River Leader's banks amongst the green Borderland hills, the small lairdship he had inherited from his father, a mere half-mile from the Earl's castle. But there was nothing for him there save a sour old housekeeper and her brother, his steward of small acres. His real home for long had been at the castle itself, where he was something of a favourite with the Countess and her children, his ability to make rhymes, tell stories and play the lute ever popular — although the frequency with which his foretellings and presagings, even casually made, were alleged to come true, caused him to be eyed a little askance at times.

The travellers were warmly welcomed after their long absence of almost three months. The Countess was a cheerful, uncomplicated creature now in early middle years, with no pretensions to beauty but a sufficiency of energy and broad acres to make up for it. She had been the Lady Christian Bruce, sister of the present Robert Bruce, Lord of Annandale, daughter of the third Lord and Isabel of Huntingdon, niece of both Malcolm the Fourth and William the Lyon. She certainly gave herself no airs on account of her royal blood. Her children took after her, so that Ercildoune and Dunbar Castles were apt to resound with noise and laughter. Unlike his monarch, the Earl Patrick was well content with his marriage, however roving of eye when abroad.

There was one of the Cospatrick family however whose welcome was rather different, just as she herself was different — they were known as the Cospatricks although, in fact being descendants of the royal house of Scotland, they bore no surname, Cospatrick being the traditional Christian name of the head of the house, Earl Patrick himself having been so baptised although he chose to drop the prefix. The Lady Bethoc was different in that, at fifteen years, she was already of a glowing dark beauty, where the others were plain, quiet where they were noisy, thoughtful instead of headstrong. And she thought that Thomas Learmonth was wonderful, and showed it quite often — to that young man's appreciation but slight embarrassment, and her family's frank amusement. Now, after receiving a smacking kiss from the Countess and sundry hugs and salutations from the other youngsters, he was granted a much softer and more lingering embrace from the eldest daughter of the house, which left him considerably affected although he sought not to show it. Practically penniless esquires, however gifted in odd ways, had to watch their steps.

That evening, around the great fire in the private hall, it was Thomas rather than the Earl who recounted the ongoings and adventures of the King's party in the South, improving on it all here and there perhaps, as is the way of born storytellers, for the delectation of his wide-eyed audience, especially the deep dark eyes of the Lady Bethoc — although he carefully omitted any references to his betters' need for feminine consolations when away from home.

Two days later they were joined by the King again as he came up Lauderdale on his way to the Scotwater, Queen Margaret's Ferry and Dunfermline.

The fact that the Council-of-State — it was that rather than a parliament, which would have required forty days' notice — had been called for Dunfermline, in Fothrif, might have served as a warning to all concerned that a new situation was about to develop. In the past dozen years, councils and a few parliaments had been called for wherever was most convenient and secure for whoever was Regent or in power at the time, however awkward for others; and the young King had willy-nilly had to go there to give authenticity to the proceedings, however dumb he had to remain throughout — for the Great Council, which had grown out of the ancient Celtic High Council of the *ri* or mormaors, the lesser kings of Scotland, required the presence of the Ard Righ or High King, to be effective. Never, in all those years of Alexander's minority, had such been held at Dunfermline, Malcolm Canmore's small, stark palace above the Forth, which would have been laughably inadequate for the safety of the ruling caucus and the housing of the great hosts of men-at-arms the lords always brought with them. The great fortress-castles of Stirling, Edinburgh, Dumbarton and the like were the favourite venues, Dunfermline unthinkable. The present royal summons sent out from Roxburgh had stipulated that no lord, baron or bishop was to appear before the monarch bringing a train of more than a score was equally significant. Thomas, for one, decided that it would be interesting to see how the magnates reacted.

2

The royal party took up residence in the little castle-palace beside Queen Margaret's great minster — Malcolm the Third had been no man for palaces before he married the sainted Margaret Atheling. It had been Alexander's real home, for his mother, the Frenchwoman Marie de Coucy, Alexander the Second's second queen, had it as her jointure-house and retained it when her husband died ten years after their marriage, to bring up her son there — when he and she were not in the grip of one or other of the warring lords.

In the tiny palace they waited. Alexander made no attempt to pack Dunfermline with his own or Earl Patrick's men — he had few enough that he could call his own anyway. Nor did he seek to provide accommodation for the other visitors — let them find their own, he said. This was, hopefully, the beginning of a new chapter in the nation's story. Let them all discover it.

As might have been expected, Alan Durward, Earl of Atholl, was the first to arrive. Equally predictable, he had ignored the decree about no more than twenty men, and came with a tail of fully ten times that number. A grizzled veteran of the ancient Celtic stock, hereditary Doorward to the High King, as his name implied, for long he had been the most powerful man in Scotland, married to one of the late monarch's illegitimate daughters, and therefore Alexander's brother-in-law. He was at present High Justiciar. When the King heard that he had arrived with this great train, however, he refused to see him, announcing that if his illustrious good-brother cared to send nine-tenths of his men-at-arms back to Atholl or wherever they came from, he would be glad to grant him audience; if not, he must withdraw from Dunfermline town to wherever he found convenient, not to return until the first day of the Nones of March, set for the Council, and then only with the permitted number of supporters.

This, of course, set not only Durward and Dunfermline by the ears but all around, and, with time enough to spread the tale quite far afield, to set the land ringing. Furiously Atholl marched off, vowing retribution.

That was only the start of it. William Earl of Mar arrived next, and without rivalling the Atholl contingent he did bring fully one hundred men with him. Not a Comyn himself, he was married to one of that ambitious and potent family, and firmly in their camp — the main opposition to Durward and the English faction. Formerly de Comines, they now cut the widest swathe in all Scotland. This earl was likewise refused audience, and banished to the Dunfermline hinterland. Others followed in quick succession, and only those accompanied by twenty or less of a train were admitted to the palace — and these were few indeed. In thirteenth-century Scotland men who could afford it rode abroad well protected.

In the King's own company there was disquiet and apprehension. All this was quite outwith anyone's experience, and they feared the worst. Earl Patrick especially was perturbed. He himself had long been a colleague of Durward's in the English faction, his mother being another of Alexander the Second's illegitimate daughters. He knew how fierce and obstinate his Durward uncle could be. He also well knew the power of the Comyns. His remonstrations with the King were given short shrift, however. The amiable and normally friendly Alexander appeared to have developed a new character, awkward as it was unexpected. Not that

Thomas Learmonth was surprised, telling [ ] [ ] that he had been expecting some such confrontati[ ] though he had not foreseen the style and scope of it. [ ] iege lord had been holding in a vehement and dec[ ] de to his nature for years. Now it seemed that the [ ] vas to be loosened.

Even True Thomas forbore to prophesy what the result would be for them all, for Scotland.

One magnate who turned up with a mere twenty-five men, and was permitted to join the royal entourage in consequence, was Sir David Lindsay of Luffness and the Byres, in Lothian, a quietly authoritative man of middle years, who had in fact been Regent of the realm for a period just before Alexander reached the age of eighteen and the regency automatically lapsed. The young monarch had always got on well with him, better than with any other of his masters in those grim years, although Lindsay was a difficult man to know, being stiff and undemonstrative. But he had a reputation for honesty, was not ambitious like so many, and was only loosely connected with the English faction, largely through his cousinship with the Earl Patrick.

"My lord," Alexander said to him, "you alone of my great lords have seen fit to obey my command that none bring more than a score of armed men to this Council. I commend your judgment."

"I thank you, my lord King. But . . . would that I could commend yours, Sire, in this matter," the older man returned bluntly. "I fear that you will have given offence to many on whom your realm must rely. Is there sense in that?"

"There is, yes. As they will find out."

"But, Sire — always they must have their tails behind them. Tails which Your Grace will find useful, necessary, when it comes to warfare."

"This is not warfare, my lord. This is a peaceful occasion, the first Great Council of my *rule*, though not of my reign. No need for any armed strength. *You* understand that. Why not others?"

Lindsay had no answer to that. Obliquely however he made his point. "This Council, Sire — some may have been ul as to its purpose. Suspicious. It is usual for such to be called on forty days' notice, as is a parliament. And called by the Chancellor, not by direct royal summons."

"But there is no Chancellor, my friend."

"Eh . . .?" Lindsay stared. Even Earl Patrick swallowed, whilst others present blinked their surprise. Bishop Gamelin of St. Andrews, the Primate, a strong Comyn supporter — indeed illegitimate son of a Comyn himself — had been Chancellor or chief minister of the realm for years.

"The worthy bishop, Sir David, is relieved of his office. As are all other officers of state — even if they do not yet know it! We make a new start. Now that I am of full years. All is changed. I take the rule that is mine. And appoint such ministers as I judge best. Of whom Bishop Gamelin will not be one!"

"But, my lord King — the Council? It will have to approve. And it will require a chairman. Your Highness presides, yes. But the business is conducted by the Chancellor. Until then, at least, you must . . ."

"Until then, *you* will conduct the business, Sir David! Act Chancellor. Who better?"

"Me? Sire — no! Not me. I am no clerk. It is not for such as myself . . ."

"I say that it is. You, who were Regent. And are now Chamberlain. You know all that is required, all the procedure. And you are honest — as are not all! It is my royal command, my friend — you will conduct the business. Under my guidance. Say no more of it . . ."

With only one day more to go before the Council, the most significant figure of all put in his appearance — John Comyn, Lord of Badenoch and Lochaber, Justiciar of Galloway, known as the Red Comyn. If as an individual he was younger, less powerful and dominating than Alan Durward of Atholl, he was at this juncture more influential, as chief of all the Comyns. It was extraordinary how the former de Comines, of no great standing in Normandy, had in the space of a century, from being modest adventurers in the service of David the First, by most judicious intermarriage with Celtic heiresses, sheer aggression and a notable ability to adapt themselves, become the most powerful family in the land, more Scottish than the Scots, with all the trappings of ancient clanship. This Red John, their chief, had delayed his arrival, and now with his younger half-brother, Alexander, Earl of Buchan, made appearance with the scrupulously correct number of twenty supporters. But he made his point adequately, nevertheless — for every one of that score was, not a man-at-arms nor even a household officer, but a full, belted knight, most of them lairds of large substance. Only the Comyn could have done this, brought what amounted to his own court with him, in the guise of a mere bodyguard — and the gesture was not lost on any, the monarch included. King Alexander could not have produced the like. Moreover the Red Comyn casually let it be known that he could have trebled his knightly tail with ease. He did not seek to take up his residence in the crowded palace either; but, after briefly and coldly presenting himself before his liege-lord, promptly retired, ejected the Abbot and his monks from the adjoining Abbey, allegedly with their eager compliance, and took over the monastic quarters for his company, so much more comfortable and spacious than the cramped old palace.

Only one other important latecomer was awaited, and he arrived that last evening, delayed by his wife providing him with a son and heir — Alexander fitz Alan, now calling himself Stewart, High Steward of Scotland, as his ancestors had been Stewards of Dol for the Normandy dukes. He arrived in haste, with only a couple of servants, an unassuming, somewhat delicate-looking young man, with whom his royal namesake was friendly. If the King was relieved to see him, he did not allow it to show.

The scene was set for decision.

* * *

The Council was held in the great minster of the Abbey which the fairly recently sanctified St. Margaret, Alexander's ancestress, had built, no other premises being sufficiently large to accommodate all who were entitled to attend. There had been nothing on this scale almost within living memory, for in the later years of his reign, Alexander the Second, a strange man of mixed virtues and vices, had been more productive of bastards than of good government, and had eschewed Councils. Since then Secret or Privy Councils had been the rule — and not many of them, for most important decisions had long been taken by two or three men, of the ruling caucus, behind closed doors. But now the King had summoned all his lords and barons entitled to attend, and the place was full. Outside, a milling host of men-at-arms, caterans and miscellaneous supporters turned the town into an armed camp and bedlam, with eruptions of fighting between rival groupings going on in every street and alley.

Alexander deliberately kept all waiting. By noon the greatest lords had taken up all the best positions in the chancel and transepts and the nave was packed. Between the chancel-steps and the high altar a table had been placed, facing down the church, with behind it a chair and at the sides two benches for the clerks. In the chair sat the Chancellor, in the rich robes of a bishop — Gamelin of St. Andrews, Primate of Holy Church in Scotland for the last eight years. The Abbot's throne-like chair had been moved into a central position between this table and the altar, and was reserved for the monarch. The entire minster throbbed with stir and noise.

In the sacristy, off the south transept, Alexander waited also, with a small group which included the Earl Patrick, Lindsay and the Steward, with their esquires in attendance. Also the Abbot Robert of Dunfermline, who had been Chancellor before Gamelin, today an agitated man. Indeed almost all there, save the King himself, looked less than at ease. Of them all, Alexander found only Thomas Learmonth able to concentrate on tossing dice with him — to the obvious if unspoken disapproval of the rest. They played for single pence, out of regard for Thomas's comparative poverty — although the King was consistently and cheerfully losing.

"It is well past noon, Sire," Earl Patrick protested. "All await Your Grace. The Comyns' men keep coming to ask when . . ."

"If the Comyns are so impatient, let them leave!" Alexander mentioned casually. "We can do well enough lacking them."

"*Can* you, Sire? They represent almost half the realm!"

"Only by my favour and agreement, Pate — remember that. Thomas — your throw. And at three, plaguey easy to beat! Ha — five! You have Beelzebub's own luck, man! Perhaps I should make *you* Chancellor — that the realm might benefit!"

"Then, I fear, I would be Dead Thomas, not True Thomas, my lord King, in a matter of days! And that requires no soothsaying!"

In the brief laughter that sally provoked, Alexander pocketed the dice and rose. "Perhaps you are right. Tell the trumpeters to sound, then, man."

So, to a stirring fanfare, the sacristy-door was thrown open and, preceded by an acolyte holding aloft the golden cross of the abbey before Abbot Robert, and a dozen chanting choristers, the King entered the great church by the south transept, followed by his party. Apart from the vacant throne behind the Chancellor's chair at the table, there was no single place left for any of them to sit. All in the minster stood for the royal entry, and for the moment the noise stilled.

Alexander paced slowly, necessarily, behind the singers, dressed simply but with a cloth-of-gold cloak thrown over one shoulder, sable-lined and bearing the embroidered red Lion Rampant thereon, set in gleaming rubies, the emblem which his grandfather William the Lyon had adopted instead of the Celtic boar — hence his by-name. Around brows and fair hair he wore the golden circlet of kingship. At the chancel-steps he turned, bowed to the altar, and then moved up to his chair-of-state. Those behind him had to find places to stand wherever they could, however illustrious.

When the singing stopped, the King, facing the great company, raised a hand.

"I, Alexander, greet you all kindly," he cried, strong-voiced. "Today, together we start a new chapter in the story of our ancient realm. I ask the Abbot Robert to pray for

Almighty God's blessing upon it, and upon the deliberations of this Great Council of State."

Bishop Gamelin the Primate, a plumply smooth man with the unlined features of a child, as it seemed, despite his middle years, raised his eyebrows at this, no doubt considering that he, as principal churchman of the kingdom, should have been asked to approach the Almighty, rather than the local abbot. But he could scarcely protest. Robert's prayer was suitably brief.

"So, my lords, under God's guidance we go forward," Alexander resumed. "I give all who have seats leave to be seated." He himself, however, remained standing.

It was a new experience for men to sit when their monarch was on his feet, to add to the other new experiences of this day.

"I have called this Council for good cause and reason, my friends," the King said when the stir subsided. "I have been High King of Scots for a dozen years, but have of necessity only reigned, not ruled, because of my insufficient years. Others have had to bear that burden for me — and for this I thank them, where thanks are due. But now all such may take rest from their labours on my behalf. I am now in my twenty-first year, and hereby take the rule into my own hands, as is proper. None, I think, shall say that I am not able so to do. I have had a sufficiency of training, I assure you! Does any say otherwise?"

There was complete silence in the church now.

"So we start afresh, my lords. But before we commence our deliberations I have two items of news for you. One happy, in that Queen Margaret has, in God's mercy, given birth to a daughter, a fine and healthy child. At London. So that the succession is now assured. A son would have been still better; but that is God's provenance and we must thank Him, not otherwise. Besides, there is time enough yet, you will concede." His glance swept over the company. "My lord of Annandale — where are you? I scarce know whether to commiserate with you or to congratulate you! You will now be much relieved, I swear!"

There was exclamation, comment, even some laughter at

that. Sir Robert Bruce of Annandale, fourth of that style from de Brus of Normandy, had been named next in succession to the throne in 1240 when, Alexander the Second still having no heir, there was growing anxiety. He was a grandson of David, Earl of Huntingdon, William the Lyon's younger brother, by a daughter, and so cousin-german to that monarch. There were many others nearer — but not legitimate of birth.

The Bruce, whatever he thought, made no comment.

"My other tidings are less joyful," Alexander went on. "King Henry, my good-sire, has received sure word from Norway that King Hakon Hakonsson has sent out commands to all his dominions to muster for war. And none doubt to where his longships will in due course point their prows! You all know well how the Norsemen have held and occupied our Western Isles and Hebrides since the time of King Edgar, and of later years have made grievous inroads on our mainland coasts. We have made many representations to King Hakon, even sent envoys to meet him. But to no effect. Ever these raidings grow more sore. Now Hakon is declaring that much of our mainland is his also, including all Galloway, Kintyre, Cowal and parts of Argyll and Lochaber. We cannot but be gravely concerned at these latest tidings — as my lord of Badenoch and Lochaber will agree in especial!"

The Comyn chief, sitting close by in one of the choir stalls, half-rose from his seat urgently — and then sat back at the King's raised hand.

"Presently, my lord — presently. In due course we shall debate what needs to be done in this grave matter. As in others. I but inform you all, that you may well consider what is best when we come thereto." He paused. "So now, my friends — to business. My lord Bishop of St. Andrews — may I suggest that you find yourself another seat?"

Gamelin turned round, to stare at the King. "Me? Why, Sire?"

"Because, my friend, that is the Chancellor's chair. And you are no longer Chancellor."

In the gasping reaction which swept the minster, none was

more surprised and outraged than the Bishop himself. When he could make himself heard, he protested.

"I *am* Chancellor, Sire. With respect. Since there is none other. I have been so for eight long years. Borne the day-to-day rule of your realm. I, I . . ."

"My lord Bishop, since you are so well-versed in rule and governance, you know better than most that subjects may not contradict nor bandy words with their monarch! I have said that you are no longer my Chancellor — so you are not. It is sufficiently simple. But if you require guidance, I will explain. When a monarch comes of full years, a new start is made. All appointments made during his minority, by whomsoever, in his name, fall. Save those which are hereditary. The monarch may reappoint or he may not. So the Chancellorship, like other non-hereditary offices, is now vacant. *You*, my lord Bishop, would not claim it to have descended to you from . . . a progenitor?" And Alexander smiled broadly.

Comparatively few present laughed at this sally, which alluded to the uncertainty of the Bishop's natal details. All were too greatly aware of the significance of the challenge which their young liege-lord had so unexpectedly thrown down, in the dismissal of his chief minister, particularly when he was the Comyns' nominee.

Thomas Learmonth knew admiration as well as trepidation, however. Alexander, by his early disclosures of the Norwegian threat to Lochaber and Galloway and the rest, was bound greatly to have perturbed the Comyns, to have made them acutely aware of the need for support on a wider scale and for national solidarity — for the Lord of Lochaber and Badenoch, as well as being the Justiciar of Galloway, owned vast estates in that south-western province. John Comyn would inevitably be wary now of rushing into dispute over the Chancellor's dismissal.

The King continued, entirely confident-seeming, even genial. "Sir David Lindsay will act Chancellor for this Council, until another is appointed. Will you take the good Bishop's chair, my friend?" He signed Lindsay forward easily. And as though in explanation, almost as an aside, added, "My lord of Luffness, Brenevil and the Byres will, I hope, have time to spare for these Chancellor's duties meantime — since, of course, his office of Justiciar of Lothian falls into the Crown, like the rest, and he will be spared *those* labours. As, to be sure, do those of the other Justiciars, including that of the High Justiciar. Appointments to all these, and other offices, will be made shortly and after due consultation. I . . ."

If it was unthinkable to interrupt the King in his speech, the unthinkable nevertheless happened. The flood of exclamation and astonishment rose from all over the church, to drown his words. It was the ultimate challenge, the dismissal of the High Justiciar, Durward of Atholl himself, the major individual in the kingdom for a score of years — not to mention John Comyn's Galloway justiciarship. The Justiciars were not just the chief justices of the land, but the officers of greatest power and richest profit, in that they controlled all appointments of magistrates and the like and were responsible for the imposition and collection of taxation and customs.

Alan Durward's mighty voice roared out above the hubbub. "Alexander! Lord King! This is not to be borne — not to be borne, I say! Beyond all belief! Have you taken leave of your wits, man?"

The noise died away to an alarmed silence at such words to the High King, even by one of the *ri* or lesser kings, in Council. Durward, massive, heavy, grizzled in a leonine fashion, was on his feet, pointing an angry finger which actually trembled with his rage. Lindsay, in the uncomfortable process of replacing the outraged Gamelin at the table, paused to watch the greater drama, as indeed did the Bishop himself.

"No, my lord of Atholl and good uncle, I have not," Alexander returned conversationally. Durward was not his uncle, of course; but as a child, it would have seemed unsuitable to call the already middle-aged husband of his half-sister, brother. So uncle it had been. "Such poor wits as I have been blessed with are in excellent shape. You should rejoice at that, since you have been seeking to mould and sharpen them for this day, for so many years! Do not miscall your own handiwork, Uncle! I am the King, of full years — and of your training. Can any deny it?"

The silence quivered as the older man sought for words, his hand still outstretched, pointing.

His monarch scarcely gave him time. "You were appointed High Justiciar in my name and by my signature and seal. Can I not, by another signature and sealing, withdraw what I granted?"

"Can . . .? *Can*, man? Any pup can bark — but does not when older dogs may show their teeth!"

"Ha — so we use kennel-talk rather than council! So be it. Hear this then, my lord. Old dogs can *lose* their teeth when young dogs' are yet at their sharpest! Think on that — all here." He paused then, and smiled. "But enough of kennel-talk, Uncle. I urge you, do not take your well-earned respite and retiral from heavy tasks so sorely. Since it must be. My lords of Badenoch, Luffness and Buchan, I think, your fellow justiciars, accept what must be more . . . civilly. Do you likewise. Eh, my lord Earl Alexander?"

Alexander Comyn, Earl of Buchan, a thick-set, youngish man of high colour, half-brother of the Red Comyn, was the third of the justiciars under the High Justiciar, that is of Scotland north of Forth. And he hated Durward. He looked at his brother doubtfully, then shrugged. "As you say, my lord King," he growled.

"As I say, yes," the King nodded. "But look not so sour, Uncle. We shall find other office for you, never fear. Less . . . trying!" And he grinned at his pun.

Durward looked around him like a baited bull, and realised that he was outmanoeuvred. The Comyns were his enemies but might have been expected to side with him in this of keeping Alexander in his place. But they were thrown into disarray, and were clearly doubtful as to where their best interests lay. And of the two other most senior members of the English faction, Lindsay had now displaced Gamelin at the Chancellor's table, and the Earl Patrick of Dunbar was obviously behind the King also, however uneasy he looked. There were many others whom he could rally to his side, of course; but in public Council there would be disinclination to come out blatantly against the King when these more important men did not. What might be done quietly and in secret, was another matter, to be sure. Scowling and muttering, abruptly Durward sat down.

Waving a hand amiably, Alexander sat also. "Sir David, if you please — to business."

Lindsay coughed and spoke gruffly. "I act here only on Your Grace's express command and not of my own wish. This is clerk's work! The first matter here is that of the King of England's unpaid marriage-portion for Queen Margaret, engaged for in the Treaty of Newcastle in the year 1244."

"Ah, yes. I am happy to tell you, my lords, that this long-standing debt is now to be paid in full. Of the remaining sum of four thousand marks, two thousand to be brought to Scotland with the Queen and Princess within forty days. The rest sent before midsummer. For this, I may say, we have greatly to thank King Hakon! For Henry fears that if Hakon defeats the Scots he will not be long in assailing Cumbria. So, he would prefer *us* to fight the Norsemen than himself! Hence his belated agreement to pay my wife's dowry — to help *me* to raise more men for the battle to come!"

There was some grim amusement at this — but the under-lying seriousness of the Norse threat was further brought home.

"We shall deal with the matters of manpower and each lord's contribution to the army, later," Lindsay went on. "That His Grace is prepared to use these moneys for the purpose of paying for added men from you all, when they are properly due to his own private purse, is, I feel sure, appreciated by all present!"

That at least produced general satisfaction.

"Then there is the matter of the bishopric of Argyll. As most will know, the good Bishop Alan has died. The nomination of his successor is, to be sure, within His Grace's provenance, for appointment by the Pope. His Grace believes that, in view of the Norse threat to the Argyll coast, amongst others, it is important that this nomination should be made

35

swiftly, for it takes time to win approval from Rome; and Holy Church's good influence on the West Highland seaboard is essential. There is no time for long competition for this office, as all must agree. If the bishopric is vacant when King Hakon invades, nothing is more sure than that he will bring a new Norse bishop with him, appointed by the Archbishop of Nidaros, who claims spiritual rule over all Norse-ruled territories. To save time, therefore, my lord King advises that Laurence, the present Dean of Argyll, be nominated. He is well-reputed and well-liked in the diocese. Is it agreed?"

Actually there was only one man competent to disagree, in that assembly, however many might have had other nominees, and that man did so.

"As Primate, I would advise otherwise," Gamelin said smoothly, from his new stance near John Comyn. "Dean Laurence is no doubt an excellent priest, but he is scarcely of the quality for the episcopate. I would nominate William, Dean of Brechin, a man of greater worth and experience." He did not add that his surname was Comyn.

Lindsay shrugged. "Does any support that nomination?"

"I do," the Earl of Mar said. He was married to the sister of John and Alexander Comyn.

"Any other nomination?"

No voice was raised.

"Vote," the King said briefly.

"Very well. Those in favour of the Bishop of St. Andrews' nomination as against the lord King's, show hands."

Everywhere men looked at each other. Now, suddenly, was the test thrown at them — to support, and to be seen to support, the young monarch in his new and unlooked for independence, which might be a mere defiant gesture without any abiding substance; or the proven, long-standing power of the House of Comyn. Hands were notably slow to rise.

There were twelve other bishops present and ten mitred abbots, all Lords of Parliament. Alexander was especially interested in how these would vote. Was the Church with him or against him? After a due period for reflection, only five of the hands of the twenty-three Lords Spiritual went up — including the Primate's.

It must have been one of the slowest votings in any Council Scotland had known. It had little to do with the worth of the candidates; the criteria were otherwise. Hesitation, watching, weighing, prevailed. When it was seen that even John, Lord of Badenoch himself had not raised his hand, some that were up actually came down. Durward sat back, his arms folded over his barrel of a chest. The clerks at the table, busy counting, looked harassed, recounting. They were, of course, Gamelin's servants.

Lindsay, glancing over his shoulder at Alexander, spoke. "Enough," he said. "No need to count. The nomination of Dean William of Brechin falls. I declare, since there is no other nomination, that Master Laurence is named to the Pope for ratification as Bishop of Argyll."

Something like a sigh rippled over the gathering. Whatever the virtue of the case, the King had won the first round.

"The next business also concerns His Holiness at Rome," Lindsay went on, level-voiced. "To pay for the great new Crusade against the Infidel, he requires large moneys. He has accordingly placed a levy on every realm of Christendom. Each abbey, priory, monastery church and parish is to pay one hundredth of its benefice, that is one-tenth of a tithe of its yearly substance — this without exception. And in addition, each lord, baron and landholder is urged, under pain of Papal displeasure and possible excommunication, to provide suitable moneys and men in proportion to the worth of his lands. This by Yuletide next."

A different sort of consternation swept the church, both Lords Spiritual and Temporal equally upset, everyone hit where it hurt most sorely. Voices were raised in heartfelt protest. Half-a-dozen men were on their feet at once; but it was Bishop Gamelin's sonorous voice which again prevailed.

"His Holiness commanded *me* to assess and collect the moneys from Holy Church," he declared. "As Primate it is my responsibility, not the responsibility of this Council. Pope Urban is to send Cardinal Ottobuoni de Fiesci as legate to all the kingdoms of Christendom on this matter. He will come to Scotland in due course. When I must have the moneys for him."

"No doubt, my lord Bishop," Lindsay said. "I feel sure that all here will gladly yield you the responsibility of extracting such siller from Holy Church — if you can! None will envy you the task, I think. But as to the others, the barons and landholders, this is a matter for the Council. Do we wish to accept and support this Crusade and the moneys policy of the Holy See?"

Into the doubtful murmurings of the company, the Primate persisted. "I am not unconcerned in this aspect also," he asserted. "As you will discover. His Holiness, to aid in this matter and to persuade weaker brethren, has given me authority to grant certain indulgences and spiritual benefits for those who make generous contributions in men and money. As remission from blame and punishment for certain grievous sins. Release from required observances and penances and fastings, as during Lent. Permission to marry within the fourth degree of consanguinity. And other most notable comforts. So, my lords — think well on this!"

There could be no denying the impact of this announcement. Piety and crusading zeal might not be in the ascendant in that gathering, but none were going to belittle the power of the Church to make life difficult, or the reverse, where it so decided. Due calculation was clearly advisable.

"What is the Council required to decide?" Durward demanded.

"Three related matters, my lord of Atholl, as I see it," Lindsay replied. "First — does the realm of Scotland support this Crusade as good and proper? And if so, does it agree to the collection of these moneys to send to Rome? And if it does, whose duty and task is it?"

"We can by no means refuse to support a Crusade to which all Christendom is to be committed," John Comyn declared. "As to payments, this appears to be a matter for each man's decision. None here may tell another what he must do. With the churchmen it may be otherwise, apparently! But no lord of Scotland is to be told by any soever what he must pay in this or other cause."

The first cheers of the day rang out for this stalwart pronouncement of faith.

Gamelin looked somewhat chastened at his chief's declaration.

Bruce of Annandale spoke up. "We assuredly want no priests dunning us for siller. We have a sufficiency of that, in their tithes and oblations. Let the justiciars collect what any man chooses to offer for this Crusade — and only that. Through the magistrates and customars. As they collect the taxation."

"But, man, did you not hear?" Durward cried. "There *are* no justiciars! The King's Grace, in his wisdom, has dismissed them!"

Laughing, Alexander raised his hand to still the din. "Never fear, Uncle — others will be appointed. And quickly." He waved a mocking hand towards Atholl. "At least, my lord, *you* need not fear this Papal levy — having already paid an ample sufficiency to Rome for your own crusade, I hear! After all that, His Holiness cannot expect to get more out of you."

Whilst everyone else looked intrigued, the older man looked uncertain — an unusual state of affairs.

"An English bishop, just back from Rome, assured me, Uncle, that you had not long since sent a large payment in gold to the Pope, in order to persuade him to legitimate the birth of your good wife, my half-sister, my father's bastard. I wonder why, at this late stage, since my good sister, the late King's earliest bastard, is now nearing fifty years, I think? Could it be, my lord, that had I not produced an heir, your own daughter by this lady could have claimed the throne? Her mother having been named lawful by Holy Church?"

Such uproar as there had been before was as nothing to the din now. For, of course, this revelation was more than just dramatic, it was alarming. Apart from the dynastic ambitions implied. Alexander the Second's profligacy in bastards, especially female ones, had provided wives and mothers for quite a cross-section of the Scottish aristocracy, including Earl Patrick and Sir David Lindsay themselves. All such, naturally, were now up-in-arms at this secret move on the part of Durward, which looked like the stealing of a march on them, since each and all might have thought to do the same.

Durward jumped up, in fury, fists clenched. "Enough!" he shouted. "Enough, I say! I will not remain here to be insulted and abused — I will not! This Council is but mummery and play-acting! I withdraw, and urge all others to do so also." And he turned to stamp down from the chancel.

"My lord of Atholl — halt you!" Alexander cried. "Back to your seat, I say. You will not leave this place before I do, or lacking my royal permission. Nor will any. That is required behaviour — all know it. Sit, man. If you, or other, seek to leave, I will have you halted by main force. And then placed in custody! As God is my witness!"

The force and vehemence of that caused much drawing of breath. None doubted that its carrying out would be attempted, with results unforeseeable, almost unthinkable — since Durward could call up men by the thousand and the King could not, save only by the support of other lords.

The older man had halted, and stood almost irresolute, he to whom resolution had always been as second nature.

Alexander gazed round them all, head high. Then he affected one of his lightning changes of stance and bearing, actually smiling. "I remind all that the most important item before this Council is still to be discussed — the raising and mustering of a great army to face and defeat Hakon of Norway. This is no light task — and it concerns you, Uncle, as much as any here, and more than most. So sit, my lord — we need your counsel as we need your men."

After a moment or two, shrugging, Durward moved back to his choir-stall and sat down.

"There are many experienced men of war here present — where I am not," the King went on. "My lord of Atholl in especial. You will all give me your advice. But first I will tell you how the position appears to me, and you no doubt will put me to rights. As I see it, we have no recourse but to await the Norwegian onslaught here on our shores. We have no great fleet of longships and galleys as has Hakon — so that we cannot challenge him at sea. And he will, no doubt, be assisted by the longships of the Hebrideans and of Man —

unless we can dissuade them first. But on land, on our mainland, he will not have the advantage of cavalry. He cannot carry horses in his ships. We therefore must hold our hands, however sore the temptation to strike sooner, so as to lure him down from the Highland West, where we cannot marshal our own cavalry because of mountains and lochs and bogs, to these Lowland shores. Our vitals, yes — but where we can bring a large horsed army to bear, which Hakon will find it difficult to counter. Do you agree with me, thus far?"

No voice was raised to contradict that.

Alexander resumed. "We must let the enemy come ashore. On the Clyde or the Cunninghame or the Kyle coasts, if we can get him there. However costly may be the waiting. Then descend upon him. Meantime seek to buy off Magnus of Man and those grandsons of Somerled of the Isles. This is how I see it, my lords — but you will now give me your wiser counsel. Also the numbers of men, horsed and afoot, which you can raise. Remembering that I shall have some small English gold to help in the matter!"

It was extraordinary how suddenly and completely different was the spirit and atmosphere prevailing in that church, changed from unease, hostility, alarm, suspicion, to involvement and co-operation. Here was something all understood and could take part in, something that affected everyone. A dozen men were speaking at once, offering men, horses, help, advice. Satisfied, Alexander sat back, leaving the rest to Sir David Lindsay.

As a council-of-war, certainly that Great Council of State was a success, ending up with a satisfactory degree of agreement on strategy and tactics, and promises of men up to over twenty thousand, with fully a quarter of the total horsed, the great ones eventually vying with each other as to numbers, as a matter of essential prestige, Durward and Comyn bidding against each other, with the Steward, Fife, Bruce, Douglas and Lindsay not far behind. But perhaps even more significant, although not all may have perceived it at the time, was the fact that Alexander emerged from it all supreme. If he was not yet master of Scotland, as well as titular King of Scots, he was at least on his way thither, and demonstrating that he knew the road.

For the last quarter-hour Thomas Learmonth, with no military guidance nor men to offer, occupied himself with composing a new rhyme.

> *The old hound growls but the young hound rends,*
> *Men wager and wonder.*
> *But when teeth are bared and the tulzie ends,*
> *The old hound's asunder!*

He was not happy with that last line. But perhaps Alexander himself would better it?

3

Despite the threat which hung over the land, Thomas for one enjoyed the summer of 1263 — even though it had its frustrations. The weather, for once, was excellent; and Dunbar, of a fine sunny summer, was a pleasant place, apt for young people, even if one dragged a leg somewhat. Admittedly it lay at the very knuckle-end of Lothian, thrusting into the Norse Sea; but, when skies were blue, it was a delight of golden beaches, dramatic cliffs and secret coves, all backed by the green Lammermuir hills. At Dunbar active folk could sail and swim, fish and hunt and hawk, ride the sheep-strewn heights or just laze on warm sands. Always the Earl Patrick and his family spent the autumn, winter and spring at Ercildoune in Lauderdale and moved to Dunbar, on the coast thirty-five miles to the north-east, for the summer. The castle here was an extraordinary structure, built on projecting rock-stacks, some actual islets, the whole linked by bridge-like corridors and vaulted passages, beneath which the tide surged and eddied, a place less than convenient and comfortable but all but impregnable, and sufficiently exciting for the young-in-heart. It guarded the port and harbour, where something was always astir. Ercildoune, in its deep wooded valley amongst the tall hills, was a good sheltered place to winter; but there was always much looking-forward to May, when the family moved to Dunbar and its coastal pleasures.

Not that there was a great deal of time for the pleasures of beach and boat and hawk and hound that summer, for the menfolk at least. For, in common with the rest of the Scots nobility, the Earl Patrick was much preoccupied with the gathering and training of armed men, with Thomas little less involved. And much training was required; for although the Earl had his own permanent corps of trained men-at-arms, a sort of bodyguard some three hundred strong, in a national emergency such as this he could raise ten times that number. But these, of course, were in the main ordinary folk, farm-workers, herdsmen, shepherds, foresters, fishermen and the like, able to bear arms but on the whole less than proficient in their use. The Earl's great Merse borderlands, to be sure, were notable for their population of tough mosstroopers and rievers, born if undisciplined cavalrymen, who all but lived in their saddles — indeed the earldom could probably provide as large a horsed contingent for the Scottish army as any other lordship in the land. On the other hand, the coastal fishermen had little use for horseflesh, and though sufficiently tough, were scarcely born soldiers; nor were those who tilled the cornlands of Lothian. So much elementary training was called for in all areas, and this had to be fitted in at different times for different places and occupations, for all these men had their own and their lord's daily bread to earn, fish to catch, hay to cut and stack, peats to dig, sheep to clip, cattle to drove, and so on.

Thomas, by the nature of things, was mainly concerned with cavalry training, as a superb horseman and no marcher. So a great deal of his time had to be spent, not in the Dunbar vicinity itself with its varied attractions, but across the Lammermuir hills in the horse country of the Merse, the great rolling plain between hills and Tweed. Here, going from village to village, from stone tower to monastery to homestead, armed with his lord's authority and a few seasoned men-at-arms as sergeants, he sought to inculcate in a recalcitrant and notoriously individualistic manpower the simple rudiments of unified cavalry tactics — to his frequent near-despair. He consoled himself, however, with the thought that all over Scotland similar efforts were going on and no doubt frustrations being suffered — although he would wager that only those who had mosstroopers to handle, like Bruce of Annandale and Soulis of Liddesdale, might parallel his own problems, with possibly Galloway also, where they were a thrawn and ungovernable lot.

Nevertheless, he did manage to spend some time at Dunbar in less military pusuits, mainly in company with the young people — who saw an esquire's duties rather differently from their father, and who anyway looked upon Thomas as more or less one of the family. The Lady Bethoc's frank admiration did nothing to discourage him from joining in sundry excursions and pleasure-parties, although perhaps it should have done.

News from furth of Lothian and the Borderland came intermittently, sometimes in the form of messages from the King or Lindsay to Earl Patrick but more often from wandering friars and mendicant priests, the great carriers of tidings and gossip, entertainers for many an evening in the hall or orchard. The situation was sufficiently dramatic, not to say alarming. King Hakon had indeed sailed from Bergen with the largest fleet allegedly ever to have left Norway, longships variously said to number between one-hundred-and-fifty and two hundred, with many merchant vessels in addition carrying troops and supplies. They were now at Orkney, said to be awaiting accessions of strength from the Norse allies and dependencies of Iceland, Shetland, the Hebrides, Ireland and Man. Alexander had sent envoys to the Hebrideans and West Highland chiefs, bearing mixed cajolings, threats and reminders of duty, to try to keep them from joining Hakon; but all knew that this was something of a forlorn hope. The Vikings had complete control of the seas, so that the isles were at their mercy; moreover most of the

Islesmen had by this time strong Norse blood-ties — and very little in common with the rest of Scotland.

There was, to be sure, the other anxiety. Whilst the general assumption was that Hakon would indeed invade by the west coast, which was almost Norse territory and the traditional scene of their operations, there was always the possibility that they might attack eastern Scotland — although no real assault on this side had been made since the days of Thorfinn Raven Feeder the Mighty. But it could not be ruled out. If the enemy was in such strength, he might do both at the same time. So Alexander was manning and strengthening all the east coast castles and forts, requiring large numbers of men for the unpopular castle-duty; also stocking up supplies. But it was a very long seaboard to guard, and the Vikings could choose anywhere to attack. Even the Lothian coast could not feel safe — indeed the Scotwater and the Firth of Forth might well offer a favoured invasion route, in that the longships could row right up Forth to Stirling, more than halfway across the land and less than forty miles of ground to cover before reaching salt water again at the Clyde estuary at Dumbarton. So Dunbar was on the alert, like the rest.

This by no means prevented the Earl Patrick's family from making the most of the fine summer weather; in fact, for the youngsters, it added spice to it all.

With the hay cut and dried in good time and the corn harvest looking as though it would be notably early, and still with no sign or word of the Norsemen moving south from Orkney, the people in general were in good heart — dangerously so, according to Earl Patrick — when, on the Nones of August, the 5th, all got something else to occupy their minds and set tongues wagging, largely in alarm. This was when, an hour after midday, and out of a cloudless sky, the sun was suddenly darkened and obscured, and for some seven minutes it was as though the summer's night had descended upon the land. Panic ensued in many quarters; and the fact that soon the shadows passed away and all was as before, did not expunge the apprehension of most. Clearly, they said, it was a sign from God, and no good sign either. The usual interpretation was that it presaged disaster —

presumably meaning that the Norsemen were going to be victorious and that Scotland was the object of the Almighty's displeasure. In vain the more enlightened — or the scoffers, as some preferred to call them — pointed out that the sun's darkening would apply equally to Hakon and his allies, like everybody else. It was interesting that in this odd situation, the two branches of Holy Church in Scotland tended to speak with opposing voices — and it was the ascendant, powerful and allegedly enlightened Romish priesthood which saw doom and the wrath of God, whilst the scorned, decadent and ignorant Celtic churchmen, whom they had largely displaced, saw it only as a natural phenomenon, without significance save astronomically. Of course the ancient Columban Church missionaries, when converting the Picts, had more or less taken over and adapted the old druidical sun-worship traditions, with its stone-circles and monoliths, even setting up their sanctuaries within the very circles — something their Roman brethren damned as heathenish. So the surviving keledei, or Friends of God, knew something about the sun, the heavens and astrology.

The young Cospatricks saw it all as an added excitement rather than any dire warning, and teased Thomas for not having foreseen it and alerted everybody.

"I am not a prophet!" he protested. "It is you who claim that I am, not myself. It is foolishness."

"Yet much that you have foretold has come true, Thomas," Bethoc insisted. "You cannot deny it. You have the gift."

"I have most ordinary sound wits, that is all. And a fondness for rhyming. I can add two parts to four parts to make six. I use my head to guess what will happen, on occasion. Sometimes, by nature, I am bound to be right."

They were sitting on the sands of a cove some distance from castle and town, a favourite haunt tucked away privily in a re-entrant of the cliffs, the golden strand divided by a natural thrusting breakwater of reef which reached out into the little bay and served as pier for a couple of small boats, a diving-platform, and also a modesty-screen for bathing — so that the sexes could undress separately and enter the water

46

decently on either side of the rock barrier. The party consisted of the Countess Christian, one of her ladies, the six Cospatrick children and Thomas.

"It is more than that," the girl asserted. "You should have faith in your own powers, not doubt them."

"She will be naming you Doubting Thomas not True!" Pate, her eldest brother, aged fourteen, announced. "*I* do not believe in prophecies and soothsaying, anyway."

"How can you say that when you know nothing about it?" his sister asked. "I would accept your opinion, Pate, on the best place to catch flukies or the best falcon to fly at snipe — but little else! Besides, Thomas — what do you know what to rhyme about? After all, you do not make verses about everything. So something must come to you to set you off. And if, as so often, what you say comes to pass, how can you declare that there is nothing more to it than just adding two to four and making it rhyme?"

"Rhymes just spring to my mind," he told her, uncomfortably, going to toss unnecessary further driftwood on the fire behind them. "There is nothing wonderful about it. I get the notion of a person or a happening, then think about how it will be most like to come about. I do that, see you, because folk are a deal more likely to take heed to any verse if there is something to come, something promised, than if it is just concerned with the present. Cozening, if you will! So there cannot be any purpose or especial truth behind it."

"Will you make a rhyme about me Thomas?" Gelis, the middle daughter, aged twelve, demanded. "Who will I marry? When? Will I have lots of babies? Make one for me . . ."

"You, Scone-face, will never marry — no man would have you!" her brother John scoffed. "And any babies you produce will have to be begotten behind a dyke in the dark, so the man does not see your face!"

"Enough of that, Johnnie!" the Countess Christian intervened. "Enough of all this profitless chatter. Leave Thomas alone. Forby — if we are going to swim this day, we had better be at it, or I for one will be past it."

"I want to fish," Alec, the youngest said. "The sea is cold."

"Fish, then — but from the other side of this skerry. Off with you, whilst we women undress."

The males duly went to take off their clothes at the far side of the long spine of rock. Thomas was a good swimmer, his lameness no handicap in the water, as in the saddle. Indeed, naked he proved to be a well-built young man, not heavy but with quite powerful shoulders, a good carriage, and slender waist and hips, only the left leg, slightly twisted from birth, to mar the picture. His limping progress down to the tide's edge was in marked contrast to his strong but gracefully rhythmic motion after he had shallow-dived into the water.

Leaving the boys to splash and shout in the small waves of the shallows, he swam out steadily towards the mouth of the little bay, heading for a tidal rock some three hundred yards out, which although itself weed-hung, offered a fine platform for deep diving to firm sand many feet down even at low tide. Here quite large flounders were apt to lie, just visible in outline under a thin skin of sand, a challenge to the good diver with a sharp eye, strong lungs and well-adjusted reflexes. Swimming round to the seaward side of the skerry, he clambered out, shook himself and stood breathing deeply for a few moments, before plunging cleanly, smoothly, steeply in again, almost straight down. He descended about nine feet, and then levelled off some two feet above the wrinkled sandy floor, to swim slowly, with quietly controlled arm strokes and winnowing feet, round the rock, right-about. The problem was to hold the breath for sufficiently long to still have some left on the landwards side, where required. The flat-fish preferred the more sheltered water there; but they were easily alarmed by diving and splashy swimming. So the actual dive had to be at the far side, and the under-water approach almost stealthy. Breath-holding ability was vital. A sunny day such as this was not the best for it, with a tell-tale swimmer's shadow thrown on the sand.

Today presumably the shadow gave away Thomas's approach, for he rounded a spur of the rock just in time to see movement rather than any shape, and a tiny stir of sand-cloud. Swiftly he grabbed down, fingers clawing. He felt slithering motion, but that was all. The trick was to get the fingers under the gills, an inch-and-a-half or so behind the pair of protruding eyes — the only place where it was possible to grip the slippery, squirming creature. So, unless the head could be seen, the chances were remote. Despite its odd shape, the fish could flap its way with astonishing speed under the sand.

Thomas had a little breath left; but it would be a pity to waste the remaining stretch of sheltered water without full lungs. He turned back, and slanted up to the surface at a gentle angle, to tread water there, breathing deeply.

Quickly he perceived another swimmer approaching. He had no doubts as to who it was. Only the Countess herself and her eldest daughter were sufficiently confident in the water to venture out thus far — and he did not for a moment think that it was the mother. He knew a distinct stirring, as he trod water, waiting.

Bethoc swam with a plain but strong and effective breast-stroke which, however lacking in the flourish beloved by some experts, at least had the advantage, from the man's point of view, of raising the girl's head and shoulders upwards at each surge forward so that most of her bosom was momentarily revealed. Panting, she came close, her long dark hair streaming behind her like stranded seaweed in current.

"You might have waited for me," she reproached, gaspingly.

He did not answer, too much aware of that green-tinted loveliness so near to him, the shapeliness little contorted or hidden by the wavering shimmer of the sea.

"You were under? Did you see anything?"

"One. Too late. I but touched it. But — there is still a chance. I have only been at this end. The sea is less cold than I feared."

"Yes. I have never caught a fish with my hands. Trouts, yes, in a burn. But not a sea fish. Can I try, Thomas?"

"It is your sea as much as mine, Beth! More, I suppose. You know what to do? Slide your fingers in behind the head. From the back. Under the gills."

"If I see one. And if I can get down far enough. I always

49

get forced up. Mother says that women are wrongly shaped for staying under. Floaters not sinkers!"

He did not comment on that directly. "You need a steep dive. Go further round this side of the skerry, to start. Out of their sight, and so that you are low enough at the right place. Keep fairly close to the rock." Then as he saw that she was in process of drawing deep breaths, pleasing as this was to watch, he shook his head. "No — not that. Not from the water, Beth. You will never go deep enough without much heavy swimming if you dive from the surface. You will require to dive from the rock."

"Oh!" she said, eyeing him.

"Only way, lass. To get deep without fuss. Not to scare the fish." He paused. "But . . . not if you do not wish to."

She looked away. "Very well," she said, and began to swim off round the south side of the skerry, seawards.

"Watch that you do not scrape yourself, climbing out," he warned, behind her. "The weed hides sharp rock. Shall I give you a hand out?"

"No need." At the far side of the barrier, clutching the waving weed, she looked up and round. "As well, I think, that we cannot be seen from the shore here, Thomas!" Then, strongly, she hoisted herself out on to a ledge of the skerry, on knees first, gleaming posterior white and shadow, then gingerly standing up on the slippery tangle.

The man watched, his heart in his mouth. Her naked beauty overwhelmed him. He had glimpsed her unclothed before, of course, in their seaside excursions, since childhood, always in the water. But never like this, standing poised before him, a woman now, no longer a child, the water running off her, hair plastered to face and shoulders, firm of breasts, round of aureole, dark of groin, swelling of hip, long of leg. She did not huddle or shrink or seek to cover herself in any way, but stood up straight and proud and free.

He did not mean to stare, but did so nevertheless.

She was seeking to take deep breaths again, but her eyes were on his rather than on the water into which she was going to dive, not bold or brazen but questioning, almost appealing. Her lips moved, but no words came.

He felt the need for words, himself. "I . . . I could make a rhyme . . . of this!" he got out, deep-voiced.

"No! No — you must not!" she exclaimed, and straightway made her dive — less cleanly than she might have done.

He followed in a surface-dive, to swim down after her, a few yards behind and a little above, appreciatively. They rounded the rock again and moved along the landward side, her fine body a delightful picture of regular, purposeful motion — even though perhaps more vigour evident than the occasion warranted. But he quickly realised that she was too high above the sand, that unless she went lower she would be unable to run a hand at the required angle along any flounder's back in order to slip under the gills. Presumably she meant to go lower when and if she saw a fish; but that would involve change of motion, extra disturbance however small, and in the split second which would be all that was likely to be granted, that would be apt to make the difference between success and failure. Should he move up and try to point this out to her somehow?

He decided against it, as likely to distract and to increase the disturbance of the water and create extra shadow — especially as it dawned on him that, instead of going lower as she went on, she was in fact gradually losing depth, not by any great deal but sufficient to require a definite downwards plunge should she see a fish. Her alleged female buoyancy, something to do with the chest formation and lungs, no doubt?

He saw the flounder's outline, a big one, at precisely the same moment as the girl did. She convulsed herself in a sort of jack-knife movement, and a hand shot down, fingers spread. But she was inches above it, and the creature darted off well before her fingers could make contact.

Instead of burrowing under, as more usual, this fish scurried off along the sand surface in zigzag fashion, and Bethoc made urgent effort to go after it. But she was too high and it too fast. Thomas's impulse was to thrust past her, below her, and grab — but he restrained himself.

She was allowing herself to slant upwards now, indeed

swimming for the surface as though in a hurry, her breath no doubt giving out. He went up with her.

Gasping for air, blinking the water from her eyes, and wiping the hair from her face, she looked at him.

"Sorry," she panted. "Too slow. Could not keep down — as I said."

He shook his head. "Difficult. Not many . . . can do it. *I* failed also." He grinned. "Bethoc bare and . . . flukie brown. Flukie safe . . . she could not stay down!"

"Poor!" she cried. "Poor — and not for the others! Or I shall hate you." She chittered a little as she threatened.

He made amends. "I am cold," he said. "I am going in. Will you try it again?"

"No, no. We shall go back . . ."

They swam slowly shorewards, companionably, side-by-side.

Hodierna Haig, daughter of another of Earl Patrick's vassals, Haig of Bemersyde, had already returned to the beach and wrapped herself in a plaid. But her mistress the Countess was still swimming about happily amongst her offspring, displacing a lot of water for she was a large and comfortably-made creature, bulging of breast and stomach—which she did not seem to mind being approximately on view, so long as she was in the water and moving.

"Where have you two been?" she demanded, but scarcely censoriously.

"Round the out-skerry, trying to catch flukies," her daughter informed. "But they were too quick for us."

"Or you too slow, with only half your wits on the business!" her mother returned. "Alec has done better, see you, with lugworm and hook. The sea is good today — warm. Although Johnnie is shivering. Considering all he eats, he puts little flesh on those bones of his!"

"If he would swim about instead of standing quaking at the edge, he would be warmer," his brother Pate declared. "Look at this starfish I have found. Has it got any eyes . . .?"

He was interrupted by shouting from the beach. A man had appeared, standing beside the party's horses on a stretch

52

of greensward below the cliff-path. Above the noises of the waves they could not make out what he was saying.

"Come closer, man!" the Countess shouted back, and beckoned. She moved a little further inshore herself, then judiciously went down on her knees.

The man, one of the castle servants, came halfway down to the tide-line. "Wat the Steward sent me, my lady," he called. "To send for you. The King — His Grace the King is come. To the castle. And none to greet him."

"Sakes — the King! What a God's Name . . .?" The Countess half-rose, recollected, knelt down again and began to waddle forward on her knees. Finding this awkward, to say the least, she got to her feet cursing and waved a peremptory hand. "Do not stand there staring, oaf! Away with you. I shall come. Away! Hody, you fool — bring me down my plaid. Quickly."

Thomas and the grinning boys swam off to their own side of the reef, leaving the females to extricate themselves.

Wrapped in a plaid herself, the Countess soon reappeared on top of the spine of rock. "Thomas," she called. "Get you back to the castle first. With all speed. Tell the King that my lord is at Haddington. That I shall be back so soon as I can. You might tell His Grace too that he should send some warning before he makes royal descent upon us — but perhaps you had better not!"

Pulling on his breeches, Thomas waved acknowledgment.

Pate was ready and eager to come with him, and together they rode fast back the half-mile to the castle.

There, the Earl's steward, in some agitation, led them to a tower's wall-walk where they found Alexander pacing impatiently, two attendants waiting a little apart and looking disapproving.

"Ha — Thomas Rhymer!" the King exclaimed. "Praise God for someone at least who may have wit enough to answer a simple question! Where is everybody, man?"

"My lord is gone to Haddington, Sire, Sir David Pepdie with him. And Home, Lauder, Cowdenknowes and Bemersyde are all gone to the Merse. The rest of us were down at the shore swimming . . ."

"Swimming, saints save us! The realm in dire danger and all at Dunbar go traipsing the land and swimming!"

"Your pardon, my lord King, but Earl Patrick and his knights are all away on the business of raising and training men. As even such as I have been doing until yesterday. Had the Countess Christian known that you were coming . . ."

"Yes, yes — never heed me, Thomas. I am plagued by problems and dolts — and so act the dolt my own self on occasion!" Alexander grinned and shrugged. "I need Patrick's help."

"It is but seven miles back to Haddington, Sire. Although my lord spoke of going on to Gifford . . ."

"I have not the time. I am on my way to Roxburgh. I heard at Soltra that Patrick was here, not at Ercildoune — so came all this way along the hillfoots of Lammermuir, instead of proceeding down Lauderdale. I need an earl, see you. I am meeting Bruce and Soulis and Douglas at Roxburgh — they will be there awaiting me, now. To plan the mustering of the Middle and West Marches. But none of these will serve for what I need. Patrick may. Can you reach him, Thomas, quickly? And give him my message."

"To be sure, Sire. I shall be with him within the hour."

"Good. Pay close heed, then — for this is fell important. John Comyn has sent me word that Ewan MacDougall of Lorn is in Galloway. What he is doing there is not certain — but only a fool would say that it had nothing to do with this Norse invasion. The Lord of Lorn — who calls himself King of Argyll and the South Isles — is in Hakon's pocket, like the rest of the Islesmen. He has no call to be in Galloway. Comyn himself is not there meantime — he is up in Lochaber putting that lordship into some state of defence. His steward sent him word. I want to see Ewan of Lorn!"

Thomas Learmonth spread eloquent hands but said nothing. He scarcely required to.

"It is not battle, fighting, that I want, see you," the King went on. "Ewan is proud, as are all of his kind. But he is the best of Somerled's kin. If I could detach him from Hakon it would be to our notable advantage. Quite apart from Galloway. He holds the mainlands of Lorn and Argyll of the

54

Scots crown; only the Isles, the Sudreys, of Norway. We have not met since I was but a youth. He hates both the Comyns and Durward — with some cause. Myself, now I am come of man's stature, he might mislike less."

Thomas nodded.

"I cannot go to him. It is unthinkable that the King of Scots should ride over one hundred miles to seek speech with one of his own near-rebel lords. So he must come to me. I could go part-way to meet him, from Roxburgh — no more. You understand?"

"Yes, Sire. Earl Patrick is to go, to persuade him. And not by force of arms. But . . . how?"

"He must use his wits. Promise rich reward. Although Ewan, being Highland and proud, is more like to respond to high talk as between equals. That is why it must be Patrick who goes. The others, although great lords, would not serve. The Cospatricks are of the ancient Celtic royal line. Patrick is also my half-sister's son. And the seventh Earl of Dunbar. Ewan would talk with him where he would spurn Bruce or Douglas, or any of Norman blood."

"And what has he to offer my lord of Lorn, Sire?"

"The hope of the lordship of *all* the Isles, under the Scots crown. Nordreys and Sudreys both. Perhaps even Man, if King Magnus Olafsson sides with Hakon, as we expect — and we can defeat them! All that."

"The *hope*, Sire? Not the promise?"

"The hope, yes. I cannot promise what I may not be able to fulfil, man. I can but try. Ewan will know that. You have it, then? To tell Patrick? Say to send me word at Roxburgh. As swiftly as may be. Ewan was last reported at Cruggleton Castle, near to Wigtown. Visiting the Galloway chieftains. No doubt on Hakon's business. I would come as far as Dumfries to meet him — say at Uchtred's nunnery of Lincluden. You have it?"

The esquire bowed.

"Then off with you, and waste no further time . . ."

When the Countess and her family got back to Dunbar Castle, it was to find not only the King departed but True Thomas also.

*   *   *

The Earl Patrick, with Thomas and a small escort of no more than a dozen of his best-mounted men, rode south-westwards directly from Haddington in the Vale of Tyne, in no hopeful nor appreciative frame of mind, with no liking for the task laid upon him. Like most Lowlanders, he deplored and despised the Highlanders, looking on them as all but barbarians, and the Islesmen especially as pirates and born traitors. To have to dash across the width of Scotland to see one, to have to treat him with the respect due to an equal, and to try to persuade him to an improbable course of action, went much against the grain. Not even to have time to go home and arrange his affairs was an annoyance. Thomas judiciously kept half-a-horse behind his master for the first couple of hours, himself not overjoyed at the Earl's insistence that he accompany him.

They went by Soltra to the Gala Water and so down to Tweed near Selkirk, to traverse the wilds of the Forest of Ettrick to the head of Annandale, halting the first night at the former Abbey of Shiel Kirk, now only a grange of its successor at Kelso. By next evening they had reached Dumfries, in Outer Galloway, where, at the Grey Friars' monastery, they learned that they would not have so far to go as they had feared; for the word was that the Lord Ewan of Lorn was heading eastwards, calling on the more important local chieftains, and was last reported in the Dee valley, at Carlingwark, apparently making for Kirk Cuthbert's Town, the chief centre of Inner Galloway, seat of the former earls thereof. There was no Earl of Galloway at this juncture, unfortunately, a source of dire weakness. The Earl Alan had died early, leaving only three daughters as heiresses, all married to Normans, their respective husbands each at least sufficiently wise not to claim more than one-third of the earldom. One was married to Alexander Comyn, Earl of Buchan; and since his brother, John Comyn the Red was Justiciar, they formed the greatest power in Galloway; but their many responsibilities elsewhere meant that they did not rule the province as strongly as it required — for long it had been one of the most unruly parts of the kingdom.

56

So the following morning the travellers pressed on, due westwards now, into Galloway proper, across the upland moors of Lochrutton to the valley of the Urr Water and on by Carlingwark to great Dee, on the estuary of which lay Kirk Cuthbert's Town.

Hitherto, none had dared to interfere with a superbly horsed and armoured company, however small, which rode under the banner of the Earl of Dunbar and March. But that evidently did not mean that their progress had gone unnoticed. Nearing the Dee valley at Threave, they found their way barred by a quite large company of rough-looking but heavily-armed men, fully three hundred strong, under a chieftain who named himself as MacLellan of Bombie, demanding to know their business.

"The King's business, sirrah!" the Earl gave back. "And, let us hope, no concern of yours! I am Patrick of Dunbar, Chief Warden of the Marches. By what right do you ask?"

"These are my lands, my lord . . ."

"Only as vassal to the Galloway lordship — and that by permission of the King's Grace. You have no authority to threaten travellers."

"I do not threaten, my lord," MacLellan assured. He was a heavily-built man of middle years and unprepossessing appearance, clearly out of his depth in dealing with someone of the Earl Patrick's calibre. "I was but sent to discover who came, unannounced and on what business . . ."

"So — you were sent? Who sent you, MacLellan?"

The other looked uncomfortable. "Not *sent*, my lord. Besought, shall we say? Since I lord it here . . ."

"Who, man — who?"

"The Lord Ewan of Lorn and the Isles, my lord Earl. He who calls himself King of the South Isles . . ."

"Ha — so Ewan sends MacLellan, does he? He who has no least authority in Galloway. But — no matter. Since he it is that I have come to see. Take me to him . . ."

Well escorted, therefore, they were conducted to the rambling, untidy hallhouse of Bombie some way east of Kirk Cuthbert's Town, in the midst of its huddle of supporting farmeries, cothouses and hovels. Galloway was still very much a Celtic province, with the Norman and Anglo-Saxon influence minimal. There, when MacLellan would have ushered him into his house, the Earl would no more than dismount from his horse. He was not going to be led before and presented to the Islesman like some mere envoy to a potentate.

"Fetch the Lord of Lorn," he commanded. "I shall see him here."

There might have developed something of a tug-of-war over this, but fortunately Ewan MacDougall did not elect to make it so. He appeared from the house after only a minute or so, a tall, fine-looking man in probably his late thirties, almost noble of carriage and feature, dark, slender, dressed in the Highland fashion of philabeg or short multi-coloured kilt and plaid, with the long calfskin waistcoat, over what was clearly a silken shirt, something neither of his visitors could sport. He also wore a shoulder-belt of intricate Celtic design in solid gold links. Beside his host the oafish MacLellan, he seemed almost of a different species.

"Salutations, friends," he called, with the soft, lilting accents of the Highland West. "MacLellan tells me that you come from the King of Scots? I am Ewan."

Despite himself Patrick was impressed, Thomas more so.

"Yes. His Grace sends his royal greetings," the Earl replied. "I am Patrick of Dunbar and March. Come to convey all due felicitations. And to command your attendance on His Grace, my lord."

"Command . . .?"

"Command, yes. As your liege-lord, and mine, His Grace commands rather than requests — as you will agree? Although, being the man he is, my Cousin Alexander would probably be happy to use the latter word."

The other stroked his chin. "Then why not *you*, my lord of Dunbar?"

"Because I am not the King, sir. And may not dispense with royal privilege, as he might do. But — he wishes to speak with you."

"I am honoured that King Alexander should concern himself with such as myself. But I am at the present much engaged otherwise. I am sure that His Grace will understand. Another time, perhaps?" That sounded entirely courteous — yet could be construed as high treason.

Patrick's lips tightened. "You refuse, my lord? You, a lord of the Scots realm, standing on the soil of Scotland, refuse the summons of the High King of Scots? Before these witnesses."

"Not so, my friend. I do nothing so uncivil as to refuse. I only would postpone the honour and pleasure. Until an occasion more apt and suitable. Surely that is reasonable. When I am, as now, engaged in pressing affairs."

"These affairs being the enrolling of Galloway subjects of King Alexander in favour of Hakon of Norway, sir! Against you own liege-lord!"

"King Hakon of Norway is also my liege-lord, Earl Patrick, I would remind you."

"For a few wretched islands! Which by right should also belong to the Scots crown."

The other said nothing.

Thomas cleared his throat, "My lords — since there are two lieges to consider, is it not a matter for some weighing, balancing? And due courtesies? Courtesies towards my lord of Lorn — but also towards His Grace of Scotland. After all, you my Lord Ewan, stand here on King Alexander's territory. If you stood on King Hakon's land, in Norway, I think that you would consider it civil to visit him, if he sought your presence? Forby, it is not so far to ride, to Lincluden at Dumfries. King Alexander is young and has heard much of the Lord Ewan."

That produced some reaction other than the Earl's frown. Thomas had judged aright.

"I would not wish to seem lacking in courtesy, sir," the Highlander said, with some emphasis on the personal pronoun. "You say that His Grace is so near as Lincluden?"

"Yes. He comes from Roxburgh, thus far. To meet you."

"*We* have ridden from Dumfries, this day," the Earl added, almost reluctantly. "Something over thirty miles. You could be there, with us, by nightfall."

"Scarcely that, my lord," Ewan gave back. "There are more courtesies than one! Certain others come here to see me this day. I would not be after disappointing them. Go you back to Lincluden, my friends. And if I may so contrive it, I shall visit His Grace of Scotland there tomorrow."

Earl Patrick opened his mouth to speak — then shut it again, glancing sidelong at his esquire.

"His Grace will be content, I think, my lord," Thomas said.

Stiffly, his two seniors inclined heads towards each other, and the visitors turned back to their horses.

"Damned arrogant, up-jumped islander!" Patrick jerked as they rode off. "If he may contrive it he will deign to visit his sovereign-lord the King! Tomorrow!"

"Yes, my lord," Thomas agreed diplomatically. "But he *will* come, to be sure. And as well not this day — for King Alexander could scarce come to Lincluden before tomorrow anyway. And it would be a pity if the bird, once netted, was to fly off again!"

"That bird would be better with its neck wrung, I say! Instead of all this gentling."

In the event, the Islesman did arrive at the nunnery of Lincluden before the King did — and even the Earl Patrick grew a little agitated lest their quarry should indeed take flight in proud impatience. They could not have restrained him physically, for he had brought four score fierce-looking warriors with him — to the nuns' distinct alarm.

But Ewan showed no signs of impatience. And when, around sundown, Alexander did arrive, with Patrick's brother-in-law, Bruce of Annandale, the Highlandman was actually at evening worship, or vespers, in the nunnery chapel.

They met, in due course, in the refectory where the newcomers were refreshing themselves after their journey. The King rose and after only a moment's hesitation strode forward, hand out, in frank and informal greeting. The other bowed, though not low, before taking the outstretched hand. They eyed each other, thus close.

"Ewan mac Duncan mac Dougal mac Somerled — well met," the King said affably. "I am Alexander mac Alexander

60

mac William. I hope that to come to this meeting did not incommode you?"

"I found it . . . possible, Sire."

"To be sure. It seemed too good an opportunity to miss. We do not often see the lord of Lorn and Argyll in our Lowland parts."

"No. I have many responsibilities, in the main otherwhere, Your Grace."

"Ah, yes. Yes, indeed. And, as well as the pleasure of greeting you, it is these responsibilities of yours, otherwhere, that I wish to speak of. Come, sit, my lord. You have eaten? Wine, then . . .?"

Warily, but with dignity, the other sat at the Abbess's table.

"My cousin of Dunbar tells me that you have problems of fealties, my lord," Alexander went on, conversationally. "To the crowns of Scotland and Norway. It is my hope that I can help you to resolve this."

"That may be difficult, Sire."

"Perhaps. But not impossible, I think. I and my royal forebears have had some experience in this matter, see you. We have had to pay fealty to the Kings of England for our great earldom of Huntingdon in that realm. But without conceding in any way the interests and independence of our Scottish realm. We do homage, therefore, adding to the oath the words '. . . always excepting the whole rights of the Kingdom of Scotland' or the like. Some such wording might serve your needs sufficiently well, do you not think?"

"Such words spoken to *which* monarch, Sire?"

"Ha — there is the rub, yes. But there seems little question when we consider it. After all, you are a Scot, my lord, not a Norwegian. And the lands you owe fealty for to me, the large mainland lordships of Lorn and Argyll, are much greater in size and value than the islands you do homage for to Hakon. Is it not so?"

"Size and value are not all, Your Grace. The people are important. Their support and their interests. Their, and my own, protection. There is a vast seaboard — and you, my lord King, are far away across the mountains. We never see you or yours. Whereas the Norsemen and their longships are ever with us. In truth, the Hebridean Sea is *their* sea, and most of Lorn and Argyll, although held of you in name, is wholly under the domination of the Norsemen, the Orkneymen and the Northern Islesmen, to say nothing of the Irish and the Icelanders. To all of whom, were I not under King Hakon's protection, I must needs pay tribute. Or go."

"So you esteem Hakon more potent a liege-lord than am I?"

"With all respect, Sire, I do."

"Then we must needs change this situation, sir. I must be able to protect my lords, else I am no true monarch, I agree. Fortunately, I had already decided to do this, to take back the Hebrides and the Isles into my own sure keeping. Loth to shed blood, I sent envoys to Hakon in Norway offering to buy back all these stolen territories. For much gold. And a treaty of peace. Hakon refused. Now he comes in force to take more. He says that he will annexe my entire western seaboard. But — none knows this better than do you, my lord!"

"I know it, yes."

"And you throw in your lot with Hakon?"

"I look facts in the face, Your Grace. As I needs must."

"Then look this fact in the face, my friend. There is a new wind blowing in Scotland. The days of my minority are past. I will be no more cozened, hampered, used. I will be true King of Scots — or die of it! The days of weak and divided rule are over. Scotland is mine — all Scotland. I intend to take back every island and every territory of the west. My whole realm musters to arms. Hakon is come to put all to the test — and tested he shall be. At sea he may be strong, but on land he cannot withstand my heavy cavalry. All Scotland is amove, I tell you. And you — you, a Scot, choose Hakon!"

The other spoke slowly, carefully. "I admire Your Grace's spirit. And commend your intentions. But there is a notably long seaboard to man, to defend. As I know to my cost. A thousand miles of beach and bay and inlet and island, cut up by lochs innumerable."

"I know it. But the same terrain faces Hakon. He will gain nothing by landing on the greater part of it. This is no Viking

62

raid. He has brought a great army, to outface me. He comes for war. And to fight me he must land where he can reach me. That you must also know. You, my lord are perhaps here to prepare the ground for him — in Galloway?"

The Islesman said nothing.

"So we now understand each other." Alexander's voice was still pleasantly conversational. "I say, I pledge you, that Scotland shall and must win in this struggle. And where does that leave you, my lord of Lorn? If you choose the wrong side? Here is what I propose. I do not ask you to join me. But I ask that you do not join the Norwegian. You have sworn oaths of fealty to both crowns. Betray neither. Go back to your own place and wait. Leave Galloway. The chiefs here are disunited and leaderless — and have no love for the Norsemen, even if they scarcely love me! They will not stir without you, or other, to lead them. Go you back to Dunstaffnage in Lorn and await the outcome. If the Scots go down, time enough to join Hakon. But I tell you, if he cannot win *without* you, he will not win with you! And you lose all, with him. Will you do this for me, and Scotland, my lord?"

MacDougall's fine features were a study. Indecision undoubtedly was not often to be seen thereon; nor indeed harsh obduracy. He toyed with his wine-cup, frowning.

"So much to lose, my friend, by taking the wrong decision now. And so much to gain by the right!" the King added.

"Gain, Sire? I see only risk, loss from either course."

"Gain, yes. For, if you choose aright, and we defeat the Norseman, then I would think to make you my lord of the Isles — lord of *all* the Isles, my friend, not just the Sudreys. Your cousin Dugald of Garmoran, who calls himself King of the North Isles, is already with Hakon in Orkney. And is my avowed foe. He must go down. Magnus of Man is also in Hakon's pocket. So, in my new Scotland, I require a sure and reliable overlord of the West. I would wish that to be yourself."

For long moments they considered each other searchingly. Then MacDougall inclined his head.

"You are generous, Sire — and courteous. I could scarce be less so and still respect myself. I shall do as you propose. I shall leave Galloway and go, not to Dunstaffnage my house, but to King Hakon. And tell him that I cannot draw sword on his behalf, owing the greater fealty to you. The rest is in your hands — and in God's!"

Alexander let out a long breath. "That is . . . well," he said simply. "When you entered this room and I saw you, I said to myself that I believed we could be friends, my lord. Let us drink to our enduring friendship . . ."

4

Thomas Learmonth, head down against the buffeting October wind off the wide Clyde estuary, rode over the echoing timbers of the drawbridge into Turnberry Castle on its exposed peninsula, assuring the guard that he was there on the King's business and summons. The place was buzzing with activity like a beehive disturbed, armed men everywhere, the new royal standard of the Rampant Lion snapping in the half-gale from the topmost tower alongside that of the earldom of Carrick. He found Sandy, son to Sir David Lindsay the Chamberlain, to conduct him to the King's presence.

Alexander was run to earth in the private hall of the Countess of Carrick — and Sandy Lindsay's knock at the door took a little while to elicit the royal response to enter. Grinning, that young man showed the visitor in without comment, and discreetly retired.

"Ha — Thomas!" the King called, heartily, from a stone window-seat at the far end of the chamber, looking over his shoulder as though he had been deeply engrossed in the view of tossing waters. "You have come . . . promptly, I see. As, of course, is commendable." The monarch sounded almost as though there might be two views on that. "Countess — this is

True Thomas, of whom you will have heard — Learmonth of Ercildoune, esquire to my cousin, Patrick of Dunbar."

Thomas turned from his bowing towards the window, to find the chatelaine of Turnberry standing a notable distance from the King, before a well-doing fire of logs. She looked attractively flushed and bright-eyed — but the hot fire could have accounted for that.

"I have heard tell of Thomas Rhymer, to be sure," the lady said. "Welcome to my house."

Marjory, Countess of Carrick in her own right, was a sprightly, lively young woman, comely, shapely and undoubtedly conscious of the fact. She was the only child of the late Earl Nigel, grandson of an Earl of Galloway. If it was a disappointment that both these Celtic earldoms had produced only daughters, at least Marjory of Carrick could nowise be described as disappointing by any standards — as the King would have been the first to agree. She had a husband somewhere, the Lord Adam of Kilconquhar, brother to the Earl of Fife — but he was at present away at Dumbarton helping to lead the Fife force in the vast counter-invasion strategy. That Alexander had chosen to make the castle of Turnberry his own headquarters for this dangerous period was coincidental. But the preoccupations of war did not mean that a man should close his mind to all social and civil intercourse — especially such a man as Alexander mac Alexander.

Thomas bowed to the lady, unspeaking.

"How goes it at Portincross?" the King asked, moving from his window. "Does Patrick find it draughty? And time to hang heavily, in all this of waiting? These unending storms."

"He makes do, Sire, like the rest of us. He is much with the Lord Alexander, the High Steward, at his house of Inverkip, where they plan the defence of all the Cunninghame, Kyle and Noddsdale districts. Or else visiting the men on guard along the whole shores. As do I."

"To be sure. Do not we all. How do they fare, in your parts? In this delay? You keep them alert, vigilant, in fair heart?"

"It is difficult, Sire. Week after week. But we strive to do so. We keep visiting all the companies, make many practice assaults, seek to keep the men busy. But it is not easy, in this weather, everlasting wind and rain, to maintain a fighting spirit. Although, to be sure, it must be as ill for the enemy, if not worse . . ."

"Aye — there you have it. I know not whether to curse these storms or to bless them! The Countess Marjory, here, says we should give praise. That we can sit comparatively snug here, with all the land behind to sustain us and to gather more men — whilst Hakon must needs sit there on that Arran, unable to sail, or at least to invade. He and his host will fare less well on that island of mountains than we here, I swear!"

Thomas's glance from his liege-lord to the lady before the fire, taking in the hall's comfort and furnishings, was eloquent enough. "Yes, Highness," he agreed. "King Hakon is unlikely to do so well, at this present!"

It was indeed an extraordinary situation. After long delay at Orkney, with only one or two mere foraging raids down the Scottish east coasts of Caithness and Ross, the Norwegian fleet had at last set forth westwards on St. Laurence's Day, 10th August, to commence what seemed an almost leisurely progress down through the Hebridean Sea and the West Highland coasts. The theory was that they had been waiting the arrival of the King of Denmark — which apparently had not eventuated. Hakon had put in at various points on that long seaboard, Skye, Lochalsh, Mull, and Kerrera of Lorn, taking weeks about it, presumably in an effort to confuse and disperse the defending forces so that, not knowing where the main invasion was going to take place, the Scots would be forced to stretch out their manpower over hundreds of miles of that most difficult coastline — which to some extent they had had to do. But Alexander had taken a chance, convinced that in the end Hakon would have to come right down to the south for his real thrust, since by no other means could he reach the vitals of the Scottish realm and so inflict any major defeat. And as the weeks passed, so Alexander's reasoning became the more generally acceptable — for it had proved

66

to be a cold, wet autumn, with early snow on the hills and all the rivers running high. Any attempt to push an army inland from the West Highland coast, through the mountains, would have been impracticable — especially for a Viking host, which misliked marching or being far from its longships. At Lochalsh, Magnus King of Man had joined Hakon, with all his strength; at Kerrera, the Islay MacDonalds: but further south still, at the Isles of Gigha off Kintyre, Ewan MacDougall of Lorn had presented himself to the Norwegian to inform him that he would not, could not, aid him against his true liege-lord, the King of Scots, and resigning his Norse-held lands there and then — a confrontation which the said King of Scots would dearly have loved to witness. Plundering the more savagely Ewan's territories of Knapdale and Kintyre, even sending raiding parties as far east as Loch Lomond in Lennox, eventually thereafter Hakon had turned the tip of the seventy-mile-long Kintyre peninsula, at the Mull thereof, and sailed into the Clyde estuary at long last, the open coast of Lowland Scotland before him — Renfrew, Cunninghame, Kyle, Carrick and Galloway. Under the lee of the great mountainous island of Arran he had anchored, towards the end of September. And then the weather, bad enough before, suddenly became worse, gales from the west battering land and sea, day after day.

So, a mere fourteen miles away across the firth, the invaders sat, storm-bound. The Vikings, the finest sailors in Christendom, were not afraid of rough seas, especially in an estuary; but to attempt to land an army on a dangerous lee-shore in such tumultuous seas would be suicidal, even without a determined defence.

This gift for the Scots was welcome indeed. Not only was it bad for the enemy morale, but every day's delay gave much-needed time to call back the Scottish forces watching the seaboard northwards, since clearly the main thrust was indeed going to take place hereabouts whatever diversions went on elsewhere. Alexander's messages to his scattered commanders were urgent; but in that vast and difficult terrain, regrouping could not be achieved swiftly.

Meantime, there was also a problem in maintaining the

morale of their own troops here, standing idle along so exposed a coastline for so long a period in such grim weather. It proved indeed to be this aspect which accounted for the present royal summons.

"Thomas," the King said. "I want one of your rhymes, see you. Make me a rhyme to meet this occasion, a notable rhyme. Foretelling the utter defeat of Hakon and the great triumph of the Scots arms. For all men to declare and speak of."

Thomas stared. "But . . . but . . .!"

"It must be strong, but simple. Such as unlettered men can tell to each other. And remember. Short, see you, but telling. Ringing in the mind. A sure prophesy."

"Sire — I, I *cannot* foretell, to order! Any more than I can rhyme to order. It is not to be done . . . so."

"Nonsense, man! You can make me a simple verse, can you not? I am not asking that it be *true* foretelling — although God grant that it may be! Only that it *says* that Hakon is doomed. Your fame as True Thomas has gone abroad. Many men will know of you and your rhymes — and more will, hereafter. Do you not see? They need cheer, encouragement, during this time of waiting. A verse of yours, to trip off the tongue, could greatly aid. It will be passed from mouth to mouth. Prophesying sure victory. But — it must be short. To be remembered and repeated. One verse only. Sit you — do it now. I will help you."

"Your Grace — how can I tell you? That is not how rhymes are made. Not as letters are written, nor shoes are cobbled! I require time, for the thing to spring up within me, the *need* of it to spur me on . . ."

"The need is there, man — sufficient for any! As for time, how long to devise four lines? Off with you — and bring me the rhyme in an hour or so. My royal command!" Alexander grinned. "How did it go, that time in London Tower? 'When the Lion of Alba makes man's estate — let those watchers watch their gait?' Something of the sort. Watch *you*, then! Go somewhere in this castle and bend your wits to the task. I want that verse sent out by my clerks, far and near, this very day. See, Thomas — you could use that shadow over the sun, on the Eve of the Transfiguration, perhaps . . .?"

In no very suitable frame of mind for poetic inspiration much less divination, Thomas went limping down Turnberry's turnpike stairs and along its vaulted corridors. He did not closet himself in any private chamber however — all of which would be perishing cold — nor in the warmth of the crowded main hall or busy kitchens. Instead he went out into the gale, to tramp along the cliff-top path above the surging, foaming tide, battered and pummelled by the wind, drenched by the drifting clouds of salt spray, stamping out his resentment on the slippery, muddy track. And before he had limped half-a-mile from Turnberry Point towards Maidenhead Bay, he had the thing forming itself in his head, more than forming, ringing in his mind, as the King had put it.

The Norsemen sailed from the Orcades, to grasp at Alba's land;
  But a greater Lord than Hakon held Alba in His hand.
He covered the sun that day at noon as sign of wrath and skaith;
  And the Norse were wrecked on Scotland, and the price was
                                                Hakon's death.

Never, in fact, had a rhyme come to him more readily, with less of chopping and changing. Blinking the mixed rain and spray from his eyes, he turned back for the castle, bemused.

Up at the door of the private hall again, his knock was only a little more promptly answered. Alexander himself opened, frowning.

"Lord — you already!" he exclaimed. "Do not tell me that you cannot find the words, man — for I will not have it! I am decided on this."

"No, Sire — I have the words. It, it came to me. On the cliff, there. Here it is . . ."

"You say so? Come in, then — to the fire. You are soaked. Marjory — a beaker of wine for our Thomas . . ."

Before ever he reached the great open hearth, Thomas was declaiming the verse, his two hearers pausing wide-eyed to listen.

"God be good!" the King said, at the end. "Save us —

that is . . . that is excellent! Marjory — you hear? Is it not a notable rhyme? '. . . as sign of wrath and skaith! The Norse were wrecked on Scotland.' Good!"

"Notable, yes — but a little long, perhaps, my lord. For rough soldiery to remember."

Thomas scowled.

"Long, yes — but it matters not, I think. They will remember the best parts. Say it again, Thomas."

This time the composer jerked and growled it out.

"Aye — good, good," Alexander said. "Grasped . . . wrath and skaith . . . wrecked on Scotland — these ring notably well. But — this of Hakon's death. Is that wise? Hakon himself is scarce like to die in any battle. Some other word to rhyme with skaith."

"No," Thomas said flatly. "That is the way the rhyme goes, how it came to me. Let it stand, Sire."

"A pity for the verse to fail for one word, man! Faith, now — could you not work in the word faith instead?"

"If Your Grace conceives that you can do better, do so!"

"Ha — hoity-toity, now! I charge you, Thomas Learmonth . . . oh, let it be! It matters not. By the time that we learn whether Hakon lives or falls, the battle will be over, won or lost. Write it down then, man — there is ink, quill and paper over there on yonder table. Then I will have the clerks to copy it, many times. Now — the wine . . ."

*   *   *

How effective was Thomas's versifying, as an improver of morale, he had no means of telling. He did hear some of their own Dunbar men repeating the words in more or less garbled form, in the days that followed; but none actually mentioned the matter to him — although he was aware of some curious glances. Not that he expected any personal questioning or discussion — he would have been as embarrassed as would have been his questioners. Earl Patrick himself scoffed rather, in a friendly way — but then familiarity does tend to produce such an attitude.

After a fashion, as it transpired, higher power did rather reinforce the rhyme's message. For although it had seemed scarcely possible, the weather actually got worse, the storm building up to a fury such as none could remember previously. The first Sunday of October, the Eve of St. Adamnan's, indeed so fierce was the gale that none of the defenders could have told whether there was an invasion in progress or not, with the air so thick with spray and spume from the battered beaches, for half-a-mile inland, that there was no seeing a score of yards beyond one's nose. Not that any force could have landed in such conditions. The popular impression was that God indeed looked like being on the Scots' side.

On the Monday morning the wind had moderated somewhat. But a slight change in its direction, from due west to south-south-west, had the effect of clearing the atmosphere somewhat, or at least blowing the spray up-firth rather than directly on-shore, so that men were able to see for some distance, even seawards. As the light strengthened, from Portincross Castle, the stark little fortalice of one of the High Steward's vassals, forty miles north of Turnberry, which was Earl Patrick's present base, what the watchers saw were a number of scattered vessels being driven up-firth, like the spray, in that wilderness of tossing white water. None could doubt, by their aspect, dispersed and apparently helpless state, that they were there unwillingly, in distress. The Norsemen would not deliberately have put to sea in such conditions, all agreed — therefore these must have dragged their anchors. Arran's bulk must be proving insufficient breakwater.

Before noon a breathless messenger arrived from Alexander, the High Steward, at Largs, some eight miles up the coast, to say that the Norwegians actually had landed there. Not in any large numbers, as yet. But if more came, the Earl Patrick was to hold himself in readiness to bring down part of his force to the Steward's aid. Meantime to keep a sharp watch in case of more landings, in the Portincross area, and to warn commanders further south. Alexander, fourth High Steward, being the territorial lord of Renfrew, Cunninghame and Kyle, was in overall command hereabouts.

By mid-afternoon, with no further word from the Steward

and no sign of any attempted landings on his own sector, the Earl sent Thomas north to Largs to discover what was happening.

It made quite a difficult journey, with trees blown down across the tracks, burns raging high, his horse having to wade knee-deep and alarmed through blankets of brown-white bubbling salt foam, even out-of-sight of the sea, and seaweed festooning bushes half-a-mile inland. But the wind was undoubtedly lessening and the rain had stopped. Occasionally the peaks of Arran could be discerned, towering vaguely to the west.

The township, haven and castle of Largs lay beneath the steep escarpment of the Noddsdale hills where they came close to salt water, and a small promontory separated two shallow bays with shelving beaches, bad for navigation — except for the deeper mouth of the Gogo Burn where was the haven. Offshore just over a mile lay the quite large island of Great Cumbrae. This served as a substantial breakwater so that, in fact, the Largs landfall became the most sheltered piece of west-facing coast of the entire firth. Which was why the Steward had chosen Largs as his headquarters, since this might be expected to be a favourite for any landing attempt.

As Thomas approached it from the south, it was to see a strange sight. The shallows flanking the river-mouth haven were, like all the rest of the seaboard, a raging, seething turmoil of tossing, spouting waters under a curtain of spindrift; but, differing from the rest, this stretch was now littered with vessels. Nine craft lay there, obviously aground, the great waves in most cases breaking right over them in clouds of spray. Most had the long, lean, low-set outlines of typical longships, their proud rearing eagle and dragon prows now in sorry decline; but three were merchant-type craft, larger, broader, more clumsy, one a great ship close inshore, its masts snapped off, lying on its side. And, crazy as it seemed, around this and between it and the beach, four or five local fishing-cobles were battling amidst the mountainous rollers, tossing about like corks. Mystified, Thomas rode on.

Largs Castle crowned a spur of a quite steep little hill half-a-mile south-east of the haven, the Norman-style stone keep, as so often, built within the ramparts of an earlier Pictish fort, the Picts having been adept at selecting the best defensive sites. Thomas was for mounting the winding track up to this when guards on foot informed him that the Lord Alexander was down at the beach, at the haven.

He found the High Steward, with a group of his knights and vassals, standing alean against the wind, gazing seawards with water-filled eyes, obviously watching the progress or otherwise of the fishing-boats. Even as Thomas came up, a corporate groan arose from the group, as one of the cobles was seen to rear up on end under a great breaker, tossing out its six oarsmen like puppets before falling over, capsized.

"My lord — why? What folly is this?" the newcomer demanded.

Alexander Stewart turned. "Ah, Learmonth — you," he said. "That is the fourth. The fourth coble to go. Two going, two returning. Only one has won back safely. It is damnable . . .!"

"But — what, my lord? What are they at? It is madness. Small boats in that sea . . .!"

"That large vessel, Learmonth, the merchanter, carries all the spoil, the treasure, gathered by Hakon on this entire venture. All the gold and siller and gear, stolen from a hundred churches and halls and towns. That is what," the Steward declared.

"Treasure! Gold! Is that what now concerns you? Is that what those men are dying for? The realm in direst danger, and siller your concern! We believed you to be in battle with the Norwegians, not, not . . ."

"So we were, man — so we were. They have retired now, yonder — we drove them off." Stewart pointed over to Cumbrae island. "A pity to let notable treasure sink to the bottom."

"Pity that men should die before your eyes for it!" Thomas returned strongly. "What happened?"

"These merchanters dragged their anchors. Over at Arran. Some longships also, no doubt. The storm drove them here, to wreck. Because they carried Hakon's treasure, he sent a

73

force under Ogmund Crow-dance to rescue it. Some of that was wrecked also." The other pointed to the stranded longships. "Some hundreds won ashore, from them and other craft. We attacked and repulsed them. Slew many and took some captive. Some were Manxmen and Islemen, and they talked. That is how we know of this Ogmund and the rest. And the treasure. They have retreated meantime. But not far. They are there, anchored now under the lee of the Great Cumbrae, only a mile off. You can just see them. They will be back. They will want that treasure . . ."

A shout drew attention to the fact that one of the cobles had managed to reach the crippled merchant-ship.

"If we can empty that ship, there will be less to bring back Ogmund Crow-dance!" the Steward added.

Thomas shrugged. "Is there anything else I have to tell the Earl Patrick, my lord?"

"Yes. Tell him that the prisoners say that Hakon has over two hundred and fifty longships at Arran — twenty thousand men! The storm is abating. He may strike at any time. God knows where. It could be at more than one point. But this Largs is the most sheltered shore, for disembarking. And he could re-assemble behind Cumbrae, where Ogmund lies now. Reform his craft for the assault. I have sent word to the King at Turnberry."

"You judge that the main assault will be here then?"

"I do not know, man. But if *I* was Hakon, I would come here. Go tell Patrick of Dunbar to be ready to come to my aid at any time, with all speed. I have had beacons built on the high ground behind here, to warn you — but whether you will see the smoke in this wind, the good Lord knows!"

"Twenty thousand! That surely is false? They cozen you, these captives."

"Perhaps. But they say that Magnus of Man has brought fifty longships, and Dugald of Garmoran another forty. Each has a crew of eighty, at least, and can carry another one hundred and fifty fighting-men. So . . ."

Practising depressing arithmetic, Thomas rode back to Portincross.

*   *   *

It was not the Steward's messengers nor his smoke-signals which alerted the Dunbar force on the Tuesday morning, but their own look-outs' observation. Soon after first light they saw the longships coming out from the shadow of Arran, a fearsome sight. But they were heading almost due north, not eastwards across the firth. Although there was still a gusty wind it was no longer a gale, the seas moderated although still rough, visibility improving.

The Earl Patrick and his vassals watched from the parapet-walk of Portincross Castle. Two matters were fairly quickly established. One that the enemy was continuing on a course which would take them through the comparatively narrow channel between the south tip of Bute and Little Cumbrae island — which meant that the assault was probably going to be in the Largs area or still further north in the narrowing estuary, possibly using the two Cumbraes as a screen. The islands, only half-a-mile apart, between them constituted a six-mile barrier off the Cunninghame shore. The other point made clear was that, daunting as all those menacing long-ships appeared, wolfhounds of the seas, there were not more than sixty of them involved. So that the majority of Hakon's fleet was still uncommitted.

This of course put the watchers in a quandary. Was this force, of possibly six thousand to eight thousand men, merely the advance party of a larger assault? Or were there other attacks, to be aimed more or less simultaneously at different stretches of the mainland coast? Eight thousand, even six, would be more than the Steward could cope with, and he would require their help. But, on the other hand, this might be only a diversion and the principal Norse thrust elsewhere, possibly to the south, likewise demanding their aid to beat off. The Earl just dared not move off northwards at this stage.

They waited, watching, in some agitation. Soon the last of the longships disappeared from their sight behind the bulk of the Cumbraes, each in its flurry of spray set up by its two-score and more oars, above which the single square sails, with their painted devices, caught the slanting beams of the first thin watery sun seen for days.

There was still no sign of any other or reinforcing fleet,

when the watchers perceived the smoke of two beacons rising from hilltops behind Largs, to the north, blowing almost horizontally in the wind but plain enough -- the Steward's summons.

Patrick reckoned that he had no option now. Alexander Stewart was in command here. The Dunbar and March contingent totalled almost one thousand — but unlike most other baronial forces, being Borderers, they were almost entirely horsed. He decided to send messengers to Boyd at Ardrossan, Lindsay at Ayr, and the King at Turnberry, informing them of the situation, and himself to take six hundred of his horsemen to Largs, leaving at least a few hundred available to help counter any other attack.

They took longer to cover the eight miles' ride than Thomas had done the day before, despite improved weather. This was because of the knights' heavier and armoured horses. These great war-chargers were magnificent animals for their purpose, almost impossible for infantry to stop, but scarcely speedy — and, of course, carrying the extra weight of heavily-armoured men. It was not long before Thomas, for one, grew impatient at progress, and prevailed upon the Earl to let him ride ahead with a couple of hundred of the more lightly-horsed Border mosstroopers, to at least offer the Steward some advance support and encouragement.

It was soon to be seen that this was much needed. Rounding the shoulder of the castle-hill, they perceived that Largs was indeed the Norwegian objective. For a full mile up that shelving but comparatively sheltered shore, the long-ships were drawn up, beached in the foaming shallows, score upon score of them. They were built for this, to be sure, shallow-draught with upturning prows which allowed them to be run up on to sand and shingle. Even so, some had come to grief, capsized or holed and sunk, for the seas were still far too wild for satisfactory landing, and there were reefs and skerries unseen beneath the lacework of white water. Men were streaming ashore still from the latest arrivals, waist-deep in the breakers, swords, maces and battle-axes held high, shields slung meantime. Some stumbled and fell, inevitably.

On the beaches hand-to-hand fighting was going on in

what looked like utter chaos. No cavalry appeared to be involved as yet. On a mile-long stretch of sand and pebbles and rocks, divided by the river-mouth but most of it to the north, the confused mass of men fought it out in small companies, groups and pairs, inextricably mixed, without any semblance of line nor front. Keener eyes were able to discern squadrons of cavalry waiting in the sand-dunes and re-entrants behind, obviously unable to engage the enemy without riding down their own foot.

Pounding on, Thomas led his company in search of Alexander Stewart. He found him, with some of his officers, sitting their horses on a low sandy ridge above the beach, staring at the mêlée.

A young man, of knightly prowess and high chivalry but unused to large-scale war, it was quickly clear that the Steward was out of his depth. He was cursing the scene of hopeless confusion before him, gnawing his lip between shouts of "Fools! Fools!"

He turned with an air almost of relief upon Thomas, as representing something he could effect. "You, Learmonth! Good, good! Look there — fools! No line, no order. I told them, I told Montgomerie and Fairlie and Graham. To hold a line on the beach. Then to force gaps through the enemy — wide gaps, so that my cavalry could drive through. Get behind the Norsemen. Roll them up. But — this! This folly! You — how many have you?"

"Two hundred. Earl Patrick comes on, with another four hundred. And the heavy cavalry. He should be here shortly . . ."

"Yes. Then dismount, man — have your men dismount. Then down there with you. Afoot. Draw so many as you can of those fools to you. With them cut a way through. Make a lane for the horse. To win through, to sweep up the Norsemen. You have it?"

"My lord — no! Not that — not on foot. Not so . . ."

"Yes, by God! The only way, man. Do as I say. A fresh, tight company on foot will rally the rest. Or enough of them. To make the gap we need."

"No, no, my lord — not there. Not these. Never! These are

mosstroopers, born to the saddle. Trained to fight ahorse, only that. To dismount them would be madness. Use your own horse for it, if you must."

"How can I? Into that rabble. They would ride down our own men. Do as I say, Learmonth."

"If you must send in dismounted men, send some of that waiting cavalry yonder, my lord. There — and there." Thomas pointed northwards to groups of horse waiting in the dunes. "Those will serve you. Better than dismounted mosstroopers."

"No — they must bide there. Between us and that hill." It was the Steward's turn to point. "Or all could be lost. Hakon is there, on the hill. And the man Ogmund. The first wave of them — they won to that sandhill. There are two thousand of them there. Only our cavalry between will keep them from sweeping down behind us, man. I dare not move the cavalry."

Thomas, concerned with the battle below, had not taken in the situation to the north where, about a quarter-mile away, a grass-grown former dune, inland a little and larger than the others, could be seen to be a mass of men. The Scandinavians did not go in much for banners, but two streamed in the wind on this hilltop, the larger the royal standard of Norway.

"Move your cavalry, my lord. If it coaxes them down from that hill, so much the better. Then, when the Earl Patrick comes up, the horse can cut them up on this level machar . . ."

"No, I tell you! Too dangerous. All could be lost that way. Before ever Dunbar comes. Best as I say. Dismount your men, Learmonth. That is my command! Rally so many down there as you can. And cut me a gap through to the water. No more talk, for God's sake!"

Thomas swallowed. "My lord Steward — I take my orders from the Earl Patrick. And he sent me to fight ahorse. As we are trained. My respects, lord — but no! But — I will make your gap!" And, without waiting for the High Steward's reaction, he turned in his saddle and waved back to his waiting squadron.

"Wedges!" he shouted, tugging out his sword. "Forward —
in three wedges. Down at them, in three. Side-by-side. A
Cospatrick! A Cospatrick!" He yelled the Mersemen's slogan.
"Forward — trot!"

His two hundred had been riding in approximate column
of threes, so that hurried forming into three arrowhead
formations was less difficult than it might have been. Nevertheless, the resultant wedges were distinctly ragged, shape-
less, with much jockeying for position as all moved forward at
the trot. But training told and some sort of order grew, all on
the move. Thomas spurred to put himself at the head of the
foremost formation, and held it back until the others drew
level on each flank. By this time they were trotting down
through low dunes and ridges of soft, blown sand — which
did not help. Then the open firm sand-and-shingle of the
main beach was before them, a seething mass of hacking,
smiting, stabbing, yelling and screaming men.

"Canter! Canter!" Thomas cried, slashing his sword forward. "Through them — through all. Right through. A
Cospatrick! A Cospatrick!"

There was only perhaps one hundred yards before the first
of the struggling ranks, but sufficient for the horses to attain a
full canter. Down upon the horde of battling foot, friend and
foe alike, the mosstroopers pounded, swords swinging, lances
still upright — since these would have caused the break-up of
the formations.

Between them, the three wedges formed a front of some
seventy-five yards. The impact, the crash and jar as this hit
the packed fighters, was dire, overwhelming. Men went
down like ninepins beneath the threshing hooves, in shrieking,
bloody ruin. There was, of course, no way of avoiding the
Scots therein, who went under no differently from the enemy.
Thomas and his men sought to use the flats of their swords in
the main, for the sake of their fellow-countrymen, and most
of the havoc was wrought by the horses, their weight,
impetus and flailing steel-shod hooves.

Learmonth, in the centre-front, knew a wild elation,
mixed with a desperate fear that he had done terribly wrong,
betrayed his own people, taken the heartless choice. But this

79

was battle, war, men slaying each other all around him. This was surely the *right* course for the battle, for Scotland. It could, indeed, lessen the carnage, shorten it . . .

All the time he was spurring, smiting, beating his beast with clenched fist, yelling the slogan. A short, wide Norse sword, deflected by his horse's charge, struck his leather-covered lame knee — but he felt nothing. A Manx stabbing-spear whistled past his cheek and struck the man on his left. A Scots dirk thrust upwards at him as its owner went down, grimacing hate, and slashed a rent in his leather jerkin. But his mount never faltered, even when it half-stumbled over fallen men; and the wedges, although losing their shape and something of their pace, beat on.

Then they were through and into the streaming tide and crashing waves.

Now for further decision, right or wrong. They had driven the required gap through the battle, a seventy-five-yard corridor of broken and bleeding flesh. But would the Steward be sufficiently quick to take full advantage of it? Bring his cavalry forward in time to exploit it, before it filled up again? No sign of them yet. But — was not his own horsed squadron best placed to do just that? Why wait?

A swift glance around decided him. Opportunity was there. His men were milling around, also uncertain what was next to be done. There seemed to be few serious casualties amongst them — although he could see three or four fallen horses thrashing about in that terrible corridor, and two riderless beasts were careering along the strand.

He raised his sword-arm. "Form up! Form up!" he yelled. "Not wedges. In column. Column of threes. Form column."

In the tide's edge turmoil they got into some sort of order. Placing himself at the head, he led the way back into the gap, at the trot, amongst the fallen dead and wounded. The horses did not like this at all, sidling and rearing.

In this formation they made a triple file perhaps two hundred and fifty yards long. It was just about the width of the battle-area of the beach. Riding up, Thomas was surprised to note how little impact his cavalry drive appeared to have had on the fighting as a whole. Apart from this bloody lane, the struggle went on as it had done before, left and right, as though they had never intervened.

Signalling and calling a halt, he turned at right angles, pointing his sword southwards. Then he cantered back down the column to roughly halfway, inserted himself in the front rank there, and waved the line forward, southwards.

It was obvious now, to even the least intelligent of his mosstroopers, what was intended. Their gap had been cut approximately midway along the beach, so that perhaps half of the total were fighting on this south side of it. But the southern section represented a situation different from that on the north. For here, after some six hundred yards, instead of a hill serving as base for the Norse main body, was the barrier of the river-mouth. Clearly, any drive by cavalry here, if successful, would have the effect of rolling up the milling foot against the river and so penning and demoralising them.

So now the long file of horsemen pressed into the fighting in a quite different tactic, not seeking to canter, not even able to keep up a trot for much of the time, but moving steadily southwards and keeping in line-abreast, seeking to drive the battling foot before them like sheep, Norse, Manxmen, Islesmen and Scots alike. Or not quite alike, this time, for now, their approach being less headlong, the Scots on that beach had time to recognise that any cavalry there must be of their own folk. So many took the opportunity to break off fighting, to try to dodge between and get behind the advancing horsemen. Soon there was quite a substantial body of foot coming along raggedly in their rear, to deal with such of the enemy as the mosstroopers failed to beat down or drive before them.

Not that the Norwegians and their allies allowed themselves to be driven, sheeplike or otherwise. These were some of the most fearless and practised fighting-men in Christendom. But they were greatly handicapped here, largely leaderless, in no formation, jammed ever more tightly together, and finding horsemen amongst them whilst still in furious fight with the foot.

Much more actual battling was involved now, for the

cavalry, than heretofore. But even so, the advantage was wholly with the mounted men, their superior height giving both increased reach and striking-power, the horses themselves a major weapon as well as hard on enemy morale. Also, the mosstroopers were fresh to the fight and under central control. Hacking, smiting, thrusting, they ploughed on into the rabble.

It became easier, in fact — if that was the word — as they progressed. For the ranks they were pressing back affected those behind, crowding them, distracting them, infecting them with uncertainty and alarm, forcing them also in a southwards direction. Strong leadership might have stemmed the tide, for the enemy vastly outnumbered the Scots; but meantime such was not in evidence.

By the time that the Borderers were one-third of the way to the river, there was a distinct drift before them; every extra few yards increased and speeded this. Before long it developed into a steady stream, breaking off fight, the Scots foot left panting and thankful, some to pursue, some to stagger off, most to fall in behind the horsemen. Probably most of the enemy did not realise that there was a water barrier cutting off their retiral.

Soon it was almost headlong flight — which the mosstroopers exploited by forcing their advance to a fast trot, shouting their slogan. Utter confusion ensued when the first of the Norsemen reached the Gogo Burn. The river here flowed between shingle banks some fifty yards apart, deep enough to be navigable by fishing-boats at all but lowest water. Today the tide was half-in, and none could cross without at least a few yards of swimming.

Not all were swimmers, most obviously. Some plunged in, throwing away heavy weapons, some raced off upstream, some even downstream for salt water, hoping no doubt to win out to their longships, some turned at bay for a last stand.

Thomas admired the courage of these last — but that did not prevent him from waving on his line of horsemen right to the river's edge, forcing the desperate defenders on into the water. There, in a lather of foam and spray, which quickly turned red-tinged, the slaughter was fierce, unrelenting. On and on the riders pressed, until their mounts were above their bellies, and men were drowning before them in scores. Even then Thomas the Rhymer was not content. The Mersemen were used to swimming their horses across Tweed and Teviot and Whitadder, greater streams than this. Right over he led his squadron, to clamber out beyond, streaming water, and to race on after such enemy as had reached the further bank, to prevent them reforming on the southern beach. Not that these probably constituted any real menace now, however many, for almost all had had to abandon their weapons, save for daggers and dirks, in order to swim.

Presently, with the fugitives so dispersed as to constitute no danger, Thomas called a halt, to count the cost. He found that he had lost about thirty men all told — although some of these would be only dismounted, their beasts disembowelled under them by ripping dirks. Many with him were wounded in some degree, though few seriously. He himself became aware of a bleeding forearm and a grazed check-bone where a dagger had been thrown at him. But considering the havoc wrought, it had been a cheap victory indeed.

Leaving half-a-dozen of the slightly-wounded to aid their more seriously-afflicted comrades, and to cross back to the former battle-ground to look to their fallen, Thomas formed up his squadron into column of threes once more, and turned north-eastwards for the Largs bridge, to rejoin the Steward and his lieutenants. They did not gallop thither however.

The Scots leadership was no longer on the sand-ridge where Thomas had left them. Indeed the entire scene had much changed. Fighting was going on now on two fronts — below, on the beach, where another and much larger cavalry force was doing for the northern half of the Norse throng there what he had done for the southern, rolling them up in the other direction; and a second battle was going on well to the north, inland, on the level machar grassland, behind the dunes and in front of the hillock where the Norwegian standard flew. This last obviously was the greater engagement, with both horse and foot involved on the Scots side. But it seemed to be largely stationary, deadlocked; whereas that on the beach was developing into another rout, with some of the enemy fleeing either north towards the hill or out into the sea, back to their ships. In the forefront of the advancing Scots cavalry, Thomas discerned the lion banner of the Earl of Dunbar, amongst others.

Clearly their services were not required down on the shore. Thomas led his people northwards towards the main battle.

It was evident as they drew near that, whatever was happening this side of the hill, there was major disorder in the Norse rear, on and around the hill itself. Men, from the shore fight, were retiring to it, as to a base, while others were streaming away seawards for the ships.

If Thomas and his men had expected praise for their exploits against the enemy right, they were disappointed. Alexander Stewart, on his new vantage-point, was much too preoccupied with the situation before him to refer to what was past — so, at least he did not berate Thomas for his disobedience.

"Learmonth — thank God you have come! At last!" he exclaimed. "See — they are working round to the hillfoots, yonder." He pointed eastwards. "Off with you. I have no other horse left to send. Head them off. Quickly."

"But — what is the position, my lord? Some come, some go. The battle seems all awry. The beach is all but cleared. But here . . .?"

"Hakon has retired — why, the saints alone know! Back to his dragon-ship. I cannot think that he is wounded, back there. Even our few archers could not shoot so far. Ogmund Crow-dance now commands, they say. He is a fighter, and attacks here. We are containing him, meantime. Currie, on our left, has done well. Made strong advance there. If Dunbar would but join him, from the shore, we could roll up the Norse right. But now — this on *our* right! These seek to work round along those hillfoots. So, go stop them, man!"

Weary now as they were, the mosstroopers had to ride off again, due eastwards behind the main Scots force, heading for the rising ground at the foot of the high escarpment which flanked all this coastline about a mile inland. There, amongst the whins and scrub-woodland, numbers of the enemy could be discerned advancing well ahead of their main array. Not any great many seemed to be involved — but more were heading that way on the Norse left. Undoubtedly this would create a dangerous situation if they won round behind the Scots rear.

A half-mile dash brought Thomas's horsemen to the scene of the trouble. Only a few Scots foot were hereabouts, amongst the trees and bushes, to oppose the infiltrating enemy, and not making much of it, over a wide, broken and slantwise front, cut up by gullies and burn-channels and fallen trees. It was far from ideal country for cavalry, likewise, but the morale effect might well be important. Thomas strung out his squadron, now numbering about one hundred and fifty, in a line some four hundred yards long, facing northwards, and with the foot to back them up and being added to as they went, moved forward. There was little or no trotting now, the terrain forbidding it.

This proved to be very different from either of their two previous engagements, more akin to a boar-hunt than a battle. For the terrain imposed similar restraints and difficulties on the advancing Norsemen; so that they could not progress in any formation or even massed ranks but had to work their way through the broken wilderness as best they could in ones and twos and small groups. Consequently the opponents came face to face more as individuals than as a force, and certainly not in any recognisable line — often without warning. It was as well, in the circumstances, that the Vikings did not much go in for archery, for hidden bowmen could have picked off the horsemen almost at will. But the short sword and the axe gave them no advantage here against cavalry lances, which now came into their own, as at boar-sticking.

The scrub and close country no doubt aided the Scots too in that the invaders would not be able to perceive that the cavalry was in fact only one line deep. At all events, the mosstroopers were able to press ahead, unevenly and with pauses to try to maintain some sort of line, but fairly consistently, thereby turning the tide of the infiltrating Norse. And once the forward enemy began to turn back, they automatically spread alarm and indecision in those behind. So that, presently, the Scots advance became assured, and more like a deer-drive than a boar-hunt, with little actual opposition.

Nevertheless, it all took some considerable time to work through those tangled foothill slopes, until they had flushed out the last of the enemy, to see them hurrying away westwards whence they had come, across the levels towards hillock and beach.

But now it was a different scene which met the eyes of both friend and foe. The struggle on the machar seemed to have disintegrated altogether, with the invaders in general and untidy retreat to their ships, the Norwegian standard no longer to be seen, the hillock site abandoned, with everywhere the Scots pressing hard. Fairly evidently the battle was over.

Thomas and his company rode down to join in the harrying process, but were really too late. They pursued a few of the last stragglers into the sea, where their countrymen on foot were loth to go at this stage; but horses as well as men were weary now, sated with struggle, and they were really only making a gesture. Thereafter, they were content to add their cheers, as the remaining longships pulled off, including King Hakon's dragon-ship which had attached itself to the wrecked treasure-vessel — obviously an aspect of the situation which had been preoccupying the monarch.

Amidst modified rejoicing, the Scots took stock and licked their wounds. Their victory was heartening and their losses comparatively modest, not one-quarter those of the enemy. But all recognised that only a small proportion of the total invading force had been engaged so far — on this sector at least. Who knew what had gone on elsewhere? Although no other major movement of shipping had been observed out on the firth.

The Earl Patrick was concerned about the safety of his own sector of the coast — for the bulk of the two Cumbraes prevented them from seeing the sea-approaches to the Portincross area. So, after fairly brief mutual congratulations and some small refreshment, the Dunbar contingent, with its wounded and dead, left the Steward and his people to return southwards. Reaction had set in, to some extent, for Thomas as for others, euphoria evaporating. Even slight wounds and bruising, once the excitement is over, can stiffen up and become sufficiently painful to nullify heroics.

Their reaching Portincross at dusk coincided with the arrival of a messenger from the King at Turnberry, seeking news and informing that there had been no word nor sign of any other invasion attempt further down the coast. It looked almost as though the Largs assault had been as much concerned with the recovery of the stranded treasure as with any wider objective.

Next day King Alexander himself arrived, with extraordinary tidings. Fishermen from Arran had crossed the firth to report that the Norse threat was in fact over — at least in these parts. At first light the entire enemy fleet had raised anchor and sailed away south by west, round the Mull of Kintyre for the open Western Sea. Look-outs from points of vantage all agreed that there was no single longship left in the Firth of Clyde — save those wrecked on the Largs shore.

The Scots could scarcely credit the news.

But a week later, with confirmatory reports from the West Highland seaboard, right up beyond Skye, that the Norwegian fleet was still sailing northwards, presumably heading back to Orkney, the King gave orders for a stand-down of his forces meantime, sent his thanks and congratulations to all, and commanded the bells to be rung and prayers of gratitude to God said in every abbey, monastery and church in the land.

Thomas returned to Ercildoune something of a hero, the Mersemen making the most of their contribution and therefore his own. He was greeted with his own new rhyme, chanted by the Cospatrick family, somewhat garbled but recognisable, now apparently become popular on all hands. The Lady Bethoc found his grazed cheek-bone and torn forearm greatly in need of her frequent attentions — indeed, Thomas almost got the impression that she would have preferred more serious and incapacitating wounds so that she could have nursed them the more comprehensively.

But this flattering attention was as nothing to the renown which came his way early in the New Year, just before Up

Holy Day, when the news reached Southern Scotland that King Hakon had died in Orkney. Apparently he had been slightly wounded at the Battle of Largs, though nothing to concern his people at the time. However he had failed steadily in health thereafter, with a mounting fever, and succumbed in the bishop's palace at Egilsay on the Eve of St. Drostan, in his forty-seventh year.

Suddenly Thomas the Rhymer's verse was on all lips again, especially the line: '*And the Norse were wrecked on Scotland and the price was Hakon's death.*'

Folk began to look at him with something approaching awe — which that young man did his best to refute, protesting that he had only written what first came into his head. When even Bethoc eyed him a little askance if he made even the most innocent reference to future happenings, Thomas Learmonth commenced to consider the advisability of giving up this versifying propensity as unprofitable, an embarrassment.

5

Thomas carefully reined back his roan mare a little, so as not to be the first to reach the summit ridge — discreetly, that it would not be apparent to the others. This was one of the drawbacks with young people, their overdeveloped competitive spirit. He greatly enjoyed their company but could have wished that it was not always a struggle as to who could be first at this or best at that, with subsequent accusations by the losers that the winner had taken an unfair advantage or was showing off or something such. Yet any obvious letting others win was equally productive of censure. The young Cospatricks were probably no worse at this than others, but it could be wearing for their escort.

He managed to make it second-equal to the top with

Johnnie, Pate in the lead — which was acceptable — Gelis and Alec battling for third place, Bethoc waiting behind with the youngest girl, Eala on her short-legged pony, as was allowable for mere females. There was, in consequence, no breathless argument on this central and highest of the three Eildon summits, such as had made a battle-ground of the first.

The views from up here were superb, on this fine May noonday, with all the East and Middle Marches of the Borderland spread out below and around them. This, of course, was one of the finest view-points in all South Scotland, the three isolated and shapely peaks rising abruptly out of the Tweed's fair valley a thousand feet and more above the river, the Trimontium of the Romans. From the ancient Pictish fort here they could look almost due northwards up the long vale of Lauderdale to their own place of Ercildoune, four miles away and far beyond to the Lothian hills; eastwards across the lower ridge of Bemersyde to all the green rolling plain of the Merse; southwards across the vales of Ale Water and Teviot, where the rival peak of Ruberslaw reared proudly, to the long blue ramparts of the Cheviots with England beyond; and westwards up silver Tweed itself and over the endless heights and hollows of the Forest of Ettrick into infinity. It was one of their favourite rides from Ercildoune — but scarcely because of that vast prospect, or not consciously anyway. At what stage views became appreciated by young people was uncertain, Bethoc alone seeming to have reached it. The challenge was the thing, the sense of achievement, the fine feeling of freedom engendered by height and isolation, the sensation that they were superior to all the feeble world down below.

When Thomas, pointing to the sweep of it all, sought words to express something of the wonder and beauty of that vista, he was interrupted.

"Race you to the last top!" Pate cried. "Wager my new falcon that I am there first, for anything you can offer!" And he dug heels into his black's flanks. Quick as he was off the mark, however, his brother John was quicker. And the other youngsters, even Eala, showed only a little less alacrity.

Looking at each other, and wagging their heads, Bethoc and Thomas followed on at a more sedate trot down into the quite deep dip before the third and westernmost Eildon summit half-a-mile away.

On that final hilltop presently, beside the burial cairn of some Pictish chief, they found a war of words in progress. Johnnie had won, apparently — but only because Eala had fallen from her pony when it had slipped on a scree-face, and Pate had gone to her aid. Johnnie nevertheless claimed the hawk wagered, declaring that nothing had been said about conditions and making up rules as they went along; and anyway, Eala had been perfectly capable of climbing back on to her own horse. Pate had just realised that he was going to lose and so had taken this opportunity to dodge defeat. Gelis sided with Johnnie, the other two with Pate. All appealed to Thomas for support.

When that young man suggested that Pate's action had been praiseworthy and so should not cost him the race, Johnnie was much incensed, declaring that it was all a trick to prevent him getting the new falcon — which he clearly coveted. Pate, denying this, thereupon proposed a new and alternative trial of prowess and endurance — namely that they race back whence they had come, over the middle summit again to the eastern hill, whoever reached the top of that first to be the undoubted owner of the said bird. This was rapturously agreed by five-sevenths of the company.

However, both Thomas and Bethoc here drew the line, enough being entirely enough, they asserted. The others could do so if they wished, but for themselves they would ride comfortably downhill to the Tweed ford below Newstead, where they would look to meet the others in due course.

Amidst scornful accusations of feebleness, craven-heartedness or mere mushy intentions of dalliance, the contestants hurtled off eastwards, and the accused set their beasts' heads to the long downwards slope.

It was quite steep, at first, and the descent took up most of the riders' attention. But presently, proceeding slantwise across the middle slopes amongst the budding bracken, with the bees humming loudly on the yellow blaze of gorse and broom and the cuckoos calling from the scattered thorn-trees, the pair could relax and enjoy the genial, sun-filled excellence of it all, letting their horses pick their own way. Although, in fact, relaxation was not the man's predominant reaction, at least.

"Is this not a joy, Thomas?" Bethoc said, at length. "So lovely a place, so fair a day — and ourselves, alone!"

"Yes," he said.

"They are very dear, to be sure — my family. But . . . tiring!" she went on. "Are all families so? Now that I am a woman, I weary of them, sometimes. Is that unkind?"

"No." He glanced sidelong at her, savouring that phrase 'now that I am a woman'. She had recently had her seventeenth birthday, and Thomas was very much aware of the fact.

"We are so seldom alone," she went on. "It would seem that we would be, often, when living in the same house. But it is not . . . easy, is it?"

How should he answer that? Implying that he had tried to arrange it so — as indeed he had, on occasion, but was hardly prepared to admit it. Or indeed that on other occasions he had actually deliberately frustrated her some-what obvious attempts — so contradictory and confused were his emotions, his desires and his fears.

"No," he admitted.

"But now, at least, we *are* alone," she declared. "And on Eildonside, with the cuckoos calling — the loveliest place in all the world, I think! Oh, I am happy, Thomas! Are not you?"

He swallowed. "Yes. It is . . . good."

"I love the sound of the cuckoos. My mother finds them tiresome, calling the same two notes all the livelong day. But I do not. They speak to me of warm and kindly but strange things, of promises, perhaps. Promises that summer comes, yes — but other things too. Of times to come, of far places, of a life to be lived, *my* life. And, and . . ." She shook her lovely head. "Do they speak so to you, Thomas? You, a poet?"

"I am no poet!" he said, almost harshly. "I am but a rhymer — which is very different."

"I say that you *are* a poet. And a good one. You have all the feelings of a poet, I know! Do the cuckoos not speak to you, Thomas? Say . . . something to you? Look — there is one, flying from that tree." She pointed, her finger making a scalloping motion as it followed the swooping up-and-down flight of the grey bird. "It does not call as it flies, see you — only when it settles. There — it has gone to that thorn-tree, beside the broom-bush, lower. And hear — it calls again. It seems to call to *us*, Thomas, calling us on. Can you not hear?"

"I hear — only a gowk mocking eternity!"

"Mocking . . .?" She bit her lip. "Thomas — we have time. We shall come much too early to the ford, before the others. Let us go sit under that thorn-tree for a little. And listen to the cuckoos. Listen — and see if you can hear more than your mockery! As *I* can. For a little while. Come."

He began to object, but she had heeled her mount forward and was off into a canter over the slantwise russet-tipped deer-hair grass below that eastern Eildon peak.

She reined up beneath the sturdy old wind-blown hawthorn — which the cuckoo promptly vacated. She had to bend forward in her saddle to avoid the lowermost branches, for it was no tall tree on that exposed hillside. The blossom was just beginning to open, more pink than white, and its sweet scent was like a caress, not yet heavy. When the man came up, on his taller horse, he could not have got underneath without his face being scratched.

"Help me down, Thomas," she said.

"But . . ." he commenced — but she cut him short.

"I said help me down, sir!" For that moment she was the Lady Bethoc of Dunbar and March, of the ancient royal house of Scotland. She had not, however, required aid in dismounting hitherto that day.

Jumping down, he went over to her side. For a long moment she looked down into his eyes, and then, with a deliberate gesture which was much too positive for abandon, launched herself bodily down into his arms.

He staggered a little, for she was no sylph, and his lame leg of doubtful support, and had to grip her the more tightly to prevent them both falling. She aided, to be sure, her own arms flung around his neck, her face against his, cheek to cheek.

And, with Thomas Learmonth, it was as though a dam had burst. In that moment all the long-repressed emotions and desires and sheer need overwhelmed his carefully-built stops and barriers. Hungrily, his lips sought hers, found them and parted them — and without hindrance. Passionately, he kissed and was kissed, urgent hands as vehement as lips, clutching her shapely, rounded, yielding person, seeking incoherent words from the said too busy lips, his whole consciousness and being seeking to be fused with the other within his embrace.

Panting, moaning a little, she strained against him, eyes closed, breasts heaving.

So they stood, lost in each other, the horses moving away a little, to crop at the deer-hair grass tentatively.

When at last, out of a kind of growing limpness, she stirred differently within his arms, the man, becoming aware, slackened his grip, stilled his lips and not exactly drew back from her but thrust her a little away from him, although still he held her strongly by the arms. He stared at her.

"Oh, Beth, Beth lass — I am sorry!" he gulped. "Forgive me — forgive! I, I . . . was carried away. Forgot myself . . ."

"Thomas, my dear, my dear — never say it! Why be sorry? It is what I want, want! What I have wanted for so long. Surely you must know it? Is it not sufficiently plain? I love you, Thomas — love you!"

He shook his head in mixed wonder, perplexity, frustration. "My heart, my sweet, my beloved — and I you! Beyond all telling. Love, yes. Adore, delight in, worship! And that you should offer me *your* love, also, is joy, joy! But — it is all the more unforgivable that I should act so, give way. Knowing, knowing . . ."

"Why, Thomas — why? When we love each other. What is there to forgive?"

"Ask that of others! Ask your father, your mother! Ask any but yourself! For it cannot be, my dear — it is not possible. For you and me. You must see it."

"I see nothing but that we belong to each other, Thomas and Bethoc. That is all. That is everything."

"Would God that it was, Beth. But we cannot shut our eyes to it. You are not for such as myself. You come of the royal house, a great earl's daughter. And I am a poor lairdling, penniless — and lame! It is beyond all hoping. Always I have known it. And sought to, sought to . . ."

"My father and mother esteem and like you well. You are almost as one of their own, like another son . . ."

"I am your father's small vassal and esquire — nothing more. He has three-score of vassals greater than I am. He has been kind to me, the Countess most generous — possibly because of my lameness. But that is all. No doubt they have plans to wed you to some great lord, as their eldest daughter . . ."

"No! Never!"

"It is their right, lass. Your, your destiny. To be a great lady. Not gudewife in the little tower of Ercildoune. You must know it, Beth — for you have wits aplenty, as well as beauty and so warm a heart."

"They will not make me wed against my wishes. And I will wed only you, Thomas Learmonth! They are good, kind . . ."

"They are the Earl and Countess of Dunbar and March, Beth. No less. Amongst the highest in the land, after the King. Nothing can alter that. And they have trusted me, put you and the others in my care. As this day. And now I do this . . .!"

She shook her head. "You are wrong, Thomas. It need not be so. If we are strong, make sure. I am not a child any more. And you are renowned, famous, even the King seeking your aid. But — let us not spoil this dear moment by fruitless dispute, my beloved. We have a little time yet. Let us sit beneath this tree and listen to the cuckoos, as I said. And, and. . ." She left the rest *un*said.

It is doubtful indeed whether they did hear any cuckoos after the first few moments sitting. There was so much else to occupy their attention. And with all that warm, eager and lovely feminity so close and quickly within his arms in fact,

Thomas Learmonth would have been no less than super-human if he had found his scruples and doubts sufficient to inhibit him from due co-operation. He was, after all, a man of sentiment and poetry.

Time in such circumstances is apt to be more immaterial than usual, and it was with something of a guilty start that Thomas realised that they had probably been there longer than they ought, in more respects than one. His companion was much less perturbed, declaring that there was no hurry. It would do her brothers and sisters no harm to wait for a little while.

Reluctant to leave that precious spot, they collected their grazing horses and rode on.

They were first at the Newstead ford, as it transpired, and had to wait for some time for the unexplained latecoming of the others. At least this spared them any sly or ribald suggestions as to how they had been passing the time. Oddly, Gelis had somehow won the final race, and therefore the falcon — which she had no desire for. So there was a new battle going on between Pate and Johnnie as to what should happen to the bird, Gelis remaining smugly non-committal. This debate preoccupied the ride back to Ercildoune. The older couple thought their own thoughts.

*   *   *

For Thomas, at least, the problems connected with his new-found romance were fairly promptly pushed into the back-ground by the course of events. For a royal messenger had arrived at the castle during the young people's absence, informing that the King intended to strike while the iron was still hot, to teach Magnus Olafsson of Man a lesson not to join in attacks against his neighbour the King of Scots. Alexander would be marching south-westwards for Galloway in a few days' time, preparatory to embarking an army to sail for Man. When he passed down Lauderdale on his way, he expected to pick up the Earl Patrick and a suitable contingent of Mersemen and Lothianers to aid in the expedition.

So Thomas was sent off recruiting once more, and lovers' difficulties relegated to the back of his mind, whatever the case with Bethoc. He did make her promise to say nothing to anyone in the meantime, however, as to their predicament.

Five days later the King arrived, at the head of a host about four thousand strong which, with the Dunbar and March contribution and those he intended to collect in Galloway, ought to give him a force of between five and six thousand — which should be sufficient to deal with the Isle of Man, and which anyway was fully as much as shipping would be available to carry. Alexander had sent orders for Ewan of Argyll to assemble the necessary craft from all the coasts down from Lorn to the Solway, at Kirk Cuthbert's Town; but he recognised possible problems in this respect.

The King proved to be in fine spirits. His unexciting Queen had redeemed herself and presented him with another child, a son and heir, to be named Alexander again. With the succession thus better established, his mounting credit in his kingdom was further enhanced. The Largs battle and the entire anti-Norse campaign had much increased his prestige — he was indeed being accorded the title of Slayer of Ravens, these days, to his amusement but undoubted satisfaction — and in general his personal authority was being established fairly consistently.

"So, True Thomas — what notable prediction have you for us on this occasion and enterprise?" he cried, when he perceived the esquire behind his master. "Tell me — can you contrive the death of this Magnus Olafsson as you did Hakon Hakonsson? He would be little loss, I swear!"

"No, Sire — no predictions," Thomas answered flatly.

"Tut, man — why so? We rely on you, now, to sustain our spirit, I vow! Do not play difficult, of a mercy!"

"I cannot rhyme lacking some need to do so, my lord King — some inner need. As I told Your Grace at Turnberry."

"Is your liege-lord's command not sufficient need, sirrah?"

"With respect, Sire — no. It has to well up within. Like some well of water."

Alexander snorted and turned away.

However, once on their way, the King showed no resentment towards the reluctant bard, and not infrequently tossed a word or two back to him where he rode behind the Earl

Patrick. He heard, in the process, much of what was said by his betters and learned in more detail what they had heard only as rumours at Ercildoune as to the realm's affairs. It seemed that in March a deputation had come south from Orkney, in the name of the new King of Norway, Magnus Hakonsson, led by his Chancellor Askatin and the Bishop of Orkney, offering terms of peace. Alexander, however, feeling himself to be in a strong position, rejected this approach, declaring the terms to be inadequate. And to reinforce that message, he had sent off two expeditions. One, under Durward and Buchan, to the far North, to the rebellious provinces of Caithness, Sutherland and Ross, long dominated by the Orkney Norse, with instructions to demonstrate in no uncertain fashion whose writ now ran in Scotland; the other under the Earl of Mar to the Highland West and Inner Hebrides, on the same errand. Reports coming back from both indicated success, with MacDonald of Islay submitting unconditionally and indeed yielding up his infant son, with nurse, as hostage; whilst the north mainland chiefs seemed to be almost eager to return to their due allegiance. Only Dugald of Garmoran calling himself King of the North Isles, remained defiant, secure in his Outer Hebridean islands of Lewis and Harris, from which only a large-scale naval expedition could dislodge him. Now this new move against Man might act as a rehearsal for just such a venture.

There was news also from England. King Henry was at war again with his rebellious barons who were demanding reforms, this time his son Edward being on his own side. But at the beginning of this month of May, Henry had suffered a great defeat at Lewes in Sussex, where Sir Simon de Montfort, Earl of Leicester, the barons' leader, with the aid of Louis of France, had not only won the day but actually captured both Henry and Edward. Alexander sounded not at all dejected as he reported his father-in-law's sad fate. So now all England was in disarray, de Montfort in approximate control, although nominally acting in the name of the King his prisoner. It was partly on account of this state of affairs that Alexander was risking this Manx invasion — which would have been highly dangerous had the English not been otherwise preoccupied,

Magnus of Man being something of a protégé of Henry for strategic reasons, and the English fleet capable of annihilating the Scots transport shipping *en route*. But now . . .

So they rode across Scotland south by west, in fine style, with indeed little of a going-to-war feeling about the entire proceedings. The Forest of Ettrick — through which lay their route — had seldom looked fairer, that late May, with everything blithe and burgeoning around them, summer ahead. Thomas was haunted by the cuckoos calling from every hillside, all the way — and not unaffected thereby.

Then, halfway down Annandale, one of the Red Comyn's vassals came hot-foot from Dumfries to inform them that the almost holiday atmosphere was in fact justified. For Magnus Olafsson of Man himself had landed at Kirk Cuthbert's Town, but not in war. He had come with only a small retinue, apparently, to throw himself on the mercy of the King of Scots, no doubt recognising the various writings on the wall.

Alexander seemed almost disappointed. He did not indulge in any hosannas, at any rate, said that he would proceed on to Dumfries, and gave orders that Magnus should be brought before him there.

Ewan MacDougall of Argyll arrived at the Grey Friars' monastery in the Nithside town the next afternoon, with the Manxmen. Magnus Olafsson was an elderly man, shrunken, indeed always undersized — although not so small as had been his father, Olaf the Morsel. Never of a cheerful disposition, present circumstances hardly helped, and he was the picture of gloom. So poor a creature did he seem, to be the successor of a long line of Viking pirates, that Alexander found himself inhibited from taking so strong a line with the man as he had intended.

"I greet you, Magnus Olafsson, less warmly than I would have wished to do," he began, after their wary exchange of bows. "I had thought you my friend and neighbour, but find you my enemy. When I had done you no hurt."

"I regret it, Sire," the other said, thin-voiced. "I was . . . but ill advised."

"Ah — so that was it? And who advised you thus ill, King Magnus?"

"I, I meant . . . mistaken. We — my Council and myself — we were ordered by King Hakon to sail to his aid. We could scarce refuse. My kingdom is small, an island. At the mercy of Hakon's longships. What could we do?"

"You could have joined *me*, your neighbour. Who also was being assailed by the Norseman. Aided me to repulse him."

"You, Sire, have no mighty fleet. To protect my island. Hakon could threaten — but he also could protect . . ."

"So you chose to play the jackal! To run to which you thought to be strongest, caring nothing for the right. And you chose wrongly!"

"My lord King — hear me." In his agitation, Magnus achieved a semblance of spirit. "For you, it is easy to speak so. You have a large kingdom, many men. Mine is small. I cannot stand alone. I must needs choose what seems best for my people. I desired no war. I sought Henry of England's protection. But he answered me nothing. What was I to do, with Hakon's hundreds of ships in the Western Sea . . . ?"

"You could have done what my Lord Ewan of Argyll here did in like case. He went to the Norseman and told him that he could not in honesty support him in arms. Braved the Raven! And now, I make him Lord of all the Isles."

"May I remind Your Grace that we are *not* in like case. MacDougall is your vassal, one of your lords. I am not."

Alexander paused. "Aye — there is the nub of it," he said. "You are not — or *were* not! Now it is time that you were! If you wish to keep your island throne. You have made it very clear that Man is indeed too small to stand alone. You require a protector. From henceforward *I* shall be that protector. Not Norway, not England, but Scotland. You shall be my vassal, Magnus Olafsson, and I your liege-lord. And your price for having chosen amiss will be that you may sleep more soundly in your Manx bed of a night!"

The older man said no word. He twisted his hands together.

"You will do homage to me for Man," Alexander went on. "And you may retain your style and title of king. But sub-king or Regulus, under the High King of Scots. You will

99

provide me with ships of war, longships or galleys, when I call for them, at any time. And an armed host of men for war, if need arises. In return, you and yours shall have right to take refuge in my realm and to call on my aid against your enemies. This is my decision. Is it understood?"

Magnus inclined his grey head.

"So be it. My clerks will write it down, for our signatures and seals. And we shall bury the past. Look not so downcast, man! You have come out of this coil passing well, I vow! It could have been . . . otherwise. Now — let us refresh ourselves with what this monastery may be able to offer us, while the clerks write. Come . . ."

Without a blow being struck or even a protest made, the ancient kingdom of Man thus became part of the Scottish realm, and Alexander's credit the higher. Yet, despite the undoubted triumph and enhancement of security, power — especially in relation to the Western Isles and Hebrides — and increased prestige, a sense of anti-climax prevailed at Dumfries, not least with Alexander himself. To have marched a gallant army across Scotland for this seemed somehow pointless, unsatisfying — though no doubt not unsatisfactory. There should be celebration — but none felt in the mood; and this minor Grey Friars establishment in the small town of Dumfries did not provide either the setting or the where-withal. The Red Comyn had a castle here but it was shut up and unwelcoming, with its lord actually a prisoner in England, captured with Bruce of Annandale whilst fighting for Henry at the Battle of Lewes — the price to pay for possessing large lands in two kingdoms.

The very next morning Magnus was despatched back to Man, and the King of Scots and his host turned to march northwards again in curiously less high-spirited style than when they had marched south. Was victory tasteless, in fact, lacking bloodshed?

6

The Lady Bethoc sighed audibly, and not for the first time, nor it must be admitted with any sort of romantic fervour as might have been suitable in the circumstances — with irritation, rather, impatience. Which was not like that quietly equable young woman. Her mother, looking up from her needlework, eyed her thoughtfully. Normally she had been apt to listen in dreamy enthralment when Thomas was entertaining them with song and lute, as he did so often of an evening; but of late there had been some undefinable change in her attitude — this restlessness. The Countess, that artless but understanding soul, nodded to herself as though in confirmation of some earlier suspicion.

Unaware of such reactions, Thomas continued to pluck at his lute-strings while he sang, low-voiced, slowly but tunefully, the sorrowful ballad of *Sir Ewain But Reproach*, and what befell that lovelorn Arthurian knight. He had a great affection for these old songs, so redolent of this Borderland, and had in fact collected a large repertoire, setting to his own melodies some that were merely spoken folk-tales. The Cospatrick family were duly appreciative of having their own permanent minstrel, as it were, in the family — and hitherto Bethoc the most obviously so.

It was May again, the May of 1265, though scarcely as fine weather as the previous year, with so far no cuckoos heard around Ercildoune. The two youngest children were off to bed; and Earl Patrick was, as so often, absent on ploys of his own which did not call for the presence of an esquire — the Countess by now schooled to be philosophical about this. Pate and Johnnie played the game of tables before the dying embers of the lesser-hall fire, with only occasional and muted bursts of argument to interrupt the music, while their sisters stitched at tapestries, like their mother. It all made a pleasing domestic scene inconsistent with impatient sighing.

When Thomas plucked the last lingering note to end *Sir Ewain*, there was a prompt shout from the boys for him to render them *Kempy Kaye and the Fusome Fug*, a scurrilous, indeed scandalous, ditty, much favoured. But Bethoc rose to her feet, dropping her needlework.

"No!" she exclaimed. "No! Thomas — I told you about the eggs. That I wanted you to see the nest I discovered down at the burnside. To tell me what eggs they were. Some strange sort of duck, I think. If we do not go now, it will be too dark . . ."

"Will your eggs not still be there in the morning, Beth?" her mother wondered.

"No. Or . . . yes — but Thomas is always too throng with ploys in the morning. Off with Father."

"She but wants to get him alone behind a bush!" her younger brother declared, grinning. "Girls' sport!"

"Johnnie — enough!" the Countess said, as Gelis giggled.

Thomas stood up. "I saw a pair of pintail flighting down Leader two days back. It could be these, nesting up this burn . . ."

"Come, then. We shall not be long."

"I have a mind to come with you!" Pate threatened, from the tables-board. "I am as good at birds' eggs as is Thomas, I swear — if not, perhaps, at some other things!"

His sister achieved an extraordinarily unkind glance from such fine and gentle eyes, and turned to hurry to the door and out. Almost apologetically, Thomas followed after.

Down through the slantwise orchard beneath the castle-mound she led him, in the cool evening air, almost at a run, skirts kilted up. Not until the fall of the ground hid the castle and its windows did she turn, to grasp his arm.

"Thomas — I have been trying to get you alone — trying for long," she exclaimed. "You must have seen it."

"I did not, no. What is to do, Beth? Why this, this haste?"

"Why! Sufficient reason, I declare! Today, I overheard my father and mother talking. They were alone, in the charter-room. I was seeking Mother, to ask her something. When, at the door, I heard my name spoken. I listened — perhaps I should not have done, but I did! They were talking of me. And, and — they plan to wed me, Thomas!"

"Lord!" he said.

"It is not to be borne — not to be borne, I say! Now that I am eighteen years they said that it is high time that I am wed. Father said that he had spoken to the Earl Malcolm of Fife at the last Council meeting. His second son, Duff MacDuff, unmarried. Colban, the elder son, is. He said it will be a fair enough match. This Duff will heir large lands. But I will not, I *will* not, Thomas!"

Unhappily he gazed at her flushed and lovely face.

"I do not know him. But I *hate* him! I will nowise wed him. Or any, but you. What are we to do, Thomas?"

"God knows! What *can* we do? Your father may marry you to whomsoever he will. You cannot refuse . . ."

"I can. And do!"

"But not to any effect, Beth my dear. It is a father's right. None may gainsay it. Especially when the father is Earl of Dunbar!"

"I will not. I will run away! If need be. If I am woman enough to be wed, then I am my own woman! And yours! There must be something that we can do. Think, Thomas — think!"

"If there is, I do not know it, lass."

"I believe . . . I believe that you do not care!"

"Save us — I do, Beth. God knows that I do. It is damnable. But, of ourselves we cannot overturn the due order of things. Would that we could."

She left him, to hurry on down through the apple trees.

He caught up with her. "Perhaps . . . once you have seen him, Beth — this Duff MacDuff. I have met him. He is none so ill. A quiet man, of my own age, I would say . . ."

"You, Thomas — you are telling me that I should *like* him! Find him to my taste? Instead of yourself? Oh, I would never have believed . . . !"

"No, no — not that. I meant that when you have seen him, you could perhaps tell your father and mother that you could not wed him. For some reason. Something about him that you could not abide. I do not know what — but you might think of something. Perhaps your father would heed you then. He loves you, and would not wish you sorrow . . ."

"Then if I tell him that it is *you* I love and would wed, should he not heed me also? You made me promise not to tell them. But I say that you are wrong in this . . ."

"No. To tell Earl Patrick of me would be the end of all. Do you not see? He would send me away from here — nothing surer."

"Then I would go with you!"

"Lassie, lassie — that is not possible, not how it could be. Think you. A great earl's daughter and a lame lairdie! We cannot traipse the country like a pair of gangrel-bodies. How could we live? My small lands are here, at Ercildoune. I have nothing but them, and your father's employ. Besides, he would soon find you, have you back — and me punished. We must think better than that."

"Thinking will serve us little — only *doing*," she averred. "And doing quickly. For they talk of a meeting. More than a meeting — a feasting here. Having the Earl Malcolm and this Duff to come, with others, so that we may see each other, know each other in some measure, before, before the betrothal is announced. How kind they are!"

"I am sorry, Beth. When is this to be?"

"I did not hear — they did not say a time. But before long — that was clear. I am to be allowed to *see* this man before I am wed! Is that not a joy!"

He shook his head, helplessly. "It will be the time, then, to say that you mislike Duff MacDuff, to find some fault in him. Sufficient to convince your father . . ."

"Then he will but find another. Only delay it all a little."

Unhappily they went on down to the floor of the side-valley of the Leader's Ercildoune tributary. At the water side, Bethoc showed him the large untidy nest of twigs and reed, wedged between the roots of a scrub-willow overhanging the stream, with its seven pale green eggs. But he could not tell her what species of duck they represented — and, anyway, she was in no mood to be greatly interested.

Seeing her drooping shoulders, woebegone expression and hearing the lack of lift and lilt in her normally musical voice, his heart went out to her and he turned to take her in his arms. Desperately, she clung to him, even wept a little. Much affected, he sought to comfort her, assuring that it would be none so ill, that they would find a way, promising that he would think of something, while he kissed her tears away. Needless to say that led to more positive embracing and passionate kissing. By mutual consent they sat down there at the burnside, and to the whisper and chuckle of the water, succeeded in forgetting for a time their sorrows and problems.

It is to be feared that they managed to forget the passage of time also, for they were still there and oblivious to all but each other when the Countess and young Pate came down to find them. Nor did they hear the others' approach.

"Guidsakes — so that is what you are at!" the Lady Christian exclaimed. "We thought that you must have fallen in the burn and drowned yourselves, at the least!"

"*I* did not think that! I told you how it would be!" Pate cried.

They started up, Thomas guilty, confused, Bethoc neither, defiant rather.

"I . . . I am sorry!" he said. "I, we but paused. For a moment or two. I was to blame . . . was carried away. It was remiss of me. I forgot myself."

"No!" Bethoc declared.

"My, oh my — it is that way, is it!" her mother commented. She looked speculative rather than censorious. "You both know what you are at?"

Not the reaction Thomas had anticipated, he hesitated. Not so his companion.

"Yes, Mother," she said. "We do."

"Aye. Young folk always think that they do, Beth. And sometimes do not. Or let matters go too far. A little of this must be sufficient. Mind it. Your father, girl, might be less . . . understanding! See that he is not troubled in the matter." She looked directly at Thomas. "You understand *me*?"

He swallowed. "Yes, Countess. I, I thank you."

Bethoc opened her mouth to speak, but her mother raised a hand.

"We shall say no more about it — meantime. Back you go. It is chill now — although perhaps you have not noticed it?"

Bethoc went to her bedchamber almost immediately thereafter. When Thomas excused himself, presently, the Countess cocked an eyebrow at him.

"She thinks that she is a woman grown, of a sudden," she said. "And so knows it all. She will learn, in time. But you, Thomas, *are* a man grown — and know now! We all esteem you well — and hope to continue so to do."

He bowed, wordless, and retired.

For better or worse, the alleged project of the MacDuff father and son being invited to visit Ercildoune to view and be viewed, was abandoned when, a couple of days later, the Earl Patrick announced that the King had summoned him and others to a great gathering at Roxburgh Castle in a week's time, when the baby prince, Alexander, would be on view — after a somewhat sickly first year of life — and would be ceremonially invested as Prince of Strathclyde and heir-apparent to the throne. This was the ostensible reason for the assemblage and celebration; but there was another and more urgent reason why the great ones of the kingdom should be called together. The new Pope Clement the Fourth was promoting the Crusade, to be led by King Louis of France, the most ambitious effort yet to free the holy places from the grip of the Infidel. And to raise the necessary funds for this, he was levying a great tax on all Christendom. The Cardinal-Deacon Ottobuoni of Fiesci was the Papal Legate sent to England and Scotland to prosecute this policy, and he had been working in England for the best part of a year. Now he was on his way to Scotland, and not only Alexander but most of the Scots magnates were distinctly apprehensive as to the visit and the demands to be made upon them. Ample reports had come northwards as to the severity of his requirements and assessments in England — and the fact that that country was in the grip of civil war and therefore bound to be a disappointment financially to the Cardinal, would be apt to make his claims on Scotland the more excessive. Bishop Gamelin the Primate had for the same period been acting as a sort of forerunner for the Legate, trying to collect moneys and making himself less popular than ever in the process. The King was anxious that what looked like being inevitably something of a confrontation with the Cardinal should be staged in conditions which would give him and his nobles and prelates any advantage possible — since the full weight of Holy Church's majesty and authority was not to be countered lightly. And by all accounts countering there would have to be. It was not that Alexander and his lords were against the Crusade. They were prepared to co-operate and subscribe; and many to take an active part. But this of being assessed and taxed compulsorily by an authority outwith their own land, and in gold and silver, not kind, in which the realm was far from rich, was obnoxious; also once acceded to, it could be used as a precedent for further exactions.

At any rate, Alexander wanted a full turn-out of his nobles and bishops to support him. And he wanted no synod, no ecclesiastical type of gathering, where the religious voice would tend to have the greatest authority. So this mainly celebratory assembly was planned for Roxburgh, and the Papal Legate invited thereto. The Earl of Fife would be there, with his sons — as would all the other earls; and since there was to be feasting and entertainment after the child-prince's investiture, and the womenfolk of the nobility were summoned to take part, it would be an opportunity to meet the MacDuffs — and save the Cospatricks the trouble and expense of providing a special entertainment.

So, in due course, the Dunbar and March family, less the younger members, set out on their fifteen-mile ride to the royal castle of Roxburgh, formerly Rook's Burgh, where Teviot joined Tweed, Bethoc at least in no cheerful frame of mind. Thomas, as usual, accompanied his master as personal esquire, the Earl Patrick treating him in as casually friendly fashion as ever — so presumably the Countess had told him nothing of the burnside incident.

Roxburgh was almost the favourite of Alexander's twenty-three castles and palaces, as it had been his great-great-grandsire David's, who had built it — despite the fact that it was the reverse of centrally convenient and so close to the Northumbrian border. Indeed that was the reason for its existence as reminder that the King of Scots still claimed Northumbria as part of his realm, however little was being done about it these days. Alexander had been born here, to be sure — as had his new son. The castle's site was extraordinary in that it occupied the summit of a narrow ridge between the two great rivers at their junction, an elongated site protected on all sides save the west, where the ridge had been artificially gapped by a deep and wide ditch which was normally spanned only by a drawbridge, On the south side the walls soared directly in cliffs above the Teviot; but on the north there was a lower shelf between its heights and the Tweed, and along this narrow terrace huddled the township of Roxburgh — which had started merely as a castleton to serve the fortress but had grown into the fourth-largest town in Scotland, indeed a royal burgh. So cramped had its site become, despite its almost mile-long straggle, that a detached extension had had to be erected some way to the west, known as New Roxburgh. With the complementary abbey-town of Kelso, or Kelshaugh, beyond Tweed to the east, the area was the most populous in southern Scotland, set in the lovely and sylvan surroundings of the green Border hills, with the Forest of Jedworth, eastwards extension of the great Ettrick Forest, lying nearby, to provide unrivalled facilities for hunting.

The entire vicinity was teeming with life and activity as the Ercildoune party arrived. Their escort was left to find its way to quarters in the new town, the old being already packed out with visitors, the lesser nobility and the entourages of the lords. The earls, bishops and great magnates were being put up in the castle itself, but even here it was uncomfortably crowded; and the Earl Patrick's accommodation proved to be less than palatial, in one of the small flanking-towers. However, they had this to themselves, Thomas's share being no more than a garderobe or mural cupboard, six feet by four, in the thickness of the walling off his lord's circular and modest chamber, the only ventilation and light being provided by a single narrow arrow-slit. Nevertheless, he reminded himself that it was better than he had had at Portincross Castle, on the Largs campaign, where he had slept in a stable.

The castle was buzzing with talk as well as people. Apparently the King had received word from the south that the Prince Edward of Chester, the Queen's brother, had contrived his escape from Dover Castle, where he and his father had been held prisoner since the Battle of Lewes the year before, by Simon de Montfort, Earl of Leicester. He was now said to be seeking to rally such of the nobility as remained approximately loyal to Henry for a resumption of the war. Longshanks had, it seemed, achieved his escape by the simple expedient of challenging his captors to a series of horse-races, to pass the time, all of which he let the others win until they were sufficiently off their guard; whereupon he outrode all — and went on riding until all were left behind. Edward was not popular with the Scots because of his arrogance; but this exploit certainly enhanced his reputation.

The other news being circulated was that the Papal Legate Ottobone, as he was called in England, had arrived by sea at St. Andrews in Fife, and that Bishop Gamelin would be bringing him on to Roxburgh on the morrow.

That evening there was a great banquet in the huge hall of the castle, with some three hundred sitting down. The heralds had a complicated and thankless task in arranging the seating in accordance with due precedence, some folk being inordinately prickly in the matter. Thomas was not; but after seeing Earl Patrick and his countess to their lofty places at the King's long dais-table at the top of the hall, he was given the little-appreciated duty of conducting the Ladies Bethoc and Gelis to their seats at the table immediately below the dais, where they were set, amongst the earls' families, one on either side of the Lord Duff MacDuff of Fife. It is to be feared that he performed his esquire's functions less punctiliously than usual, despite the fact that Bethoc no doubt needed support and encouragement.

Duff MacDuff certainly showed no particular gallantry at this encounter, looking more embarrassed than eager, lovely a picture as Bethoc made. He was a somewhat stolid young man, strange for one who was half a Welshman, his mother being the daughter of Llewellyn, Prince of Wales. Still only in his late teens, he was quite good-looking in a black-browed, sallow fashion, slender of build and richly dressed. Gelis obviously found him to her taste — which was perhaps as well, for her sister half-turned her shoulder on him as soon as she sat down and promptly engaged in determined converse with her neighbour on the other side, William, son and heir of the Earl of Ross, a considerably older man safely married.

Thomas's own seat was well down the hall at a very secondary table — although even this was carefully graded, with the earls' esquires seated above those of lesser lords and barons, but still below the most junior knights. Whether fortunately or otherwise, this placing gave him a clear view of Bethoc and her immediate neighbours — which did not tend to make him the better company for his own neighbours.

When all were seated, trumpets sounded heralding the King's entry, and all rose. Led by the High Sennachie, Alexander strode in, a little quickly for the Queen on his arm, he bowing and smiling right and left, she keeping her eyes lowered. Behind them came a nurse carrying the precious infant on a cloth-of-gold wrap. Instead of going directly to his seat, Alexander escorted his wife to hers and leaving her at the table, led the nurse and child down from the dais to make a circuit of the hall, showing off the princeling to all, a father most proud, to the oohs and ahs of the ladies and the self-conscious grins of the men. An heir to the throne, sound of body and, hopefully, of mind, was desperately important for the peace and security of the realm, any doubts about the succession being a sure cause of trouble and possible revolt on the part of ambitious alternative incumbents.

This parade over, the child was removed, the King took his place at the dais-table and all could sit. The banquet commenced, to the accompaniment of music from instrumentalists led by the King's *clarsair* or harpist, one Elias, from the minstrel's gallery.

Throughout, Thomas's glance seldom strayed far from Bethoc and her companions. As time went on he almost began to feel sorry for Duff MacDuff. Surely seldom had a partner at a feast, and a prospective husband at that, received so little attention, much less encouragement. William of Ross, on the other hand, must have felt himself to be next to irresistible — and his wife, on his other side, sadly neglected. MacDuff may very well have wondered whether perhaps there might have been some mistake as to which of the Cospatrick sisters he was destined for, since fifteen-year-old Gelis could scarcely have been more forthcoming, her gaiety and laughter quite a feature of the evening.

Entertainers were brought in during the later part of the meal, although so full was the hall that there was little space for their performances — singers, dancers, tumblers, gypsies, a Muscovy bear-leader, even a white horse from Hungary which actually danced to music. Such banquets as this were apt to develop somewhat rowdily, as the wine flowed; but on this occasion all was kept under fairly strict control by the sennachies and heralds, at this stage at least, spirited guests being firmly restrained.

When the lavish eating was over, at last, and before serious drinking began, a trumpet-blast stilled the clamour and gypsy-dancing, and the King rose, signing to all others to remain seated.

"I greet you all in warm regard," he said, "and invite you to join with Her Grace and myself and my friends and councillors here, in our joy that our ancient throne is now garnished and buttressed by the blessing of a son and heir. God be thanked, he is growing strong and well after sickness at the start. So now it is time to make plain to all Christendom, friend and unfriend alike, that this Scotland is in good heart, firm in her purposes, stout in her arms, assured in her destiny. We have defended our shores, defeated the invader, recovered most of the territory that had been lost to us, gained the Kingdom of Man, and established peace with Norway by treaty. Now we have a prince to succeed. I call for Alexander — one day to be the fourth of his name as King of Scots."

As all rose to their feet cheering, the dais-door was thrown open and the child brought in again, not by his nurse this time but by two heralds resplendent in Lion Rampant tabards of red and gold. They carried him round to the front of the dais-table, where Malcolm Earl of Fife, Hereditary Inaugurator of the old Celtic kingdom, and John, Bishop of

Glasgow, representing Holy Church, came forward, the Bishop taking the baby from the heralds, the Earl laying a hand on the little cloth-of-gold shoulder, the infant choosing this moment to look up and around, yawning hugely.

"In the name of the *Ard Righ Albann* and the lesser *ri* of this realm, of which I am one, I, Malcom MacDuff do hereby declare before you all that this Alexander mac Alexander mac William mac Henry mac David mac Malcolm is the true and only Tanister and Heir to the Throne of Scotland," the Earl proclaimed, loud voiced. "To which end, as sign and symbol . . ." He turned towards the King, who reached across the table with a gold and jewelled chain, which Fife placed approximately around the child's neck. " . . . I now invest the said Alexander as Prince of Strathclyde and Cumbria. Hail the Prince!"

The applause was lost in a blaring flourish of trumpets from the back of the dais which seemed to shake the very smoke-blackened timbers of the roof — and unfortunately so startled the new Prince of Strathclyde that he burst into loud wailing. The Bishop's efforts at pacification proving unavailing, the Queen herself came anxiously round from her place, took her son, and with no more success as soother, hurried with her protesting offspring from the hall.

Grinning widely, the King held up his hand to still the mixed acclaim and laughter. "My son has no ear for music, it seems!" he declared. "Her Grace will reason with him. I thank you, my good lords, for your kind offices," he added, to the Earl and Bishop. "A more expeditious investiture I have yet to witness!" He picked up his silver goblet. "I now ask all present to rise and raise their wine-cups, to drink with me to the health and prosperity of Alexander, Prince of Strathclyde — and to swear your support for him in all time coming."

When this was honoured with loud enthusiasm and much shouting, the King again claimed silence.

"On this happy occasion it is my pleasure to declare my gratitude and great esteem towards all who so ably and bravely distinguished themselves at the affray at Largs and elsewhere, in the defence of our realm against the Norsemen.

Much of courage and daring and devotion was displayed in those days, not only on the Clyde shore but up and down our coasts. Most must go unrewarded and unsung. But to one or two I can show some small appreciation. I call on these to come forward herewith, all of whom contributed nobly to the victory — the Lord Colban of Fife; the Lord David of Strathbogie; Robert Bruce, Younger of Annandale; William Comyn, son to the Lord of Badenoch; and Alexander of Lorn, son of Ewan, Lord of the Isles."

When, amidst loud applause, these five made their way up to the dais, the King ordered them to kneel in line before him, and calling for a sword from the High Sennachie, he tapped each on his shoulder with the flat of the blade, commanding him to be a good and true knight, in the fear of God and lealty to his liege-lord, until life's end. And so to arise — Sir Colban, Sir David, Sir Robert, Sir William and Sir Alexander. Adjuring them all to make their vigils and take their knightly vows that same night, he sent them back to their places under a shower of congratulations.

Alexander held up his hand again. "I have not finished, my friends," he resumed. "Others amany distinguished themselves in the warfare now so happily past, and these I can only thank warmly from a full heart. But three in particular, not great lords or their sons, rendered especial service which calls for especial recognition. One of these, already knight, died on the field of battle, at Largs, having repeatedly led sallies against the enemy, rallying our flagging line. This was Sir Peter Currie, vassal and chamberlain to the High Steward of the realm. Another to whom we owe much also is vassal to the Steward, Malcolm Wallace of Elderslie, who took Sir Peter's place when he fell, and most gallantly led that company throughout the remainder of the battle although twice wounded. I command Wallace of Elderslie to come up before me."

This created a considerable stir, for Wallace was only a small laird, of the old Cymric stock, as his name implied, of whom very few had heard. A big man of early middle years, he came self-consciously forward from the bottom end of the hall.

As they waited, Alexander went on. "The third I name to you bears a style most will have heard tell of, although fewer will know him. But we all owe much to him. For while the realm awaited the onslaught of Hakon and his hordes in some fear and alarm, this young man raised our spirits, assuring us of the victory, and most strangely insisting that King Hakon himself would die. Not only this, but he led part of my lord of Dunbar's array in the battle, with as great spirit and success as in his foretelling. I charge Thomas Learmonth of Ercildoune to come forward — True Thomas the Rhymer!"

There was much exclamation and comment. Flushing, set-faced, Thomas rose and limped between the tables, passing just behind Bethoc and Gelis, to climb the steps to the dais.

Alexander smiled at him as he took his place beside Wallace. "Ha, my friend — did you foresee this?" he asked. "On your knees, man — one knee will serve for you. Down with you both."

Scarcely believing that it was happening to him, Thomas knelt, and felt the tapping of the sword on each shoulder, heard the same words as said over the earlier and loftier five, and then the command to arise, Sir Malcolm and Sir Thomas.

The King actually stooped to lend him a hand to stand upright, on account of his lame leg. They were also given the instruction to hold their vigils that night and take their vows. Then they were dismissed, with Thomas being urged jocu-larly to go make a rhyme out of it all.

In a daze he stumbled off, only part-aware of the varied reaction demonstrated around him — for the knighting of such comparatively humbly born men as these, however valuable their services, was not always approved by the nobility; knighthood was not only an honour, it marked the major dividing line between the ruling class and the ruled. Once a man had received this accolade his entire status was changed and a respect was owed to him, by all, such as was really only suitable for the high-born. In consequence, by no means all of the distinguished company felt called upon to cheer.

But at least there were no doubts about the attitude of one of the most high-born there, for on his way back to his table, Thomas suddenly found Bethoc in front of him, on her feet, hands out, eyes shining.

"Oh, Thomas, Thomas my dear!" she cried — and those nearby at least could not fail to hear as well as observe. "How good, how very good! It is most splendid, most right. I am so happy . . ."

He took her hands, but squeezing them turned her round to propel her back to her seat. "Thank you, thank you, Lady Bethoc, for your good wishes. And you, Lady Gelis." Deliberately he bowed towards the other girl, as well as to others around who felt constrained to murmur congratulation. A final pressure on Bethoc's hand and he disengaged himself firmly, and went limping onwards to his place down the hall, leaving his love biting her lip.

His lively reception by his companions at the senior esquires' table was interrupted by trumpeting and the High Sennachie's announcement that the central trestles would be cleared away for dancing but that wine would continue to be dispensed at the side tables for all who wanted it. The musicians to assemble.

In the stir and movement that followed, Thomas contrived to slip outside into the soft May dusk, anxious to be alone with his thoughts for a space. He was overwhelmed, to put it mildly. Never had he anticipated or even considered that knighthood would come his way, lame as he was. One part of him was pleased, elated, to be sure; but another was concerned, all but perturbed, wishing it otherwise. For in a moment his entire situation was altered by this whim of the monarch's, and not necessarily for the better. It was well intended, undoubtedly; but there would inevitably be many complications. He could not foresee them all, as yet; but one did stare him in the face. He could no longer be the Earl Patrick's personal esquire. Which meant . . . what? Would he have to leave the Earl's employ? And therefore the Earl's house? Knights were not *employed* by great lords, nor by any — not King's knighted men. His new rank and status might sound very splendid, as Bethoc had said — Sir Thomas

Learmonth of Ercildoune, Knight; but Ercildoune's few sorry acres and little stone tower would nowise support his style and title, indeed had not been able to support him hitherto, his father having been an amiable spendthrift who had frittered away his inheritance. So Thomas could not just join the Earl's group of senior vassals, who supported him on great occasions and at war — since his lands were not such as he could live on. He was now a misfit as well as a cripple, neither fish nor fowl. It was all very well for King Alexander to make large gestures like this — but *he* did not have to live with them!

He hirpled off round the parapet-walk of Roxburgh's curtain-walls, staring into the evening shadows and seeing nothing.

After a few circuits of the castle perimeter and little clarity of mind he recognised that he would have to return to the hall. His absence might well be remarked upon; and one did not leave the King's presence without the royal leave. Moreover, he should have at least a word with Bethoc. Dear, loving Bethoc — it had grieved him sorely to have to seem almost to reject her as he had done back there; but it had been necessary, for her own good. It was to be hoped that her greeting to him as he came down from the dais would be seen by at least the major part of the company as merely the friendly if impetuous gesture of her father's daughter towards a favoured servant.

Back in the hall, he found dancing in progress, hearty rather than elegant, as the King preferred, and gaiety unconfined. The Queen had evidently not come back — she was no more of a dancer than was Thomas — and Alexander was stepping it out in lively fashion with Marjory, Countess of Carrick. In all that whirlpool of movement and colour and laughter, he could see no sign of Bethoc. But he discerned Gelis dancing with Duff MacDuff.

The Earl Patrick, wine-cup in hand, presently appeared at Thomas's side . "So my friend — here is a surprise!" he said. "Sir Thomas Learmonth, no less — and myself bereft of an esquire!"

"Yes, my lord — surprise indeed. I do not know what to

think. I would never have sought this. His Grace is kind —
but I fear that he has scarce considered the, the
circumstances."

"Perhaps not. But we cannot change it now. There can be
no unknighting you, man!"

"No. What am I to do, my lord? I have been in your
service since I was but a child, as page and esquire. Now
what? You know my . . . state."

"We shall have to consider it, even if Alexander did
not — since it changes all. But — you could not have remained my esquire for ever, Thomas. One day you would
have had to leave my house — since esquiring is a young
man's employ. Perhaps as well now as later." The Earl
sipped his wine. "Beth was much . . . affected, I saw. She
has retired to her chamber. Unsuitably early. Leaving,
leaving . . ." He did not have to finish that, his glance seeking
out young MacDuff and Gelis. Clearly he saw these two
problems as linked.

Thomas made no answer.

"Her mother has gone to her. I think that neither will be
back . . ."

This dance over, the King came sauntering round the
company of his guests, chattering, rallying, paying compliments to the ladies, in excellent spirits.

"Look not so glum, you two," he exclaimed. "You might
be mourners at a burial! What's so ill? Is your new dignity
weighing so heavy, Sir Thomas?"

"You have cost me a good esquire, Sire!" the Earl said.

"Tut, man — the realm has gained a better knight. Think
beyond yourself, Patrick. We need such as True Thomas for
more than just Dunbar and the Merse."

"*Need*, Your Grace . . .?" Thomas echoed.

"To be sure. My kingdom needs men of wits and vision,
cunning with words, able with pen as well as with sword."
Alexander lowered his voice a little. "Too long I have had to
rely on churchmen for such services — and churchmen and
clerks, even the best of them, are not always to my taste!
Especially as they too often look for approval and preferment
to that Gamelin of St. Andrews. The Primate loves me no

more than I love him! So — never fear, Thomas, there will be work for you."

The new knight looked from the king to the Earl. "I, I shall require new employ, yes."

"And you shall have it, my friend. Tomorrow, for a start. Tomorrow, when this plaguey Cardinal and Gamelin come, there will be much debate, much holy talk — aye, and holy threat! Much chaffering and bargaining. At which the churchmen will be the more proficient, I swear! You, Thomas, will be there, to act as clerk also, *my* clerk. Oh, I have many bishops and abbots and the like who mislike Gamelin and take my side. But they are churchmen nevertheless, they *think* like churchmen. And with a cardinal straight from the Vatican calling the tune, I would prefer to have a scribe with less divided loyalties! Even Archdeacon Wishart, my Chancellor, could be less than single-minded in this. So bring your quill and paper, Sir Thomas, to the great talking, and write, note, mark, at my elbow. I will have a place for you. Is it understood?"

"I think so, Sire." Evidently the King had taken more thought over this knighting than they had given him credit for.

"Then, man, since you have a vigil to perform this night, and I require your wits to be sharp tomorrow, I suggest that you waste no more time here drinking wine! There will be seven of you at it in my chapel here, I would think — a mite distracting! So you might be wise to go early. And be not too long about it either — for tomorrow's sake!"

Bowing low, Thomas gladly made his departure.

He would dearly have liked to go to their flanking-tower for a word with Bethoc. But the girls were having to share a chamber with their mother, and the Countess apparently would be there now. So he went direct to one of the castle's basement well-chambers, called the lavatorium, where attendants, male and female, kept great cauldrons of water heated on a fire which was never allowed to die out. There, stripping off his clothing, he performed the ritual bathing preparatory to vigil. Thereafter, cleansed in body if not in mind, he made his way to the royal chapel set on one of the rocky knolls of that elongated ridge within the perimeter walls.

In the dim light of two or three flickering candles he perceived one other worshipper already kneeling before the altar in silent devotion — Sir Malcolm Wallace. No doubt the five sprigs of nobility knighted earlier were all much engaged meantime celebrating. Saying nothing, Thomas went and knelt at the other side of the chancel from the older man. He had brought his sword, as required, and laid it in front of him on the stone floor, hilt towards the altar.

Feeling self-conscious and far from spiritual, he bent his head and sought to school his thoughts. The vigil was the traditional preparation for knighthood, although for those knighted in the field or, as it were, by surprise, it had to be performed after the accolade was bestowed. Originally it had entailed a night-long session in some holy place, alone, communing with the Creator, or at least His saints, before taking the knightly vows. But since the sort of men apt to be knighted, soldiers, lordlings, men of action and the like, seldom had the aptitude for intensive prayer, meditation and contemplation, the thing had become scaled down to such period as the aspirant could manage without either falling asleep, getting cramp, or otherwise making nonsense of it all. But a couple of hours minimum was expected.

Like many another before him, Thomas found it all very difficult and unsatisfactory. To empty his mind, for it to be filled with the right thoughts, visions and decisions, was more easily said than done. However determinedly he sought to discipline his consciousness, however sternly he concentrated on the knightly ideals of worship, chivalry, service and the rest, he constantly discovered himself to be thinking about other things, and usually quite unsuitable things — particularly Bethoc and her delectable person and what was to be done about their forlorn love for each other. At other times he was deep in speculation over his new and not very clearly defined duties on the King's behalf next day. Or else wondering where he was to go when he had to leave the Earl's house, and on what he was to live. And interspersed amongst all were lines and phrases to add, or already written, for the great task he had set himself, to translate and interpret for the Scots the splendid epic of *Sir Tristrem*, from the original Celtic-Cymric, in his efforts to demonstrate that he was not just a rhymster of jingles, however unusual.

He did achieve some purposeful thinking, some dedication to the knightly conception, in all this, however, but it was spasmodic and distinctly incoherent.

Kneeling on the stone floor became an increasing trial, especially for his lame leg.

How long he had been there he did not know when there was an interruption. Three of their new fellow-knights arrived, and somewhat noisily — Colban MacDuff, David de Strathbogie and William Comyn, in the best of good humour and fortified with wine. They clattered around, tripped over unseen obstacles, exclaimed at the dimness, and hailed the pair already there, when they perceived them. If vigil-keeping had been difficult enough before, it was clearly going to be all but impossible now. Wallace demonstrated his acceptance of the fact by raising his sword upright before him, muttering his vows, and rising to leave the chapel.

Thomas fairly quickly did the same, holding up the sword by the blade so that the long two-handed hilt made a cross between himself and the altar. Kneeling thus, a little shakily on account of his cramped joints and the weight of the weapon, he silently repeated the words of the undertaking to seek to love God, honour the King, serve the needy, cherish the helpless and women in distress, and remain a good knight until his life's end, Christ and His saints aiding him; in the Name of God the Father, God the Son and God the Holy Spirit.

Thankfully he rose to his feet and limped stiffly off.

Sounds of revelry were still emanating from the hall as he passed, on his way to his knightly couch in the wall-closet.

*   *   *

In the morning, the Cospatrick sisters were late in appearing, and Thomas had no opportunity for private talk with a notably subdued Bethoc, although he did manage to squeeze her arm, unseen he hoped, and received a brief wan smile in return. Gelis, on the contrary, was in fine fettle and excited, making a great play of calling him *Sir* Thomas and bowing whenever she managed to catch his eye. The Countess was kind and gave the young man a kiss of congratulation, but otherwise she and her husband were somewhat restrained with all concerned.

Bishop Gamelin and the Cardinal-Deacon Ottobone of Fiesci arrived in mid-forenoon, with an impressive train, led by a mounted choir of chanting choristers.

Thomas was summoned to the lesser hall shortly before midday, where one of the royal chaplains somewhat sourly showed him a small table he was to share with this Master Reginald, just behind and to the left of the King's throne-like chair. A much larger table was in front, seated for about a score, with a similar large chair, actually the Queen's, opposite that of the King's, for the Papal Legate. Benches filled the hall for the Lords Spiritual and Temporal, the magnates, chiefs, officers and sheriffs of the realm. Men were already arriving to fill these, amidst much clamour.

The royal entrance, presently, was stage-managed with some care. Papal nuncios, being personal representatives of the Pope, were entitled to receive very special courtesies, even from kings — if not necessarily always all they deemed suitable. So, on a flourish of trumpets, doors were thrown open at each end of this lesser hall and two processions entered simultaneously, Alexander leading in his earls; and the Cardinal, followed by Gamelin, with a file of clerics. But it so happened that the king's door was further from the great table than was the Cardinal's, so that the latter reached his chair first and so had to stand awaiting Alexander's arrival like everyone else.

Cardinal Ottobone, more properly Ottobuoni, was not the typical smooth churchman which so often emanated from Rome, but a tall, craggy, stooping figure, cadaverous, with a great beak of a nose, dark bushy eyebrows and a stern eye, formidable to say the least, as the English had found him to be. Beside him, Gamelin looked unimpressive — and Alexander seemed very young and boyish however seemingly confident.

The King bowed, but in a modulated degree. "Illustrissimo — we all greet you, and through you the Holy Father, with due respect and acclaim. May I call on you to commend our deliberations to Almighty God?" he said.

The Cardinal raised a hand glittering with rings. "The Supreme Pontiff bestows on you all his blessing and enjoins on you all proper obedience. God be with us," he declared briefly, and sat down, all red robes and eagle-like peering.

Deliberately Alexander remained standing, as must all others. "We much esteem the good will of His Holiness and will endeavour to retain his approbation! And yours, Illustrissimo, and yours. Whilst remembering the due needs and well-being of our own realm. All have my permission to sit."

From his chair, the King continued. "We understand, sir, that your visit is concerned with furthering the Crusade against the Infidel, declared by the late and lamented Pope Urban the Fourth and endorsed by Clement the Fourth, his present Holiness. We would assure the Pontiff, through yourself, that we in Scotland are wholly in favour of this noble enterprise and will do all in our power to aid it. Alas, unlike King Louis of France — who I learn is to lead the Crusade — I have only an infant son, and no brother, to leave in charge of my realm, and so cannot myself participate. But a number of my earls and lords have already expressed their intention of taking the Cross, some here present — the Earl of Carrick, the Earl of Atholl, the former Regent, Sir David Lindsay, Sir Robert Bruce of Annandale and others. Also we shall set aside certain moneys from our Treasury to hire men and to supply the project. So, Illustrissimo, much of your task is already achieved for you!"

If this was calculated in some measure to take the wind from Ottobone's sails, it was less than successful. "That is gratifying, King Alexander," he said in a heavily accented, grating voice. "May it mean that my requirements will be met with the minimum of unseemly reluctance, such as I have experienced in England, and so our arrangements be settled with expedition. I would ask, however, why this large gathering, King of Scotland. Surely the said arrangements could have been more conveniently decided in a small company of two or three rather than in hundreds?"

"In some degree you answer your own question, my lord Cardinal. In that you name me King of Scotland. That I am not, but King of *Scots*. There is much difference. I am but the High King, *Ard Righ*, the greater king of this realm. There are lesser kings, these my earls. They and many others are concerned in the taking of the realm's decisions. And to advise. They are here of right."

The other shrugged. "As you will. Your Highness will not, I think, require much advice — for the matter is in the main clear and not for debate." Ottobone turned to the Italian secretary on his left. "The lists," he ordered. "I have here lists made of all earldoms, lordships, baronies and manors, as well as the lands and temporalities of Holy Church, in this kingdom. All carefully compiled for me by the Bishop of St. Andrews here. These give the annual rentals and values of all, painstakingly ascertained. His Holiness's requirements are clear and not to be questioned. An especial levy of one tenth is imposed herewith on all Christendom for the requirements of the Crusade — this in Christ God's blessed Name. This levy is mandatory upon all, without exception and without reduction, on pain of the most stern displeasure of His Holiness. Previous attempts to recover and cleanse our blessed Lord's holy places have failed through lack of men and moneys. This must not be again." The Cardinal placed his beringed hand on the stack of papers his secretary had put before him. "These lists are many and full. I cannot conceive that they should be read out here, any or all of them. Is it agreed?"

There were resentful murmurs from all over the hall.

"My lord Cardinal," the King said. "Certainly we cannot read out and consider all the lands and baronies of my kingdom — God forbid! But — nor can we accept without question your — or Bishop Gamelin's — assessment of values and taxation. That would be quite . . . insupportable. These lists will have to be examined closely and well considered. Values vary. Moreover, this of a tenth of all yearly value, is surely iniquitous! Greatly too much. No property could stand such levy, over and above the Church's own yearly requirements here and the realm's taxation. It is not possible."

"It is possible and mandatory, Highness, for all the rest of Christendom. Is your Scotland alone to be exempted?"

"Not so. But what is not there cannot be produced! In especial in gold and silver. This realm is not rich in moneys. In goods and gear, in such as cattle and grain and wool, in hides and coals and wax, we have sufficient for our needs most years. But you cannot take these on your Crusade. And to turn them into gold and silver would not be possible, moreover would lower the value of all. It is not to be considered."

The uproar from the hall did more than underline Alexander's objections.

"Yet considered, and more than considered, it must be, Sir King," Ottobone rasped. "Failure to produce the required revenue will be met by the fullest rigours at the disposal of Holy Church — the fullest, I say!"

"May I speak, my lord King?" Gamelin put in, over the growling of the company. "The Holy See permits us time to produce this revenue. Half-a-year for the first payment, other payments later up till a year after. Two harvests will therefore be in. This will much ease the matter. We have been most heedful, have taken all into consideration . . ."

"You, my lord Bishop, have indeed been heedful, I think!" Alexander stared at the Primate. "But not for *our* good and welfare! Only for your masters in Rome, I say! You have been all too busy."

"Sire . . .!" Gamelin's protest was lost in the resentful cries of many.

The Cardinal held up his hand, glittering but clawlike, in commanding gesture. "I charge all here to have a care!" he exclaimed. "Bishop Gamelin has done only as he was strictly enjoined. As every other Primate and Metropolitan has had to do. The Supreme Pontiff's orders are explicit and apply to all. And the price of disobedience, for great as for small, is . . . excommunication."

There was a notable hush as that dreaded word was enunciated. It was the ultimate sanction, and there was no denying its terrors and menace. Even for such as were sufficiently free-thinking or sceptical as to doubt whether in fact it would mean everlasting damnation hereafter, all knew that its imposition would entail grievous hardship and loss meantime. For it meant that the Church would inevitably have to withdraw all its many services from the excommunicated and his family — and the Church's influence in everyday life was great and all-pervasive. The obvious necessities such as marriage, baptism and Christian burial would be refused; but as well as these others, such as nursing in sickness — which was almost all done by monks — the use of the hospices which were the only shelter for travellers on most roads; the services of mills, tanneries, breweries and other needful facilities in many areas, run by the Church; the use of ferries, almost always manned by lay-brothers; protection against spells and witchcraft, an ever-present threat; and so on. None there underestimated the price to be paid of offence to the Vatican.

"Sir," the King cried. "This is surely inconceivable? To impose dire excommunication for mere failure to pay moneys! Or *some* moneys — since we are not refusing all contribution. I cannot believe that Christ's saving grace could be withheld from any because he paid insufficient gold!"

"It is not for insufficient payment that excommunication will be pronounced, Highness, but for the direct disobedience to the Holy Father's command. And for obstruction of the great work of the Crusade in Christ's service. Be in no doubt, such will be the penalty imposed on all who do not comply — from the occupants of earthly thrones down to the tillers of their soil!" Again the Cardinal's hand banged down on the pile of paper. "I am assured that these assessments are fair, true and just. Indeed I have scanned them and would consider that they err on the side of too great leniency." And he turned to glare accusingly at the Primate.

"No, Illustrissimo. Or . . . or, not leniency. I have sought not to be harsh. I have recognised special difficulties and problems — that is all."

"As this, Bishop?" Ottobone pulled out a paper partly bent over, as marker. "The Abbey of Lindores is here valued at but the paltry sum of two hundred and sixty pounds. No single English abbey, however small, is assessed at less than double that sum. Yet this Lindores is noted as possessing ten parishes and eighty ploughgates of land. For but two hundred and sixty pounds?"

Gamelin coughed, as the Abbot of Lindores from the body of the hall rose to protest. "Illustrissimo — Lindores' lands are but poor, infertile," the Primate declared. "On the heights of North Fife and Fothrif. Not to be compared with many another house for wealth. This I have ascertained . . ."

The first brief smiles of the session were produced by this defence, since all there — save perhaps Ottobone himself — knew well that Lindores was in Gamelin's own diocese of St. Andrews and paid tribute to him as bishop.

Thomas had been scribbling on a paper during this exchange. He pushed this forward at the King's elbow. Glancing over it, Alexander nodded.

"My lord Bishop," he intervened. "On which year's valuation did you make your assessments?"

"The most recent, Sire. The last year for which we have returns. I sent for these from all bishops and sheriffs."

"But last year was a particularly good year, my lord, you will recollect. An excellent harvest. And the grass good, so that the beasts were fat and they calved and lambed well. The year before, 1263, was much otherwise — storms and dearth and invasion. Only God knows what *this* year will bring. It is unfair, surely, to assess on an unusually rich year?"

"You have *had* the riches and can therefore pay Almighty God His due!" the Cardinal grated.

"Sire — that is false reckoning," Malcolm, Earl of Fife, objected. "We required last year's revenues to replenish the year before's losses. I, for one, have no spare gold wherewith to pay this churchman's grasping levy."

The surge of agreement and support from all around was vehement, even some of the bishops and abbots joining in.

"Is this man to be the first to seek the pronunciation of Holy Church's anathema?" Ottobone thundered. "I warn him, and all others, that such talk could cost him dearer than a little gold!"

"The Earl of Fife, Cardinal, is my senior earl and Hereditary Inaugurator of this realm," Alexander said. "He is entitled to speak, and for many."

"Then he should choose his words with more care, Sir King! I promise you that I do not bear the Pope's authority in vain!"

"Was there not a general valuation made in the reign of your royal father, Sire?" Malise of Strathearn put in, diplomatically. "If I recollect rightly, this might serve better to base the assessments on than last year."

"That was twenty years ago, my lord," Gamelin said. "There has been much improvement since then . . ."

There was more outcry in the hall, some agreeing that the old valuation would be a fairer basis, others shouting that Strathearn had sold the pass by conceding any such valuation at all. Throughout, Thomas was writing busily. He pushed this second note forward. It read:

Offer payment in goods, whatever assessment. Moneys not available. Grain, hides, wool, delivered at ports and havens. The Pope's ships to come for all. Not possible for Rome. But will give him pause. Cannot then accuse of refusal to pay.

Alexander glanced round, when he had read this, one eyebrow raised quizzically. Then he lifted his hand for silence.

"My lords — and my lord Cardinal. This profits little. The Holy See is determined on payment. And we, of course, are faithful supporters of Holy Church. So whatever is the valuation decided upon, we must pay a due proportion in the end. I suggest that we assure the Cardinal-Deacon of our willingness. And pay by despatching our dues, in kind, to the nearest port and harbour to our several lands. We do not have the silver or gold in this realm to send to Rome. So we will send our cattle, grain, wool, hides, ale, wax, salt, coals — each his produce. We have no shipping sufficient to carry this enormous tribute, so we will take it to our sea-coasts and His Holiness will send the vessels to collect it. Thus all will be satisfied and our duty done." He beamed on Ottobone.

There was silence throughout the lesser hall as all considered the implications of this. Some men raised their eyebrows, some glanced at neighbours, some grinned outright. The Cardinal did none of these. His hawklike features were still. He stared ahead of him for moments on end, his gaze apparently concentrated on the King's chest.

"That would be . . . difficult, Highness," he jerked, at length, his voice less certain than it had been hitherto. "So much shipping required. His Holiness does not command so many ships. I fear that it is not possible."

"His Holiness commands the entire shipping of Christendom, does he not? As all else. Not only *our* poor tithes! He can command whosoever he will to uplift and carry our tribute — since we do not have the craft. The King of Norway, see you, has the greatest fleet on the seas. Command him. The English have much shipping. Call on them, as part of their payment. France, likewise. Flanders. Many shipping lands, all paying service to the Pope. We will pay ours, at every port. In goods which will sell for much gold in Rome and elsewhere. This is best, our answer to all."

"I fear, I fear, Highness, that I cannot accept this, cannot agree. It would be difficult, I say . . ."

"I do not ask you to accept or agree, sir! As King of this realm, under God, I charge you to go tell what I have offered to His Holiness himself. That Scotland will pay in full, on the final assessment. And the payment will be awaiting at our ports within the time specified. *We* at least will have fulfilled the Pontiff's injunction. He cannot say otherwise — nor you, sir! So our business is thus happily concluded."

"But, but. . ."

"But nothing, Illustrissimo. You will convey our duty and obedience and goodwill to Pope Clement. And we thank you for coming to us. Now — this audience is over." Alexander rose to his feet.

So the assembly ended as it had begun, with all standing save the Papal Legate. After a few moments that stooping but impressive scarlet-clad figure got up, glared around him tight-lipped, inclined his head briefly towards the King, and omitting the customary benediction, turned and stalked for the door by which he had entered, his entourage bobbing heads before hurrying after. Gamelin stood unhappy, undecided, before he too bowed and followed the others.

As a great tide of relief and applause swept the hall, Alexander swung round, to clap Thomas on the shoulder.

"Well done, my friend — well written!" he exclaimed. "True Thomas again — with the agile wits! We had him there, I say! My thanks, Sir Thomas Learmonth, my thanks. And when it is in my power to serve you in turn — come to me, man, come to me. I shall not forget this day . . ."

Making his genuflection, Thomas made his limping escape also.

7

"I tell you, Thomas, that we have reached the end of this road!" Bethoc declared, low-voiced. "The parting of the tracks. Or — *I* have. There is no more hoping, nor praying, nor waiting. Even you must see it."

That hurt. "Even I! Save us, Beth — think you that I do not recognise it all? Grieve over it as much as do you? Curse the fate that comes between us . . .?"

"Neither grieving nor yet cursing will serve now," she asserted, strongly if quietly. "Only acting will avail. And I am going to act — whether you do or no."

He glanced at her sidelong. They were riding up Leader from Tweed, in the narrows south of Cowdenknowes, where the constriction of the wooded bluffs shouldering the river's course forced them into proceeding no more than two abreast. The Countess Christian, with her two ladies, was ahead; Gelis, moody and withdrawn today, imagining herself to be sorrowfully in love with one reserved for her unappreciative sister, rode alone just in front, with their escort of men-at-arms some way behind — for the Earl Patrick had remained with the King meantime for some high council. It was the first time in the dozen miles since leaving Roxburgh that he and Bethoc had had opportunity to speak privately — and Ercildoune lay less than two miles ahead.

"Act . . .?" he wondered.

"Yes, act, Thomas. Either with you, or alone. I am going to leave. Leave Ercildoune. It has come to that." Her level tense tone spoke of quiet desperation. "And leave quickly. It has to be soon, at once indeed. Father is determined that I wed Duff MacDuff. He will heed me nothing, saying that he knows best, that I am but a silly girl who may sometimes be humoured in small things but not in great. He is bringing the Earl of Fife and his sons to Ercildoune, after this Council and tomorrow's hunting in the Forest of Jedworth, with the King. And our betrothal will be entered into then and announced to all. But I . . . I will not be there to hear it, Thomas! I will not marry Duff MacDuff."

He rode on, frowning, silent, for a little, and it was the girl's turn to look sidelong at him.

"Have you nothing to say?" she demanded, at length.

"Where will you go?" he asked — not wanting to know, but only to give him a little time.

"Does it matter? Far away, it must be — for I will not be chased and brought back. Into England, perhaps, where my father's writ does not run. I can do it. I am a good horsewoman. I have little moneys — but I have jewels, gold things, which I can sell. I am sure that young Dod Home, the falconer's son, would go with me, as servant. He likes me well, and is at odds with his father and elder brother. I would go south, by secret ways, into Northumbria . . ."

"No," he said, decidedly. "Not that. We will go north."

She drew a quick breath that somehow trembled. "Thomas! You, you mean . . .?"

"Yes, my dear — we go together. Since you are set on it, show me the way — I see that it is the only way." The dammed-up weight of all his desires, his love and emotions, his endless debatings with himself, burst through at last. "Oh, my heart — think you that I have not longed, ached, craved for this, these long months? Even schemed for it, God knows — then sought to cast it from me. I believed that I could not do it to you, lass — I *could* not! But, now . . ."

"Now, I force you to it, Thomas?"

"No, no — never that. But — I see that it must be. There is no other way out. Now. If you go, anyway, how can I not go with you? Since it is what I have yearned to do. But — you have counted the cost, Beth?"

"Yes. And deem it a light price to pay. Lighter now — oh, so much lighter, Thomas. To go with you."

"We will be hunted, homeless fugitives . . ."

"But together. That is all that counts." She paused. "With me. But *you*, Thomas — you must count the cost also. I am selfish, perhaps. For you, it could be a dear-bought love indeed, I fear?"

"No. Not so dear as it was, as it would have been before. For all is changed with me now, Beth. This knighthood. I am no longer your father's esquire. I could no longer dwell on in his house. I would have had to go, anyway. Seek new employment, somewhere, somehow. My small lands cannot support me . . . or us! No, in one way, a change had to be made. The King it was saw to that!"

"Thomas — now that you are knight? Will it not aid us? No longer a mere esquire. For me to wed a King's knight will not seem so, so ill a match?"

"Not so, lass — forget that. A knight's wife is something better than an esquire's. But great earls' daughters are destined for great lords' sons. Not for poor knights, landless and without employ. The Earl Patrick, I promise you, will see me as no better goodson for having been knighted."

"The King? Would he not aid you? Clearly he thinks highly of you, Thomas. And to the King, all is possible . . ."

"He said to call upon him, yes. If I required his aid, one day. Perhaps he would do something. But — your father is his friend, as well as one of his earls. His kin, also. I fear that he will be less than pleased with me."

They had come to a somewhat wider stretch of the river-line, with the party able to marshal itself in closer order again. Their chance for talk privately came to an end.

"How shall we do it?" Bethoc demanded urgently. "It will have to be quickly. Tonight or tomorrow. For Father will be back."

"I will think of something. It will have to be tomorrow. Much to consider and do before. I will think, lass — and somehow warn you. Now — no more of it. None must suspect anything . . ."

Few newly-created knights, surely, ever spent the first evening of their enhanced state — and after vigil and vows — in such wits-cudgelling and guilty planning. To remove himself from the Cospatrick family to allow his mind to concentrate on the multiple problems before them, he betook himself for a long walk, to climb the White Hill of Ercildoune, behind the castle, dip down beyond and ascend the higher summit of the Black Hill, above Cowdenknowes, where he sat on the overgrown rampart of the ancient Pictish fort and watched the sun sink behind the hills to the west, mind far away. When in the May dusk he returned to the castle, he heard the first cuckoo of the season calling — and took it for a good omen. He made his way to the private hall, with the lamps lit, more or less decided on what was to be done, or at least attempted. To Bethoc's eager, expectant look, he allowed himself, and her, only a quick nod.

Later, when bed was being agreed on, after a tiring day, he suggested as casually as he could, that if the day was fine, tomorrow he and the young people might make another excursion to their favoured Eildon Hills, since soon he would have to be away on his travels, and he for one would much enjoy such a day before he went. The Countess's protests that there was no reason in the world why he should consider leaving them, just because he was a knight, were drowned in the shouts of acclaim of the other members of the family. He caught Bethoc's eye and she inclined her head. They would make a fairly early start, all agreed, and have a good long day of it.

So, next morning, grey but mild, after an early panic that it might rain, the young people set out for the Eildons. If Bethoc's and Thomas's horses seemed more heavily burdened than usual with alleged picnic provisioning, the others did not comment on it. Bethoc's leave-taking of mother and home could not be allowed to be obvious, the tears in her eyes hastily blinked away. Thomas himself felt emotionally upset and grievously at fault, for he had long received so much kindness in this household. But the Countess must be given no least inkling that they planned anything unusual; and so farewells had to be of the most casual.

Their ride down Leaderside thereafter, at least for the two eldest of the party, was silent, with none of the flush of excitement which might have been looked for at the start of an elopement. Nothing of this was noticed, of course, by the rest of the family, concerned only with the day's adventures.

It was at the Newstead ford of Tweed that Thomas made his suggestion. He was worried that Bethoc and himself might not be left alone; for Gelis was now just that little bit older, and changing her attitudes to life, eager to be considered a young woman and no child, indeed seeing herself intermittently as lovelorn and suffering at the heart. So that the old-time racing challenges might well not work with her any more. He therefore proposed something different — that they should have a competition rather than any ordinary race. Gelis was particularly fond of collecting and pressing wild-flowers and grasses; so to ensure her co-operation, the project was that all should make their way, by different routes, to the little loch which they all knew at the far side of the West Eildon Hill, on the edge of Bowden Moor, gathering specimens of plant and flower and leaf as they went, to meet soon after midday and see who had collected the most interesting and unusual items. And to ensure that Pate and Johnnie did not refuse to take part in so unmanly an exercise, it was made part of the conditions that they had to go over the tops of the three hills on their way, their favourite ride, and to bring down a selection of high-growing plants, such as blaeberry, cranberry, heaths, stonewort and the like. Bethoc and Thomas would take the north side of the hills, Gelis, Eala and Alec the south.

As, all unsuspecting, the other five rode off, the two conspirators looked at each other.

"At last!" Bethoc exclaimed, and reached out to him. "Thomas — at last! We are . . . free! Alone. We can go. Oh, my dearest!"

"Go, yes. But first we must seem to do what we said. See — we shall be in sight of Pate and Johnnie up there on the hill. For some time. If they look back, they will be able to see us — until they cross the shoulder of the East Hill. If we went off now, it would seem strange. And none must know *where* we go, which airt. So — we must seem to climb some way up, and westwards, as though we too headed for Bowden Loch. Then, when we are out of sight, we turn down to Tweed again, and off. Come."

They rode slantwise up, west by south.

"The cuckoos, Thomas — hear them! Our own cuckoos!" Bethoc said. "How good! And, see — is that not our tree? Our Eildon thorn, where, where . . .!" She pointed.

He nodded. "The same. I remember that spur of rock nearby, rising out of whins . . ."

"Thomas — let us go to it. Just for a moment or two. It was where we, we came together. Now, we are to be together for always. Let us start it there, under our thorn-tree."

He was glancing up, half-left. "They are still in sight — so can see us also. Will still see us at that tree. But — yes, as well there as anywhere. We can seem to be picking our first flowers, leaves, if they look down . . ."

They came to their gnarled hawthorn of the year before, and again she launched herself into his arms, to dismount, in eager embrace. But it had to be but brief contact, in case they were being observed. Part protesting, part laughing, the girl went down on hands and knees on the grass, to seem to search for plants, Thomas doing likewise.

"Pate and Johnnie will not care what we do," she said. "We need not be so careful."

"Safer," he insisted. "There must be no suspicions. You are to be betrothed to Duff MacDuff, probably tomorrow. They must not see their sister in *my* arms. But — not long now . . ."

Soon the two mounted figures, over half-a-mile away now and five hundred feet higher, dropped out of sight behind a spur of the east summit, and the pair beneath the tree could rise. But though Bethoc would have lingered in this spot which meant so much to them, the man would not hear of it. The brothers would climb into sight again, out of the hidden hollow, on the final ascent. By that time they themselves must be well out of view down in the woodlands flanking Tweed, or all might be hazarded.

So hastily they remounted and rode off downhill, as fast as they dared put their horses to the rough ground, Thomas glancing back and upwards, over his shoulder.

They saw nothing of the boys, nor of any other sign of life save grazing sheep, soaring larks and flighting cuckoos, before the lower scrub woodland received them into its cover.

At the riverside road, this south side of Tweed, Thomas reined his beast round left-handed, westwards.

"Where, my dear?" she asked. "Where are we going? What now?"

"We ride westwards, lass — far and fast. West and still west, to country where we are not known. Praying that meantime we are not seen — or not recognised. We have an hour yet before noon — many hours riding ahead of us. You said that you are a good horsewoman — and I know it. Now is the time to prove it!"

"Yes, my love — never fear. I shall not fail you. But *where* are we to go? Do you know? Or do we but ride on uncaring?"

"Not that, no. I have thought much on this. We must go somewhere not only where we are not known but where we will not be searched for — for nothing is more sure than that your father will search for you, high and low. So we keep away from all places where he might think to find us, or where others might send him word of us. And that must include King Alexander's Court, meantime."

"But you said that you would seek the King's aid . . .?"

"Yes — but not yet. Not until the searching has died away. So we must go where we may lay quiet for a time. One or two such places I have in mind, Beth."

"Good!" she nodded, cheerfully. "Good. I shall enjoy that, Thomas — lying quiet with you! The quieter the better, I say!"

"It has been my dream, lass. But — first we must wed."

"Ye-e-es. But — how? Where? Who is to wed us?"

"I have a notion on this, to contrive it. You remember Friar Nicolas? The monk of Houston, the small monastery near to Dunbar? Who used sometimes to come to act chaplain to your father at the castle."

"Nicholas, yes. He it was who christened Eala, was it not, at Dunbar. The dark friar, with the limp."

"Yes. Our lameness drew us together somewhat, I suppose. But I had occasion to serve him, one time. He came to grief with your father. You will not remember, if you ever knew. It was over three years ago. Over the Earl's encroachment of the monastery lands at Houston on the Tyne — the mill lands and dues. Your father claimed that they were his. Nicholas can have a high temper — he was bastard of one of the Douglas lordlings. And your father higher! I succeeded in persuading him, the Earl, to give way on this — for truly the land was the monastery's. Not only that, but not to report Nicholas to his superiors in the Trinitarian Order, as he threatened to do. I made a rhyme about it, for him, I remember. But, wisely, Friar Nicholas moved away from Houston thereafter. He is now Sub-Prior at the monastery of Faill, near to Ayr — the Trinitarians call their priors ministers. So he is Sub-Minister at Faill. And I think that he would wish to oblige me, if not you."

"Would he . . . would he risk Father's wrath again?"

"Faill is a long way from Dunbar or Ercildoune. In the High Steward's territories. We would hope that it would be long before the Earl learned who married us. If ever. And Brother Nicholas has a mind of his own . . ."

"How good if he will do it, Thomas — how good! This Faill — is it so far away?"

"Far enough for our purposes. Not much less than one hundred miles, I would say. Across the rigging of Scotland. I passed it on my way to Portincross and the Largs battle."

"Then, then we shall not reach there by this night?"

"No," he agreed, briefly.

They rode on, thoughtfully.

The Tweed makes a great bend southwards a couple of

miles west of New Melrose, and the travellers were able to cut off a corner and at the same time avoid the populous areas where the Allan and Gala Waters came in from the north, by swinging away over the higher ground, by Huntlyburn and Faldonside, to return to the great river again at Cauldshiels. Thereafter they remained with Tweed mile after mile, following its sylvan course in the deepening valley ever westwards, by Yair and Elibank and Innerleithen, to Peebles. It was easy riding, with a good, well-defined track all the way, the incoming burns all easily forded, the marshland crossed by stone-set causeways. A month or two earlier, with the melting snows filling the watercourses and flooding the valley-floors, their progress would have been less speedy. As it was they made excellent time, keeping up a steady fast trot which enabled them to cover eight to ten miles in each hour without straining the horses.

After Peebles, the valley grew narrower and less straight, the country becoming ever more wild, the flanking hills higher. They were deep in the Ettrick Forest now, and the haunts of men growing few and far between. Bethoc had never been so far as this. But still they made good time.

They left Tweed at last, at Broughton of Tweedsmuir, forty miles from Melrose, where it swung away southwards towards its source, and followed instead the lesser valley of the Biggar Water, still westwards. The character of the land was changing all the while, now becoming bare, with fewer and stunted trees, heather and moorland predominating as they lifted towards the watershed of Lowland Scotland, from the east-flowing rivers to the west-flowing. At Culter, near to the great castle of Boghall, seat of the Baldwin Flemings, whom David the King had imported into Scotland a century before, they were over fifty miles from the Eildons. Sir David le Fleming was a friend of Earl Patrick's; so they carefully avoided the vicinity of his house. The sun was beginning to sink behind the mighty mass of the isolated hill of Tintock before them, soaring over the Clyde valley. Their mounts, although tiring, were not yet done by any means; and Bethoc declared that she was ready to go on for some time yet. But Thomas knew that once out of this Clyde vale they had a lengthy stretch of very rough and upland country to traverse, bleak hills and empty moors where they would be hard put to it to find shelter for the night. He decided that they must halt at the first likely place they came across. They were keeping well away from all castles and manors, not just Boghall, where they might have to give an account of themselves, even if they were not known. It would have to be a hospice or other churchman's establishment — there were unlikely to be any monasteries in these harsh uplands.

Riding south-about around the vast bulk of Tintock, they came with the sunset to the scattered herdsmen's village of Wiston, where Wice, another of David's Flemings, had established a small church and parish. The priest's house was as modest; but in such a remote area he would probably be quite used to putting up benighted travellers, since there was little alternative shelter save the shepherds' and foresters' cabins.

The incumbent proved to be an old man of frail and not very cleanly appearance who, when asked if he could shelter them overnight, eyed them searchingly before he committed himself, seeming to pay particular attention to their clothing and the quality of their horses. Bethoc was afraid that he would turn them away as shameless sinners and unwed. But Thomas had a shrewd guess that it was otherwise.

"You can pay, young sir?" the old priest quavered. "I am a poor man and cannot afford to provide for all comers."

"I can pay," Thomas agreed.

"Yet you travel without groom or servant?"

"Is such required before we may seek entrance at the door of Holy Church, Master Priest?" But Thomas put hand in pocket and held out a silver piece. "Is this sufficient warranty?"

"Ah, yes." The other reached out a gnarled hand to grasp the coin. "It is needful, sir. I am much troubled by sorners and their like who pay me nothing. And I am no better provided than they. This is but a poor place. But I have a fine large chamber for you and your wife, yes. You will rest well. And a leg of lamb to sustain you. My man will see to your beasts. Come . . ."

They were shown into a bare, loft-like apartment above the priest's own room, straw on the floor, its only furnishings a few mattresses, really just sacks filled with more straw, some old plaids for blanketing, and two small tubs, one with water, one without. But the place seemed dry and clean enough, once two pigeons had been expelled.

"Can I ask you to spend a night in this?" Thomas asked, shaking his head. "You, an earl's daughter?"

"To be sure you can," she said. "It is none so bad. As bairns we played in worse than this. But — you heard, Thomas? What he said. 'Your wife!' So, so . . ."

"Yes. I heard. I did not correct him lest he refuse us and turn us away. Where else we might find shelter tonight God alone knows . . .!"

"No, no, my dear! I am complaining nothing! I rejoice to be called your wife — what I have longed for. It was, it was but the first time it has been said." She turned and opened her arms to him. "Oh, Thomas — is it not wonderful? Tomorrow, God willing, I will be truly your wife. Truly and for always!"

"Tomorrow — but not tonight!" he reminded, looking around him as he kissed her hair.

They shared the priest's evening meal of thick broth, cold mutton and stale bread, washed down with rough ale, and made no complaint. Thereafter, a single candle was given them, and their host gestured towards the stair which was little better than a ladder. Clearly their entertainment was over.

They chose to go outside for a little, to ensure that their horses were being cared for, as well as for their own natural requirements — since such did not appear to be catered for indoors, unless those tubs represented the facilities. They also collected their horse-blankets, which were used below their saddles. In the twilight, the girl did not delay unduly in returning to the house, the man more dilatory, almost reluctant, strangely. In their upper room, she took the lead.

"These straw-mattresses put together, and two deep, should be sufficiently comfortable," she declared, in a practical tone of voice. "One of the plaids over them, then one of our horse-blankets. These at least we know whom they last covered! Then the other above, and a second plaid on top. That will be best, I think."

He cleared his throat. "Beth — this is . . . difficult. It was no intention of mine to put you in such, such position. You put yourself in my care — and now this! I am sorry, lass."

"I am not," she assured. "See — help me with these mattresses."

"But — see you, I will put *my* sacks over in the corner there. The least I can do. Perhaps I could contrive a screen for you, out of these plaids. If there was something that I could use to hold them up . . ."

"My foolish Thomas — what need have we of a screen? And why hide in corners? We love each other, do we not? Belong to each other now. Will wed, we pray, tomorrow. We have made our choice, taken the great step. Are we now to be afraid of this lesser step? And it sheer delight! To spend all this night in each other's arms. Have you not dreamed of this, Thomas? I have."

"My dear — dreamed, yes. You do not know how much and how often. But not thus. Not . . . unwed. I have taken you out of your father's house, from his protection. Not to take advantage of you now! We must wait, lass."

"I had not thought that you would be so . . . nice!"

"It is not that. Only that I am responsible for you now. Honour you, must cherish you . . ."

"So much ado about lying side by side on a sack of straw!" she exclaimed almost hotly.

"If it were only that . . ."

"Whether it is more than that is of *your* deciding, is it not?"

"I fear, Beth — I fear that I might forget myself, fail to hold myself back . . ."

"Then I must seek to remind you! If it is so important." She was continuing to arrange the mattresses and covers into the one wide couch, not two. "I had scarce thought of you thus, Thomas. You, who led in battle, who outfaced the King, confounded the Cardinal! So . . . timorous!"

"Timorous!" He all but choked. "Lord — you do not know what you say, girl! What I am saying now, seeking to do, is harder, sorer, than anything I have ever done. To have you here, mine for the taking — and not to take! Think you that is easy? Timorous?"

"I am sorry, then. But — is a priest's word or two so important? It is *God* who makes us man and wife, is it not? Not the priest's words. There is more to marriage than churchmen's mumblings!"

"Aye — there are our vows, taken before God. And before witnesses . . ."

"Vows we can take here and now, if you so wish."

He shook his head. "Beth, Beth — how can I make you see? Have you forgotten? Or perhaps you never truly knew. Two nights ago I took vows, yes — the most solemn I have ever taken. Before God's altar. My knight's vigil. I swore then, on the cross of my sword, to keep faith, to maintain chivalry, to honour and protect women always — and the woman before all in my mind then, as ever, was you. I swore, by all that I held holy, to honour, reverence and cherish *you*, in body as in soul and spirit. But two nights gone. And now . . .!"

She rose and came to him. "Thomas — forgive me. I had not understood. You must do what you believe is right. Forgive me. Only, only . . . I do love you so!"

He clasped her to him more fiercely than he knew, so that she all but cried out. "And I, lass — and I! I love and want you with every inch of me, every part and particle of my being. But — we must start aright, Beth, on our journey together. It is important, yes — not only for my vows . . ."

"Yes. So be it." She drew down his head, for his lips to meet hers.

Long they kissed — and despite their words, it was deep and uninhibited, passionate kissing. And the man's hands were almost as eager, outlining, moulding her rounded person, squeezing, caressing, exploring — and meeting no least resistance. Words and resolutions and sentiments were all very well, but . . .

It was the girl who found breath and words first. "My beloved — what fools we are!" she whispered. "Is this not sufficiently wonderful? A heaven in itself. Just you and me. Enough bliss for any. For this night, at least! Let us be content, well content, with what we have. Within your vows. In joy. The long night together. Close. Holding each other. Holding each other's wills, if need be, as well as our bodies. Together. We, we can do it, can we not?"

"We can try," he said huskily. "You will have to help me."

"And perhaps you me."

She went to sit down on the mattress, to pull off her riding-boots and then unroll her silken hose. At the sight of her white legs, gleaming in the candle-light, he spoke, from stiff lips.

"Beth — no more, of a mercy! Keep your clothes on. If I am to retain my reason!"

"But — you have seen me naked, Thomas. In the sea. And out of it, that day . . ."

"That was different. If I am to lie beside you, this night, woman . . .!"

"Very well. But I must take off my gown. I cannot sleep in it. You, you can bear with me in my shift, Thomas?"

"I . . ." He started to answer that but got no further. He took off his own tunic and boots, that was all.

Bethoc's shift was a simple, elementary garment, suitable for warm-weather wear beneath outer clothing, and there-fore moderate in scope, starting as it were late and finishing early. When the man lowered himself, almost gingerly, on to the couch beside her, any idea that her feminine charms would be appropriately muted had to be dismissed. Even in the dim lighting the white shoulders and the swell and division of her bosom made themselves entirely evident, not to mention the shapely legs as far as mid-thigh. Hurriedly he reached down and pulled up the covers, amidst a strong smell of horse.

"Lord!" he said, part comment and exclamation, part prayer.

Her smothered laughter, as she turned to him, arms encircling, was little help.

His attempts to keep himself stiff, tense but impervious, were markedly unsuccessful. The girl's delectable person seemed to fit so naturally and rightly into and against his own that such frozen rigidity on his part was impossible of maintenance, an offence against all sensibility in fact. Gradually he relaxed, bodily at least, if scarcely in mind and awareness — and perhaps not all his bodily parts at that. And when her hands sought and found his arms, carefully held close to his sides, and drew them around her, he had to accept that he was in for a more testing time even than he had anticipated.

"Kiss me, Thomas — *Sir* Thomas!" she commanded.

No chivalrous male, however new-knighted, could refuse such appeal. He kissed her hair, the scent of it not wholly submerged in that of horse. Then moved lower to her brows, her nose, then her lips. There he lingered — although that is inadequate description of his activity there. And presently, all too well aware of the tumult in her breathing, to say nothing of his own, he felt it incumbent on him to give her respiration some relief at mouth and nose, and so slid his busy lips lower still to the column of her neck. Shapely and long as this was, it was only inches and natural progression to work down to where the softly firm projection of prominent breasts positively demanded attention and acclaim — with the shift-top little impediment. In that heaving haven of delight he thereafter all but drowned and sought no rescue, only dimly aware that it was his turn to be having his hair kissed.

Awareness is a state which may grow by degrees, to be sure, and while one part of the mind may be very much conscious of immediate conditions and developments, such as contours, texture and the intriguing rise and fall of a warm female chest structure, with its effect upon male lips, plus their counter-effect — another department could be all but unaware of activity in a different sphere even though there might be some similarity of contour and general attraction. Awareness in this latter respect, in fact, was brought home to the man only by Bethoc gently but firmly removing his right hand from behind her, from the region of her buttocks, and returning it to her front, above approximately the waist-line.

"Oh!" he said, raising his face from between her breasts. "I . . . I am sorry."

"So am I," she murmured. "But I promised . . . to help!"

"Yes . . ." He began to draw away a little, jerkily. But she pressed him close again, even urging his head back from whence it had lifted.

"Bide you there, near my heart, my dearest," she instructed. "We are doing very well. Only . . . perhaps we should keep our hands up, above, our middles. If vows are to be kept!"

"M'mm. Yes — indeed, yes. Forgive me, Beth. I promise, I promise . . .! Oh, lassie, lassie — I know not whether to shout with joy or weep with, with . . ."

"Do neither," she advised. "Or the old priest below will be up, enquiring. And what would you tell him? Just kiss me, Thomas my love, and keep on kissing me. Kiss me to sleep — if you can! I did not close my eyes once, last night, I swear. And tomorrow night may be, be . . .?"

With that injunction he sought to comply. For himself, he had never felt less somnolent in his life.

Astonishingly, the young woman did sleep some time later, before so very long; and although her companion was slow indeed to follow her example, he nevertheless gradually achieved an alternative state, an unexpected and extraordinary sense of sheer satisfaction and well-being, almost peace. To hold this dear, warm, desirable and utterly trusting woman asleep within his arms, to listen to her calm and regular breathing, to feel the quiet stirring of her winsome body, so conscious of every lovely part of her, was an experience so profound and gratifying, far beyond mere pleasure, that he was able to put thwarted physical desire from him and lie there in a glow of sheer well-being and felicity.

Eventually he too slept.

He wakened to the sound of the priest moving about below, and daylight, to find their situations reversed, with Bethoc lying watching him within his arms. They savoured each other, and their joy in waking thus together, before rising to wash as best they could in the water-tub, the girl singing her happiness even in that. As for the man, he was loath to see her don her gown, over that excellent shift, as previously he had been to see her doff it.

They breakfasted on porridge, oatcakes, honey and more of the cold mutton, and were on their way without delay, evidencing their general satisfaction with life by presenting the surprised cleric with another silver piece.

Now they had to ride through the bright morning hills, west by north seven miles to the valley of the quite large Douglas Water, down which they turned southwards. Thomas had come this way to Largs, indeed the Dunbar contingent had spent the night at Douglas Castle. They now carefully avoided its vicinity therefore, keeping to the far side of the river. Fortunately, they saw none of the Douglases, and presently were able to leave the populous lands of the valley and swing away due westwards into the empty hills again, still loftier heights these, with the great Cairn Tables dominating on their left and marking the boundary of the large sheriffdom of Ayr.

It was bleak country in the main, but they made no complaints, happier and more at peace with circumstances than they had ever been. Bethoc sang to rival the larks and the wheepling curlews, and Thomas declaimed nonsense rhymes.

By noon they had reached the River Ayr itself, and thereafter it was but a matter of following it down the dozen miles through ever more gentle country, by Sorn to Mauchline. They were on the borders of the High Steward's and the Countess of Carrick's territories here; but they anticipated no recognition problems; for both these great ones and their entourages would be with the King still. Alexander was known to be going to Stirling in a day or two, taking his Court with him, for the beginning of the annual summer solstice celebrations at the King's Knot there, traditional echo of the old Pictish sun-worship days, now tending to become something of a saturnalia.

They left the Ayr valley at Failford, to follow the incoming Faill Water for some four miles, by Tarbolton, until at length they saw the Trinitarian monastery of Faill itself, set in pleasant green rolling pasture-country, the most attractive place they had seen since leaving Tweed.

Faill was not a large establishment, with only about a

dozen monks and perhaps a score of lay-brothers; but it was a busy, well-doing, self-contained and practically self-supporting community, these Red Friars being strong on industry and the more practical aspects of Christian endeavour. Also they had a reputation for living well, despite a disciplined code. They were expert cattle-rearers, in that pastoral land, and their monastic activities included butter- and cheese-making, a tannery, a boot and shoe workshop, with saddlery, a tallow factory and a glue-making plant. They also went in for fish-rearing on a large scale in the many surrounding ponds and lochans. And their brewery was famous, as indicated by the popular jingle:

> The friars of Faill drank berry-brown ale,
> The best that ever was tasted;
> And ne'er went short of the fat of the land,
> So long as their neighbours' lasted!

The travellers were well received by Friar Nicholas — now *Prior* Nicholas indeed, the previous Minister of Faill having died and Nicholas appointed to succeed him. He was a dark, gaunt man in his early thirties, young for his position, a typical Black Douglas — which may have had something to do with his early promotion — and though sombre-seeming, possessed a keen sense of humour as well as a hot temper. Whatever his religious qualifications, he was obviously an efficient administrator and man of business.

He looked from one to the other of his visitors, shrewd dark eyes speculative. "Faill is much honoured by the presence of the Earl of Dunbar's daughter, and the renowned True Thomas," he said. "However unexpected. The Lady Bethoc is much enhanced in beauty since last I saw her — a full woman now, and a fair one. Escorting her must be a notable privilege, Thomas! I rejoice that you found your way to Faill, wherever you are bound. How can I serve you?"

"You can marry us!" the girl declared simply.

Even the worldly-wise churchman raised his brows at that. "Marry, lady? Yourself and Thomas here?"

"*Sir* Thomas," she said. "The King has knighted him. Yes,

we would wed, Sir Prior. And, of your goodness, so soon as may be."

"So-o-o! Here is a surprise indeed. And you come to my humble self! I am privileged, as I say, lady — but I wonder why?"

"It is sufficiently simple, Nicholas," Thomas said. "We believed that you would do it for us. And knew not where else to turn."

"Usually earls' daughters are wed by bishops, are they not? The Earl Patrick knows many bishops, I feel sure."

"Earls' daughters do not usually wed humble and impoverished knights, my friend. And it is not the Earl Patrick who contrives this wedding!"

"Ah! So I take it that you have . . . run away?"

"We love each other, Sir Prior," Bethoc declared. "My father would have wed me to the Lord Duff MacDuff. That I would not. So — we came away."

"And came all the way to Faill! What of the Earl Patrick? How far is he behind?"

"We believe that he can know nothing of where we are," Thomas assured. "We have been very heedful, made our plans with care. Left no traces, we hope. Our going would not be discovered until last night. We did not know to whom else to go but you, Nicholas."

"To be sure, I see your problem. Have you considered, in all this, that whosoever marries you may well earn Earl Patrick's displeasure?"

"Yes — that I recognised also. But believed that you might be prepared to brave that, knowing you, Nicholas."

"Ah — so that is my reputation! Perhaps you are right. Very well — I shall do it. Since I know and esteem you both, and see no good reason why you should not wed. I do not think that my lord Earl could injure me here. Nor this house. So be it. When do you wish this, this union to take place?"

"So soon as you can, or will. In case . . ."

"In case, yes. It would be a misfortune if all was halted at the last moment. As well, if Almighty God is going to join you together, that He is not . . . impeded! What preparation do you require, Lady Bethoc?"

"None, Sir Prior — save to cleanse myself from journeying. I am as prepared for this in mind and soul as ever I shall be. I have prayed for it, sufficiently."

"As you will. Within the hour, then — in the chapel . . ."

So, presently, in the briefest and most simple of ceremonies, in the presence of two senior monks as witnesses, the couple exchanged the necessary vows, Thomas produced and fitted his mother's wedding-ring, and the Minister of Faill spoke the required words and pronounced them man and wife, whom no man was to put asunder, here or hereafter. It all took only a few minutes to forge a lifetime's bonds.

Bethoc was scarcely able to accept that this was all, that the thing was done — and could not be undone short of a specific Papal edict. Her gratitude towards Nicholas was most manifest.

Thereafter the monastery even produced a wedding-feast of a sort, something undoubtedly never before attempted on the premises. If hardly up to the standards which might have been reached in an earl's castle, there was no lack of viands, supplemented not only by the famous brown Faill ale but by a more potent brew distilled apparently from honey, plums and buckthorn berries, a speciality of the establishment.

Despite these appreciations of God's good provision, the Trinitarians had a strict daily discipline of worship, and after the repast it was time for the evening office of compline. The newly-weds felt that the least they could do was to attend this, so back to the chapel they went for another half-hour. Thereafter the monks retired to their dormitory with the dusk, for they would be up again for early matins at five o'clock. On this occasion the visitors found no complaint over such premature retiral. Besides, they also thought that it would be wise to be on their way as early in the morning as was convenient for their hosts, with another long day ahead of them.

"Where do you intend to go?" Nicholas asked, as he escorted them to their chamber in the guest-house. "I would think that Earl Patrick will be no laggard in his search for you."

"That we do not doubt," Thomas acceded. "So we seek to go where we are not likely to be looked for. When I was at

Largs fight, there were two islands lying offshore, a mile or so — the Cumbraes. I was told that there is a small house or cashel of Celtic monks still subsisting on the larger isle — the Keledei. I swear none would look for us there — if they will take us in."

"You say so? I had not heard of these. I did not know that there were any of the Columban heretics remaining south of the Highlands and Hebrides. Although, to be sure, these islands are all but part of the Hebrides. I have never been there . . ."

"Few have — which the more commends them to us. There we would hope to lie low for some while, until any search dies down."

"And then what, my friend? You cannot hide away like conies for ever. You will have to emerge one day. What then?"

"The King, after he had knighted me, told me to come to him if I required his aid. Once the noise has died away, I will go secretly to Alexander and seek his help. Scotland is large. Surely he will find some employ for me."

Nicholas looked less than convinced. "But what will you *do*, man? Until such time — if ever?" The Minister glanced at Bethoc. "Having a wife, delightful as this, is scarcely full occupation for such a man as yourself. After, h'm, the first few days! You are not one to idle away your days in hiding, with any satisfaction. Not for long."

"True. But I have a large task in view, for myself. Indeed, I have already commenced it. You will have heard of the great story of *Sir Tristrem?* About one of King Arthur's knights and the wife of the King of Cornwall."

"Heard, yes — who has not? But know naught of it. Was it not written by a Frenchman?"

"By Thomas of Brittany, yes — but only secondly. It is a Cornish and Celtic story, a mighty epic. Many hundreds of fyttes or verses. From the Breton-French it was translated and altered somewhat into the German. But it really first came from Wales. Few here can read it in these tongues — a great work lost to Scotland. So I am going to translate it into our own good Scots tongue. For all to read — and those who cannot read, at least to hear and enjoy, spoken by minstrels and sennachies. And not only to translate but to make familiar, to make use of Scots names and places. Make a poem of it."

"A noble project indeed," the other allowed. "But more like clerks' work than knights'!"

"Perhaps. But the tale is that of a knight and his love for Isolde, who was above him in station. So it may be that this lame knight, now wed to an earl's daughter, might aspire to it!"

"He has already written the first part," Bethoc added. "I have seen it. Starting on our own fair Eildon Hills. One Thomas continuing, indeed improving, the work of another. It is good, good . . ."

Bidding them a good night, with one raised eyebrow and a murmured benediction, their benefactor left them to it.

Their apartment in the guest-house at Faill was very different from the previous night's at Wiston, plain but adequately furnished, with two large beds and blankets, a garderobe with water and slop, skin-rugs on the clean-scrubbed floor, coffers for their clothing, and lamps. The monks had even put in fresh-cut flowers for the newly-weds. Not that the couple had more than briefly appreciative eyes for more than each other.

"At last!" Bethoc exclaimed, as the door shut behind them, arms wide to him. "Husband!"

Like the chamber, Thomas himself was very different from the night before. If then he had seemed a reluctant lover, hesitant and lacking fire, now his bride could make no such complaint. Eager, urgent, even masterful, he went to her, all but sweeping her off her feet. Nowise backward nor restraining, she was nevertheless next to breathless as she found herself as good as carried to the first of the great beds. All his inhibitions gone, his only restraints now were lest he too greatly hurried and outplayed her. She was, he well knew, a virgin, as he was not, and was entitled to some gentling.

He found himself helping her off with her clothing, with no suggestions to the contrary. But when she lay completely

naked before him, suddenly bashful, hands and arms seeking
to cover herself however inadequately, he as abruptly knew a
different emotion, compassion overcoming passion, true love
and affection tempering desire. He drew back.

"My dear, my dear," he said, chokingly. But he did not
cease to feast his eyes, at least.

Her own eyes had been tight shut for a few moments. Now
she opened them, to gaze up at him. And at his expression of
deep concern and tenderness, she moistened her lips, almost
visibly willed herself to relax, achieved a smile, and then
sitting up, spread her arms open.

Her loveliness was beyond all telling.

He drew a long, quivering breath and began to divest
himself of his own clothes. But he did it without withdrawing
his enthralled gaze for even a moment. And she watched,
tongue-tip fitful.

Murmuring endearments, reassurances — and having to
keep himself from escalating his murmurs almost to shouts —
he took her then, as gently as he knew how, promising that
they would do better, better, hereafter, that they had all
night, that it was so good, splendid, wonderful . . .

"Yes," she breathed, "yes, yes!" Convincing herself,
seeking to reassure him.

It took time and patience and understanding, as well as
love. But they had all these, and the night was long, thanks to
monkish discipline. Long before its end they were finding
fulfilment, man and wife indeed.

*   *   *

On their way early next morning, yawning but finding no
fault with their world, after a smiling farewell from Nicholas
and his friars, they rode north by west through the pleasant
Ayrshire pasturelands of Craigie and Dundonald, to ford the
River Irvine and reach the sea at the salt-pans of Kilwinning
Abbey, north of Irvine Bay. Eight further miles of the coast-
road brought them to Portincross Castle; but they avoided
this, where Thomas was known, pressing on another nine
miles to Largs.

It was strange for the man to be back in that place in such

151

changed circumstances, war and stress and crowds gone, it now only a small, quiet fishing township, with no signs of the drama of two years before. It all seemed different somehow, larger, more open, the distances greater — although the Cumbrae Isles looked the same and no further off than he had remembered them, the larger island's northern tip little more than a mile offshore. Nevertheless, when Thomas set about trying to arrange passage over that narrow stretch of water, he found it not so easy. Local fishermen were quite prepared to take them across — although obviously much surprised at anyone wishing to go; but the horses were the problem. None of them had craft capable of carrying the beasts; and the travellers were not prepared to leave them behind. It was advised that they return southwards for some three miles, to the haven of Fairlie, opposite the south end of the island, where there was a system of signalling by beacon to the monks who dwelt on Cumbrae Mor, and who had their own ferry-scows for the transport of their livestock to and from the island. There was good grazing over there, it seemed, and the churchmen had quite large flocks and herds; moreover some of the mainland farmers summered their stock on the island pastures at a small charge, so that the monks were quite used to ferrying animals.

They retraced their steps therefore, to Fairlie — which in fact, owing to the coastal contours, was almost twice as far away from Cumbrae as was Largs but opposite the less rugged and more fertile southern end of the larger island, where evidently was the cashel or Celtic monastery. There, on a knoll above the boat-strand, was the beacon, in the shape of a gibbet from which hung an iron basket in which were tarred and pitch-pine timbers to set alight. The keeper of a small alehouse lit this for them, producing a satisfactorily vigorous red flame and great clouds of dirty black smoke. He also provided modest refreshment while they waited.

They had, in fact, a lengthy wait, for this was no regular ferry and there was apparently no constant traffic with the island, save at times when the cattle and sheep were being transported in spring and autumn or market-time. Here too the locals were much exercised as to what was drawing the young wayfarers over to such God-forsaken place. Thomas's brief assertion that they had business with the Columban abbot was only doubtfully received.

When at last the beacon-signal was answered by the appearance of a boat coming across the two miles of the sound, the visitors were disappointed to see that it was no scow but quite a small craft, rowed by only two oarsmen although with the assistance of a square sail — clearly not large enough to carry their horses. The ferrymen proved to be two cheerful and quite brawny young men, not notably monkish save in their black and somewhat ragged leather-belted robes and their forehead tonsures — as distinct from the crown-of-the-head Romish sort — who eyed the visitors with frankest interest, Bethoc in especial, and declared in soft, Highland voices that it was a long time since the island had had any guests with horses and of their quality, and so they had not brought one of their flat-bottomed barges. There was, unfortunately, no time to go back and fetch one of the heavier craft before evening worship; but if the travellers wished to see their abbot that night, they would take them over forthwith and come back for the horses in the morning.

With this the couple had to be content.

So, taking their saddle-bags, they left their beasts in the care of the alehouse-keeper and boarded the boat for their two-mile row, against a light westerly breeze, to Cumbrae Mor.

Their oarsmen proved to be a notably friendly pair — and as obviously inquisitive as the fisherfolk to know what brought such gentlefolk to their island — but being Highlanders, were much too polite for direct questioning. Failing to obtain much information, they nevertheless were quite forthcoming as to their own situation and that of the Columban monastery, which they called an abbey, all Celtic Church monastic establishments using that style, and under the rule of abbots. Abbot Drostan, it seemed, was a very holy man of great age, with fourteen monks at the Abbey of St. Colm itself and two more at the detached chapel and farmery of St. Vey up at the north end of the island. Cumbrae Mor was over three miles long and comprised three thousand acres, they said. The Church — the true Columban Church, that is — had been established here from the Blessed Columba's days; indeed the name of Cumbrae should really be Cymri-ay, the Isle of the Cymric-speaking ones. Norse overlords from Arran had latterly made life difficult for them but now, after Largs battle, these were gone and they were left in peace to work and worship. Although it was said that the King had now given the Cumbraes to the High Steward at Renfrew, as reward for his leadership at Largs, so far he had not troubled them or even visited.

Cumbrae Mor proved to be shaped rather like an arrowhead with the forked base enclosing between headlands a wide and deep bay into which the boatmen steered. At the head of this was a jetty and above it, on the gentle hillside, was the Abbey of St. Colm or Columba.

A greater contrast with the monastery of Faill would be hard to imagine, for two religious establishments only twenty-five miles apart as the crow flies. Instead of excellent and well-designed dressed-stone buildings, handsome masonry and carved ornamentation, regularly laid-out, compact and orderly, here was a scatter of hutments and cabins within a grassy rampart, little more than hovels of dry-stone and turf, some apparently living-accommodation, some cattle-sheds, stables, barns and storerooms, ramshackle and in no sort of order. One of the smaller buildings, of the same style as the rest, proved to be the chapel, a mere low-browed thatched cothouse with a low door and four small windows, nothing sacred-looking about it — save that outside, placed apparently haphazard, were five of the most magnificent high crosses that it had been Thomas's privilege ever to see, of intricately-carved stone with early Christian symbols, Pictish animals and elaborate interlacing designs, treasures of man's artistic and devotional dedication by any standards. The newcomers were all but struck dumb with surprise at all they saw.

They were conducted to one of the huts, no different from the others, from which an old bent man emerged to greet them, dressed exactly as were the two oarsmen except in that his black robe was green with age and rather more ragged and stained. His toothless smile was beaming, however, and his welcome warm, with no doubtful scrutiny of the strangers. It was not often that their poor house was honoured with guests, on Cumbrae, he declared — although his toothlessness, allied to his sibilant Hebridean voice, made his words a little difficult to understand.

Thomas had been rehearsing his speech in his mind, since there was no blinking their problems if they were not permitted to stay here.

"We have come, as you might say, seeking sanctuary, Sir Abbot," he said frankly. "My wife and I. She is the Lady Bethoc of Dunbar and I am Sir Thomas Learmonth. We love each other deeply. But she was to wed another. So we came away, were wed yesterday, and now seek refuge for a while where we will not be looked for. Will you, sir, permit that we stay here on Cumbrae? We can pay for our lodging. We require very little save shelter and feeding. And I will gladly work at whatever is required."

"My lord Abbot — please!" Bethoc said.

The old man looked from one to the other. "Do not name me lord, young woman," he said, but gently. "We have no lords in this Church. I am but the humblest of Christ's servants. And if you come to me, in the name of Christ, seeking sanctuary and what I can give, who am I to refuse it?"

"You, you will take us in, then?"

"I can no more turn you away than I could a starving beggar, my dear. Even if you have . . . transgressed."

"We have transgressed only in that we have wed without my father's approval, sir. He would have married me to a man I have no regard for, when I loved Thomas and have done since I was a child. Is that transgression?"

"Who am I to judge? I can only accept you in Christ, as you are. Pray for your well-being. And do what I can to further it, whatever. The rest is in God's good hands. Only, I would warn you, we live but simply on this island — for such folk as you. Our Church does not set great store by riches and the like."

"So much the better, Abbot Drostan," Thomas asserted.

"Although I am now wed to an earl's daughter, I am but a very poor knight with no love for riches and but little of the world's goods . . ."

"But Thomas has his own riches!" Bethoc put in strongly. "He is a poet, and a noted one. Thomas the Rhymer."

Clearly the Abbot had not heard of True Thomas. But he looked at the embarrassed young man with a new eye nevertheless — for unwittingly Bethoc had struck a notable chord. The Celtic Church, although dying before the sustained onslaught of the Romish one, backward in many ways and utterly lacking in hierarchy, organisation and power, had always had the greatest respect for matters cultural and the arts. Indeed it was one of the accusations of their Roman critics that they were all but heathenish in this respect, as in others, propagating secular and ungodly songs and themes, tales and designs — as witness their barbarous stone crosses — retaining many of the arts and customs of the pagan, sun-worshipping Picts, revering things that the Vatican had solemnly declared to be anathema. So Drostan was disposed to look the more warmly on a poet, especially one who claimed to be poor and a rejector of riches, moreover one evidently prepared to defy the power of worldly authority. Nodding his white head vigorously, he took the poet's arm to lead them off through the scatter of hutments to a cabin on the outskirts, stone-and-turf and thatched like the rest. He ushered them inside. This was theirs, he said, for so long as they wished to occupy it.

Despite their declarations of the virtues of simplicity, the new arrivals' breaths did rather catch at the basic austerity of their allotted quarters. There was a beaten-earth floor, two bunks, a large box, a wall-cupboard, a basin, jug and wooden platters — and that was all. Abbot Drostan made no apologies, however, although he added that blankets and deerskins would be forthcoming. Also that they would be having the evening meal shortly — a bell would summon them. Meantime, if they would excuse him, he would give the necessary instructions to his brethren.

Left alone in that bare cell they stared at each other.

"Oh, my love — what have I done to you!" Thomas exclaimed. "Brought you to . . . this! From Ercildoune Castle to, to . . .!"

"To a safe and secure place where we may be together, Thomas. That is what I have wanted and what you have done. This is none so ill, my dear. It is clean. And we shall make it more comfortable, never fear. These people are kind, good. And the Abbot is a saint, is he not? We shall do very well."

"But . . . a hermit's cell!"

"I am no shrinking flower, my heart — I am my father's daughter in that, at least. Consider how it would have been had they *refused* us, turned us away. Then indeed we should have had cause for worry. But not here, now . . ."

Their oarsmen came with the saddle-bags from the boat. Even to have some of their own things about them helped. Then more monks arrived with blankets, plaids and half-a-dozen deerskins, these to pile on the bunks to form mattresses of a sort — although once the monks were gone they promptly pushed the two bunks together to make one and so could make do with three of the skins, and the others, put on the floor to form rugs, at once made the place look better. When the hollow clonk-clonk of a Celtic saint's bell summoned them to the largest building of the establishment, the eating-house with kitchen attached, Thomas was beginning to feel less self-critical and apprehensive.

The dozen monks, of all ages, most evidently welcomed the novelty of having visitors, especially a poet and a lovely young woman. They were a cheerful and utterly unpretentious lot, with a strange mixture of innate Highland courtesy and somewhat crude manners. They were less obviously disciplined than were Nicholas's Red Friars, but they clearly greatly loved and respected old Drostan. The meal was as simple as all else, but the food plentiful. Instead of wine or ale they drank a fiery spirit which they called *uisge-beatha* or the water-of-life; but this was sipped in small quantities and the visitors left it alone.

When, later, they retired to their hut and couch, neither thought to find any fault, being otherwise preoccupied. The entire establishment was closed down and asleep by soon after sundown.

Next day, while the ferrymen sailed their large flat-bottomed scow across to the mainland to collect the horses, Thomas and Bethoc went walking, to explore some of the island, the man's limp notwithstanding. They discovered that these Keledei, the Friends of God as they called themselves, were not the sole inhabitants, there being perhaps a dozen small farms, crofts or shepherds' and fishermen's cottages scattered here and there about the southern portion of the island. But all were more or less dependent on the abbey, either employed by the monks, or their tenants. Cumbrae Mor, in its three and a half miles, comprised quite a variety of country and scenery, a central hill mass rising to some three hundred feet above the sea, divided approximately down the centre by a valley known as the Glen of St. Ninian. There was a considerable area of tillable ground and good pasture at the southern and broad end; while the northern tip was more rocky and moorish, with heather and scrub. There were small cliffs, both coastal and on inland escarpments; and the strange feature of two great dykes of outcropping rock, like enormous walls, running parallel across the island, one terminating on the east in a rugged hill shaped like a crouching lion, indeed remarkably resembling the well-known Arthur's Crag at Edinburgh, in miniature. Much of the shoreline was rock-bound, but there were some small sandy bays, with headlands and offshore skerries. Stone-circles and standing-stones stood here and there, indicating that this had been a centre of worship for long before Christianity came. Cattle and sheep grazed in fairly large numbers, also herds of small, sturdy ponies.

The newcomers enjoyed their walk and approved of almost all they saw that bright sunny morning — although admittedly they were in a state of mind the reverse of fault-finding. They decided that they would be quite content to remain at St. Colm's Abbey for an indefinite period.

However, when they returned to the monastery, it was to find Abbot Drostan with changed ideas. It seemed that some mainland fishermen had put in at the abbey-haven, as often they did, to barter fish for meat or honey or cheese, and these had observed the two thoroughbred horses being ferried out from Fairlie, so different from the rough local garrons or island ponies — and had asked the inevitable questions. The monks had attempted to parry their queries, but there had been no denying that two visitors of some quality had come to Cumbrae and that one of them was a woman. Tongues therefore would most certainly wag and no doubt further enquiries would be made at Fairlie and elsewhere, human nature being what it was. Therefore, Drostan said, if their young guests wished to remain in hiding and undisturbed, he regretfully felt that they must leave the Abbey.

Grievously disappointed, the couple protested that surely they could counter the possibility of discovery and danger by lying low and keeping out of sight when callers reached the island? After all, such must come by boat, and boats could be watched for . . .?

The Abbot shook his old head. He had a better notion than that, he divulged. The Abbey had a small subsidiary or dependency at the far north end of the island, dedicated to the Blessed St. Vey. Once it had been an independent cashel, but now only two monks remained there at any one time, looking after the sheep and cattle of that remote part of their domain and catching the lobsters for which that coast was famed. The visitors could go there. There was accommodation and to spare, and the St. Vey monks had no direct communication with the mainland. Nobody ever went there save from the Abbey itself. A more secure refuge would be difficult to find.

So the following morning, with their ferrymen as guides, mounted on island ponies, Thomas and Bethoc rode off northwards up St. Ninian's Glen, distinctly doubtfully. The Abbey monks seemed loth to see them go, too.

Their doubts vanished an hour or so later when, descending from a sort of pass below the Aird hill which rose at the extreme northern tip of Cumbrae Mor, by a series of grassy but rock-ribbed terraces, they came to a cliff-top apron of old turf and whins, protected by the ultimate

headland of Tomont's Ness, called after a Viking called
Thormod Foal's-leg they were told. On this lofty shelf, with
the wrinkled sea spread sheerly below and magnificent
prospects across the firth to the large island of Bute and all
the blue mainland mountains of Cowal, was a cluster of
cabins within a grass-grown rampart, on a smaller scale to St.
Colm's, surrounded by sheep-folds, byres, barns and bee-
skeps. No doubt in winter storms it would be a dire and
exposed eyrie indeed; but on a sunny day of June it was like a
corner of heaven, out of the world, lost in dreaming peace
and beauty.

Its two custodians, quiet men of middle-years both,
introduced as Dungal and Comgal, although they must have
been highly surprised, if not taken aback at the arrival of
secular visitors come to stay, accepted them without question
— or nearly so — and with the most friendly of greetings.
Indeed acceptance scarcely came into it, their evident
pleasure in the young company that descended upon them
unannounced being simple, unaffected and heart-warming.
They smiled and smiled, patting their guests on the shoulder,
giving little skips of satisfaction, offering them creamy milk
and bannocks dripping with honey, and nodding to each
other as though confirming that they had always anticipated
some such joy. Thomas had a shrewd notion that Bethoc's
youthful beauty was very largely responsible — but found no
fault with that.

They were taken on a tour of the establishment and offered
any one of half-a-dozen hutments similar to that at St.
Colm's. A burn ran tinkling through the cashel, providing
convenient washing and sanitation facilities; and the
newcomers selected a cabin at a little bend of this, which
turned its back on the rest and faced out over that
tremendous vista of sea and islands and mountains. Comgal
and Dungal hurried to clean up and plenish it for its new
occupants. Labouring hugely, with the help of the guides,
they even dragged a smallish Celtic stone cross over, to stand
it before the doorway, to watch over them, than which no
more notable gesture and tribute could have been offered.

By the time that their former escort left to return to St.

Colm's, the latest denizens of St. Vey's, preparing to settle in, were as happy as their hosts seemed to be. Bethoc declared herself to be the most fortunate bride in all the world.

Hand-in-hand they stood in their doorway and gazed out over as fair a prospect as any man could hope to see, while their hosts heedfully hurried off to leave them in peace.

8

The weeks that followed were more like a dream than reality, and afterwards became ever more difficult to believe that they had ever been. Nothing in the lives of the newly-wed couple seemed to have any relevance to their life on Cumbrae's northern tip. Everything seemed to be different, ambience, tempo, priorities, interests, work, simply being. And, of course, the fulfilment of their mutual love and understanding of each other, all in a perpetual glow of scenic beauty and colour such as they had not realised existed. That the weather was consistently kind helped, undoubtedly.

From the first they were made to feel that they belonged to this tiny community, and after the first day or two they took their part in its daily rhythm of work and worship as a matter of course. Not that either of these was taxing or any trial. The work was unhurried, basic, elemental — herding, fishing, digging peats and soil, tending the lobster-creels, spinning wool, weaving blankets and the like. And the worship consisted largely of singing and contemplation, formal services reserved for Sundays. There were specialised activities, of course, at which the newcomers could only look on and admire — lettering and illuminating scriptural texts and sacred scrolls, carving in stone and wood, tending the bees. But with all this there was ample leisure, time to laze in the sun, swim in the sea, clamber amongst the cliffs, gaze out over the breathtaking prospects and talk or be silent. Dungal and Comgal made the best of companions, the most attentive of hosts — but were careful to leave the young people alone a great deal, not to intrude on their privacy.

Bethoc adapted herself to the timeless round of their days as though born to it, more easily indeed than did Thomas who continued to have feelings akin to guilt on the score of idleness for a few days, perhaps an echo of Prior Nicholas's doubts. The young woman was content to do nothing for hours on end, although she worked hard enough when occasion called. She became indeed a notable shepherdess, milked the cows, churned milk, strained honey, melted wax and introduced variety into the diet. Also she made a home out of their cabin so that it was scarcely recognisable, carpeting the floor with skins, hanging blankets on the walls, contriving a table and benches from boarding and always having wild flowers as decoration. The tiny chapel, too, bare as the rest save for a rough stone altar on which stood a lovely cross of intricately-carved silver and a bronze saint's bell, she presently grew bold enough to deck with flowers also, and drew no reproaches from the monks.

They learned a lot about the Celtic Church, now in fatal decline, and about the story of this tiny corner of it. They knew, of course, that it had been introduced to a pagan, Pictish Alba, from Ireland, by Columba and his famous Brethren, in the sixth century, after an earlier missionary effort by St. Ninian had come to naught. They also knew that it had been the Church of the land for four centuries, until Queen Margaret, the Saxon wife of Malcolm Canmore, had conceived herself to have a divine mission to convert, persuade and mould it into adherence to Rome and obedience to the Vatican, a determined and effective policy completed by her sons, especially King David, the present Alexander's great-great-grandsire. What they did not know much about was its beliefs, practices and observances, now damned as heretical by religious authorities and surviving only in small pockets here and there, mainly in the Highlands and Hebrides. They learned that it had no dioceses as did the Roman Catholics, indeed very little central organisation at all — which had much aided in its being brought low. But it did have bishops, although these were not the Church's rulers but had especial priestly duties and responsibilities concerned with ordination and the sacraments. The rulers — if that term could apply at all — were the abbots, under the leadership of the Abbot of Iona. But these controlled only their own abbeys and cashels and did not form any real college, although they formerly had met in council at intervals. Priests were permitted to marry, although comparatively few did, and certain offices had become hereditary — another cause of weakness and degeneracy. But the essential faith had been kept fairly pure and undefiled, based on the early apostolic ministry, without the accretions and hierarchical pretensions of the papacy, and largely uncontaminated by the world, simple, basic, a people's Church wholly monastic, with little or no interest in church buildings, fond of open-air worship, communicating in both bread and wine, unconcerned with wealth and land-owning, going in for a minimum of liturgy, penances, fastings and sentences of damnation. To the young people, perhaps in their innocence, it did not seem to merit the fierce and prolonged campaign against it and the scorn with which its remains were viewed by orthodox churchmen.

As to this St. Vey's itself, the present small establishment was in fact something of a transplant as well as a mere shadow of the original. The earlier cashel of St. Vey had been on the other island, Cumbrae Beg, in its heyday a fair-sized monastery. But Viking raiding brought it low, like so many another, and it was decided that it was better to try to defend one island rather than two. But the St. Vey survivors did not wish to be absorbed into St. Colm's, so they established their new cashel on this unaccessible tip of Cumbrae Mor where for some time it had maintained an independent existence. But eventually, with the decline of the Celtic Church, it became a mere appendage of the larger St. Colm, useful for the care of livestock at this northern end of the island.

Each day of their stay, Thomas decided that he would get down to his work on *Sir Tristrem* — and each day he failed to do so. Somehow there was always something else to do; or if, in fact, nothing was being done but thinking, contemplating loveliness and infinity, he was not quite in the mood for poetic creation. He frequently felt that he *ought* to be, that with all the peace and beauty, leisure and sheer satisfaction which filled their days, he should be inspired as never before. But it did not seem to work that way. Of course *Sir Tristrem* admittedly was scarcely a peaceful and pastoral idyll but an epic of guilty passion, treachery, heartbreak and sacrifice. He consoled himself with the thought that there would almost certainly come more appropriate conditions for dealing with such.

During those halcyon weeks they saw little of their fellow-men, save for Comgal and Dungal, extraordinarily so considering that the populous Cunninghame area of the mainland was not much more than a mile away. Frequently they saw fishing-boats quite near at hand, but these avoided their rockbound coast; and their little cliff-foot sandy bay, favourite as it was for their swimming, had no attractions for fishermen. They were careful, when themselves out fishing or visiting the lobster-creels, to watch out for and avoid other boats. But the island's fisheries were accepted as belonging to the monks, and they were not much troubled by poachers, the anathemas of even the Celtic Church being considered sufficiently effective, probably, not to be worth provoking. Actual visitors, by land, there were none. Brothers came up from St. Colms every few days, and once Abbot Drostan himself made the journey to see how they were getting on. He was able to reassure them that there had been no real enquiries made about them, not on the island at any rate, although the ferrymen, when they landed at Fairlie, were apt to be asked what had happened to the young gentlefolk. They said in reply only that they had moved on. Whether or not the Earl of Dunbar was making a great to-do searching for his daughter was not vouchsafed and the monks did not ask. The only other people the fugitives saw throughout were an elderly shepherd and his wife whose cothouse at Figgatoch was the nearest neighbouring habitation, almost two miles away at the head of a small side-glen, a quiet, uncommunicative pair who posed no threat.

So six unforgettable weeks passed, and gradually Thomas became restless, some feeling of guilt growing upon him. Bethoc would have been well content to continue there more or less indefinitely, at least until the winter brought very different conditions. But the man was made otherwise. There was an impatience in him, an urge to be up and doing, some drive to meet the challenges of life and a recognition that this lull had to come to an end sooner or later. Also the weather broke down — and three days of driving rain, blustering winds, slate-grey, white-veined seas and mountains blotted out, altered life up in their cliff-top eyrie not a little.

Reluctantly Thomas came to the conclusion that it was time to make a move. The distress of Dungal and Comgal was touching; but they made no sustained attempt to dissuade their guests. On the next appearance of monks from St. Colms, Thomas asked them to inform the Abbot of their decision to leave, and the hope that it would be possible for the ferry-scow to take them and their horses, by night, to some different part of the mainland coast where they could be put ashore unobserved.

And so, on the afternoon of the Eve of St. Blathmac, they took a moving farewell of their good friends at St. Veys at Tomont's Ness, in mutual esteem and commendation to the good God's blessing, and rode down Ninian's glen for the last time, Bethoc almost tearful. At St. Colms their going likewise produced most evident regrets; but Abbot Drostan declared that he knew that their stay must be only temporary. He told them that he had arranged their transport, after nightfall, to a point well south of Fairlie where, at Brigurd Ness, the shoals of Southannan Sands gave way to a shelving beach on which their horses could be landed. So they had their final meal with the Columban monks — who refused to charge any moneys for their stay, claiming that not only had they been welcome guests but that they had worked adequately for their keep. Bethoc insisted, however, on leaving with Drostan a gold chain and small crucifix which she had possessed since childhood.

Just before midnight they were disembarked into the shallows of the mainland shore at a quite empty stretch, in the two-thirds dark of a cloudy late-July night, said their goodbyes to the crew and splashed their mounts to land, to head due eastwards for the dimly-seen mouth of Crosbie Glen. Their feelings were mixed, to say the least.

*   *   *

Travelling thus by night, it was necessary to keep to a recognisable road if they were not to get lost in country Thomas did not know. This entailed quite a detour southwards, up this glen through the Crosbie Hills, over a small pass and down to the township of Dalry on the River Garnock, belonging to the Abbey of Kilwinning. They had come some nine quite difficult miles by then, in a couple of hours, distinctly out-of-their-way — for they were *en route* for Stirling where Thomas hoped either to find the King or to learn as to his present whereabouts. But now they could turn north-eastwards up the valley of the Garnock for Lochwinnoch, which they reached with the dawn. The High Steward's baronies of Paisley and Renfrew were ahead, and these they thought it wise to avoid. So they swung away eastwards by the Braes of Gleniffer to the valley of the White Cart and so to the royal burgh of Rutherglen on the Clyde, forty-five miles from their start, which they reached weary but in good spirits in the afternoon. They passed the night at the Hospice of the Blessed Virgin there, without being asked to give any special account of themselves.

Next morning, across Clyde, they could head due north for the Kelvin valley, which they reached at Kirkintilloch, in three hours, no more. Now the barrier of the Kilsyth Hills lay before them, but with Stirling only a score of miles north by east as the crow flies. By early evening the soaring mass of the castle-crowned rock and all the winding links of the Forth lay before them. Thomas went carefully now, for if the Court was still in residence here they could be recognised. At the Hospice of St. Ninian, on the southern outskirts, he intended to leave Bethoc whilst he went forward to prospect. But the friar in charge made this unnecessary by informing them that the King's Grace had left Stirling ten days previously, to go to the summer palace of Kincardine in the Mearns.

They were faced, therefore, with further journeying in a big way, for Kincardine lay at the far end of long Strathmore in the jaws of the Mounth, almost one hundred miles to the north-east. But in a way they were well enough content, for they felt that the further they went northwards, away from their own part of Scotland, the less likelihood there was of being heard of and identified.

It took them almost three days' steady riding to reach Kincardine, by Strathearn, St. John's Town of Perth and Dunsinnane to the head of Strathmore, and down that fair and mighty vale, the second-largest in the land, through Gowrie and Angus to the Mearns. Not once were they challenged as to identity or otherwise, or inconvenienced save by weariness and inclement weather. They avoided abbeys and major monasteries, as well as the castles and hallhouses of the lordly ones, putting up at small and modest hospices for travellers.

Kincardine Castle proved to be more of an old-fashioned hallhouse than any major fortified strength, really no more than a hunting-seat, lying amongst the outliers of the great heather mountains of the Mounth, at the mouth of a deep, steep glen which probed into these heights northwards. Again Thomas thought it wise to leave Bethoc at an alehouse in the castleton while he went forward to the palace alone, and in some trepidation.

He discovered, however, that the King was out hawking presently. But he managed to obtain an interview with one of the royal secretaries, who proved to be the same chaplain Reginald with whom he had shared a table behind the King at Roxburgh Castle during the confrontation with Cardinal Ottobone. This Reginald greeted him with a mixture of astonishment and disapproval, but could not refuse Sir Thomas's request that the monarch should be informed that he sought private audience, very private. He would be at the village alehouse until sent for. From the guard at the castle gatehouse he sought information as to the nobles and personalities attending presently on the King — and was relieved to learn that the Earl Patrick at least was not one, indeed that only a very small group had accompanied

Alexander here, for the deer-driving. Unfortunately Colban MacDuff was one of them.

The alehouse was situated on the west bank of a sizeable burn which flowed out of the glen known as Strathdevilly above, and which provided the water for the castle moat. Thomas found Bethoc down at the burnside watching the peat-brown waters in a half-dream, and was glad enough to join her in this quiet activity, for they were tired indeed from long riding. This Strathdevilly was a pleasant place to idle, birchwoods leading up to the darker forest of Caledonian pines and soaring above these the huge and dominating Highland mountains which made their own Eildons seem but hillocks.

It was a warm day and lulled by the murmur and chuckle of the stream they were both almost asleep, despite their apprehensions, when they were aroused by the baying of deerhounds and clatter of hooves as the royal hawking-party returned from the hill, riding through the castleton no more than a couple of hundred yards from them, the King at the head. Thomas could no longer hide his anxiety. What would be Alexander's reaction? He had, he was well aware, offended against the established order of things, behaved badly in the eyes of authority and custom. The King might well refuse to see him, much less help him; might even apprehend him and send Bethoc back to her father. They had discussed all this time and again, and the girl had indeed advised avoiding the royal presence altogether. But Thomas had declared that they could not remain fugitives indefinitely. The King had told him to come to him, if in need. Moreover, he owed Alexander an explanation, owed him more than just the normal allegiance. For his knightly vows included an especial duty and service towards the monarch who had knighted him. They were wed and no one, not even the King, could unwed them. All of which did little to nullify present anxieties.

Whatever Thomas had feared or anticipated regarding Alexander did not prepare him for what transpired, however. They were about to return to the alehouse in expectation of the hoped-for royal summons when they perceived a man coming striding purposefully down to them, a couple of loping deerhounds at heel — and perceived split-seconds later that the strider was their liege-lord himself. They started up in major confusion.

Alexander's fair and comely good looks were not often disfigured by so black a frown. He jabbed out an accusatory finger as he came up.

"God's mercy — both of you!" he exclaimed. "By the Mass — you come here? You dare to come to *me*, Thomas Learmonth? Demanding audience. After, after what you have done!"

"I did not mean for you to come to me, Sire — as God is my witness! I but sought . . ."

"Sakes, man — if I had let you come to me, granted you audience in yonder castle, all Scotland would have known of it in a day or two! You may be prepared for that, but I am not! All the realm has been looking for you. Then lame Thomas Learmonth comes hirpling into my presence! Some of these with me here know you well. Indeed Colban MacDuff is here. How think you *he* loves you? I have sworn my secretary to secrecy — but I could not swear them all. Do you not see how ill a position you put me in, man? Myself, the King, compounding your shameful conduct, your infamy, taking part against my cousin, one of my own earls?"

Thomas began to speak — and then stopped as the implications behind Alexander's words dawned upon him. "You mean, Sire — you mean that you will not, will not move against me? That you will be merciful, understanding? Not to hand us over, to those against us . . .?"

The King cleared his throat strongly. "Do not crow too soon, Thomas! And you, young woman. I have not yet decided what I shall do. I know what you deserve . . ."

"Sire," Bethoc intervened, forgetting that kings must not be interrupted. "You will not take part against us, surely? I am your kin also, you will mind. And my, my husband is your very good and true servant, who has served you and your kingdom well . . ."

"*Husband* you say, girl?"

"To be sure. Your Grace did not think that we would live together in sin? We. were wed the day after we left Ercildoune."

"So — wed!" Alexander stared from one to the other. "There are more kinds of sin than one, see you. Think you marriage will commend you the more to your father? Or to the MacDuffs?"

"Perhaps not, Highness. But to God, and all godly men and women, it may mean more. We are man and wife. Had I wed Duff MacDuff, loving Thomas, *that* would have been sin, and my marriage vows shameful hypocrisy."

"H'mm." Alexander kicked a stone into the burn. "Who wed you?"

"Must we tell you that, Sire?" Thomas asked. "It was truly done, by the prior of a monastery. Would it not be better that you did not learn whom? Better for all?"

"You have the devil's own insolence, man! But — perhaps you are right. In this, at least. But — where in God's name have you been? All this time. Patrick has searched the land for you. We were almost beginning to credit this tale of fairies and spirits! It was scarcely believable that a lame knight and an earl's daughter could disappear from man's ken completely. And now you come here, to my palace, full of virtue and telling me what it is best that I know!"

"We were on an island, Sire. In the care of kindly monks, Columban monks. Need you to know where?"

"Save us — Columban monks on an island! The Hebrides, then. What next? I will say this for you, Thomas — you can be relied upon to do the unexpected and set all by the ears! Not only in your prophesyings, it seems. Small wonder that the Merse folk believed this nonsense about a fairy queen!"

"Fairy queen?" Thomas wondered. "What is this? You said spirits and fairies, before, Sire. What folly is this?"

"You mean to say that *you* did not invent it all, man? To hide your tracks. They say, these Merse and Tweedside folk, that you were seen, by some foresters, riding down off the Eildon Hill. With a fairy queen all dressed in green. And so are gone, with her, beyond the ken of men!"

"Lord . . .!"

"My riding-cloak is green," Bethoc said, practically. "And we were on the Eildons."

Thomas shook his head. "Ignorant fools! But — anyone who knew me there, should have known the Lady Bethoc also, Sire. I cannot understand this."

"It is all over the land, now, folly or none. Your fame as a rhymer and soothsayer has seen to that . . ." the King was saying, when again he was interrupted.

"Thomas — *Sir Tristrem!*" the young woman cried. "Your poem. The Queen of Elfland in her grass-green gown. How you make it to start, by the Eildon Tree . . .!"

"Mary Mother!" Thomas said.

"What is this?" Alexander demanded.

"It could be — aye, it could be that. It is the great epic story, Your Grace — *Sir Tristrem*. You will know of it. I have been contriving to translate it into our Scots tongue. From the original Cymric. A poem. It is long, a mighty work. I have been at it for some time. I had thought to place the start here in Scotland, instead of in Brittany and Cornwall and Ireland, to make it more real to our folk. So I started it on the Eildon Hills which I know well, under an especial tree there. With Thomas — not myself but the French writer, Thomas of Brittany — lying asleep, when the Queen of Elfland comes riding by. This as introduction, to account for much that is strange and miraculous in the tale . . ."

"Ha — this sounds like enough. But is it known, this poem of yours?"

"No. But I have written it down on many papers. Versions of it. To get it right. The papers were all left, to be sure, with my other things, at Ercildoune. When I came away. They could have been found, read, this tale noised abroad . . ."

"That is it, Thomas — I am sure that is what has happened," Bethoc said.

"It could be," the King agreed. "With your repute as an oracle, almost a wizard, such a tale could be taken up by the credulous and the unlettered."

"But not by my father and mother!" the girl asserted. "Who would be the ones who would read Thomas's papers."

"No-o-o. That does not sound like the Earl Patrick. Yet he

might *use* the story. Even as he hunted for you, might he not? He is sore hit, that any daughter of his, and his eldest child, should make him seem a laughing-stock by running off with his esquire, his former esquire. The finger pointed at him, he might well be glad to make use of this witchcraft and superstition. You both being bewitched by this being in green. I can see it, yes. I can see Patrick publishing that story abroad."

"Perhaps. But what difference does it make?" Thomas said. "He will seek us none the less urgently."

"True — but others may not. It could have that difference. Others, the common folk in especial, might not wish to work against the unseen, to cross this fairy queen and the powers of the other world. You have disappeared so completely. Folk will believe it. So — you must stay disappeared, I say!"

"Yes, Sire — so say we. But . . ."

"Then why come here, man? Why come to me? And risk all."

"Because you told me to, Highness. After the knighting. You said if ever I needed your help, to come to you."

"M'mm. Yes, you served me well, before Largs and with that Ottobone. But — can you not see how you discompose me in this, confound me? What you have done puts you outside my help, Thomas. The King cannot be seen to be aiding a lowly knight against one of his great lords — against two of them since this young woman was promised to the son of the Earl of Fife. However well I wish you, my hands are tied. I am *Ard Righ*, the High King, and these are my lesser kings. We must support each other — or at least seem to. And Patrick is also my friend as well as my kinsman. I cannot take your part."

"Could you not, secretly, Sire? Could I not still serve you, in some way, unknown to others? I must do something, work at some task. That is why we did not remain on the island with the Keledei. Have you no task for me, some privy service? Far away, perhaps? Where we will not be known, looked for, but I will still be your leal servant?"

Alexander frowned at him, fondling a deerhound's shaggy head. "Lord, man — how can I tell you that? Would you have me to send you as envoy to some other monarch? Thomas Learmonth, a disgraced fugitive! It is not to be considered."

"Not a foreign envoy, no. Something much less fine. Something wherein I could be your private liegeman, a tool for your royal hand? As a secretary, perhaps, far away, such as few others might wish to be. For a time, until all this is forgotten . . ."

"God knows — *I* do not! I cannot think of anything such, now. See you — I must go back, or there will be talk. Bide here tonight. I will consider it. I promise nothing, mind you. But I will come to you, or send you word, in the morning. Meantime, do not show yourselves nearer to the palace than this alehouse. You understand?"

He left them then, all in a state of some agitation.

The suppliants retired early, to wrap themselves in their cloaks and plaids in a communal apartment shared with lords' men-at-arms overflowed from the palace, noisy and uncongenial company to whom they gave no account of themselves. But in view of their other problems, this was a minor one.

In the early forenoon the chaplain Reginald came to instruct them, sourly, to ride on up the Devilly-side a mile to where they would see the remains of a Pictish fort surmounting a hillock above the burn, unseen at the far side of which was a grove of old pines. To wait there, and remain hidden.

At least it was no curt royal refusal and dismissal, however curtly conveyed.

An hour or so later Alexander came riding alone to the rendezvous, hounds at heel and hawk at wrist. He was in a more cheerful mood, and more like himself.

"I have thought of a way in which you could be of service to me," he announced, without preamble. "And sufficiently far away for you. I have long been concerned with the position in the north of my kingdom, in Moray and those parts, where the descendants of MacBeth and Lulach hold sway — the old Celtic line. There is no true Earl of Moray now, but one or two think to call themselves that. They may aspire even higher, for whilst *I* descend from David, sixth son of Malcolm Canmore and Margaret, the MacEths descend from his elder brother Ethelred. Moreover, the MacWilliams there descend from Duncan the Second, who was King for a little space, son of Canmore *before* he married Margaret. Both of these, therefore, could make some claim to my throne. They have not done so, save in drunken boasting, I am told — but they keep their distance from me and from each other. They never come south, and act as all but independent princes up there. You will know most of this, Thomas?"

The other nodded.

"So long as Alan Durward held Mar and Atholl, and Alexander Comyn held Buchan, I could rest easy. Both are strong men and ambitious, and though they hate each other, they hate the Moraymen more. They together formed a strong barrier between Moray and the South. But now Durward is old and sick and Buchan has taken the Cross and gone on this Crusade, with David Lindsay and Adam of Carrick. I feel less secure. And I do not altogether trust the other Comyns. They are too powerful, *too* ambitious. And now Fergus Comyn, Buchan's younger brother, has married the daughter of Gillespic MacWilliam. Which I mislike greatly. If Alexander of Buchan does not come back from the Crusade . . .!"

In silence, they waited.

"I used to be kept informed of what went on in Moray by Durward and the Comyns. Now I am not. I could use someone whom I could trust, up there, to be my eyes and ears. You, Thomas. And none will know you there."

The other drew a deep breath. "Moray!" he said. "Moray — yes, we might be safe in Moray."

"As to safety, I know not! But you could serve me usefully there."

"But — how could it be contrived, Sire? How would I live, in Moray. A land I know nothing of. How send you word . . .?"

"The Priory of Monymusk, man — the Priory of Monymusk! On the borders of Mar and Buchan and Moray.

It was founded by Malcolm Canmore, on royal land. Monymusk is a Crown barony, large, rich as such northern baronies go, with the Priory but sitting in a corner of it. The Sub-Prior has hitherto acted as my steward — but it never was a satisfactory arrangement and now he is past it and the Crown's interests fail. You, Thomas, shall be royal steward at Monymusk and serve my interests there, managing the Crown lands to better purpose. And minding what goes on in Buchan and Moray. Forby, there are two other royal baronies in Mar which you can bring into a better state. Even one in Moray itself — Darnaway — of which I have heard nothing these years. You shall go steward all these for me, from Monymusk. How say you?"

Distinctly doubtful, Thomas looked at Bethoc — and saw her eyes shining even brighter than usual.

"My lord King!" she exclaimed. "This is good, good. You are generous. Thomas — is it not truly kind? What you require — and could scarce hope for. You will go to this Monymusk . . .?"

"To be sure he will go!" Alexander said. "It is my royal command. I want neither of you here, in any south parts of my realm, for one day longer. You will go forthwith. See — here is a paper, with my signature and seal, naming you steward of Monymusk and my baronies north of the Mounth, with all authority to act as such in my name. Only Master Reginald my secretary, and myself, know of this. Your messages and moneys will be sent to him, him only. And he will inform me. You yourself will not venture south of the Mounth — until I say so. Is it clear?"

Thomas inclined his head. "As you will, Sire. I know little of stewarding — but I will do my best. How am I to send you the messages, thus secretly?"

"The monks, man — the friars. That is the beauty of it. These churchmen, these wandering friars, roam the land. They are ever at it. None interfere with them, the minions of Holy Church. Every abbey and monastery is being visited all the time, and each sends out its own emissaries. You will use these, from Monymusk Priory, to my Master Reginald, chaplain. None will be the wiser. And you will soon learn your stewarding. You had better — for I shall expect much improvement, as well as information!"

"Yes, Sire. And . . . I thank you. I am grateful."

"You should be. Now — off with you, both, before folk come seeking the King. As ever they do. You do not deserve it — but God go with you! Since you have chosen to challenge all, I hope that you are happy. You, lass, keep this lame knight of mine from other follies than wedding you! And Thomas, when next you foresee the future, foresee the consequences of your own actions! Godspeed!"

They bowed, silent, as the monarch remounted and rode off whence he had come.

"Alexander — by the Grace of God!" Thomas murmured, then.

"Yes — and thank God for him! What now, my dear? What now?"

"Why — Monymusk, Beth. Wherever that is! Monymusk and a new life. Beyond the Mounth . . ."

Part Two

9

The Augustinian Priory of Monymusk in Strathdon proved to be scarcely as well-doing an establishment as that of Faill of the Trinitarians; nor yet as welcoming and friendly as that of St. Colms of Cumbrae. But it was a fair enough place, in pleasing, indeed highly attractive country, smallish by southern standards but something of an outpost of the Romish faith in an area where the Celtic Church still was more than a memory — so that something of the reverse position to that of St. Colms prevailed.

The newcomers were surprised by what they discovered, in many ways. For one thing, the country itself was very different from what they had anticipated. Like most Low-landers they had believed that all the lands north of the Mounth, the vast northern barrier of the Eastern Highlands, were a harsh, barren, almost savage terrain, populated by semi-barbarians and wild caterans. Hence Thomas's lack of enthusiasm for being sent there. In fact, once they had crossed the admittedly fearsome mountain passes above Strathdevilly and Strathfinella, for some fifteen daunting miles, they had found themselves in quite lovely and far from frightening country of great open pine forests, wide green valleys, fair spreading, rolling pastures and considerable tillable land, a territory ever tinged by blue mountains which were now coming into full heather-bloom, but far from a wilderness or in any way poverty-stricken. It was a land of great east-flowing rivers in broad straths, of which the Dee and the Don were the largest; and far more populous than they had expected, and by folk none so different seeming to those of Strathearn, Gowrie, Angus and the Mearns. Admittedly they spoke mainly the Gaelic or Erse, and dressed in stained and ragged tartan cloth and plaiding, men and women alike. Also the men carried weapons noticeably more generally than they did in the South, and bore themselves as though prepared to use them — although not once were the travellers in any way threatened; quite the reverse. Likewise, even the cottars and shepherds and the like tended to wear what might be described as heavy jewellery — largely required by their style of clothing, to be sure, but unexpected in such humble folk — of beaten and intricately-worked silver set with large clear stones, brooches, clasps, buckles and so on.

Monymusk, they found, lay about midway up the long and major valley of the Don, a delectably-sited, rambling establishment sitting at a bend of the fine river below the tall, wooded hill of Pitfichie and just a mile or so south of the lofty and shapely cone of Benachie, a notable, isolated mountain which dominated all this Garioch area of Mar. The Priory itself was less extensive than that of Faill, manned by about a dozen monks, most of them oldish. Although of course a Roman order, these friars were in fact more like the Celtic brothers of St. Colm's than Nicholas's Trinitarians, being Highlandmen and under much looser discipline. Indeed the monastery was merely a Romanisation of a former Columban cashel here, re-instituted by Malcolm Canmore to mark his victory over Moray rebels at Pitfichie in 1078; and something of the former atmosphere persisted still in this remote area. Not to put too fine a point on it, Prior Nicholas of Faill would have condemned Monymusk as a lax, easy-going and all-but degenerate house — with its small kirkton nearby apparently largely the haunt of concubines for the monks, Prior Andrew however actually keeping his own woman conveniently on the premises in the guise of launderer.

The new arrivals had been received with only moderate warmth, on the assumption that a royal steward being billeted upon them must imply dissatisfaction with things as they were, and could therefore only lead to changes and discomforts. But when Thomas not only made it clear, but proved by his conduct, that his role and concern had nothing to do with matters religious or monastic but only with the better management of the King's baronial lands, he became accepted as more or less harmless. At least there was no problem as to accommodation for Bethoc. It would have been unthinkable in a more strictly-run monastery for any woman to be in permanent residence within the precincts. But here this rule was already breached. The couple were allotted vacant premises once occupied by the Sub-Prior — who was now old and doddery and not fit to have his own quarters, and so slept in the general dormitory. Since this was the same individual who had been nominally responsible for any surveillance there had been of the royal lands, it was scarcely to be wondered at that matters had fallen into disorder and neglect. At any rate, none at Monymusk were in the least distressed at having the responsibility lifted from their monkish shoulders.

Bethoc soon had the Sub-Prior's house turned into a home of reasonable comfort.

So they settled into life at Monymusk, that autumn, without any real difficulty, in the Priory but not of it, indeed seeing remarkably little of the friars in any intimate respect despite the close proximity. They had their own domestic quarters, their own entrance, their own corner of the neglected orchard as their garden and pleasance, their own stable and presently their own servants, man and wife, even their own cow and poultry.

And Thomas was busy, with much to learn and enquire into, and the neglect of years to try to put right — and he took his new duties seriously. His first task, obviously, was to visit and explore the baronial lands and to discover how the King's interests therein were being served. He found the Monymusk barony itself to be very large, of some twenty-thousand acres, of which only about two thousand were in the monks' hands. It extended up and down the Don for many miles, and included the royal burgh of Inverurie — but this was administered by its own magistrates and did not come under Thomas's responsibilities. Westwards it included much of the Vale of Alford, all of the hill masses of Pitfichie and Corrennie and much of the Back of Benachie. The majority was hill and forest, but there was also much excellent pasture and considerable riverside land fit for the plough, with many small farms and crofts and some quite large tenantries. None of these, great and small, actually welcomed the new steward. They had had matters their own way for long and were ready to anticipate interference and harassment. Thomas sought to be tactful, moderate, fair; but he could not shut his eyes to much that was amiss, rents in arrears, land unutilised, husbandry poor, stock of wretched quality, drainage non-existent, heather and bracken allowed to spread in the low ground, streams uncontrolled by flood-dykes. Used as he was to the much more advanced farming of the Lothians and the Merse, all this struck him forcibly. But he recognised also that improvement must be a long-term project and that he had not been sent north to antagonise the tenantry. Conditions up here were very different from south of the Scotwater, he realised well, the ground higher and less fertile, Highland cattle smaller, tradition quite otherwise, industry not looked upon as any special virtue. The folk were not exactly lazy but were more preoccupied with other matters than toil — sociability, singing and dancing and story-telling, hunting, fighting, great talking and great drinking, and just doing nothing in a deliberate sort of way.

Thomas, then, was not popular, however careful he was, however resigned to making haste slowly. But he was determined that the rents should be paid — and they were on the whole very low, some ridiculously so. That autumn and winter he made a survey of all lands and rentals, with comparisons — and learned a lot about human nature as well as property and produce values in the process. He was enlightened, as well as often astonished, by what he found, discovering that some of the largest tenants paid the smallest rents — or failed to pay them; and that sub-letting was rife, some of the sub-tenants paying more than their principals. The rents were nearly all paid in kind, of course, there being very little coin in this land, such silver as there was tending to get melted down for making brooches and gewgaws; so that most tribute had to be bought by dealers in corn and stock — and these were apt to come to special arrangements with certain landholders, to the detriment of others, and also of the royal revenues. The millers were especially open to corruption, for baronial law required that all barony tenants must have their corn ground at the barony mills, and this allowed unscrupulous millers to overcharge.

In his efforts at reform and improvement, Thomas's means of persuasion and pressure were limited and not the most suitable. If advice and remonstration were ineffectual, he really had only two sanctions which he could impose, penal raising of rent or eviction from the holding — neither of which he was wishful to apply. He could, of course, seek the aid of the sheriff of the earldom, at Aberdeen. But again he was loth to do so. The sheriff was the Crown's law officer in theory; but in practice he was the earl's man, usually appointed at the earl's instigation, often a kinsman, and much more apt to uphold his earl's interests than those of the distant king, or even simple justice.

And Thomas made a point of keeping as far as possible from William, Earl of Mar, and therefore from his sheriff. He had seen him at court, an elderly man of stolid, not to say bull-like manner, with little to say and a reputation for harshness. There was no reason to suppose that he had ever noticed anyone so lowly as the Dunbar esquire; and he had not been present at Roxburgh at the time of the knighting. But he could have heard of True Thomas — and the lameness would be an unfortunate lead to identification. They were bound to meet sooner or later, for the chief seat of the earldom was at the Dun of Invernochty, some thirty miles up Strathdon from Monymusk; but the longer it could be put off the better. The Earl was said to be in indifferent health, which might help. And at least he was no friend of Earl Patrick, any more than of the King.

In his new situation Thomas found his knighthood to be of considerable advantage, gaining him the respect and authority he much required. His name and style, however, did not appear to produce any sign of recognition. It looked as though his fame, happily, had not penetrated north of the Mounth.

During that winter of short days and long lamp-lit evenings before aromatic birch-log fires, he was able to get on with his *Sir Tristrem*. But it was an enormous task, demanding in three distinct respects: first in the translation itself, then in the imaginative transference to the Scots usage and terminology, and finally and most vitally, into the making of real poetry out of the result. With this last he was seldom satisfied, and rewrote continually, despite Bethoc's chidings — who was greatly interested and sought to help.

The basic story was sufficiently dramatic and linked with the semi-legendary King Arthur, some claiming that Sir Tristrem was one of his famous knights. He was the son of a celebrated Cornish chieftain and the nephew of King Mark of Cornwall, from whose court at Tintagel he was sent on a mission to the High King of Ireland. Here he fell in love with the beauteous Isolde, daughter of that King, his passion being reciprocated. On his return to Tintagel he was injudicious enough to extol the lady's beauty and virtues sufficiently for King Mark himself to desire this peerless woman for wife. The two monarchs agreed the match, and Tristrem, despite his distress, was sent to escort the princess to Cornwall, where she was duly wed. It was not long however before Tristrem proved that his love and desire were stronger than his duty and moral code, and a guilty association developed between him and the Queen, against all his knightly and her marriage vows. When at length King Mark was apprised of this, Tristrem fled, first to Wales, was forgiven, returned, recommenced the association and had to flee again, this time to Brittany. Here his good looks and knightly fame attracted the attentions of another high-born lady, the similarly-named Yseult, daughter of the Duke of Brittany himself. They were wed; but Tristrem never forgot Queen Isolde. Wounded in a battle, he lay at death's door, gangrene in his wound. He believed that Isolde, having great skills in medicine, alone could cure him. A ship was sent to Tintagel with the plea that the Queen should come to save his life. He urged that if she should agree, a white flag should be flown from the top-mast, on its return, to inform him; if not, a black one. She came, and Yseult saw the white flag; but in her jealousy told Tristrem that it was the black one. He sank back in despair, and died forthwith. When the Queen landed and found her lover dead, she herself expired with grief. They were buried together in a single grave, and a rose-bush and a vine planted above each body. In time these grew and intermingled so that none could separate them.

This was the story which was being told and sung, in various versions, all over Continental Christendom by the minstrels and troubadours. Thomas of Brittany gave the Cornish-Welsh tale wider fame; but it had been given greater currency by being translated into the Germanic tongues by the minnesinger Godfrey of Strasbourg, from which it had even been converted into a Norse saga. Thomas, good at languages, was only doing what many another had attempted — but was seeking to make fine poetry of it in the process. But it was no light work, for there were three parts, with a conclusion, totalling three-hundred-and-nineteen stanzas.

When spring melted the Highland snows, *Sir Tristrem* was put aside, there being so much to be done outdoors. Thomas had been able to visit only the near-at-hand properties during the recent months, and by no means all of them. He now wished to inspect the other two royal baronies in the Mar-Buchan earldoms — Drum and Fyvie. Drum lay a score of miles to the south, on the Dee between Aberdeen and Banchory St. Ternan; whilst Fyvie lay about thirty miles to the north on the borders of Buchan and Strathbogie. He felt that if there was anywhere for him to learn about what went on in Moray, it would be at Fyvie, for the Moray border was not so far away. He decided to go there first, so that he might possibly have some word to send south to the King. Hither-to, although he had sent moneys, and reports about the properties and tenants, he had learned nothing of any special significance regarding what Alexander wanted to hear.

In late April, by which time most of the snows were melted, save from the mountain-tops, and the rivers had become fordable again, before he set off, Bethoc informed him that she believed that she was pregnant. That sent him rejoicing on his way.

*　　*　　*

Thomas and his man Donald rode up the valley of the upper Ythan northwards where it emerged from the narrows of the Braes of Minnonie, on a track above the flooded haughlands, the hills now drawing back and ancient beech-woods clothing the lower slopes, fairer country than he had looked for. Donald, the husband of their serving-woman at the Priory — he appeared to have no surname but was vaguely connected with the Forbes clan — was quite good company, a man in his mid-thirties and a great storyteller and gossip, but knowledgeable and effective and good with animals. They got on well, and Thomas learned more about the people and country from Donald than from any other single source.

He could not tell him a great deal about the Fyvie area, however, for it was something of a *terra incognita* to the rest of Mar. Indeed, although the thanage of Formartine was in theory and name a division of Mar, with Fyvie its chief place, it was more often looked upon as part of Buchan, the borders being vague and the Buchan influence the stronger. The dominant house was that of the Norman le Chien, allied to that of Comyn, and le Chien tended to look north to Buchan rather than south to Mar, the two earldoms seldom on good terms. Sir Reginald le Chien, calling himself Thane of Formartine, had a reputation for being a man not to cross. Thomas seemed to remember having heard of him, in some connection.

They were trotting over the russet smooth carpet of the hanging beech-woods, unusual trees to find so well-grown thus far north, when rounding a projecting crag, they found their way barred by a group of five rough-looking men dressed in miscellaneous tartans, mounted on shaggy garrons and having hands on sword-hilts. Not liking the look of them, Thomas reined up and then round quickly, gesturing for Donald to do the same; they were much better-mounted on tall southern horses and ought to be able to outride these people fairly easily. But behind them they discovered another four of the caterans moving to block their retiral. It seemed that they were in an ambush.

"What is this?" Thomas demanded, facing front again. "Who are you and what do you want?"

"More to the point, cockerel — who are you, who ride so bold through Fyvyn without let or leave?" a red-bearded individual returned, and drew a short-bladed stabbing-sword to emphasise his point.

"I require neither let nor leave from you or any man, fellow. I am the lord King's representative on the King's business. Out of my way!"

"Which king is that?" he was asked, amidst hoots of appreciation from the others.

"King Alexander, High King of Scots, man. With a sufficiently long arm to punish those who interfere with his servants, I promise you."

The spokesman turned to his companions. "Have we heard of this long-armed king who would think to send cockerels to crow in Fyvyn?" he wondered, in a sing-song voice, to hearty assertions to the contrary. "No? Myself, I have heard of only one lord here, and that is the Thane of Fyvyn."

Thomas endeavoured to speak through the cheers and jeers. "You speak of Sir Reginald le Chien? Are you servants of his? If so, take me to him. At once."

"Ho — is that the way of it? You are in haste to face your Maker? For you will hang, little man — oh yes, you will hang, lacking Thane Ranald's permission to ride here. Nothing surer. He is good at the hanging. He keeps a crowded gallows! But, hech aye, we will find room for you two, never fear." He laughed even louder than the others, and pointed. "Your sword, cockerel."

"No! How dare you! I am Sir Thomas Learmonth . . ."

But he could have saved his breath. The caterans, shouting, closed in swiftly, efficiently, and before he had his long sword half-out of its sheath he found his arms pinioned in a fierce grip, whilst he had his face slapped, left and right, by the red-bearded man.

"Bind him!" that individual ordered. "Ropes."

They were all mounted, and in the circumstances, however effective, there was considerable milling about and jostling on the part of the attackers. In the confusion Donald, very wisely, took the opportunity to depart the scene.

Finding that the men behind him had come to help in the business, leaving a gap, he pulled his mount round, kicked its flanks, and plunged off whence they had come. He was riding Bethoc's fine horse, and though some of the caterans rode after him, it was quickly apparent that they could never catch him up. A corner of Thomas's mind, despite his stress, was able to applaud that the man had had the wit to perceive that he was better away, and hopefully winning aid, than remaining uselessly with his master.

So, humiliatingly tied round with rope, the King's steward was escorted up the Vale of Fyvie, or Fyvyn as they seemed to call it here, his lip bleeding from the face-slapping.

The vale was very fair, even if Thomas was in no state to appreciate it. But the valley-floor, which should have been drained for tilth, and the river banked against the spates, was grievously flooded throughout, and the place's potential as productive land badly neglected — a situation tending to preoccupy that young man. Presently, out of the waterlogged haughlands rose a long, low whaleback of ridge, fairly narrow and perhaps a mile in length, seemingly surrounded by the floods. This feature very much drew the eye, even as jaundiced an eye as Thomas Learmonth's. For it was not exactly crowded but very much occupied with buildings. At this south end was what appeared to be a small monastery, whilst behind it and slightly higher was a towered church and graveyard. Further north was a quite large town-ship, more closely-huddled than was usual in that country. And, on the summit of the ridge, dominating all, a square Norman-type keep rose on an artificial mound or motte, stark and strong. The entire place, within its barrier of spreading waters, had something of the appearance of a citadel, there amongst the empty hills.

They splashed across river and flooding by what was evidently an underwater causeway, and trotted up past monastery and church and village to the castle. Between the two last, on a knoll, was erected a double gibbet from which dangled no fewer than eight corpses, in various stages of decay apparently.

An outer curtain-wall surrounded the motte on which the

keep rose, defended by a deep ditch with drawbridge. The courtyard this enclosed contained a number of lesser lean-to buildings, kitchen, brewhouse, bunkhouse, stables and the like. But it was up the steep slope to the tower itself that Thomas, dismounted, was propelled with rough pushings, to be thrust into a small, vaulted basement chamber, lit only by two arrow-slits but otherwise devoid of feature or furnishing. There he was left, arms still bound by the rope, and the heavy door slammed on him, and barred.

If Thomas's temper was hot when he was immured in this comfortless cell, it had time to cool. For he was left alone therein, bound as he was, for some hours, from mid-afternoon until some time in the evening, with such light as was admitted through the narrow slits beginning to fade. He heard the clatter of hooves and some authoritative shout-ing considerably before that, from the courtyard, but no approach was made to his prison. He tried shouting for attention, but to no effect.

At length voices outside heralded the throwing open of his door, and men came stamping in. But it was now so dark in the cell that Thomas could see little of the newcomers. How-ever the same applied to them, so that a strong and com-pletely non-Highland-sounding voice declared vehemently that its owner was not an owl and for God's sake to bring whoever they had lurking in there upstairs to the hall, where at least he might see what sort of game they had snared for him.

So Thomas was dragged out and pushed up the winding turnpike stair to the first-floor hall, a large chamber, stone walls lined with hangings, with an enormous fireplace on which logs blazed, lit by many candles. The remains of a meal littered the table, wolf and deerhounds helping them-selves. A man stood with his back to the fire, waiting.

From his treatment and the style of his captors, Thomas had assumed that their master would be, if not as uncouth as his minions, at least some boorish barbarian. But the man before him now was quite otherwise, handsome and tall, almost elegant indeed. In his early forties probably, he had long, narrow features, short dark hair, thin down-turning moustaches and a trim pointed beard, his eyes notably bright — but not in the least friendly-seeming. He was dressed in hunting-clothes, but of stylish mode.

"Ha — is this all?" this man exclaimed. "A cripple! On my soul, sorry sport!"

"Expensive sport, you will find, sirrah!" Thomas put in, spiritedly. "I do not know who you are. But if these oafish caterans are yours, you and they will pay dearly for this, I promise you."

The other raised dark eyebrows, unspeaking, and flicked a finger towards the red-bearded man who stood beside Thomas. That individual grinned and, without other warning, turned and struck the prisoner a vicious blow on the side of the head, sufficient, on account of his lame leg, to fell him to the floor. There he added a kick for full measure.

The man by the fire gave a brief laugh. "Tell me what sort of payment you suggest, friend?" he said.

Biting his lip, swollen as it was, Thomas remained silent. One of the deerhounds came and licked his face.

"Answer, fool!" the other barked. "When I speak to you."

"I speak to none, tied with rope and struck to the ground," Thomas grated.

"Ah — the rope incommodes you? Have him up, MacFirbis, and untie him. So that he may enlighten us. But — keep your rope to hand. It will serve to hang him with, hereafter!"

Thomas was hoisted and unbound. He stood swaying, dizzy.

"Now — speak. Who are you, and by what effrontery do you think to ride through my territories without my express permission?"

"That is easily answered. Since these are not *your* territories."

The dark man stared. "Do I hear aright? Are you of sound mind, fellow? MacFirbis — your playful buffet must have scattered this poor cripple's wits. He raves. He doubts if these are my territories — I, who am lord here at Fyvie, Sir Reginald le Chien, Thane of Formartine, Lord of Inverugie and Sheriff of Banff and Nairn."

"But *not* Lord of Fyvie!" Thomas declared flatly. "For Fyvie is a royal barony. The King's own, and in his own hands. And I am the King's representative."

There was a moment or two of complete silence in that chamber, save for the snuffle of the dogs and the crackle of the fire. Le Chien gazed at him.

If Thomas had any momentary advantage in this, he pursued it. "His Grace is going to be displeased, I think, Sir Reginald le Chien. When he hears how you have treated his steward. King Alexander sent me from Kincardine Castle. To look to and steward his baronies of Monymusk, Fyvie, Drum and Darnaway. Of the rule of which he has long been dissatisfied. How think you he will consider this?"

"God's Death — you rave, man!" the other exclaimed. "You have brought me a madman, MacFirbis!"

"He will hang well enough, whatever, my lord," the red-beard declared, hooting. "Mad, lame or no."

"No doubt. But first, we shall win ourselves instruction as to his royal authority. As one of His Grace's thanes and sheriffs, this should much concern me!"

"That also is simple," Thomas said. Reaching into his doublet, and wincing with the pain of bruised ribs, he brought out from an inner pocket the King's signed and sealed paper, which he carried with him as commission, now somewhat bent and scuffed. He tossed this down on to the table.

Sir Reginald frowned, and at first seemed as though the last thing he would do would be to step over and pick it up. But after a moment or two curiosity overcame arrogance, and he moved to inspect the document.

Reading, his handsome features underwent a transformation. His lips, beneath that cruel moustache, first slightly opened and then tightened. His frown changed its character from hauteur to some perplexity. He looked up.

"This, this says *Sir* Thomas Learmonth . . .?" he said.

"That is so. I am Sir Thomas Learmonth."

"M'mm." Le Chien stroked his pointed beard. "You are knight?"

"I am. Knighted by His Grace's own hand."

The other put down the paper and took a turn back to the

fireside, clearly at something of a loss. "Why did you not say that you were knight?" he demanded.

"Would you, or these, have heeded? I was the madman, you recollect? I did tell this red dolt my name and style — but he heeded me as little as did you."

"How was I to know? A lame man . . . I know none such knighted." Most evidently le Chien was more exercised by Thomas being a knight than by his position as King's steward. A knight himself, of course, he no doubt was concerned that proper respect should be maintained towards the dignity.

"Did His Grace err in knighting a lame man?"

"I did not say that . . ."

Thomas took a chance. "Who knighted *you*, Sir Reginald?" he asked. He was fairly sure that it had not been the present King; for he had never heard of this le Chien spoken of at court or involved in the affairs of the southern part of the realm, since Alexander had been of age to knight anyone. And it was nearly twenty years since Alexander the Second had died. But earls could knight. This man, he understood, was half a Comyn. Therefore the probability was that it was one of the Comyn earls, Buchan most likely, who had conferred the accolade. And an earl's knighting scarcely held the cachet of a king's one.

The other did not answer that. "If you had sent to inform me that you intended to visit Fyvie, all this need not have happened," he said instead, stiffly.

"Must any man, royal representative or none, have *your* permission before he travels through the King's realm, sir? If so, I have not heard of it. But . . ." He turned to glance at the man MacFirbis and his minions. ". . . I am not used to discussing the King's affairs before such as these, le Chien."

"Ah. No." Sir Reginald waved a dismissive hand at the others. "Begone," he said briefly. "And, MacFirbis — have fresh meats sent up for our guest. Sir Thomas — a cup of wine . . .?"

"I do not choose to drink wine in this house!"

"Come, man — be not so prickly. Mistakes can be made. *You* made one by failing to inform me of your coming. It would have been courteous, as well as wise. Let us say no more of this, then. Here — drink. You could do with it, I swear!"

That at least was true. Thomas was feeling faint as well as dizzy and sore, for he had eaten and drunk nothing for many hours. Sustenance was called for — and he was unlikely to be able to obtain it anywhere else in the near future. He accepted the proffered beaker.

"Sit, Sir Thomas — here, near the fire. You have come from Kincardine Castle, you say? I know it well. I was Sheriff of the Mearns, there, until two years back."

So that was where he had heard of this le Chien. The alehouse-keeper and some of the men-at-arms at Kincardine had been talking, that night back in August, of this former Sheriff, of his drastic methods of justice, his refined savageries, his almost unlimited power, with the Comyn backing; until he had been replaced by the King, allegedly at the behest of Alan Durward, Earl of Atholl, in that old man's feud with the Comyns. Thomas recognised now that he would indeed have been wise to have learned who was in control here at Fyvie before he ventured into this lion's den.

"You left Kincardine?" he said carefully. "For good reason, no doubt?"

"For good reason," the other agreed, but did not elaborate. "I am Sheriff of Banff and part of Moray, now."

"Ah, yes — part of Moray." That was worth remembering, in the circumstances. "I do not understand your position here, Sir Reginald. You named yourself thane. But you cannot be Thane of Fyvie, since it is a Crown lordship."

"Not of Fyvie, no. I am Thane of Formartine, and Fyvie is the chief messuage of Formartine." The other replenished the wine-cup. "To what circumstance do I owe this visit, Sir Thomas? What brings you to Fyvie?"

"His Grace is dissatisfied with the returns from his northern baronies, sir — that is why. He is much concerned. Revenues are withheld, malpractice is rife, and there is grievous neglect of the land and what it should produce. I am sent to effect improvement."

"Improvement? Not at Fyvie, I hope?" There was a steely sound to that.

"I have so far no reason to believe that Fyvie is any better served than the King's other baronies here, Sir Reginald."

"You are scarcely in a position to say, my friend — since you have not inspected it."

"I saw something of the land as I rode here — flooded haughs and pastures, neglected rigs, cothouse ruins . . ."

"This is a chase, sir, a royal hunting-forest. Not cornlands and cattle country."

"Yet producing no chase or other revenues — or not for the Crown, at least! The papers at Monymusk Priory show little or nothing from Fyvie these several years."

"That old fool of a Prior! Or Sub-Prior. What does he know? What papers could he show, as to Fyvie? I do not render account of my affairs to monkish dotards."

"No? He was acting as King's steward, nevertheless. Until I came. But you must have an account to render to *someone*, sir. For this royal barony. Papers. Even if you do not send them to Monymusk."

"To be sure."

"Then I would wish to inspect them, Sir Reginald. My simple duty."

"I do not keep them here. They are at Inverugie, in Buchan. At my house there."

"That is . . . unfortunate. Can you send for them? How far to Inverugie? Twenty-five miles? Thirty? Near to Buchan Ness, is it not?"

The other looked thoughtful. Then servitors arrived with food to replenish the table — which Thomas now made no bones about attacking. Le Chien left the room whilst his involuntary guest ate.

When he came back, he announced that he had been seeing to the preparation of a suitable bedchamber for the visitor, who must be tired after his long journeying. They must be up early, for he was leaving for Inverugie in the morning and he would take Sir Thomas with him.

That sounded suspiciously like a command, which Thomas was prepared to resent. On the other hand, if he was to uncover the state of affairs of this Fyvie barony, it appeared that the quickest way to do it was to go to Inverugie anyway.

He swallowed his objections, therefore, as he finished an excellent meal. No more desirous of prolonging the evening's confrontation than was his host, he retired forthwith.

On their journey next day, at the head of an armed troop, Thomas at least *looked* as though he rode as colleague and equal of his knightly companion, although he had the distinct impression that he was as much a prisoner as ever and that if he announced that he had had enough and desired to return to Monymusk, this by no means would be tolerated. Le Chien was affable enough, today, and in fact interesting company, talking easily and well-informed — although he asked a lot of shrewd questions as well as informing. These Thomas was notably careful about answering. He was knowledgeable about national affairs, considering how far removed was his situation from Scotland's centre of government — much better-versed than was his listener. He told of the death, last autumn, of Magnus of Man, and prognosticated trouble with his successor, Godfrey. He disclosed that all was now changed in England, that after Prince Edward Longshanks had made his escape from Dover Castle, that ruthless but effective character had managed to rally his father's scattered and depressed supporters and attacked the rebel barons' leader, Simon de Montfort, Earl of Leicester, at Evesham, where there had been a great battle and victory for Edward. De Montfort and many of his lieutenants had been killed; but not content with that, Edward had thereafter initiated the greatest slaughter known in England since the Conqueror's days, methodically slaying not only the prisoners but all the survivors of the rebel army that could be found, and their supporters, in a blood-bath of unparalleled ferocity. So now Henry the Third sat his throne again, although it was his son who ruled. Le Chien indicated that it was his opinion that King Alexander would have to come to terms with his aggressive brother-in-law sooner or later.

Sir Reginald also spoke of the reported progress of the great Crusade, the Seventh, under King Louis the Ninth of France. This had been intended to proceed to Acre, near Tyre, but had turned aside to Carthage, to further the ambitions of Charles of Anjou, Louis's brother, King of the

Two Sicilies, who desired to add that part of the caliphate to his kingdom. The Crusaders were now besieging the chief city thereof, Tunis, in dire conditions. There had been many deaths, more of fever than of wounds. Sir David de Lindsay, the High Chamberlain and former Regent, was dead. Also David de Strathbogie, the new Earl of Atholl who had displaced Alan Durward. And many another. Whether they would ever get to the Holy Land, in these circumstances, was doubtful, despite all the Papal urgings and support.

Le Chien was in a position to know all this, and more. His wife, the Lady Mary Comyn, was a sister of Red John, Lord of Badenoch, chief of the house; and also of his half-brother, Alexander Comyn, Earl of Buchan, the High Constable, who had likewise taken the Cross. Thomas gathered, indeed, that whilst the Constable was away crusading, it was his brother-in-law, le Chien the Sheriff, rather than the difficult third brother Fergus, who was running the affairs of the earldom of Buchan. This was interesting, for it was, of course, the activities of Fergus Comyn up in Moray, which most exercised the King meantime, and was the main reason behind Thomas's own presence in the North.

They rode, hounds trotting behind, back down Ythan to Gight, then north-eastwards through the rolling, barish Buchan countryside some twelve miles to reach the South Ugie Water at Bruxie. Thereafter it was but a matter of following that quite large river down, due eastwards, by the famous Abbey of Deer, once one of the bright lights of the Celtic Church, through the Howe of Buchan ten miles to the sea where, on the north shore of the estuary of the Ugie, under the St. Peter's Head of Buchan Ness, the castle of Inverugie rose high and dominant out of its protecting marshlands.

Inverugie was quite the largest castle Thomas had seen since he crossed the Mounth, a powerful Norman stronghold, consisting of a mighty square donjon-keep of five storeys, with massive gatehouse drum-towers as well as four subsidiary angle-towers at the corners of the high courtyard curtain-walls, all surrounded by a double moat-system reinforcing the natural defences of the marshy surroundings. As the little cavalcade trotted over the timbers of the lowered drawbridge between the drum-towers, and the heavy gates clanged shut behind, Thomas felt more of a prisoner than ever, whatever his host's present comparative amiability.

The Lady Mary showed no delight in the arrival of their guest. She was a cool and haughty woman, of an age with her husband, thin, sharp-featured but with fine eyes. Obviously very much aware of her Comyn blood, Thomas's knighthood did not impress *her*, at any rate. He was provided with quarters in one of the angle-towers across the courtyard from the main keep, given a servant, and there left more or less to his own devices.

Later the servitor came to escort him to the private hall in the keep for the evening meal. There Sir Reginald presently arrived, to inform that the Lady Mary sent her compliments but had a headache and would eat in her own chamber. With the castle's captain and the chaplain they sat down to an excellent repast. Le Chien made all the conversation.

Thomas learned something of the background and situation of his host. His father, Bernard le Chien, descended it was said from one of the Conqueror's hound-keepers — hence the name — had been the first of Inverugie, coming north in the Comyns' train and marrying the heiress of the place in the usual way. He had left his son a fair heritage; but Sir Reginald had increased this many times over. He himself had two sons, Reginald le Fils, who had recently married the heiress of the head of the powerful Flemish family of de Moravia, Sir Freskin, and who was now, in his wife's right, Lord of Duffus, in Moray; the other, Henry, a priest, was presently Precentor of the Cathedral of St. Machar at Aberdeen — and apparently the right hand of the ageing Bishop of Aberdeen.

All this confirmed in Thomas's mind, that this le Chien was ideally situated to be a source of information as to what went on in Moray, if he could be persuaded to talk. It would have to be very carefully attempted, obviously. He did not venture to ask, meantime, about the Lord Fergus Comyn — but was at least glad to gather from the reaction of his host to mere mention of his name, that he did not approve of this brother-in-law. He did not risk going further at this stage.

The captain and chaplain taking their departure almost immediately after the meal was over, Thomas perceived that the servant had come to escort him back to his tower-room. He asked when he was likely to be able to see the Fyvie papers. Le Chien answered that his steward, who dealt with such clerks' matters, was absent at the moment, but would no doubt return soon. He bid his guest a good night.

Thomas's chamber was comfortable enough, with a good fire and all facilities, plus this servant to minister to him. Nevertheless he could not rid himself of the feeling of being held captive, held as it were in suspension, for purposes unknown.

Next day brought him no further forward. He was left severely alone in fact; and when he went in search of le Chien, he was told that my lord had gone about sheriffdom affairs; also that the land-steward was still not available. Fretting, he managed at least to collect paper and ink and tried to get on with *Sir Tristrem*. That evening he ate alone in his room.

The following afternoon, le Chien returned, bringing with him a rather furtive-seeming individual in monkish habit who turned out to be Master Ralph, the steward. Thomas noted that his robe still had crumbs adhering, which gave the impression that he had not travelled any distance to get here; he suspected that he might have been on or near the premises all the time. Also his fingers were new-stained with ink — which could well imply very recent busy writing.

Nevertheless, when Sir Reginald left them together before Thomas's fire, being much too lofty a man to engage in such mundane matters, the man Ralph produced only one brief paper. This was no more than an elementary summary, purporting to show that after all essential costs and expenses had been deducted from the Fyvie barony's total rental payments for the past year, the sum of a mere 124 merks remained to be remitted to the Crown as due revenue.

Unbelieving, Thomas stared at the man, "This is . . . out of reason!" he declared. "For the entire barony? How can it possibly be? So little. How many acres, man? How much, to produce *this*?"

"On Fyvie?" The other shrugged. "Perhaps eighty thousand. But it is, in the main, chase. Hill and hunting-forest."

"Nevertheless, even such great chase will produce much. And I saw many farmsteads, villages, mills, tilled lands. There is the township of Fyvie itself, with its multures, brew-house, tannery and the rest. This 124 merks is, is a mockery!"

"Expenses are large and prices low. There was great flooding. Long snow. The folk cannot pay . . ."

"Cannot? Or will not? Or is it Sir Reginald? Is he so generous a master that he remits all their rentals?"

"No, no. But . . . times are hard. Even this sum will leave my lord out-of-pocket, sir."

"That I take leave to doubt! Sir Reginald clearly does very well. What are these great expenses? I saw little of dykes to restrain the flooding, little of drainage, bridges unrepaired. You will, to be sure, have papers to account for such expenditure. Also total rent-rolls. These I would see."

The steward pursed his lips. "It will take time to produce these."

"Time? I have waited already for long. And you will at least have last year's papers? And earlier years. I have seen no word, at Monymusk, of *any* moneys sent there from Fyvie. I will require many papers, my friend — and honest ones!"

The other looked unhappy, but said nothing. When he had produced his one and only document, Thomas had been fairly sure that he had heard other papers rustling, from the pocket inside the voluminous monk's habit. But he could hardly say so.

"Have you not brought your full papers with you?" That was the best he could do.

"No. No — my lord said . . ." The monk's voice tailed away.

"Then you must produce them. Before I can accept this paltry sum, for transmission to the King's Grace. Go get me your figures, and at the earliest, Master Ralph."

The steward hurried off.

Later, when Thomas was summoned to the hall for the evening meal, he found only one other diner besides their host, a young man of a smooth look and a cold eye, pale, thin, unforthcoming.

"My son Henry, Sir Thomas — new come from Aberdeen," Sir Reginald introduced. "And come with interesting tidings."

This newcomer accorded Thomas only a frosty greeting. He was markedly unlike his father — who at least had a lively personality to go with his handsome if somewhat satanic features; more resembling his mother.

"Henry tells me that he has been talking to your wife," the older man went on. "A notable young lady, it seems!"

Thomas drew a quick breath. "My wife? Why? Where? You have been to Monymusk?"

Sir Reginald did the talking. "Not so. The lady came to Aberdeen. Evidently she was concerned as to your whereabouts, Sir Thomas. Came seeking the good offices of the Sheriff, to find you. Wifely, was it not? And when she could not reach the Sheriff, went to the Bishop — for whom Henry here acts as coadjutor."

Thomas looked from one to the other. The man Donald must have returned straight to Monymusk and reported the ambush. Bethoc, dear Bethoc, earl's daughter as she was, had gone directly to the highest authority available, to come to his aid. He nodded, unspeaking.

"A spirited young woman," le Chien went on. "You did not tell me that you were wed to the daughter of the Earl of Dunbar and March, my friend."

"Should I have done? Does it concern the issue between us, sir?"

"Ah, now — I think that it does, yes. So high-born a lady. The Lady Bethoc, is it not? This, I say, could alter much."

"Because my wife is an earl's daughter? Will that alter the fact, Sir Reginald, that you have been failing to pay the Crown its due revenues from Fyvie, for years? That your steward now presents a wholly false account, and offers the paltry sum of 124 merks for so great a barony?"

"You do not suggest, Sir Thomas, that there is anything false about Master Ralph's accounting?"

"Until proved by fullest figures, I must conceive him . . . mistaken. Grievously so."

"So!" Le Chien turned to his son.

That young man smiled thinly. "In Aberdeen diocese we are not altogether ignorant of what goes on in the southern parts of this realm, sir," he said. "Holy Church has good ears. It had not escaped my lord Bishop's notice that the Earl of Dunbar's daughter was amissing. Had run off with a man of, shall we say, lower estate? When she was promised to the Earl of Fife's son. Perhaps a year past. And that the two earls were both searching the land for this errant pair, intent on due retribution. But could nowise find them. Now it appears that the search could be ended!"

Thomas, tight-lipped, said nothing.

"The matter is the more intriguing in that the man sought is reputed to be a notour mountebank or soothsayer styled Thomas the Rhymer, who impiously claims to be able to foretell the future, contrary to God's laws. It is scarcely to be wondered at that the Earl Patrick seeks to recover his daughter from the clutches of such a one."

"Tut, Henry — Sir Thomas is our guest," his father reproved, almost genially. "Moreover, knighted apparently by the King himself. My friend, tell me — was this knighting performed *before* you ran off with the lady? Or after?"

"Before, naturally. I was knight when we left Ercildoune together. I mislike the term 'ran off'. The Lady Bethoc would nowise agree to wed the Lord Duff MacDuff. We two had been fond for long."

"Ah, true romance! But against her father's wishes, and he a great earl." Sir Reginald sighed, and stroked his beard. "Your commission from King Alexander to come north and act his royal steward — was that also given before your, er, romantic departure? I notice that the paper is not dated."

Thomas hesitated. He had no desire to implicate his liege-lord, who had so befriended him, in any move which might seem to be against the interests of two of his greatest lords.

"If His Grace did not wish to date the commission, who am I to say differently, sir?"

"I see . . ."

"Unless this man's commission is itself false? A forgery?" Henry le Chien said.

"Could I forge the King's royal seal — even if I would?" Thomas demanded.

The servitors came in with the steaming platters, and the three sat down to a meal, excellent as ever but scarcely appreciated by the guest at least. Sir Reginald did not seem in the least uncomfortable and talked amiably enough on sundry subjects unconnected with their controversy, with little help from the other two. Clearly he enjoyed his food and did not wish to spoil it by acrimonious dispute.

The eating over, however, and the wine being savoured, he returned to the issue between them.

"Sir Thomas," he said, "it seems to me that we are, shall we say, mutually beholden. We perhaps need each other's goodwill, do you not think? I jalouse that we might be sufficiently good friends, as two knights should be, to the advantage of both."

Warily Thomas looked at his host.

"Put it this way. You, I think, have no wish for the Earls of Dunbar and Fife to come up over the Mounth seeking you, and perhaps taking your wife from you? And I would not wish for the trouble of petty probings into my affairs at Fyvie or elsewhere. If my steward has been remiss in his accounting in the past, he will no doubt improve, on my instructions. Your duty is done, then. So we accommodate each the other, and none is the worse off. How say you?"

Thomas clenched his fists on the table-top. "What you are saying, sir, is that unless I agree to overlook your withholding of the royal revenues over the years, you will send to inform the Earl of Dunbar of my presence at Monymusk? That is the threat?"

"Did I say that, man? Henry — did I say anything such? I merely suggested that by being friends instead of continuing this unseemly bickering, we could serve each other better, to the hurt of none. Certainly not of the King's Grace, whose best interests you undoubtedly would be serving, likewise."

Pushing back his bench, Thomas rose. "I will not barter my honour, and the King's trust, for your silence, sir," he said.

"No? On my soul, you sound the pompous ass! Go sleep on it, Sir Thomas. Consider well. Consider, when you ride back to Monymusk tomorrow, whether you will leave behind you a powerful friend and associate. Or . . . otherwise! I, to be sure, would not send informations to Earl Patrick of Dunbar. But who knows who might learn of this matter? In the Bishop's household at Aberdeen. Who might hear of it. Henry, here, who manages the old Bishop's affairs, could see to it that none did. Consider, my friend. And a good night to you."

Thomas did consider sufficiently thoroughly; indeed he did not sleep for long hours. He acknowledged to himself that it was easy to talk of honour and the like. But apart from his own interests, where lay his first duty? To the King? Or to Bethoc? Was not his wife, with child, now his prime concern? If her father learned that she was up here, he would come for her, nothing more sure. To take her away. Whatever happened to himself, they would be parted. Was this the price to pay for improving a tiny part of the royal revenues? If this was unfair reasoning, were Alexander's interests to be best served by reporting and seeking to fight this powerful baron, even so? Might he not be of more use to his monarch up here in the King's goodwill than offended? What of Moray? Might not his influence and information be of more use to Alexander than a few more merks?

So Thomas debated with himself before, at last, he slept.

He was called to breakfast with his host, who seemed in excellent spirits.

"Well, friend — have you had a good night? And come to a wise and kindly decision?" he was asked genially. There was no sign of the son Henry.

"As to wise, I know not. But I have thought long. And come to some conclusion, sir. I hope that we may come to . . . an agreement."

"Ah! Good. That *is* wise, I say. I thought that you would see light, being a man of some wits. No good would be done to the King's cause, or your own, by stirring up trouble here."

"It is the King's cause that I am concerned with, Sir

Reginald. I do not wish my goodsire of Dunbar to come for his daughter, no. But His Grace's trust in me is the more important. I have come to believe that these Fyvie moneys are less vital to him than something else you may supply."

"Something else . . .?"

"Information. About Moray. Continuing information. The King is much concerned as to what may go on in Morayland. He hears little or nothing from there now. Since old Durward of Atholl is displaced, and the Earl of Buchan has taken the Cross. There are not the same safeguards against revolt. Always there has been danger from the Moraymen, led by descendants of the older royal line, MacEths and MacWilliams. His Grace needs eyes and ears in the North. That, indeed, is the major reason for my presence here."

"So that is it! I confess, I wondered why a man such as yourself, a knight and seemingly close to the King, should come here to be a steward."

"I was set both tasks. But I conceive the first to be the more vital. If you will aid me in this of information, of keeping watch on Moray, I will, will refrain from reporting on the Fyvie barony."

The other eyed him narrowly. "What do you want of me, in this?"

"Nothing that it is not already your duty to give His Grace, as a sheriff and leal subject, sir. But I conceive you to be in an especially good situation to provide information. You sit here, on the edge of Moray and Strathbogie. Your elder son is Lord of Duffus, in Moray, married into the leading house. And your good-brother is the Lord Fergus Comyn, married to a daughter of the old Celtic line . . ."

"I have no dealings with Fergus. He is no friend to me and mine."

"Nor to the King, perhaps. You may have no dealings with him. But you could hear what he is at, learn of any danger to the realm. And inform me. His Grace, I swear, would be grateful."

"I see." Le Chien nodded. "Yes, I see. I perceive also, that I was much mistaken in you, my young friend!"

"There is more than the Lord Fergus to watch, to be sure. This Moray is all but a closed land. Much could go on there that the King, in the South, knows nothing of. He wisely desires to be better informed. The Church there must hear much. Your son, the Precentor of Aberdeen, might be able to learn something. Holy Church is always . . . knowledgeable. As we have seen!"

"Better than Henry — the Bishop of Moray, Archibald, is of the de Moravia house. Kin to my son Reginald's wife. And he does not love Fergus and the MacEths and MacWilliams any more than do I!"

Thomas perceived that he did not require to convince le Chien further. "It is a compact, then, Sir Reginald? You send me all the information you can glean. I leave Fyvie's affairs to yourself. And you send no word south as to my presence here?"

"With all my heart, friend. And — you will inform His Grace of my good offices? My leal duty?"

Grimly, Thomas nodded, and held out his hand, less than proud of himself, however relieved.

When presently he rode off southwards, he at least had the satisfaction of leaving in his bedchamber a rhyme he had composed the previous morning after a most vivid dream — the first such he had penned for many months.

> *Inverugie by the sea, lairdless thy lands one day shall be;*
> *And beneath that hall's hearth-stane, the tod shall bring*
> *her bairnies hame.*

10

Bethoc at least had no doubts as to the rightness of her husband's course. Thankful for his safe return, she declared that not only had he done all that was possible, but that co-operation with le Chien was the best policy anyway, in the King's interests. She was not greatly concerned with moneys, rents and the like, and doubted whether Alexander would be, either, compared with the security of his throne from possible Northern threats. From a woman's point of view, Thomas had nothing at all with which to reproach himself. It did not appear to occur to her, nor did the man point it out, that if she had not gone to Aberdeen on his behalf, in the first place, and revealed her identity, the deal with le Chien might not have been necessary.

For some time thereafter it was as though Thomas had never gone to Fyvie and no arrangement had been made with its lord. No communications therefrom arrived at Monymusk. By constantly questioning others, however, especially wandering friars, he learned much more about Moray in general, thereby much enhancing his understanding of the situation regarding dangers to the kingdom, or at least to the present occupant of the throne. The province was vast, the greatest in size in all Scotland, stretching as it did from the Norse to the Hebridean Seas, and scarcely to be considered as an entity. Great lordships therein such as Badenoch and Lochaber were to all intents independent, as were many ancient thanedoms in the low-lying eastern parts, such as Brodie and Dyke, Cawdor, Invernairn and Cromdale. Indeed, these eastern parts, the wide coastal plain known as the Laigh of Moray, it seemed, presented no threat to the Crown, fertile, long-settled and reasonably peaceful territories. It was the far-flung uplands of Braemoray which were the menace, the wild clan lands where the caterans dwelt, enormous, all but impenetrable, lawless — these indeed a constant threat to the Laigh also, which the Highlanders looked upon as legitimate prey. It was there that the dispossessed descendants of the earlier Celtic kings, MacBeth, Lulach, Donald Ban and Duncan the Second, driven out by Malcolm Canmore and his sons by Margaret, had taken refuge, and had proved impossible to dislodge. Whether any of these had real hopes or intentions of trying to wrest the throne back was open to doubt. But Moray had once been a semi-autonomous kingdom of its own, the realm of the Northern Picts and their successors; in fact at times the government of all Scotland had been conducted from there, MacBeth's own favourite seat being at Spynie in the Laigh. So there could always be ambitions to return to some such status.

Thomas had sufficient to occupy his attentions other than possible threats from Morayland. He was now finding his feet in the Monymusk barony, and that spring and summer became ever more immersed and involved in the actual tasks of improvement which he had urged on the tenantry, indeed finding much satisfaction in the process. To find himself the authority over a large tract of country, in a position to influence much that went on, was something of a heady challenge to a young man whose own acres had been modest indeed. With many of the larger baronial tenants he could do little, beyond seek to persuade and coax. But others he could sway and stimulate, especially amongst the smaller men, to whom his inducements represented much-needed better-ment. He organised co-operative efforts in various areas of the property, in scrub-clearance, dyke-building, drainage and new tillage — and thereby even managed to interest some of the larger, lairdly holders, who had tended to look upon actual production from the land as beneath their dignity. Moreover there was a fair amount of neglected territory, mainly in the Don valley-floor itself, which was not in any tenant's or sub-tenant's hands, and on which Thomas him-self could go to work. He employed labour to bring some of this into production. Boldly he used some of the King's rents to buy cattle and sheep to pasture and fatten. All this to serve as demonstration. He even stirred up the Priory monks to greater efforts. He was fortunate in that he had been reared in the Merse and Lothian, where farming methods were probably more advanced and production greater than any-where else in the kingdom; and being handicapped by his lameness and to some extent debarred from much of the more manly and war-like preoccupations of his kind, had always taken an interest in the land, however scanty his own Ercildoune inheritance. Now, in this comparatively back-ward northern territory, he found himself to be something of an expert, an innovator and improver, and with the royal authority behind him. His enthusiasm grew — although frustrations multiplied also.

Sir Tristrem, it is to be feared, languished.

He visited the other large barony, Drum or Drum Moluag, to the south, in the great Dee valley near Banchory St. Ternan. Here, although he met with no adventures such as had greeted him at Fyvie, he discovered a similar neglect and lack of care for the royal interests. In this barony, another chase or hunting-forest in the main — such being what the earlier kings had sought out for themselves — there was no major single vassal, like le Chien, but a number of lesser tenants who had for long been allowed to go their own way and more or less decide their own rents — with consequent chaos. Things had not gone quite so far as at Fyvie, owing to the fact that the next barony westwards, up Dee, was that of Onele, with its great castle of Coull, belonging to Alan Durward; and Durward's influence had in the past spread in some measure to Drum. He had ruled Scotland off and on during the long minority of this Alexander, and had, it seemed, largely appropriated for himself the revenues of these royal lands. So this property, so conveniently close to his own, had until recent years not been permitted to go to seed so far as had Fyvie. Thomas sought to ensure that the process was now reversed.

All these summer months Bethoc carried their child, in the main joyfully and without complications.

Then, in early September, when Thomas had begun to fear that le Chien had resiled from their bargain and had no intention of sending him information — although admittedly no word came from the South either, to suggest that the fugitives' whereabouts had been reported — a friar from the Priory of St. Mary at Fyvie arrived at Monymusk with a sealed letter from Sir Reginald. It containd nothing of any urgency, but at least indicated that le Chien had not forgotten their compact. He informed that a large gathering, of Braemoray chiefs and leading caterans, had taken place at the remotely situated castle of Lochindorb in Cromdale, which belonged to the Lord Fergus Comyn. The purpose of the meeting was not clear, but it must have been important, for many scores of these chieftains and captains of clans and bands attended, including representatives of both the MacEths and the MacWilliams. Sir Reginald said that he was trying to discover more; but obtaining information about such people and places was difficult. This secrecy in itself might be significant. But at least the timing of the meeting, so late in the campaigning season, especially for the Highlands, indicated that no large movement of forces was likely for this year.

So Thomas had something to send to the King besides reports on rents and moneys. There was no proof that this gathering of chieftains meant revolt, of course; but clearly le Chien thought that it had been some sort of council-of-war.

In the months following, Thomas's preoccupations changed notably when Bethoc's time came and she was brought to bed of a fine son. Her labour was sore but mercifully short, with the Abbot's laundress-concubine acting as midwife. During the birth process Thomas, like many a husband before him, vowed that he would never father another child upon his suffering wife, cursing the entire business. But when the infant was in due course born, cleaned up and presented to him for inspection, he knew an enormous pride and satisfaction. Bethoc, tired but content, declared that he was perfection, and was to be called Thomas also, young Tom he would be — Thomas William, indeed, to remind all that he was descended from William the Lyon, at five removes, the present King's grandfather, whose daughter Ada had married the fifth Earl of Dunbar. The present proud father was a little doubtful about this choice of names; but in his euphoric state would have conceded anything to Bethoc. And there was no question but that, when he paced the floor thereafter with his son in his arms in attempts to stop him bawling, it helped a little to be able to remind himself that this noisy morsel was the product of a line of kings which reached back before recorded time.

So, in domestic bliss and feeling a little more secure, they passed their second winter since leaving Ercildoune.

One matter, however, distinctly disappointed Thomas.

That was the complete absence of any communication from the King, or his chaplain, any acknowledgment of his own reports and moneys. He was prepared to accept that Alexander could be much too busy, and too lofty, to write letters to a lowly knight and steward, who was under a cloud anyway. But he could have sent an occasional message through the chaplain Reginald, given some indication of his reactions towards the increased revenues coming from Monymusk the accounts of improvements on the properties, and especially some comment on the reported Lochindorb gathering and its implications. But nothing came. Bethoc advised not to be concerned. Kings and great ones were like that; they could be kind, on impulse, or the reverse, and then pass on to other and higher affairs and seem to forget entirely their earlier unbendings. It might be that Alexander now had reason to discount the possibility of trouble from Moray. But that was no concern of theirs. Thomas had done what he was sent to do. They were now very comfortably settled at Monymusk; they appeared to be safe from attentions from the South. They had each other and now Tom William, with a full life to live. Thomas should do only his duty and let the rest be. Which was practical woman's talk.

Lack of direct communication from the monarch did not mean that they were without all news from the South. The usual mendicant friars intermittently brought tidings to Strathdon — their usefulness in this respect being one of their principal assets, ensuring open doors for them wherever they went. From such they learned that a permanent peace agreement had been reached with the new King of Norway, under which the Hebrides and Man were permanently ceded to Scotland — although not Orkney. That Edward Long-shanks, now that he had licked his father's rebellious barons into shape — and slaughtered vast numbers as warning against further uprising — had actually taken the Cross at Northampton, and was planning to join the Crusaders, although apparently not just yet, for there was word that he would engage in a number of activities first, including a visit to Scotland to say goodbye to his sister Queen Margaret Plantagenet during the forthcoming summer; a strange gesture for one who hitherto had shown no brotherly interest whatever. Also that Cardinal Ottobone had sought permission for a second visit to Scotland — presumably dissatisfied with his financial campaign so far — and had been refused by King Alexander. Moreover that the King had come to a complete rupture with Bishop Gamelin, the Primate, partly over Ottobone but also over the Bishop's excommunication of one of the King's friends. Oddly, as a result, the Primate was said to have taken to his bed at St. Andrews, refusing to arise, as a sign of displeasure. And so on.

There was one item of news conveyed which concerned the hearers more personally. Malcolm, Earl of Fife had died and Sir Colban was now the ninth Earl and chief of MacDuff. So one offended earl was gone. They doubted whether Colban would be so upset about the rejection of Duff, as husband, as his father was reputed to be, since he and his brother were not on the best of terms.

It was the beginning of May when the next word arrived from le Chien. He informed that there were rumours abroad in Moray that there was to be a major rising once the harvest was in, with all the upland clans involved. That this was no mere scare, exaggerated, seemed to be confirmed by the Church authorites in the Laigh, who had been quietly informed that no threat was posed at that rich, coastal-plain area, the usual target for such clan adventures, so long as the folk there did not interfere in any way. Which sounded ominous.

Thomas got a special monkish messenger off to the South with these tidings without delay. The hay should be in, with normal conditions in the Highlands, by early July, two months. So there was no time to waste.

On this occasion, the same recognition appeared to have dawned on the King, and for the first time there was a reaction, and a swift one. Within nine days a fast royal courier, no wandering friar, came to Monymusk with a letter from Alexander. It was brief and to the point. Thomas was to present himself at Kincardine of the Mearns by St. Brendan's Day at the latest, and to bring Sir Reginald le Chien with him. That and no more.

This cryptic command presented Thomas with no minor problem, needless to say. St. Brendan's Day was the 16th of May, a mere six days hence. And in that time he had to find le Chien, persuade him to accompany him, and then make the southwards journey across the Mounth. Whether this could be done in the time was doubtful. Without actually cursing his liege-lord, he left Bethoc at least in no doubts as to his feelings.

The messenger arrived in the evening, and was very weary with hard riding. A start was made with first light, northwards, Thomas taking the royal courier with him, as well as the man Donald, after his last experience in those parts.

However, this time they covered the twenty-nine miles to Fyvie without incident, only delayed a little by the courier's tired horse. But it was to find only the red-bearded MacFirbis in charge. That character appeared to be not at all abashed at the arrival of his former victim, indeed welcoming him with something of a flourish, from amongst his grinning henchmen. He informed that the Thane unfortunately was not in residence. He had been at Fyvie until only two days back, when he had gone off down Ythan to hawk for waterfowl in the marshlands of that river's estuary. It seemed to Thomas a strange time to go fowling, at the height of the nesting season; but MacFirbis explained that the terns should have arrived by this from wherever they wintered — and hawking for terns or sea-swallows was a notable test for any falconer, the birds' agility in the air being renowned. The Thane, who prided himself on his hawks, had gone to challenge the Laird of Forvie, near Ythan-mouth, an acknowledged master of the sport.

They spent a brief night at Fyvie, more comfortably than on Thomas's previous visit, although the feeding was a deal less fine. With time pressing direly, they were off again with the sunrise — which meant only a few hours of sleep, for in May in the North the darkness period is short.

Down Ythan twenty-three miles they rode, at speed, past Gight and Methlick and Ellon, until they came within smell of the sea, the land levelling to coastal marshes enclosed within far-stretching sand-dune ridges, fairly typical of

Buchan. Here the Ythan, partly dammed up by sand, spread wide in meres and reed-beds, a paradise for waterfowl. On the north shore of this, protected from the sea by the long line of dunes, was the barony of Forvie, on slightly higher ground, owned by Sir John de Turing, another Norman with Comyn affiliations, with its hallhouse, church and village.

They were fortunate enough to arrive in time to catch le Chien and his host and rival falconer just before they set out for the day's sport. Sir Reginald, surprised as he was to see Thomas, greeted him in at least superficially friendly fashion.

"Oh my soul — our knight of the pen and purse!" he exclaimed. "De Turing — this is Sir Thomas Learmonth, steward of royal baronies. What brings you here, my friend? Do not tell me that Sir John, too, is to come under your scrutiny? Forvie is no royal fief, surely?"

De Turing, a solid, square-faced, florid man, snorted. "It is not, by God! *I* am lord here." He looked Thomas up and down, clearly unimpressed. "*Sir* Thomas Learmonth, did you say?"

"Just that. Of His Grace's own knighting, no less!" Le Chien turned. "Do I take it then, friend, that it is myself you have come seeking?"

"Yes, Sir Reginald. And on the King's behalf."

"You say so? Then the matter is . . . private?"

"Yes." Thomas glanced at Turing, who humphed sourly, and stalked off.

"You told the King of my — my concern on his royal behalf, then?"

"I did." Thomas reached into a pocket for Alexander's brief letter, and held it out.

"Lord!" le Chien said, reading. "His Grace is . . . forthright! This is difficult, man."

"It is. For us both, no doubt. But — it is a royal command."

"But — so soon? St. Brendan's is but three days hence, is it not? Why this haste? I cannot just leave all and go. Like some cur answering its master's whistle!"

Thomas almost replied that le Chien meant the dog, and the King was the master of even such as he. But he restrained himself. "There is need for haste in this situation — you yourself wrote so. And I conceive that His Grace can make the journey up Kincardine only at that time. He will be coming a long way to meet us. Probably from Roxburgh." He did not add that almost certainly Alexander had chosen Kincardine out of regard for his *own* situation, so that Thomas need not venture further south and into danger of being recognised.

"A plague on it — I cannot just ride off southwards now, Learmonth! I must go back to Inverugie first. To settle certain affairs . . ."

"How far to Inverugie from here? Twenty miles?"

"More. Nearer twenty-five."

"But not difficult riding. Coastal riding all the way. If you left now, you could be there in four or five hours. Settle your affairs and leave again at first light tomorrow, and you could be at Monymusk by two-three hours after noon. So we could reach St. Ternan's Hospice at Banchory on Dee by night. And over the Mounth, by Cairn o' Mounth, the next day. Kincardine before nightfall."

"Lord — you are a pusher, Learmonth, lame leg or none!"

"I do not find it to affect my riding, Sir Reginald. Shall I see you, then, tomorrow after midday? At Monymusk?"

"Save us — I suppose so. Although it is devilish inconvenient . . ." the other grumbled.

So Thomas was able to go back to his wife and son for the night, which was more than he had hoped for.

*   *   *

In a way, Thomas's lameness held its advantage for once, for the magnificent le Chien could not allow a semi-cripple to seem to outdo him in horsemanship or anything else. So the Lord of Inverugie and Thane of Formartine arrived at Monymusk next day dead on noon, and with a tail of no less than forty horsemen, presumably as indication of his power and prestige — although Thomas saw them only as likely to be a nuisance and delaying factor.

In the event, although they got away earlier than anticipated, they reached Kincardine next evening rather later than projected, since forty-odd men can never ride so fast as two or three, especially over rough mountainous country and passes. When they clattered up to the castle, with sundown, Thomas was in some doubts as to whether he should proceed inside with the others or go to wait at the castleton, as before, in his rather odd circumstances. But he did not want to seem too humbly retiring in front of le Chien, and decided to risk it. He could always make a discreet retreat if it seemed necessary.

However, it became apparent from the first that there was no large company here with the monarch meantime, few men-at-arms in evidence, few horses in the stabling; indeed Sir Reginald's forty minions outnumbering the rest. And when they were conducted up to the lesser hall, there was certainly no stir of courtiers about the place.

The other Reginald, the chaplain, received them, a stern, unsmiling individual, but shrewd and obviously much trusted by the monarch. He appeared to be no more delighted with le Chien than with Thomas.

Alexander came striding in, and they bowed low.

"So — you come just in time!" he exclaimed. "I am to be off in the morning. You have taken your time, Thomas!"

That young man swallowed. One could not contradict one's sovereign lord. "There was a deal of territory to cover, Sire, beyond the Mounth. We have hastened."

"Have you? You, Sir Reginald, I have not seen for long. You would have travelled the faster, I swear, lacking your army! Why bring such numbers to *my* house? Were you uneasy in your conscience as to your reception?"

"Your Grace jests! In unsettled times, and places, a troop of men can ensure safe travel and so avoid delay."

"My side of the Mounth, sirrah, is kept in better order than yours, then! I rode here with but eight men and a priest! Does Mar and Buchan require stronger governing — as well as Moray?"

Le Chien warily held his peace.

"I have come here at considerable inconvenience," the King went on. "I have been here for two days, waiting. Pressing matters take me south again in the morning. I hope that my trouble was not unnecessary. You, le Chien — you believe this stirring in Moray to be dangerous?"

"Dangerous for someone, Sire, yes. Whether it is you, or other, we do not know for sure. They keep their moves fell secret, in Braemoray. It is a mighty and difficult country to reach . . ."

"I know all that, man. I asked you if the trouble there was like to be dangerous — to me? I care not whether these outland clans slaughter each other. But if they aim against my throne and the realm's peace, then I must be concerned. In the last five reigns, the only armed risings within Scotland have come from Moray. Is this to be another?"

"I cannot say for certain sure, my lord King. But I can see no other reason for the reports received but of a major armed endeavour against some great target. Holy Church in Moray has been given to understand that *their* interests in the Laigh are not threatened. My son, with the Bishop of Aberdeen, hears that Mar and Buchan are not the objectives. It cannot be clans to battle amongst themselves, for the great gathering in September at Lochindorb included almost all the chiefs and leaders of the Highland north, many of whom are sworn enemies and at feud with each other. To unite such, the cause must be no petty one. I believe that it can only be invasion south of the Mounth."

Servitors had brought in ale and cold meats and the travellers were invited to set to. As they ate and drank, the King paced the floor, uncaring about the rule that none must sit when the monarch was on his feet.

"This Fergus Comyn?" he asked. "Is *he* behind it all? What sort of a man is he? The brother of my Great Constable! I do not think that I have ever met him. What is the style of him? What does he want? Is he dangerous? He is your good-brother, is he not, le Chien?"

"He is, to my sorrow, Your Grace. A strange man. Ever at war with his own kin and kind. No friend of mine, nor of my lord Earl. He elects to live far from Buchan, up in that grim hold on an island in Lochindorb, deep in Braemoray, a house of his half-brother the Lord John of Badenoch. And has chosen to wed Gillespic MacWilliam's daughter. What he wants I am not sure. But I do not think that Fergus himself is the true power behind all this. He does not have it in him. He is a limited man, ambitious but without the ability to lead . . ."

"Who, then? Who? Could it be his goodsire, MacWilliam?"

"It could be, yes. He is namely as a strong man, a leader. He is not young now, but he remains vigorous. And he has a sore grudge against your house. The matter of his daughter, the child, you will mind, slain at Forfar. Even so long ago. He is of the royal descent and could claim the throne — which Fergus could never do. Or perhaps seek to divide your kingdom — make himself king over Moray and all the North. The old Celtic realm."

"How much support would he have for that? In the North?"

Le Chien grimaced. "Not a little, I fear, Sire. Your Grace seldom honours us, north of the Mounth, with your presence. Many there know little, care little, for what goes on in the South. They hold to the old ways, speak a different language, cherish the Columban Church . . ."

"And love not me, their King!"

"They scarce know you, Sire. But they know Gillespic MacWilliam."

"Aye. So you think that my kingdom is in danger of breaking in two? Why now? Now, when I am strong? Not before, when I was young, weak?"

"Because now the guards are down, the barriers fallen. So long as Durward held Mar and Atholl, John Comyn held Badenoch and Lochaber and Alexander Comyn held Buchan, you were safe. Now Durward is old and feeble and has lost Atholl and most of Mar. Earl William of Mar is no fighter. John of Badenoch is governing Galloway for you. And your Constable, Alexander of Buchan, is gone Crusading, taking many of his best knights with him. The barriers are down, my lord King."

"A curse on this crusading folly! It has already cost me dear — beyond Ottobone and his moneys. David Lindsay, my Chamberlain, dead of the fever. David de Strathbogie dead of wounds. Carrick, they say, is sorely sick. Others besides. If Buchan himself were to die . . ."

"That, Sire, I would say is where Fergus Comyn comes into this. The Earl Alexander has left behind at Kinneddar as heir only a boy, John his son, aged seven years. If he did not come back from this Crusade, like these others, Fergus I think would grasp for the earldom, in place of his nephew. And if MacWilliam succeeded in detaching the North from your realm, Fergus of Buchan would be the greatest man in the North, next to its new king."

"It could be — yes, it could be. So we must halt this affair, and Fergus Comyn with it, before it becomes more dangerous. Thomas — you wrote that you esteemed the danger to be after the hay is in? July?"

"Yes, Sire. The Highlandmen will never move far before the winter feed is assured for their cattle."

"That gives us eight weeks, no more. The plague of it is this of Edward Longshanks, my good-brother. He is to come to Scotland this summer, for the first time. To say farewell to his sister, the Queen, before he goes crusading. God knows why! I mislike the man — as he mislikes me and my kingdom. The last thing that I would wish is to have to go fighting rebellious subjects while he is here. Or to have a rising in progress, even if I take no part. And to tell him not to come would be as bad, appear weak, feeble. It is damnable! So — somehow this Moray trouble has to be halted. Halted altogether if possible — but at the least, until after Edward has gone."

His hearers looked blank.

"The thing should not be beyond our wits," Alexander went on. "You, Thomas, have notable sharp wits, as I have discovered. And you, le Chien, are no dullard. How is it to be done?"

Neither of his knights produced instant suggestions.

The King came over to lean on the table and stare at them, almost accusingly. "You will go to them. To this Lochindorb. Both of you. And you will talk Fergus Comyn and Gillespic MacWilliam out of this adventure. You hear me? It should not be beyond you."

"But . . ." le Chien began.

"No buts!" he was told, flatly. "These are my commands. You will have free hands. You will concede what you must.

But these would-be rebels must be persuaded to put off their rebellion! At least for this summer. Afterwards I should be able to deal with them."

Sir Reginald shook his head helplessly.

"I do not think that you would say that we should go sword in hand, Sire." Thomas said carefully, knowing his monarch better than did the other. "But if go we must, we cannot go *empty*-handed."

"Who said that you should? You must have something to offer. Or some threat to make. Or both. You must use your wits, as I say. Judge how best they may be persuaded. Offer powers, honours, favours, moneys. Promise grievances to be considered. In my name. But halt them."

"And if we promise more than Your Grace is prepared to perform?"

"That will be for me to deal with in due course."

"That could leave us — or *me*, at least — in a sore position, my lord King," le Chien pointed out. "*I* have to live there, beyond the Mounth. I cherish my name and repute."

"So do I, sir — so do I!" the King barked. "Think you I will forget my royal honour? Interpretations may have to differ a little — that is all. But, see you — I will warrant that your name and repute will nowise suffer, man. David Lindsay my Chamberlain is dead. How would Sir Reginald le Chien, High Chamberlain of Scotland, sound?"

The other swallowed audibly. 'Your Grace . . .!" was all even that self-assured individual could get out.

"Yes, then. You contrive this for me, and you shall be Chamberlain, in room of Lindsay. With the emoluments of that office!"

"I, I thank you, Sire — thank you!"

"It would aid, Your Grace, if you would give us some hint of what to offer on your behalf," Thomas said. "That we have the wherewithal to bargain, yet do not commit you to too much."

"I have told you — powers, favours, riches, Find what they want, short of an independent realm, and go some way to meeting them. This Fergus should not be too difficult. He could be Justiciar of Moray. There is none such meantime.

Fine pickings for justiciars! A knighthood. I would not want such a one as Earl of Buchan, or Constable, if his brother does not return. But he could have the guardianship of his nephew, and so control the earldom's revenues until the youth comes of age. MacWilliam would be more difficult, I think. But there has been no true Earl of Moray now for long, since Malcolm MacEth died — however many have named themselves that. Gillespic might be tempted with that. Not a promise but a consideration — for the MacEths would not like it. But — that might help to sow dissension between these two houses, which might be to our advantage!"

The others looked less than convinced.

"When would you wish this to be done, Sire?" le Chien asked. "When to go to Lochindorb?"

"I leave that to you. But it must not be long delayed, if there are only eight weeks. We do not want any rebel army mustering. It is always difficult to send home a mustered host, empty-handed. Best that they should never assemble. So you must go before mustering starts. And leave time for word to be sent to all the chiefs. June. Go next month."

So it was left to the two very doubtful envoys — although le Chien, obviously elated by the prospect of the chamberlainship, which would make him one of the great officers of state, was at least prepared to swallow his doubts meantime.

Later, weary with long riding, and early to his couch, Thomas was surprised to have his liege-lord visit him in his bedchamber. Struggling up in some confusion, he was told by Alexander to lie back and not be a fool.

"I want a privy word with you, Thomas. This le Chien? How do you judge him?"

"Since you, Sire, propose to make him your Great Chamberlain, you must adjudge him passing well yourself!"

"Tush, man — do no take that tone with me! How do you see him?"

"Able, Sire. Clever. Ambitious. Quick to perceive his advantage. Or otherwise."

"Aye. But do you trust him?"

"No."

"I thought not. You too are able, clever, quick-witted,

Thomas — but you cannot hide your inner feelings. You think that *I* should not trust him?"

"That is for Your Grace's own decision. But he is unscrupulous, less than honest, and arrogant. So I have found him. Ready to change his course if the wind changes."

"As are many, Thomas, many. And kings have to use such able, unscrupulous men in managing their realms. I have a new Chancellor, William Wishart, Archdeacon of St. Andrews, who is I think the most unscrupulous rogue in my kingdom. But clever — and good at dealing with other rogues! So long as *I* hold the whip. That is kingship, God help me! No — I would not trust le Chien too far, either. Only as far as his self-interest impels. But he is the man to deal with these Moraymen. They will pay more heed to him than ever they would to you. But it is necessary that you go with him. You *I do* trust. Watch him. Your wits are sharp as his, I swear. Use them. I do not seek to buy *you* with offices and the like, Thomas. But then — you are already in my debt, are you not?" Alexander grinned suddenly.

"Yes, Sire — very much so. I, I am entirely in your royal hands."

"To be sure. Fortunately for you they are strong hands, Thomas lad. Never fear, I shall look to your interests well enough. And I have hinted as much to the Earl Patrick! Aye — and how is that earl's wayward daughter? The fair Bethoc?"

"She is well, Sire. And happy. As am I. Thanks to you. We have a son . . ."

"Lord so Patrick is a grandsire! But knows it not. I doubt if he will rejoice! But I do, Thomas, for your sake." Alexander paused, looking almost embarrassed. "Tell me — have you been making any rhymes, of late? Divining? Foreseeing the future?"

"Not in any great matters, Sire."

"Great? How to judge what is great and what is not? You *have* foreseen something, man? What?"

"Only small things. Nothing to concern your Grace or your realm."

"Nothing of the North? This of Moray and beyond the

Mounth? Come — out with it, Thomas. You are always so plaguey close. Let me judge whether it concerns me, or no."

Thomas shook his head, but rose naked from his bed and went over to his clothing, which lay on a bench. From a doublet pocket he took a folded paper and handed it to the King.

"Three of them!" Alexander commented. "Three verses of the one? Or three different rhymes? What's this, i' faith? Waterfalls? Watershed? Here's a nonsense!"

"I told you, they are small things. Naught for you . . ."

The King read out:

> "*At the waterfall on the watershed,*
> *When is seen the nest of the ring-tailed gled;*
> *The Lands of the North shall all be free*
> *And one king reign over kingdoms three.*"

"What a God's name does that mean, man?"

"I do not rightly know, my own self. It came to me some mornings back, before I rose. Just those words. No picture. Nothing else . . ."

"But — how can you write down words of which you know not the meaning? What waterfall? What watershed? Which King? And what three kingdoms? These Lands of the North — is that Moray?"

"I know no more than your Grace. It could be Moray, I suppose . . ."

"Moray was once a kingdom. So Moray and Scotland could be two. What of the third?"

Thomas shrugged, and hid his nakedness under the blankets again.

> "*Fyvie peace shall never see*
> *So long as there three stones shall be.*
> *One into the highest tower,*
> *One into the lady's bower,*
> *One beneath the water-gate,*
> *These three stones hold Fyvie's fate.*

Here's another riddle! Fyvie is the barony of mine that le Chien holds, is it not? What then is this?"

"I saw these three stones, Sire, as I rode. Rode two days ago, beside Sir Reginald. They were red, like blood. One set in the tower, one in the wall of the lady's chamber, one beside the gate which controls the water to feed the moat. What they mean I cannot say. Save that Fyvie will not prosper whilst they are there."

"Sakes, man — can you not do better than that? Who does this concern — le Chien or myself? What is amiss with Fyvie?"

"Much amiss, I think, Sire. As many dead men, hanging from its gallows tree, would wish to tell you! If I knew what those stones signified I would say so. Or to whom the warning applies. But I do not. These rhymes come to me out of no will of my own. Sometimes I can understand them, sometimes not. I am sorry . . ."

"The last one," the monarch went on.

> *"If ever maidens' malison shall fall upon dry land,*
> *Let naught be found on Forvie's glebes*
> *But thistles, bent and sand.*

Now that makes as little sense as the others! What does it mean? Forvie? I think that I have heard the name. Where is Forvie?"

"It is a barony in Buchan, Sire. Held by Sir John de Turing, a Comyn knight, brother to Sir William, Lord of Foveran. I was there to find le Chien. To bring him to you here. And that night I dreamed a dream. I saw three young women facing the sea, at Forvie. It is on the coast. They were cursing sorely, shaking fists at sea and sky, weeping. For their inheritance had been stolen from them by evil men. Then I saw their curses, their malisons, returning landwards from the sea. As a great dark cloud and wind. That blew and blew. It swept away those maidens. And when it was finished, all the barony of Forvie was gone likewise, all its hallhouse and church and township, its meadows and glebes, its rigs and pastures. All lost under a level plain of blown sand. Sand, all sand — a desert."

"Lord!" the King said. And again, "Lord! You make unchancy company of a night, Thomas Learmonth! I wonder that the Lady Bethoc can thole sleeping with you! Do you never dream more kindly, man?"

"Often, Sire. Bethoc makes no complaint. Most of my dreamings are nonsense. As are most folk's. As indeed may be these. But — your Grace *asked* me for any rhymes I had made."

"Aye. Well — if you dream of me this night, dream gently, for Mary-Mother's sake!" The King handed back the paper. "Better to dream not at all, I say. A good night to you Thomas. And . . . watch le Chien hereafter!"

In the morning, as the two parties mounted to ride their different ways, the larger northwards, the King's southwards, Alexander, from his saddle, spoke to le Chien, farewells said, as though in an afterthought.

"De Turing of Forvie, Sir Reginald? You know him? I have heard tell of him. He is brother to Foveran, is he not? What is his situation?"

"Situation, Sire? You mean, at Forvie?"

"His barony. Who will heir it? He is no longer young, I think. His brother? Or has he sons to follow him?"

"No sons, your Grace. But he has three daughters. None wed, as yet. He could have grandsons . . ."

"Save us!" the King muttered, and reining round, spurred away.

II

The fine isolated peak of the Knock of Braemoray had been rearing before them for hours as, after leaving the greater valleys of the Findhorn and the Divie, they followed that of the rushing Dorback Water upwards, southwards by west, in its narrower trough through the high heather moorlands, on the third day of their eighty-mile journey. At the farther side of that shapely pointed hill, their guides told them, only a few miles lay Lochindorb.

It was a strange terrain, not at all as Thomas had imagined it. He had looked for a land of great mountains and cliffs, of glens and corries, of lochs and pine-forests, true Highlands. Instead it was wide, farflung, open moorland, ever rising in vast shelves, up and up, grass and heather and peat-bog, seemingly limitless prospects on every hand save ahead where rose the ultimate ridge crowned by this Knock peak, with broom and scattered thorn-trees and birch-scrub here and there, but no forests, no mighty mountains. Admittedly these endless shelving moors were not quite what they seemed to be, cut up by deep hidden ravines in which rivers rushed in foaming, peat-stained haste, such as this Dorback. Tucked away in these valleys were the occasional dwellings of the folk, the dreaded caterans presumably, low-browed huts of turf and reed-thatch, with pens around for beasts in winter. Yet never did they see a soul in any of these small, almost furtive communities, not so much as a barking dog. It was the time of the shielings, their guides asserted, when the people moved up, with their flocks and herds, to the high summer pastures. The travellers were not wholly convinced. The young folk might mostly have gone shieling, yes; but not the old, surely, the sick and the infants? Moreover, fires of peats were found in some of the cothouses, smothered and black but still warm. The caterans they judged, were none so far away, but hidden, watching, warned of their approach. This feeling of being watched all the time had been with the horsemen these last two days, since they had left wide Spey. They seldom saw a soul but were aware that the land was not empty, however vacant-seeming the vistas.

That company, of course, would make a sufficiently daunting sight for any shyly inclined inhabitants, for le Chien had insisted on being escorted by almost his full strength of armed supporters, some one hundred and twenty men, a necessary prudent provision he claimed, in such unsettled territory. A cavalcade of this size would be safe from attack by even one of the greater cateran chiefs, he judged; and at the same time it ought to ensure word of their coming being conveyed to the people they wanted to see. Thomas considered it too ostentatious, but was not consulted.

It was late afternoon, two days short of Midsummer's Eve, when they at length surmounted that long ridge above the Dorback, on the flank of the Knock, and reined up to gaze out over an abruptly changed prospect. It was as though they had reached another land, that this escarpment at a sharp bend of the valley marked the limits of Braemoray and that the true Highlands stretched before them now to infinity. Forests covered that land, not dark, tight-packed trees in serried ranks, but scattered open woodland, growing out of heather, pine and oak, birch and hazel, a sea of greens and browns, out of the rolling waves of which thrust great hills by the score, bare-topped, rock-ribbed, shadow-slashed, to distant blue mountains everywhere, many still streaked with the dead white of snows. Throughout it all was the glimmer of sun on water, burn or river, waterfall, lochan and peat-pool. But nowhere that they looked could they see a major sheet which could be Lochindorb, the Loch of Trouble, which they sought.

The guides said it lay immediately ahead nevertheless, behind the first major crest, a mere three miles. It lay in the midst of the Forest of Leanich, they declared, the finest haunt of the great woodland stags in all Scotland.

As they rode down into the quiet glades of that limitless forest, even Sir Reginald le Chien fell silent.

They continued to follow the line of the Dorback Water until presently it swung due westwards to round the spine of higher ground which their guides had pointed out. And, sure enough, beyond this the woodlands opened out and the hills withdrew somewhat, to reveal the placid waters of a large loch mirroring the colourful scene, out of which this Dorback flowed. About two miles long and less than half of that broad, it lay embosomed in grassy slopes and patches of tilth, these dotted with the cabins of a sizeable population. And in mid-loch, towards the northern end, was a small island on which reared a stockaded fort, above which, from a tall pole, flew a blue flag bearing the three golden garbs, or wheatsheafs, of Comyn.

At the sight — and the recognition that here at least there was to be no hiding away of the country-folk, for, some way down the east side of the loch opposite the island could be seen a large crowd gathered — Sir Reginald ordered his own two banners to be unfurled, one the blue with silver crosses of le Chien and the other the selfsame Comyn garbs. Thus identified, they trotted on.

After all the long miles of apparently empty land, it was strange to be riding now past watching folk, people singly, and in groups, who stood and stared but offered no greeting, silent. Most here were women and children and some old men.

When they reached the denser crowd however, it was different. Here all were men, and armed men, hundreds strong, in ragged tartans, fierce-looking but as silent as the others. They were massed behind a timber jetty at which two flat-bottomed ferry-boats were moored.

The visitors scanned the waiting ranks, le Chien and Thomas raising hands in salutation — which was nowise returned. They could pick out no obvious leaders.

"We greet you kindly," Sir Reginald announced, carefully. "We seek my kinsman, the Lord Fergus Comyn."

This producing no least reaction, Thomas tried. "Is the Lord Fergus here, friends? Out in yonder hold? We have come far to speak with him."

The only response was one or two fingers pointing down at the moored boats.

Taking this to mean that they should embark, presumably to find Comyn in the castle, they were faced with the problem of numbers. The boats between them would not hold a quarter of their company, less if any of the horses were to be carried. To leave most of their troop here on the mainland was awkward, and meant of course that they would be entirely in Comyn's power out on his island. On the other hand they could scarcely insist that he came to them; the fact that he had not done so already, yet had all these caterans assembled, presumably meant that he intended to stay where he was. They decided to take a mere dozen men with them, and row out. Having come all this way, they could hardly do other.

Dismounting then, they left all the horses with the mass of their men-at-arms with low-voiced instructions by le Chien to be very much on their guard, and if he did not return or send word within an hour or so, to take hostages from amongst this crowd and threaten to hang them unless satisfaction was forthcoming.

Embarked, they were rowed out the quarter-mile to the castle, all ill at ease. As they approached they could see that the island was in fact artificial, a crannog such as the Picts often built for defence, founded on great oak trunks and heaped stones. Clearly the loch was not very deep. It was a major defensive structure, fully an acre in extent, with the superimposed fort taking up every square yard of its surface. This was no Norman castle but a hallhouse and subsidiary thatched-roof buildings within a tall and massive timber stockaded perimeter, again of oak trunks from the surrounding forests. Obviously it had been there for a long time, and would be all but impregnable.

The island's jetty was not before the heavy gates but some way to one side, so that people disembarking had to walk along a very narrow path between the water and the stockade, here provided with a kind of gallery or brattice from which they could be assailed on their way to the entrance. Armed men looked down on the visitors from this, heavy stones poised.

The gates however were open. Flanked by supporters a tall and very thin man, dressed in Highland style, stood therein. He was of middle years, gaunt featured, head almost like a skull, and of sour expression.

"Reginald le Chien!" was all he said, as his visitors came up — and there was no welcome in his voice.

"None other, my good-brother," the other answered, heartily. "Here's a fair meeting. Do I see you well, Fergus?"

The Comyn ignored that. "Why are you come here?" he demanded harshly. "With that host of ruffians!"

"To see you — what else, Fergus? To see my wife's brother. My ruffians, as you name them, are but for our protection on a long journey. As no doubt are yours, here."

"What brings you one hundred miles with one hundred men, to see me? You who have never before looked my way, le Chien?"

"Sufficient, Fergus — sufficient. But not, I think, to shout out before all and sundry here at your gate!"

Grudgingly the other acceded to that, and with no further greeting and scarcely even a glance at the lame Thomas, turned and led the way within.

In the hall at least the Lady Matilda, formerly MacWilliam, a rather worn, tired-seeming woman but kindly, exhibited more of the traditional Highland hospitality and hastened to bring the visitors food and drink. Her father Gillespic was in direct descent from Duncan the Second, Malcolm Canmore's eldest son, and therefore senior in line to his other sons by St. Margaret, from the last of whom stemmed Alexander. Fergus Comyn's belated marriage to her had worried the King somewhat, but so far the match had produced only two daughters.

Her husband had no small talk, found Thomas beneath his attention and was not the man to wait patiently for elucidation of a visit he found not to his taste.

"What do you want of me?" he demanded bluntly, as his guests ate and drank and his wife fluttered about nervously.

"Only your attention," le Chien said easily. "And in due course we would look for your thanks. We are come for your own good and welfare . . ."

"That I do not believe, for a start! You, le Chien, never willingly did aught in your life that was not for your *own* good! So have done with such talk and come to the bit."

His lady bleated unhappily.

Unruffled, his brother-in-law shrugged. "Is it not possible that the matter could also be to my benefit? If something less than yours. All our benefits, indeed, in these parts. But yours, and MacWilliam's in especial."

At mention of that name, Comyn's strange eyes narrowed. "Ha — so that is it!" he exclaimed.

"That is it, my friend," le Chien nodded. "Your projected rising. All is known, you see. Disaster awaits you. We come to tell you."

Comyn drew a hand over his long, bony jaw and chin. "Have you lost your wits, le Chien? To come all this way to tell me that? Think you that we are bairns here in Moray? To be frightened by such talk. We know what we do, and care not who else knows."

"Do you, man — do you? You plan to raise the North against King Alexander. But the King knows it all. And is not idle whilst you wait for your hay-harvest. He musters his fullest strength . . ."

"We can defeat his fullest strength, fool! Strength! I say weakness, rather. Alexander is weaker than ever he has been, today. His best leaders are gone from him, on this fool Crusade. Taking their thousands with them. Durward is old and done. Buchan, Mar, the Mearns, Angus and Atholl lie open to us. Think you any there will halt us? Our time has come, at last. The usurping line of the Margaretsons will end with this Alexander — God be praised! We in the North can raise a thousand men for Alexander's hundred, I tell you. The clans will rise, as never before. We can thrash Alexander — and will!"

"Can you? I wonder. And can you thrash Edward Longshanks also, brother?"

The other stared — as indeed did Thomas Learmonth. "Edward Longshanks . . .?"

"Himself. The Plantagenet — the First Knight in Christendom. Fresh from his great victory at Evesham. Edward marches north to Scotland, friend, to his good-brother's side. Indeed he may already be over Tweed. Have you not heard?"

Comyn moistened his thin lips. "You, you jest! Cozen me . . .!"

"Not so. He comes. You do not think that one would wish to see his sister's throne endangered? So you must deal with Edward as well as Alexander. Believe you that you and your friends can handle the victors of Largs and Evesham both?"

Thomas moved uncomfortably on his bench at this blatant deceit; but le Chien did not so much as glance at him. Clearly Comyn was much perturbed, as well he might be, for Edward Longshanks' reputation, not only as a warrior but as a clever, ruthless, indeed terrible opponent, had been growing with the years. He turned to pace his hall-floor in agitation.

His sister's husband struck again whilst the iron was hot. "I heard on fair authority that Edward slew twelve thousand after his victory at Evesham, beyond those who fell in the battle. He takes no prisoners, that one! He devastated the homes and lands of all who had opposed him. If he would do that in his own father's kingdom, what would he not do in Scotland? I charge you to think well on this, my friend."

Thomas was in a quandary. It angered him to be a party to this shameless deception; but to deny it was scarcely possible without utterly wrecking their purpose, the King's purpose — Alexander had told him to watch le Chien; but more than watching was required here. What could he do or say? Was there some alternative approach which might be effective, to change the emphasis? A more honest persuasion?

"My lord Fergus," he said. "What ails you at the King's Grace? Why seek to bring him down? He has done you no hurt. He is a better king than Scotland has had for long years. What so ails you that you would rise in rebellion — the friend of both your brother, my lord Constable, and your half-brother, the Lord of Badenoch?"

Comyn might not have been prepared to submit to such interrogation from so insignificant a questioner had he not been so upset over this of the Prince Edward of England.

"He and all his line are usurpers!" he exclaimed. "Descendants of the Saxon bitch Margaret!"

"Yet Scotland has accepted them for near two hundred years. Your house of Comyn not the least."

"The more shame. My precious brothers have done sufficiently well for themselves, yes, in supporting that infamous line, father and son. Constable of Scotland and Governor of Galloway! But myself? Not so much as a sheriffdom. Nothing!"

So that was it — jealousy of more illustrious brothers, unsatisfied ambitions, the sour resentment of a stay-at-home younger son of no great character.

"If His Grace has overlooked your qualities and excellences, my lord, might it not be because you are not seen at his court? He will lack knowledge of your worth. This could be put right. A no doubt suitable recognition made for past, h'm, neglect. Indeed, I think that we could promise it, my lord."

"Oh, undoubtedly!" le Chien said, but with a mocking smile.

"My worth is overlooked until I rise in arms to prove it!" Comyn declared.

"Perhaps. But, as I say, you have not put yourself into the King's presence for him to learn of your parts. And the fact that your brothers have not pressed your claims should not be blamed upon His Grace."

"What does Alexander offer, then?" That was sufficiently blunt.

"That is scarce for us to say, my lord. But it would be substantial. Have you any especial desire? A justiciarship, perhaps . . .?"

"His Grace might find it cheaper, Learmonth, to forget any such gestures towards our friend now that Edward comes. And instead offer his puissant good-brother an abundance of the sport he so dearly loves — killing. And so be done with the problem of Moray, the MacWilliams and the MacEths once and for all. Before Edward goes off crusading." Le Chien shrugged. "Myself I would so elect, I swear!"

Thomas said nothing.

Comyn looked from one to the other, doubts and uncertainty chasing each other across his cadaverous features. "What can I say?" he demanded. "I do not know what to say. I must consider — consider well. Consult. Consult my friends . . ."

"I think that there is only one whom you need to consult, in truth," his brother-in-law said. "Gillespic MacWilliam. He it is put you up to this, I swear? And we go to see him now."

The other seemed part-relieved, part-alarmed. "Now? You go to MacWilliam now?"

"To be sure. He is your master, is he not?"

"Curse you, le Chien — watch your tongue! In this house. I hold you in the palm of my hand, I'd remind you! I . . ."

"Tut, man — I but meant that MacWilliam it is who put you up to this business, is it not? You yourself would have remained loyal enough — as we can assure the King. So we must see MacWilliam. And thereby preserve you! Where is he to be found?"

"He is at Loch-an-Eilean, in Badenoch."

"How far?"

"Twenty miles. Twenty-five. By Spey and Dulnain and Nethy, to Rothiemurchus. Loch-an-Eilean lies therein."

"You can give us a guide? Good. Then we can be halfway there by nightfall."

With Comyn far from pressing them to wait or to stay the night, a move was made with minimum delay. With a cateran on a rough garron as guide, they were rowed back across the loch to their waiting men-at-arms, still surrounded by the wary, watching crowd.

Mounted, and on their way southwards along the loch-shore, le Chien said, "We were best not to linger there. Fergus is best left a prey to his own fears. But this MacWilliam will provide tougher sport, I think."

"I would not name that sport, back there," Thomas said. "I do not congratulate you, Sir Reginald, on your methods. Lies and deceit will never ennoble a cause. This of Prince Edward . . ."

"Sound not so smug, man! I am not concerned with ennobling any cause — but with winning it. And winning it with the least hurt to any. To my fool good-brother, to His Grace, to this MacWilliam or other. If, shall we say, I place a different interpretation on Longshanks' visit to Scotland than you do, and this helps the King's cause, who is to say that I err? Moreover, he may be coming north for more than just to see his languishing sister. Who knows, with that one? Our liege-lord does not want him — but he comes. Let us use his coming, then, to good purpose, if we may."

The fact that Thomas was nowise convinced did not make him able to change the other's attitude.

Leaving Lochindorb's wide hollow, they climbed through

open slantwise woodlands up and up, some five hundred feet, to lofty tree-dotted heather moors again, with the sun sinking behind their right shoulders, to cast long purple shadows over a colourful land. After eight rough miles on what seemed to be a drove-road, they began to descend to the great strath of Spey at the point where the Dulnain joined the larger river. Crossing the latter in the dusk, by a ford below a group of standing-stones, eerie in the half-light, they camped for the night in the haugh of Ballifuirth, to dine on fresh-killed beef, which Thomas managed to persuade le Chien at least to pay for.

In the morning they were into the greatest pine-forests in the land, of Abernethy and Rothiemurchus, a vast terrain of mighty, ancient Caledonian pines, red of trunk and bough, rich green of foliage and heady of scent. The six-score-strong column had to string out notably to traverse such territory; but this attentuated progress was reduced to actual single-file when, just before noon, their guide led them off the strath-road left-handed to mount towards a narrow and high pass through a lofty barrier of hill, which he named The Sluggan, meaning the throat. This was a short-cut over into Rothiemurchus apparently, to save many miles.

It made a steep ascent, by a rushing burn, more cascade than stream, with the trees thinning as they climbed. A couple of steep winding miles they rose, with the column half-a-mile long by the time the leaders reached the summit — where involuntarily they reined up, struck despite themselves by one of the most impressive prospects which it had ever been their lot to see. Before them, as behind, the land dropped away into an enormous amphitheatre, a dark-green rolling sea of trees, mile upon mile, wherein blue lochs gleamed, backed by a tremendous, snow-streaked mountain range of soaring, cliff-hung, corrie-slashed giants, hitherto hidden by the intermediate hills they had now surmounted, closing all the southward vistas as far as the eye could see, dominant, brooding but serene.

The Monadh Ruadh, the Red Mountains, their guide told them, the highest range in all Scotland. He ran off, in his lilting Highland voice, the names of the nearer individual summits — Cairngorm, Cairnlochan, Beinn MacDhui, Braeriach, the Sgoran, to his gazing hearers. Although the appreciation of scenery and natural beauty was not by any means a major preoccupation with any of them, the sheer scale and grandeur of what presented itself before them here left them bemused.

Their bemusement cost them dear for, eyes on that prospect, they for a while neglected the automatic careful scrutiny of their flanks, elementary for any cavalry force. And so were utterly taken by surprise and confounded when, just a little way beyond the summit of the Sluggan, suddenly a horde of kilted Highlanders leapt out at them from the juniper-bushes on either side of the narrow track, swords and dirks drawn.

There was an immediate chaos of shouting men, clashing steel and whinnying and rearing horses. In single file, as the riders had to be, there could be no concerted defence. One hundred and twenty mounted men can make a formidable force — but not when strung out over half-a-mile. Because the track was so narrow and winding, the horsemen had no warning, no time to draw their swords, before their leaping assailants were upon them, grasping at the horses' bridles, lunging at the riders, pulling them out of their saddles. Little was clear in that abrupt and overwhelming ambush save that the attack was not confined to the leaders of the column but proceeding simultaneously behind them, certainly as far back as the summit of the pass and probably beyond.

Thomas found himself dragged sprawling to the ground by four brawny caterans, with dirks pointed at his throat. There was no sense in struggling. Le Chien presumably felt the same way — as evidently did each and all of their men-at-arms in sight, for there was an ample sufficiency of attackers to ensure odds of at least four or five to one.

It was all over in a minute or two, the alarmed horses proving their adversaries' greatest problem. Gripped firmly, the Buchanmen were hustled together into an ever-growing and unhappy group of rueful captives, their arms taken from them. Their guide seemed to have disappeared. No explanations were offered them, no statements made, however much le Chien and Thomas protested, demanded reasons and threatened consequences. With minimum delay they were formed up into parties of roughly a dozen, each surrounded and escorted by guards of fully four times that number, bristling with weapons, and led off, marching down the track southwards. More Highlandmen led the long file of riderless horses behind.

After the first few minutes of the march down into Rothiemurchus, Thomas's ire and concern was at least somewhat ameliorated by amusement over the poetic justice of le Chien's situation. It was all so notably similar, if on a larger scale, to his own rude apprehension by Le Chien's minions at Fyvie those many months ago.

They were marched, at a trying pace for men not used to walking, through what seemed endless miles of forest very similar to that of Abernethy, even more lovely had they been in a state to recognise it, most of the way following the headlong course of a brawling, peat-brown river which flowed from a large loch directly below the rampart of those mountains. Despite his limp, Thomas found the marching less difficult than le Chien seemed to do, who kept demanding that if they must be harried along in this outrageous fashion to God knew where, at least let them sit on their horses like the knights they were. They received no answer.

After what Thomas guessed might be as far as five or six miles, the weary, stumbling prisoners were brought to the shore of another forest-girt loch tucked within a re-entrant of the steeply soaring heights, a jewel of a place scenically, smaller than the one they had seen before, perhaps a mile long, less than half that in breadth, only one-third of the size of Lochindorb but likewise possessing an island. And on the island a fort also, a modest stone castle, smaller again than Comyn's stockaded hallhouse.

"Loch-an-Eilean, the lake of the island!" Thomas guessed. "MacWilliam, for a wager."

"A curse on him — I thought that it must be he who had ordered this!" le Chien agreed. "Insolent fool! Why? Why — when we were on our way to see him?"

236

Here, although there were boats available, they required no ferry to take them out to the island stronghold. For, leaving the men-at-arms and all but a small group of their captors at the township of cabins beside the loch-shore, the two principal prisoners were at last restored to their horses, and with their immediate guards mounting also, were led splashing into the water.

Riding in close double file, their leaders twisting and turning their beasts with a careful precision, those behind following exactly at the others' heels, they zigzagged out to the island on what was obviously a narrow underwater causeway. Thomas had heard of this Pictish defensive device whereby only those who knew every foot of the precise hidden stonework plan could make the crossing, in three feet or so, with deep water on either side.

It was quickly evident why so few came out with them, for the total area of the island proved to be less than an acre, and the tiny courtyard reached through a narrow pend in a high curtain-wall, was sufficiently crowded with the horses they brought. Here the captives were dismounted and led to a squat, square, granite-built keep, and up its turnpike stair to the hall on the first floor, thrust inside and the heavy door slammed on them. Throughout, their captors had hardly addressed one word to them.

"Damnation! Savages! Barbarians!" le Chien burst out. "Treated like dogs!"

"At least we are put in better accommodation than was I when I was thrown into a cellar at Fyvie by your MacFirbis!" Thomas pointed out grimly. He glanced round the apartment, small for a hall, like the rest of this castle, no more than thirty feet by twenty but comfortable enough with adequate plenishings, colourful wall-hangings, wolf and deerskins on the stone-flagged floor and a small fire smouldering on the wide hearth.

Sir Reginald snorted but said no more.

"Did you see who was watching our arrival, hiding himself in a doorway of the courtyard down there? Our guide from Lochindorb. So we were led into that trap. Somehow MacWilliam must have known of our coming, He must have been warned. Only the Lord Fergus could have done this. Sent messengers hotfoot, much faster then we travelled . . ."

The door opened and a man came in, limping. "A good day to you, my friends," he said, deep-voiced but mildly. "I bid you welcome to my house. You have travelled far and will be weary. We must see to your refreshment."

They both stared, Thomas not only struck by the appearance of another lame man and by the curious dichotomy between this greeting and the manner of their arrival, but by the extraordinary looks of the speaker. Here was quite the most noble-seeming individual he had ever set eyes upon, a man almost elderly in years, slightly built, with fine, regular features, a high and wide brow, a leonine mane of greying tawny hair, dark lustrous eyes and an expression of warm concern. Anybody less like the picture he had envisaged of a Highland cateran leader would have been hard to imagine.

"This, this is intolerable!" le Chien got out. "To be treated so. Assaulted and manhandled like, like common felons. Driven for miles, like cattle. Brought here without a word being spoken. Our protests ignored. And now — this! This mockery of false welcome!"

"False welcome, sir? Why do you say that? My welcome is honest. Whilst in my house you are my guests and I greet you as such. Even if you did trespass against our Highland honour and customs. I am Gillespic."

"Trespass! *We* trespass? My God, sir — were we not set upon, assailed, dragged from our beasts? Knights assailed by your unwashed ruffianly horde! And you talk of trespass and honour!"

"I regret it if you were inconvenienced, sir. Especially since you are of knightly rank. But would it not have become you more to have demonstrated your respect for others' rights and sensibilities, in chivalric fashion, by not invading another's territory with a large armed force? Unannounced. By not so much as informing me, the thane of this lordship of Rothiemurchus, that you intended to enter it in armed strength?"

"We were coming to see you, man. On the King's business. In your lawless Highlands travellers require armed protec-

238

tion — as your caterans have most assuredly demonstrated!"

"I do not propose to further offend, since you are now guests in my house, by a profitless exchange of insults. But I would ask you, Sir Reginald — for I take it that you are Sir Reginald le Chien of Inverugie, called Thane of Formartine? Yes — then I ask you how you would say if *I* marched into your Buchan lands of Inverugie with a force of what you name my lawless caterans, lacking *your* permission? Poorly, I would think. But enough of such talk. You are here, whatever your business, and I welcome you. Whilst you are at Loch-an-Eilean it shall be my endeavour to accord you every courtesy and comfort, to the best of my poor ability." MacWilliam turned directly to Thomas. "You, sir, I do not know, to my regret. So forgive me for not addressing you by name."

"The Lord Fergus Comyn, then, did not inform you, sir? I dare to say that he would not consider it worth the mention — even if he remembered it! My name is Learmonth, Thomas Learmonth of Ercildoune in Lauderdale, a very humble man, merely a messenger. But . . . the King's messenger!"

"Ah! But you are knight? Or did Sir Reginald not mean it so?"

"Yes, I am."

"Then this poor house is the more honoured. We do not see many of knightly rank here behind the Highland Line. His Grace Alexander seldom raises his eyes this far! Nor did his predecessors. So we must cherish you the more? Must we not?"

Thomas was careful in his response. That there was something of mockery, of slight, in the other's polite words, could hardly be doubted. Yet the man uttering them, aside from looking the part, had the right, surely, to mock. For if anyone in Scotland should have been of at least knightly status, this man should, direct descendant of their ancient kings, in the senior line, more senior than Alexander's.

"Our cherishing, sir, like our desserts, should not be on account of ourselves but because of our royal mission," he said evenly. "The King's Grace could not send lesser than knightly envoys to such as yourself, my lord Thane."

Le Chien first frowned at this, then changed it to a thin smile. But he held his peace.

"Ah — so you are envoys?" MacWilliam said. "Envoys — or messengers, which? There is a difference, is there not? The first can treat — the other but bears a message."

Thomas inclined his head, recognising that they would have to go very warily with this one.

"Yes. But even royal envoys will probably treat better on a full stomach, I think," the other went on, smiling. "So come you, my knightly friends. A meal should be ready in another chamber."

They were conducted to a lesser room on the ground-floor, vaulted and backing on to the kitchen obviously, where a notable variety of cold meats and fish was set before them, to le Chien's evident satisfaction, their host waiting on them with courteous attention. He assured them that their men were being provided for, across the water, forbearing to complain about the numbers.

The edge of his appetite — and so of his temper also — abated, le Chien took the initiative. "Your good-son and my good-brother — Heaven help us both! — must have sent you hasty word of our coming, sir. As well as providing a guide to lead us into your trap! How much of our mission did he tell you?"

"That King Alexander knew of our intended move, Sir Reginald. And was concerned enough that it should not take place to send you up as emissaries. Little more than that. Save that you rode with a large force of armed men, and might well intend to grasp at my person, as a means of enforcing your cause!"

"If he thought that, Fergus is a bigger fool even than I esteemed him! But, yes — we come on behalf of His Grace, who knows of your projected rising and would halt it before it becomes war. He has no desire to draw sword against his own subjects unless he must. However misguided!"

"As is both commendable and discreet! I too wish no bloodshed — if our just requirements can be met by reasoned agreement. Although I am not sanguine, from previous experience. But, my friends, distinguished as you are, I fear that the cause we support is scarcely to be negotiated and settled by such as yourselves."

"We are here as His Grace's chosen representatives, sir. With powers . . ."

"Then Alexander must much lack great lords. Whom he can trust. Or else does not esteem my cause of major importance. In which case we will have to instruct him . . . otherwise. I represent the senior line of the royal house, I would remind you."

"*A* senior line . . ." le Chien began, when Thomas cut in quickly.

"At least we can discuss your cause and intentions, sir, however modest *my* personal standing. So that His Grace may be better informed and apprised."

"Alexander is quite fully informed and apprised, young man — save perhaps as to our strength and determination! I have made it my business to see that he is, these years past. But until we reach for our swords, he has paid no least heed. And now he sends only two knights, however excellent, to Gillespic — who should be sitting on his throne! Has he no earls left to him?"

"His earls, no doubt, are all meantime greeting Prince Edward of England, who has come to Scotland, sir," le Chien said. "Did Fergus not mention Edward Plantagenet?"

"Ah, yes. He did say something of Longshanks. But what has the Plantagenet to do with this matter?"

"Let us hope, for your sake, nothing, sir! Since he is reputed the fiercest warrior in Christendom. And ever spoiling for a fight!"

"Are you threatening me with the Englishman, Sir Reginald? For if Alexander would seek to use the enemy of our country against his own subjects, then assuredly that is proof that he is unfit to occupy the throne which should by rights be mine."

"Not so, sir — not so," Thomas intervened. "His Grace sent no threats. He will, to be sure, defend his position with all the strength at his disposal. And no doubt punish rebellion thereafter. But our mission is to seek to prevent anything such. To discuss . . ."

"Alexander knows our grievances very well, Sir Thomas. Apart from sitting on a throne which should be mine, if birth means anything — since he descends from an eighth son of Malcolm Canmore whilst I descend from the eldest son. Apart from that, we here in Moray and the North are wholly derided and rejected. Our voices are never heard in the South, our causes neglected. When the Norsemen or the Orkneymen or the Islesmen raid us, as they do, no help comes from Alexander. He never visits this part of his realm. The laws he and his council makes do not suit our needs — yet he would have us obey them. He demands our taxation . . ."

"But does not get it, I swear!" le Chien interjected, grinning.

MacWilliam ignored that. "And now this levy for the Crusade is to be laid upon us! Tithes of our stock and produce. To be sent down to the Laigh seaports before Hallowmas . . ."

"That, sir, is wholly against His Grace's own wishes. It is wholly a Papal decree. For all Christendom," Thomas put in. "The King fought the Cardinal whom the Pope sent to impose it. I was present. But Holy Church will declare excommunication on all who disobey . . ."

"Holy Church, young man? You mean the Roman rite! What is so holy about that arrogant, imperious dominion, so far removed from the humble, patient Christ as it is in the mind of man to conceive? We here prefer the ancient Church of our land, given us by the Blessed Columba. Do not preach Holy Rome in Badenoch, I advise you!"

"I do not, sir. Only say that this of the tithe and levy is not of the King's doing, but against his wishes. If this has helped to bring you to the verge of revolt, then it is mistaken . . ."

"I do not like the word revolt, Sir Thomas. I but seek my rights. And it seems must do so with the sword drawn, since my kinsman Alexander heeds no other. And my complaints go far beyond this of the tithes. It is but the latest, to spur me to action."

"I think, sir, that it is not so much this tithing for the Pope which spurs you to action, as the fact that so many of the

King's lords and their men are presently out of Scotland on Christ's Crusade!" le Chien declared bluntly. "So you feel that His Grace is weakened, and now is the time to strike him, to grasp for his throne!"

"Again I do not congratulate you on your manner of speech, Sir Reginald!" the other said, almost sadly. "I do not conceive this Crusade to be over-much concerned with the Lord Christ. Is it not concerned, rather, with grasping new domains and kingdoms for the friends of the Pope and King Louis of France — Carthage, Tunis and the rest? Far from the Holy Land. And as for choosing to strike now, since we face the whole might which Alexander can bring against us, must we wait to strike when he is strongest? Would *you*?"

"I would not strike at my liege-lord, back-turned or no!"

Thomas bit his lip. He and le Chien saw their envoys' duties very differently. "Sir," he urged, "from what you say, the way you list your grievances, I jalouse that what you seek principally by this rising is not so much the throne of Scotland — although you claim it should be yours — but the righting of wrongs which you claim are done to Moray and the North. That is your first aim — and, to be sure, it will be the aim of most of those who would rise with you. The betterment of this great earldom, and with it the improvement of their own lives and interests — that will be what they seek. Rather than merely putting yourself on Alexander's throne. Am I not right?"

"The one could well result from the other."

"Perhaps. But I think that there can be no doubt as to which holds the priority. Likewise which would be the most readily attained! I suggest, sir, that you cannot really hope to unseat the King's Grace in a single short campaign. And thereafter have yourself accepted as King of Scots by the whole realm and its nobility. Not many know you. Perhaps they should, but they do not. It is too much to hope for."

"Especially with Edward Longshanks to consider," le Chien threw in helpfully.

MacWilliam made no answer to that.

"If this is so," Thomas went on, "surely you may achieve much of what you seek without recourse to fighting. Clearly you are an honourable man, who would avoid bloodshed if you could. The King is prepared to revive the earldom of Moray, presently merged in the Crown. With all its powers. Would that not greatly improve the situation? For a start?"

The other stroked his chin. "That would much depend on who became earl," he said slowly.

"No doubt. But . . . clearly the choice is limited."

"Certainly it would be. *I* would claim to be the Earl of Moray, in such case."

"Yes, sir."

"Have I Alexander's assurance that the earldom would be mine?"

Since Thomas could not answer that honestly, he had to temporise. "Would the MacEths resign their claim, sir? If they would, I believe the King would confirm it to you." It was the best he could do.

"The MacEths, Sir Thomas, descend from the fifth son of Malcolm Canmore, I from the first. Eth, or Ethelred Margaretson, was never king."

"But he *was* Earl of Moray! As were his sons, Angus and Malcolm MacEth," le Chien pointed out.

"Only because the then King made them so. Can this King not do likewise?"

"I suppose that he could . . ."

"And would, sir, I say, if you could assure him that the MacEths would accept it," Thomas said. "And not rise in arms in their turn, and plunge the North into war. Either against himself or against *you*. Can you so assure?"

MacWilliam turned to pace the floor two or three steps, and back. "I believe that I can," he said carefully. "The MacEths are now settled mainly far in the North. In Ross and Caithness. Kenneth mac Kenneth MacEth, head of that house, now has Strathnaver from the Earl of Orkney, his kinsman. He looks northwards now, rather than south. He no longer looks to gain the earldom of Moray, I think."

"I would question, sir, whether that would be sufficient warranty for the King."

"As would I!" le Chien agreed strongly.

"Indeed! All the North accepts my word. Is it insufficient for Alexander? Or for you, his messengers? If I give my word that I shall see that Kenneth MacEth accepts me as Earl of Moray, will that not serve? It is all that you will get — for I can do no more."

Sidelong Thomas glanced at his colleague. Those words seemed to indicate that their mission was, in the main, accomplished. MacWilliam was going for the earldom of Moray rather than the throne. And sufficiently keenly to stake his power and reputation on being able to convince the MacEths to agree to it. Therefore there would be no rising in the near future, at least, with the situation and the distances involved. Alexander would win his breathing-space — the object of their journey.

"We must accept your assurances, indeed," he said, picking his words. "And urge His Grace so to do. As, I think, we can promise you, sir. As to the rest . . ."

"Aye, as to the rest. As Earl of Moray, with all powers of that office, I would be able to do much to improve our situation here, to right many wrongs, ensure that justice is done in and for the North. But there are still issues on which we should require the *King's* assurances. In especial, aid from the South to repel invasions. We should not have to *ask* for this, since we are part of Alexander's realm. But . . ."

"That you can be assured on, sir, I would swear. The King is strong now. Since he came of full age and took the rule into his own hands, the days of weakness are past. Any invader of his kingdom would find that he had King Alexander to face. As did Hakon . . ."

"Nevertheless, I would require specific assurance."

"As, no doubt, would the King! As to *Moray's* armed support to aid him in *his* warfare!" le Chien added, significantly.

"If I was earl, that support would be part of my compact and undertaking." MacWilliam addressed hmself rather pointedly to Thomas. "There is also the matter of the justiciary. It is intolerable that there should be no Justiciar of Moray . . ."

"Fergus, your good-son, sees himself as Justiciar, I think."

Sir Reginald chuckled. "Were you considering buying off MacEth with it?"

Coldly the other eyed him. Thomas rose from the table.

"Surely we have enough?" he said. "The position is clear, in all important matters. Lesser things can be dealt with at a later date. I, for one, am well content. I believe that the King will be also. And you, sir, will have achieved your principal aim, yet kept your sword undrawn. Reason will prevail."

"I hope so, my young friend — I hope so. For I am a reasonable man. But — I warn you, and through you, Alexander, that my sword remains to hand! If there is delay or holding back, it will be drawn. If the clans are not to assemble and march in a few weeks time, I will have to assure them that their cause is gained. And quickly. They will scarcely be easy to convince. Once we assemble, and cross the Mounth, there can be no turning back without notable bloodshed. Tell Alexander that. And you, Sir Reginald le Chien — remember that Buchan would be on our line-of-march!" Their host paused. Then he changed his tone of voice and his expression. "Enough, then, my friends. If you have eaten a sufficiency. Bedchambers await you. Wine therein. Company also, if so you desire. Young women will come across from the township. Such other hospitality as it is in my power to provide. Say but the word. I would suggest that you remained my guests for some days, to taste what Rothiemurchus has to offer in sport and entertainment. But I am concerned over time — as you will be. We have not long to set affairs in order. And Alexander is far away. I would not wish to delay you."

"Never fear — we shall ride in the morning," le Chien told him. "If we can be assured that there will be no more attacks and ambushes by your caterans!"

"On the contrary, you will be escorted comfortably, on the swiftest road back to Buchan," they were informed. "Now — to your chambers . . ."

Thomas, for one, was well content to bed down with little delay thereafter, without availing himself of the further Highland hospitality proffered. It had been a long and full day.

They left Loch-an-Eilean next morning under what amounted to a large guard of fierce-looking clansmen mounted on shaggy garrons, MacWilliam himself accompanying them for half-a-day's journey. They rode eastwards along the wooded skirts of the great mountains, by the larger loch which they had trudged past the previous day and which their host called Morlich, and then over a high, narrow pass, in the throat of which lay a small jewel of a lochan, the water a strange green such as the Lowlanders had never before seen. Le Chien remarked that it would make a notable place for an ambush; but this went without comment. Beyond, they were into the vast area known as the Braes of Abernethy, tree-scattered, which ever-rising brought them, by another and still higher pass, to the deep, sudden and lonely valley of the Braan and so down to the Avon in its wide strath. Twenty-five upheaved miles from Rothiemurchus, where Glen Rinnes left Strathavon north-eastwards, MacWilliam said farewell to them, and turned back.

"Six weeks, my friends," he reminded, warningly. "Six weeks at the latest and we march. Unless I have Alexander's written agreement to the matters raised. But since it would be better to ensure that the clans never mustered, rather than they should have to disperse once they had done, four weeks. You have four weeks to get Alexander's letter of agreement, and confirmation of the earldom, to me. I shall be waiting. God speed!"

As they rode up Glen Rinnes beneath its isolated cone of mountain, le Chien snorted. "Thank God to be quit of that insolent barbarian!" he exclaimed. "Spare me from having to deal with Highland upstarts."

"Would you, with a Norman-French name, call the senior descendant of our ancient line of kings upstart?" Thomas demanded.

"Tush, man — he is the fifth generation since King Duncan, who was a barbarian himself, I dare to say! That kind needs firm handling. You were too soft with him, too respectful, by half."

"I *do* respect the man. Respect his honesty — which is somewhat rare, I find! And recognise that he has much right on his side. You, Sir Reginald, were over-hard. You could have wrecked our cause, the *King's* cause, by your harshness."

"Nonsense! That sort has to be shown that though he may be master of a pack of caterans, outside his heathenish mountains and glens he is no more than a brigand chieftain. Earl of Moray — save us!"

"Nevertheless, Earl of Moray is the price Alexander must pay for peace. Forby the price he authorised us to offer. Earl, with all powers. You must leave the King in no doubts as to that. In equity, as well as to prevent the clans from marching."

"I will leave you to advocate such sorry counsel, my friend!"

"No. You it must be. For I cannot risk to go south of the Mounth, to the King's Court. You know why. I play my part here. You it must be. It is you who are to be the Chamberlain, is it not? You must go without me, Sir Reginald. But — I will send the King a letter, never fear . . .!"

They rode on, their mutual lack of sympathy strong as ever.

12

The Lord High Chamberlain of Scotland dandled young Tom William Learmonth on his knee genially. Clearly he was well pleased with life and himself, a man of worth and ability enjoying his just deserts and prepared to accept the Learmonths as more tolerable than heretofore.

"Yes, I saw this one's grandsire, your father, Lady Bethoc," he said. "He is well, to be sure. It grieved me not to be able to inform him of his felicity and of your well-being. But I held to my compact with your husband here."

"My mother, Sir Reginald? Did you see her?"

"No, my dear. She was not at Court. But I have news of your brother, Patrick. He is to wed my own niece, Marjory, daughter of the Earl of Buchan. All is arranged . . ."

"Pate to wed!" Thomas exclaimed. "And to a Comyn! He is but a laddie . . ."

"Nineteen now, Thomas — since I am twenty-one. Have you forgot? I do not know this Lady Marjory. But I would wish her as happy a match as mine! Dear Pate . . .!"

"Well said!" le Chien approved. "Although *you* chose something of an uncomfortable husband, Lady Bethoc! Do you never long for your old life and home, you a great earl's daughter?"

"I often long to see my family again, Sir Reginald. But for the rest, no. I am well content here at Monymusk."

"One day you will go back."

"Perhaps . . ."

"When that time is ripe, we will go — not before," Thomas said shortly. "This Lady Marjory, Buchan's daughter? Your niece. Is she . . .?"

"She is young, yet. But fourteen. But a fine spirited creature. She will make an excellent Countess of Dunbar one day, I do assure you!" Their visitor sounded still more satisfied.

Thomas frowned, glanced at Bethoc, then shrugged, and changed the subject. "What news have you for us from the Court, Sir Reginald? You saw the Prince Edward Plantagenet?"

"Yes. He is a mighty arrogant devil, that one! Although he was in a good mood, for him, they say. The Court was at Haddington, in Lothian. Not far from your own Dunbar, my dear. At the nuns' abbey, there. Longshanks had brought hundreds with him. As the new High Chamberlain, it fell to me to find them all quarters and feeding — a plaguey business, for which I got little thanks. He is not an easy man to please, is Edward. The King mislikes him, with cause, and left much of it to me . . ."

"The burden of high office!" Thomas commented. "But — he is gone again, now?"

"A week past, yes. That is why I could not get away before this. Six weeks I was there. Now he is gone back to Northampton. To prepare for setting off on the Crusade. I could wish that *he* was one who would not come back from it! But, a curse on him, he is of the kind that will!"

"What did he come for? Did you discover? He has never shown any interest in the Queen his sister, hitherto."

"It is hard to discover his reasons — the King has kept silent on this. It could be that it was partly to warn Alexander not to think of trying any ventures to take back Northumbria and Cumbria while he was away crusading. It may be that he sees his good-brother as a danger to the realm he will inherit before long — or the northern parts of it. Old King Henry, they say, is weaker and all but gone in his mind. Crazy."

"I do not understand why Edward goes crusading at all, in these circumstances."

"I see it as a shrewd move for greater power when he gains the English throne. It is said that King Louis of France is gravely sick, at this Tunis. He will not long be able to lead the crusading army. So Edward will make it his business to replace him. If he succeeds in this, and in the fighting, he will be the acknowledged first prince of Christendom. That will serve him very well when he becomes King of England. He desires much of North France — not only Normandy, Anjou and Maine, but Brittany, Picardy and Artois also. That is where his heart is — he is more Frenchman than English. If he has a heart! But he has a head, assuredly! I think that he came to warn Alexander not to adventure anything. But — it was, in the event, a boon to our liege-lord, in that we were able to use his presence as a threat to MacWilliam."

"*You* did that. I did not!"

"The more fool you! It well served the King's cause, I swear! The caterans did not march."

Bethoc, glancing anxiously from one to the other, took the child from le Chien and left the room.

"It is not through deceit that the peace of this realm can be secured," her husband declared, strongly. "The King met MacWilliam's requirements — as was wise." Although it was now early September, and this was the first of le Chien returning from the South, royal messengers had in fact gone up to Rothiemurchus within the time appointed, conveying Alexander's agreement to MacWilliam's demands and the promise of the earldom of Moray, with the justiciarship for Fergus Comyn. Whatever had been the reaction of the many individual chiefs, the general muster of the clans had not taken place. For the time-being there was peace in the North.

Le Chien shrugged. "His Grace was, perhaps, weak in this. But he has other matters on his mind. And, I think, it may be that Longshanks is behind this also. You know that the Cardinal Ottobone desired to come to Scotland again, over this of the tithes for the Crusade — which are not forth-coming, as you would expect! Bishop Gamelin is still in his bed at St. Andrews and has given up — he can make nothing of it. His Grace refused the Cardinal permission to come, and Ottobone retaliated by summoning, in the name of the Pope, all our Scottish bishops and some of the abbots, to attend on him at London, to account for their failure. For once the churchmen found their courage, and at Alexander's behest refused to go. But they did send two of their number, Dunkeld and Dunblane, with the Abbot of Dunfermline and the Prior of Lindores, to go reason with the Italian. And what did that insolent Florentine do? He declared that all the Scottish tithes and payments which were denied him were now forfeit, and were to be the property of King Henry of England, to help pay for his son Edward's crusading venture! It is scarcely believable, but vouched for by the returned bishops. Scots revenues given to the King of England by this Italian clerk!"

"How could he do that? It is impossible, beyond all crediting . . ."

"He has done it. Impossible that Henry could ever collect the moneys, perhaps! But do you not see what is behind it? The threat that the English might march north to collect the moneys, and with the Pope's blessing — pretext for invasion. I believe this is Edward's shrewd work, he put Ottobone up to it, part of what he came to Scotland to tell Alexander. A warning. While he is out of England crusading, there is the threat of English invasion all the time — since he knows well that the moneys will not be paid. A safeguard against Scots adventures! For he could return, as leader of the Pope's Crusade, with all Papal authority — and no doubt much of the crusading army — to impose his will on Scotland. He is a clever man is Edward Plantagenet. I tell you, that one looks well to the future — and sees himself not only as the First Knight of Christendom but as Emperor of the West! Canute, they say, dreamed to be that. I see Edward on the same road."

Thomas shook his head, wordless.

"So we shall have trouble with the Plantagenet, mark my words. He is uncle to Alexander's son and heir, mind you — which could be dangerous. *You* are the foreteller of the future, my friend, are you not — not I. But I foresee trouble. I am not much of a believer in prayer — but perhaps we should pray all the saints to see that, like so many another, he does not come home from this Crusade! For which, I vow, his only concern is to gain him power and put the Pope and all Christendom in his debt."

"You may be right. King Alexander, at least, will be warned, on his guard. He can be rash, but he lacks not for wits . . ."

"And fortunately now he has got good advisers. Chancellor Wishart, there, is a man after my own heart, shrewd, strong, not too dainty and nice! For a chuchman, he sees notably straight. A clever rogue, in fact! Bishop John of Glasgow has died in France, and Wishart has got that bishopric in addition to being Archdeacon of St. Andrews and all his other benefices. With Gamelin, the Primate, a spent force, he is ruling St. Andrews, so has the two greatest bishoprics in the land in his grip, as well as being principal officer of the realm as Chancellor. With Red John Comyn of Badenoch, my other good-brother, acting High Justiciar in room of his absent brother of Buchan, and my humble self as High Chamberlain, Alexander at least should not lack good and effective counsel!"

Thomas made silent prayer to the Almighty to preserve his liege-lord from the parcel of scoundrels with whom he appeared to have saddled himself. Who would be a monarch? Or was he, Thomas Learmonth, prejudiced?

*   *   *

Affairs of state left at least Thomas alone thereafter for a period, and he was able to devote himself contentedly enough to being steward of royal baronies and husband and father. And to *Sir Tristrem*, which that winter of 1268-9 made major advance. By the time that spring brought the press of outdoor work and travel to supersede his literary efforts, he reckoned that he was halfway to completion of his epic task. He was far from satisfied with the quality of his poetry and story-telling — although some parts he could not help being pleased with — but Bethoc at least thought that it was all magnificent.

Their son grew apace. At eighteen months he was a fine, sturdy toddler, of a notable lung-power, phenomenal energy and an enquiring mind, with a propensity for exhausting his parents. Fortunately, the priory monks made a favourite of him and he spent much of the time countering the monastic peace.

In this, his third year at Monymusk, Thomas was able to see considerable results from his reforms and improvements in the productivity of the royal lands, both those under his own control and the much more extensive tenanted holdings. This engendered an atmosphere of well-being and a kind of satisfaction throughout the barony, with a distinct reduction of the grumbling and suspicion which had hitherto accompanied his insistence on his policies of drainage, land-reclamation, increased tilth and stock development. Enhanced yields and quality, and the prices gained thereby, resulted in a foretaste of comparative prosperity — as well as the ability to pay the royal rents. Thomas's visits to the tenants, great and small, began to be less unpopular, to his own very real satisfaction — for despite his serious and slightly stern-seeming manner, he was a man who felt the need to be liked.

He was able to send increasing moneys, as well as fair reports, to the chaplain Reginald in the South, however, little in the way of acknowledgment came back.

News from Moray and the North was scanty. Le Chien was little at Inverugie and Fyvie now, spending most of his time, necessarily, at Court; and although his elder son, Reginald le Fils as he was known, Lord of Duffus, was supposed to substitute for his father as informant, little came from him. From the other son, Master Henry, Precentor at Aberdeen, there was nothing. But such news as Thomas did glean, mainly from peripatetic friars, was reasonably satisfactory. Braemoray and Badenoch were never haunts of tranquillity and order, with raiding and feuding endemic; but by and large conditions appeared to be fairly peaceful, certainly with no large-scale unrest. The new Earl of Moray was beginning to make his authority felt over a wider area — although he did not as yet make any moves towards the low country of the Laigh — and there were no reports of MacEth restiveness, further north. And Fergus Comyn as Justiciar justified his appointment by hanging offenders in large numbers. Whether this activity would improve the general quality of life in these parts remained to be seen. But at least the pressure was no longer on the King to take a hand.

If Alexander was no more communicative than heretofore, either, towards his northern steward, an indirect connection came about early in the summer. Returning home one evening from a visit of inspection up Strathdon, Thomas was met by Bethoc in the orchard.

"There is a man come to see you, a strange man," she reported. "From the South. He says that the King sent him. Scott is his name. He is past middle years and an unchancy manner. His eyes . . . stare! He frightens me a little, somehow . . ."

Thomas found the visitor eating very normally, however unusual his appearance. He was a spare, stooping individual, probably in his mid-fifties, with greying straggly hair and beard and bushy eyebrows, on a curious top-heavy-seeming head, the bulging over-large brow set above very narrow features and a rat-trap jaw, which now munched vigorously. But it was the eyes which made the greatest impact, dark, vivid, piercing and without evident eyelashes, despite the luxuriant eyebrows, restless, challenging, uncomfortable by any standards. He was richly dressed although travel-worn.

"Welcome to my house, sir. I am Thomas Learmonth. My wife tells me that you come from His Grace. And that your name is Scott."

"King Alexander suggested that I call upon you, yes, Sir Thomas." The man's voice was high-pitched, squeaky, not deep as somehow might have been expected from his looks. "Yes, I am Scott — Michael Scott of Balwearie. Of whom you may have heard? Since I understand you to be a man of some small learning . . .?"

"Michael Scott! The, the . . .?" Thomas swallowed the word wizard which had sprung to his lips. "The famous . . .?" He floundered.

"The same, sir — the same. Astrologer-Royal to the Emperor Frederick the Second, of blessed memory, and Count of the Holy Roman Empire. Now knighted by our King of Scots. As you have been, it seems." That last sounded just a little as though he considered it unfortunate.

Thomas cared nothing for that. He could scarcely believe that this was the celebrated Michael, one of the most renowned figures in Christendom, known as Michael the Mathematician by the learned of a dozen nations and Michael the Wizard by the commonality everywhere.

"Sir — here is a wonder, a great wonder! And honour. To have *you* in my poor house. Hardly to be credited. I rejoice that it is so — but what brings you to Monymusk, Sir Michael?"

"You do, young man — you do. I have come solely to see you. And hope that I may not be disappointed!" That was accompanied by an admonitory shake of the finger. "From what King Alexander told me, you should interest me. These rhymes of yours. Foretellings. I wish to enquire into them."

"They are nothing, sir. Nothing of any importance or worthy of consideration by such as yourself. Mere jingles and verses that come to me. Small things . . ."

"I shall be the judge of that. And if they are indeed, I shall be much displeased, sirrah! Since I have travelled far into these barbarous parts to see you. When I could have had better things to do. I trust that the King's Grace has not misled me."

With no answer to that, Thomas made his escape, to clean himself up and to seek to set his wits in order. He confessed to Bethoc that this man Michael impressed if not alarmed him much more than did any other he had ever met, kings, lords and cardinals included. He was the greatest mathematician, astronomer, philosopher and necromancer of the age, son of a Fife laird but product of the universities of St. Andrews, Oxford, Paris, Padua and Toledo. Bethoc was less smitten.

Later they sat around a birch-log fire, for the evenings still held a chill, and Thomas was put through what amounted to a professorial interrogation by their formidable visitor. He started by producing a paper which proved to be none other than a copy of the rhyme once given to the king:

> *At the waterfall on the watershed,*
> *When is seen the nest of the ring-tailed gled;*
> *The Lands of the North shall all be free,*
> *And one king reign over kingdoms three.*

Reading this out, Sir Michael pointed at Thomas.

"This is what took my attention," he said, almost accusingly. "Alexander showed my this rhyme and asked me what it might mean. He said that you, who had written it, did not know — although you had made other prophecies which had come to pass. Do you still say that it means nothing to you?"

"Nothing which signifies, sir. The words just came to me, as so many another. They were sure words — but what they refer to, which waterfall, which watershed and what gled, I know not."

"Yes — this of the gled. It was that in especial which touched me. The gled properly is the kite. But no kites could be spoken of as ring-tailed. But here in Scotland other hawks can be known as gleds. And one such is known as the ring-tail — the female hen-harrier. Rare indeed. Few know it — and fewer know it to be called ring-tail. Alexander did not. But *you* must have done?"

"Yes. I have heard of them, the hen-harriers."

"Have you ever seen one?"

"No-o-o. Not knowingly. Only heard of them."

"Then why in this rhyme? Why describe a bird, a rare bird, which you have never seen. Or . . . did you see it with an inner eye?"

"No. Leastways, I think not. Some things I see clearly enough, and then write down. Some I dream of only. Others just come to me — the words do. As did this."

"Unsatisfactory!" the other declared, severely. "Here is lack of all science, all true design and comprehension. You appear to have been given a gift, man, a talent —— but do not cherish it, do not follow it up and improve it. A sin, Sir Thomas, a sin! Were it not for this of the ring-tail, the harrier, I would have no more to do with you, sir! But . . . I have made a study of birds and fowl. Indeed of all God's dumb creation. There is much for man to learn therefrom — although so few perceive it. And the King said that you frequently brought fowl and animals into your rhymes. Is this true?"

"It is, yes, I suppose. I am interested also, in a small way . . ."

"Thomas knows much about beasts and fowls, sir," Bethoc put in, strongly. "Few know so much. Many of his prophecies speak of birds. Tell him, my love . . ."

Embarrassed, her husband frowned, shaking his head.

"There was that one, that strange one, about the raven and the crow . . ."

"Ha!" Scott said. "The raven is a fowl of notable omen. The Norsemen know that. What is this of a raven, sir. Inform me."

"It is but another pointless rhyme, Sir Michael — pointless and worthless. I wrote it down. But see no sense in it . . ."

"Let me be judge of that. Out with it."

Sighing, Thomas shrugged and recited, level-voiced:

> *"A raven shall come o'er the moor,*
> *And after him a crow shall fly*

> *To seek the moor withouten rest,*
> > *After a cross is made of stone;*
> *O'er hill and dale, both east and west.*
> > *But wit well, Thomas, he shall find none;*
> *And he shall light where the cross should be,*
> > *And raise his neb up to the sky;*
> *To drink of gentle blood and free,*
> > *Then ladies waylowaye shall cry . . .*

Och, I mind not the rest!"

The other eyed him keenly, thoughtfully, now. "And this — this came to you how? A dream? A vision?"

"No. I know not — the words but came, one day. Out of a great sorrow, somehow, I mind — a sadness. I do not know, I tell you. I cannot explain it, sir."

"Yet it is clear that it foretells a battle, sir. A great and sore battle, a doomed affray. Where many good men shall die. The raven symbolises the older pagan faith — always that. The cross is Christ's. So the battle is between these. It could be a Crusade. But it is the crow which survives, see you — the jackal of the air, who drinks the gentle blood. Not the raven. And the cross is gone. The crow shall light where the cross should be. And drinks the free and gentle blood for which the women will mourn. So the winner of this evil fight is neither the cross nor raven, the old faith or the new; but the carrion-eater, the scavenger, who fights not for any faith but for blood and power!"

"Oh, Thomas . . .!" Bethoc quavered.

That young man looked sceptical. "Why the *stone* cross? And the moor . . .?"

"Stone endures. It is symbol of the eternal. So the cross itself, Christ's cross, being eternal, is not overthrown. It survives this — it will always survive. It was not there, you will mind. The gentles who fell came seeking the stone cross. On the moor. They did not find it. A mistaken quest. And the moor — that means a wide, far-flung place, empty. A lost cause in a desert land!"

"Dear God — the Crusade!" Bethoc breathed.

"It could well be."

"You, Sir Michael, a man of learning and renown — you do not take these notions, which come to me without desire or reason, to be of any true worth or seriousness?" Thomas demanded, in some agitation. "*I* do not. Or, leastways, not usually."

"I cannot say," the older man admitted — and looked distinctly annoyed at having to concede anything such. "There is much here to ponder. Are there other such verses? Which might guide me?"

"Only small things. About houses and places . . ."

"Wait you. The King told me of another. About three women wailing on a shore . . .?"

"Aye — that was different. I saw, as in a dream, these three maidens cursing. At Forvie of Buchan. And saw all that fair barony covered in sand.

If ever maidens' malisons shall fall upon dry land,
Let naught be found on Forvie's glebes but thistles, bent and sand."

"M'mm. That is a lesser thing. Of but local significance, I think. But — if ever it comes to pass, this of the sand, I shall be interested to hear."

"Sir — how do you think to test these things? You, a man of learning and knowledge and science? You speak of judging, of comprehension. And you have come all these long miles to question me. To what end? How shall you judge and discern? What will make your consideration and testing any more sure than are my foolish and obscure rhymes themselves?"

Scott glared, with those strangely piercing eyes. "Young man — you do not compare untutored and blind predictions with the distilled wisdom of the ages, as shaped and calculated by judicial astrology and the mathematics of the heavens! The one differs from the other as does a flickering candle to the eternal effulgence of the sun itself!"

"I do not doubt it, Sir Michael. I only ask, out of my ignorance. These things do not come to me of my own wishing or decision. I seek guidance. I know nothing of astrology, less of necromancy and little of mathematics. But you, versed in them all, since you came, must have some methods by which to satisfy yourself, of investigating and deciding if there is any worth in them?"

"To be sure, I have. But think you that I can explain to the unlettered the studies of a lifetime into the occult sciences of ancient civilisations? You would comprehend nothing . . ."

"Sir — my husband is far from unlettered!" Bethoc intervened stoutly. "He is able to calculate and is conversant with other tongues. And he is a notable poet. He is composing a great poem on Sir Tristrem and Isolde."

"No doubt, lady. But that is little to the point. By his own confession he knows nothing of true divination, of the zodiacal geometry, of the importance of the animal kingdom, linked with the stars in their courses, by which the Creator guides the affairs of men and of angels. How can I begin to instruct him? When, at Toledo alone, I translated and amplified no fewer than eighteen great volumes of Aristotle's *History of Animals*? Such is the complexity of the matter. All that I can say is that all knowledge of the future, as of the past, is written in the heavens. There to be read by those few, those very few, who by laborious study and the taking of pains, seek out the truth. All is governed by strict laws, disciplines and mathematical precision. Past, present and future are one, to be interpreted by patient application and calculation. By such timeless authority I will in due course seek to test such of your unwitting predictions as may seem worth the labour. Better I cannot do, sir."

Thomas shook his head. "This is all far beyond me . . ."

"Of course it is. You will have to give me times, young man — hours, days and seasons. When these predictions came to you. So many as you can. This is vital . . ."

"I cannot do that, Sir Michael. I do not remember. Not clearly or exactly. I took no especial heed of times. I cannot recollect . . ."

"To be sure you can, man. Every thought and perception which enters the human mind, consciously or unconsciously, remains. It can be resurrected. By will and discipline. You must see to it. Or my whole journey is wasted. See you, the heavens are divided into twelve equal circles or houses. These remain immovable. But every heavenly body passes through each house, be it the House of Life, Riches, Brethren, Marriage or other, every twenty-four hours. The points of entry and exit, of passage and course, therefore, are of supreme import — and these can be calculated in minutes and even seconds."

Helplessly his hosts eyed each other.

"Tomorrow, Sir Thomas, you shall exercise your sluggard wits. Under my instruction. And we shall see." Scott rose. "Now, lady — my bed. I am weary . . ."

Long thereafter husband and wife sat up discussing, arguing, cudgelling their brains, before eventually seeking their own couch, in a kind of despair.

Yet, next day, it was astonishing how, under Sir Michael's guidance, insistence and commands, domineering as they were, Thomas was able to put dates and hours and sometimes even minutes to the genesis of not a few of his rhymes and visions, dredging up the required information which he did not realise that he possessed. He even brought to mind two or three items which he had quite forgotten, although nothing which appeared to him to be of any real significance.

Scott was interested in the actual physical conditions under which these predictions had been produced, and asked whether there was any place near-at-hand where such had evolved and where he might be taken, if possible at the same hour of day. Thomas could think of only one where these conditions might be met, which happened to be the one about the ring-tailed gled on the watershed. The thing had not come to him on any watershed but merely when he was riding quietly along Donside, one day, returning to Monymusk. So they rode thither that afternoon, where their visitor stared about him and took careful note of various aspects of the scene, and especially the position of the sun at the given hour, calculating where it would have been at the time of the year in question. Apparently the sun was of prime importance in these matters, being as it were master of the heavens, under the Creator, as recognised by the early sun-worshippers — on whose lore much of astrology seemed to be based. To Thomas it appeared pointless, a waste of time. But the Mathematician saw it otherwise.

"This of one king reigning over kingdoms three, sir?" the younger man enquired. "Do you see it as of any importance? Three kingdoms could mean anything — or nothing. Man is a kingdom, now ruled by Alexander. Dugald of Garmoran they say is dead — King of the North Isles. Some called Ewan of Argyll, his cousin, King of the South Isles. The rule over such kingdoms as these is scarcely worth foretelling? Indeed already is come about."

"There are kingdoms and kingdoms, Sir Thomas. What is important is to test and discover whether these predictions of yours are true, have any worth when measured against the proven standards of judicial astrology. If they have, then they will not be concerned with petty things, with kingdoms such as Man and the Isles. But, I would vouch, with great. Are there not three great kingdoms in these islands of Britain? Scotland, England and Ireland? *There* would be a consummation worth the foretelling!"

"Lord!" Thomas said. "Lord — Edward! After the Crusade. The crow! The jackal of the moor! Already the Plantagenets lay claim to Ireland . . ."

"It could be — but need not. To jump to immediate conclusions, young man, is major error, indeed a sin. The future is not foretold by ignorant and uninformed guessing! But by long and patient work and study."

Suitably chastened but uneasy in his mind, Thomas led the way home.

Sir Micheal Scott rode off southwards next morning, leaving a strangely disturbed pair behind him. Normally Bethoc's sound common-sense protected her from the doubts and forebodings which often afflicted her husband. But this visit left its mark on them both. Thomas, for his part, resolved to eschew predictions in future, if at all possible, and stick to simple poetry.

13

Thomas was not tested in any major way on his abstention from prediction in the months that followed, no urge presenting itself, no circumstance arising. It could be, he recognised, that his state of mind on the matter itself was partly responsible, his doubts and inhibitions, consequent on Scott's visit, having that effect. Nor did he receive any guidance or help, one way or the other, from the master, any word at all indeed. They had not expected any very speedy development, in the circumstances, since the Mathematician had told them that he intended to return to Brunswick and to start a new study of medicine which, he claimed confidently, with his mastery of the sciences of astrology, chemistry and anatomy, should make him more valuable than ever to the rest of mankind. No immediate communication, therefore, was to be looked for. But as month succeeded month and another year dawned and grew, the pair at Monymusk began to fear that the celebrated Michael had either forgotten his foray north of the Mounth or else had come to the conclusion that Thomas's curious attributes were in fact not worth further consideration, not gifts and talents to be cherished, as he had suggested, but fatuous, not to be confirmed by the stars in their courses and therefore of no value, if not actually bogus.

The reaction to this growing inference on the part of man and wife was strangely different. Thomas, the more he thought about it, came to recognise that he was the more relieved. He had never had any real pride nor satisfaction in his predictings, and to be a prophet — especially one fairly consistently prophesying woe — was an uncomfortable situation, conducive neither to personal satisfaction nor to popularity. Bethoc, on the other hand, saw Scott's failure to communicate as ill-mannered, a further proof of intellectual arrogance, if that was needed, a source of offence and indignation.

In time, of course, they largely forgot all about it.

The years 1269 and 1270 were satisfying ones for Thomas Learmonth on the whole, years of fruition as far as his present task was concerned. Land management was a slow process, most efforts taking a long time to prove and justify themselves and to bring folk their due harvest. But when they did begin to do so, the resultant burgeoning was gratifying indeed, basic and essential. To make two grains of corn grow where only one had grown before, is perhaps one of the greatest satisfactions known to man.

But the more the land under his care flourished, the busier he became in consequence, the heavier the demands on his time and energies. Perhaps he should not have involved himself so deeply in it all; that was scarcely what Alexander had sent him north to do. But it was not in that man's nature to set his hand to a task and not to put his heart into it as well. So his time was all too fully occupied for most months of the year — so much so that Bethoc complained, now and again, that she and their son were being neglected for what was, after all, no abiding concern of theirs. One day they would go back where they came from, where they really belonged, leaving all this behind. Would the King then thank him proportionately for all that he had achieved? Thomas had no certain answer to that — but was not seriously affected by the argument.

At least he was not greatly exercised over what they called affairs of state. The North was less disturbed than it had been for many a year — and Thomas could feel that he had played some small part in bringing that about. MacWilliam the Earl appeared to be both widening and tightening his grip and so far with fair acceptance and worth-while results. Le Chien spent his time almost wholly in the South now, become a great man in the realm. As for Alexander himself, when he did not require Thomas's services he tended to ignore him — which was probably always the way with rulers, almost inevitably. The kingdom seemed to be in the midst of a very welcome period of peace and prosperity, according to such informants as came to Monymusk; the harvests were excellent for the third year in succession — so obviously Thomas had been fortunate in the time in which he had started his land-improvement.

It was late summer, with the harvest in even in the Highlands, that the first word reached Monymusk which was destined to upset not only Thomas's busy routine and resolutions anent his odd endowments, but much of the North itself. It came by the usual means, mendicant friars bringing news that King Louis of France had died in North Africa, and that Edward Plantagenet — who had delayed his departure all this time — had promptly set off to take charge of the Crusade, with much flourish and gallant show. This in itself, although interesting, would not have greatly affected the Scots, especially those dwelling north of the Mounth. What did concern them was the accompanying report that the Crusaders in general were dying like flies, from some outlandish fever of those parts, and that one of the victims was none other than Alexander Comyn, Earl of Buchan and High Constable of Scotland.

These tidings made a great impact, for Buchan was not only the greatest figure in the North but one of the most powerful men in the kingdom, with vast lands and influence; and when such departed, the filling of the vacuum thereafter was apt to affect many. Although at Monymusk Thomas was not directly involved, he had an uneasy feeling that so basic an upheaval as this was bound to touch him sooner or later.

His fears were substantiated within the month. Reliable information reached him that the Lord Fergus Comyn had acted, and swiftly, not content with being Justiciar of Moray. He had descended upon Kineddar Castle, on the Deveron, the principal seat of the earldom, taken over the guardianship of his ten-year-old nephew, and proclaimed himself Earl of Buchan and acting High Constable. What the new Earl of Moray thought about this was not reported.

Thomas, perturbed, sent off a courier in haste to the King. Reaction from the South was more swift and positive than heretofore, with instructions. And the instructions were brought by no less a personage than the High Chamberlain himself, who arrived at Monymusk only nine days later — which implied much flogging of horseflesh. He declared that Thomas was to accompany him north to Kineddar forthwith, to inform Fergus Comyn that he was *not* Earl of Buchan, much less Constable, that he was to yield up his nephew, young John Comyn, to his other uncle — himself, Reginald le Chien — and to retire whence he had come, by royal command. His excellent brother, Alexander of Buchan, was not dead after all, only sick, and now on his way home to Scotland. It was all a false report, a mistake — and the greatest mistake on Fergus's part in having taken the law into his own hands thus. The King's displeasure was extreme.

Thomas was struck dumb for a few moments, even more so than the news might have warranted on the face of it. He moistened his lips.

"This is . . . a wonder!" he said, at length. "Uncanny. Not dead. Two nights ago I dreamed a dream. A sore dream. Of two brothers. The one went on a far journey — the elder. And while he was away, the other stole his inheritance, his all. Then, after a long time, he came back. His brother at home refused to acknowledge him, declared him to be no true man, only a ghost, the shade of his brother, an unquiet spirit. And drove him away. In my dream I, too, was unsure whether the elder was indeed alive or only a shade. So the younger drove his brother away. Until, one day, riding in woodland, the elder appeared again before him suddenly, in reproach. The horse stumbled at the unchancy apparition, then shied, and the rider was thrown. His head struck a tree and his neck broke. Dead. I saw it all."

"You say so! And these brothers were the Comyns?"

"The younger was Fergus, yes. The other I could not swear to. He was never clear to me, in feature, as I say. Even whether indeed he truly lived or was but ghost."

"Man — that could mean little enough, in the pass we are in. Sakes — I could have dreamed the like myself! Any could, who knew the circumstance."

"Ye-e-es. Yet the death was sorely clear. I saw the place

most surely. I saw the tree-trunk where his head hit. I heard the neck snap, even! I saw Fergus's shoulder-belt catch in the stirrup-leather, so that he was dragged off behind the bolting horse, his head bumping this way and that, loose, loose . . .!"

"M'mm. You are welcome to your dreams! Myself, I prefer to sleep in peace. But you can tell Fergus your dream when you see him, for sure!"

"I do not see why I should go. *You* can tell him about his brother, and the King's message, well enough without me."

"Not so. You must be there. Fergus and I do not love each other, you will mind. He might doubt my word, alone. The more so that I have to take into my keeping our nephew John. Until his father returns. He may consider I but covet his power. You he has no reason to doubt. Forby, it is Alexander's command."

So next day they rode northwards together. Le Chien chose to go by Inverugie, naturally enough, where they could spend the next night; it would take them no great distance out of their way. It was when, breasting the lip of the upper Ugie valley and passing the circle of standing-stones high above the Abbey of Deer, that Thomas felt a catching at his throat. His companion was pointing down to the Abbey and telling him how William Comyn, the father of John and Alexander and Fergus, who had gained the vast lordships of Badenoch and Lochaber by his first marriage, to the Celtic heiress thereof, and the earldom of Buchan by his second, had in gratitude endowed a new Cistercian monastery here, fifty years before, replacing the Columban cashel on the same site, when he was interrupted.

"This is it!" the younger man exclaimed, chokingly. "This is the place. That crag . . .!"

"What place, man? This is Aikey Brae. I know it well. I have hunted here often. Out of Deer Abbey."

"This is it, I tell you! Where he fell, died. Fergus. This is all as I saw it. The crag, the open woodland. Aye, and yonder great tree. That is it. Aikey Brae, you say . . .?"

Doubtfully le Chien eyed him and spurred on down the hill.

Thomas was no more warmly welcomed by the Lady

Mary le Chien at Inverugie than on his previous visit; but at least he was installed this time in a respectable guest-chamber in the main keep and not as a sort of semi-prisoner in an outlying angle-tower. For that matter, the lady showed no great joy at her husband's return, either. Evidently he did not take her to Court with him.

It was a further thirty miles west by north to Kineddar in the valley of the Deveron, a strange situation for the main castle of Buchan, since the Deveron itself was the boundary of Moray. No doubt it had been erected there partly as warning to the Moraymen, partly to dominate the important mid-Deveron ford of Dunlugas, partly as possible springboard for further Comyn conquests northwards. But its position would undoubtedly much have facilitated Fergus Comyn's present take-over, which might have been less easy if he had had most of Buchan to traverse to reach it.

The castle was impressively sited on top of a prominent bluff above the ravine of the Kineddar Burn which, twisting, defended it on three sides. The fourth side, the neck of this lofty peninsula, was cut with the usual deep ditch, spanned by a drawbridge. Highlanders were in evidence in large numbers, but there was no attempt to interfere with the newcomers, nor to prevent their approach. Presumably Comyn felt entirely secure.

That did not mean that he welcomed his visitors when they were brought to his presence — indeed he kept them waiting for a considerable time, although they saw him chatting to some chieftains as they were led into the lesser hall. When, at length he had them fetched before him, he was frigidly haughty.

"What brings you two to Kineddar?" he demanded, without preamble. "Little good, I swear!"

"Unkind, Fergus!" Sir Reginald reproached. "Last time we came to you, did you not become Justiciar of Moray as a result?"

"No thanks to you, le Chien, I'll be bound!"

"Tut, man — that is as ungrateful as it is uncivil. I . . ."

"Watch how you speak, sirrah! And refer to me as Lord Earl of Buchan."

"That I cannot do, Fergus, in all honesty. Since you are *not* Earl of Buchan."

"You were ever a fool, le Chien, as well as arrogant upstart. Why my father permitted that you wed our sister, God alone knows! He must have been inclining to his dotage! But — even a fool should be able to see plain facts. I hold Buchan in the cup of my hand."

"You may hold Kineddar, Fergus. But that is not Buchan. We have ridden all day through Buchan and not seen one of your caterans until now. But that is not why I say that you are not, cannot be, Earl of Buchan. It is because Alex, your brother, is not dead. And so is still Earl."

The other showed no least sign of surprise or shock. He merely stared at his brother-in-law blankly. "You lie," he said levelly.

"Not so. It is the truth. Sir Thomas, here, will confirm it."

The younger man hesitated. "Such is my information," he said carefully. After all, apart from his dream, he had only le Chien's word for it.

"You are less assured than your fellow-liar!" Comyn observed.

"No man calls me liar!" Thomas said tensely.

"Then speak truth. My brother is dead. His son is but a child. So I am Earl of Buchan. And in fact as in name."

"You are wrong, Fergus," Sir Reginald insisted. "The King had sure word. He it is that sent us. Alex is not dead. Sick, yes — but alive. And bettering. Sufficiently so to be coming home. He is on his way, from this Tunis. You have jumped too soon, good-brother. A deal too soon!"

"I think not. It is you who err."

It was not often that le Chien lost his curious temper and casual assurance. "You stubborn dizzard!" he exclaimed, voice raised. "Think you that I would come all this way to tell you what could be disproved in some short time? That I would claim Alex to be alive if he was not to be produced? He has had a fever — like so many another who took the Cross. For a while he was sorely sick and there were fears for him. But he won through and is sufficiently bettered to travel. That is the fact . . ."

"But not *all* the fact, le Chien." The other actually produced a thin smile. "You are so knowledgeable — name me the name of his fever?"

"God knows what it is called! Some outlandish distemper from those hot desert places . . ."

"Exactly, my friend — an outlandish distemper indeed. Notably so. It was leprosy!"

His hearers both drew gulping breaths, involuntarily, as they stared at Comyn. For the moment they had no words.

With a kind of grim triumph, Fergus nodded. "Leprosy, yes. My informant was better than yours, it seems. Unless you knew this, and hid it? One of Alex's own esquires came, by ship, to Kinnaird haven. Sent home because he had lost an arm in the fighting. He revealed that my brother was leper. Struck by the hand of God! That was the sickness. If my brother is not dead yet, he is as good as dead. Dead in the eyes of God, Holy Church and man. And I am Earl of Buchan!"

Appalled, the others heard him. If this was true, of the leprosy, then Fergus Comyn was not exaggerating. The dread disease was so loathed and feared by all the nations of Christendom that each had enacted the most stringent laws against the sufferers, the Romish Church agreeing vigorously — although not the Columbans, who took a more sympathetic view, St. Fillan himself, one of their most prominent missionaries, having been a leper. But for nine-tenths of Christendom, including the realms of Scotland and England, the leper was declared by law to be dead already — indeed a burial service was conducted over his person after midnight, as the Church's final gesture, before he was driven out from the company of whole men. Not only could the leper not associate with his fellow-creatures, nor live in any town or community, but he could possess no property, hold no office, his wife could remarry and his children were proclaimed orphans. God was held to have frowned upon all such, cast them from Him and turned all mercy away from them, for some presumably unforgivable sins — so man, in judgment and self-protection both, could do no other. Only the Celtic Church and the Brethren of the chivalric Order of St.

Lazarus of Jerusalem who devoted themselves to nursing and aiding the sufferers, thought otherwise. The fact that the leper was a great earl and High Constable of Scotland would be immaterial; even King Baldwin the Fourth of Jerusalem had paid the grim price.

For once le Chien was thrown completely off his stride. "We had . . . no word . . . of this," he muttered. "No word . . ."

Thomas spoke, and in contrast his voice was definite, sure — all but astonished as he was himself to hear it.

"The Earl Alexander is not leper," he said simply.

Le Chien looked at him, blinking.

"Liar — what do you know?" Comyn cried. "I tell you, he is. The esquire had no doubts, who had seen him. Why should you? You can know nothing."

"On the contrary, my lord — I *know*! Your brother is whole. I *saw* him. He is no leper."

"Saw him, man! Are you crazy mad?"

"No. I saw him. First in dream. But I saw him again. Moments ago. Clear as I see you. In this chamber. And he was no leper. A man whole, himself. Weakly but sound of person and wits. Either he is recovered of the affliction, or his esquire mistook . . ."

"Fool! Do you expect any to believe such vapourings? Such lies!"

"Heed you, Fergus — heed you!" le Chien put in, quickly now. "Sir Thomas Learmonth is a noted seer, in the South." He grinned. "True Thomas they name him. He has foretold many things. Be not so hasty in this, I counsel you." It was not to be supposed that the man believed what Thomas had seen; but he was clearly prepared to exploit the opportunity for doubt in this awkward situation.

"Faugh — lies and bairns'-talk! Lying Thomas, I say! He will require to lie more convincingly than that to change my brother's fate, and mine!"

"Aye, yours . . ." Thomas began, and swallowed. "My lord, you have thrice now called me liar. I do not lie. In especial as to what I see, what comes to me. In all truth, I believe that Earl Alexander is no leper. And will be proved not to be. I urge you to reconsider your position . . ."

"You may save your lying breath, sir!"

As Thomas shrugged, helplessly, le Chien changed stance somewhat.

"Leper or none, we have the King's commands for you, Fergus," he said. "Which you will disobey at your peril. You are to cease to call yourself Earl of Buchan. You are to retire from this Kineddar to your own place. And you are to hand over to my keeping the boy John Comyn, our nephew. Until his father's return. This by royal decree. I have it here, in this writing . . ."

"You but beat the air, le Chien. I tell you, I am and will remain Earl of Buchan. And I will remain my nephew's guardian and keeper — as is my right. You may tell King Alexander so. I swear he will think twice before sending an army here to seek change my mind! And there is none other who could do so — Gillespic MacWilliam will not try! Tell him that he does not know how useful an earl he has got in Fergus Comyn — a deal better than that of Moray. I can keep all the North secure for him."

"You are being very unwise, Fergus. Apart from earning the King's wrath, when your brother returns you must fall . . ."

"Not when he is seen as leper."

"But . . . if he is *not* leper, man . . .!"

"If he is not leper, then I will hand over his son to him and return to Lochindorb — that you may promise the King. No more. Now — I would see the backs of you both! You may eat down in my kitchen, you and yours. Then begone — for you will not pass a night under my roof. I have seen sufficient of you, God help me!" And Fergus Comyn turned and stalked from his lesser hall.

Downstairs amongst the servants of the kitchens in the lean-to courtyard buildings, where they were not too proud to eat before setting out for the hospice of St. Comgans at Turriff, which they had passed five miles to the south on their way up, le Chien grinningly commended Thomas on his quick thinking.

"This of the leprosy was a sore surprise," he conceded. "It

was a notable ruse to proclaim that you had seen the Earl, to make a vision of it. Even though Fergus could not believe it, he was not unaffected. You troubled him . . ."

"It was no ruse — it was the truth. I *saw* the Earl. Of a sudden, there before me. More clearly than I had seen him in the dream. Whole and himself. No leper. I knew that it was all false, a mistake or a lie. So I spoke."

The other shrugged. "As you will. This foreseeing has its uses . . .!"

When Sir Reginald went out to ready his escort — without which he never rode far — Thomas remained behind. He got out his belt-satchel containing quill, inkhorn and paper, with which *he* was seldom parted. He did not require actually to compose his writing, for the words seemed to come of their own accord.

> *Though Thomas the Liar thou callest me,*
> *The true tale I shall tell to thee.*
> *By Aikey-side thy horse shall stall,*
> *He shall stumble and thou shalt fall.*
> *Thy neck-bone on the tree shall break,*
> *The dogs of thy bones a meal shall make.*
> *Despite thy high house and thee,*
> *Thine own belt thy bier shall be.*

Finished, he took the paper over to the great open arched fireplace, and put it into the salt-recess beside the oven to dry for a moment. Assured that the ink would not smear, he read it over, hesitated, and then folded the paper and took it to the chief cook.

"Give that to your master, the Lord Fergus," he said, and went out into the courtyard to join le Chien and the others for their ride southwards.

14

How many letters Thomas had written to the King during those years at Monymusk he had lost count, and got precious few back — and those from the secretary, the chaplain Reginald. But in the late spring of the next year, 1271, he did receive a letter in Alexander's own hand-of-write, and a notable communication in more than that. Notably delivered also, for it came by the hands of no less than the High Constable and the High Chamberlain of the realm, riding in suitable style. Thomas did not open the heavily sealed missive until the illustrious visitors had gone on northwards, and they did not linger long at Monymusk.

Alexander, Earl of Buchan looked frail, gaunt and bent, as though he had aged at least a score of years since Thomas had last seen him in the flesh, instead of seven. But he was no leper, that was clear, nor had been, for there were none of the tell-tale marks, the white patches of the skin, the malformation of the fingers, the absence of eyebrow-hair, which even the few who recovered never could hide. He had, apparently, reached Scotland, by ship, in November, and after wintering in his Lothian house of Winton, gained by marriage with his de Quincy wife, he now felt strong enough to make the journey north to his own seat of Kineddar and to come to a reckoning with his brother Fergus, le Chien almost gleefully accompanying him. Thomas was able to inform them that reports from Moray said that Fergus had fairly recently discreetly returned to Lochindorb, leaving the boy John and his mother little the worse at Kineddar. He did not add that there was no word of Fergus having broken his neck or otherwise come to grief, at Aikey Brae or elsewhere — although, to be sure, time-limits tended to remain unspecified in all predictions.

When he had privacy to peruse the royal letter, Thomas was much exercised. It read:

Thomas,

I greet you heartily. You and your long suffering lady may now return to your own place. And when summoned come to my Court. I have received a letter from Sir Michael Scott in Brunswick. Amongst other matters of greater worth on which I sought his aid, he tells me that he has made sure enquiry and calculations as to yourself and your soothsaying. He has come to the conclusion that you are honest although ignorant, and the stars foretell your continued usefulness to my realm. He says that if you would but devote yourself to the study of astrology and other useful and excellent sciences, instead of wasting your time on poetry and the like, you might still better serve your liege-lord and mankind. He adds that he has divined that, as well as to myself, you have it in you to be of some worth to the noble houses of Cospatrick and Comyn. This, I vow, does not seem to me great divining. But I bethought me to show his letter to Patrick your good-sire. He was prepared to swallow his wrath, nurtured sufficiently long. If Michael's advisings hold any truth, Patrick would not wish his house to suffer. Forby he sorely longs for a sight of his eldest daughter. As does his Countess Christian. So you may return, Thomas. I shall send up a clerk to continue your work at Monymusk. Then come.

I wish you well.

ALEXANDER R.

He hurried with the letter to Bethoc.

"Oh, Thomas!" she exclaimed, reading. "Is it not wonderful? At last! We may go back. My dear mother! To see her again. And the others. After all these years . . ."

"You are happy, my dear?"

"Yes! Yes! I have longed for this."

"You have not said so."

"Perhaps not. What was there to say? We made our choice. Nor ever regretted it. But — never to see them! Cut off from all we knew . . ."

"And our life here? What we have made of it. All we have built up. To leave it all. Six years of our lives."

"Six years, yes. Six good years, my love. We have been

275

happy here. But — this is not our place. Not where we belong. This is a different land, different people. One day we would have to go back. You know it. Better soon, whilst we are yet young. And our son, little Thomas William. It is time that he learned from whence he came. They have never seen him."

"You have kept all this to yourself, Beth. Why?"

"Nothing was to be gained by talking of it. You were well enough content. Busy. Talk would have changed nothing. But now — what of yourself, Thomas? You are not displeasured?"

"No-o-o. It is for the best, no doubt. Yet — we have made a place here. Achieved something. To leave it all, unfinished — for what? We do not know what may be our lot in the South, hereafter. I cannot be your father's esquire again, even if he would have me."

"The King will see that you do not lack employment."

"Perhaps — perhaps not. And would we wish to live the life of the Court?"

"His letter says that you are to go. You cannot stay here, as his steward, if he recalls you."

"No . . ."

In the event it was months before there was any change, autumn before a middle-aged Cistercian friar named Simon came north to be the new steward. He proved to be a Comyn of sorts, almost certainly illegitimate, and apparently lacking all knowledge of land-management and husbandry. Thomas suspected that he was, in fact, a nominee of le Chien's, installed here to cause the least possible interference with that man's interests in Fyvie and elsewhere in Mar and Buchan. He was civil enough, however, and seemed ready to learn; and in the interests of the barony and its tenants, Thomas set about the education of Brother Simon, conducting and introducing him over much of the two earldoms in the process — and making his own farewells as they went. As a consequence, it was early November, with the first snows beginning to whiten the hilltops, before the Learmonths finally said goodbye to Monymusk and with mixed feelings commenced their journey southwards across the Mounth.

The Priory monks, it transpired, were actually sorry to see them go, Tom William in especial, now four and a favourite with all.

Although late in the season for relatively comfortable travel, they were fortunate in the weather, and moving by necessarily easy stages — for not only had they the child to consider, usually riding pillion behind his father, but they were lumbered with three pack-horse garrons loaded with possessions which they had accumulated, these led by the man Donald, who would return with them to Monymusk in due course. Covering some twenty miles each day, they took a week to reach Dunfermline, for the Forth crossing by Queen Margaret's Ferry. At the palace there they learned that King and Court were at Roxburgh in Teviotdale, another sixty miles to the south. Ercildoune was two-thirds of the way there.

It felt strange, two days later, to be riding down their own Lauderdale again, after the years of absence, the familiar scenes affecting them both, the child now tired of travel and uninterested. But the thought of their reception at Ercildoune grew dominant and silences lengthened.

At the castle, however, they discovered that the family was not at home, indeed seldom now stayed at Ercildoune apparently, living more or less permanently at Dunbar for some reason, only the house-steward left in charge — who greeted them warily. They were in some doubt as to whether to go on down Lauderdale to Tweed and Roxburgh, in case the Earl and Countess were there with the King, the steward not knowing; but they decided to try Dunbar first. Bethoc had a feeling that even if her father was with the Court, her mother was less likely to be so; and she would much prefer to see her mother before she had to face her formidable sire, if that was possible.

So they spent the night in the castle, with Thomas feeling somehow guilty to be sharing Bethoc's old bedchamber with her, even though it looked as though it had never been in use since she had left it. The great house seemed altogether different, however, empty and echoing. They were glad to leave it, next morning, to head north-eastwards for the thirty-five mile traverse through Lammermuir.

Even Dunbar, as they rode down the grassy slopes of the Doon Hill, looked different. They were apt to remember it, of course, as the summer-time home, a place of glowing red stone set on the edge of the blue plain of the sea, flanked by golden sands and backed by leafy woodlands. But in November it was not like that, the sea leaden veined with white, the trees bare, sands less than golden. The castle perched so oddly on its linked rock-stacks, was intermittently almost hidden in clouds of spray from great surging breakers. But the Earl's flag flew from its topmost tower. The travellers did not know whether to be relieved or otherwise.

Trotting down through the township, they were struck by their odd reception. At first glance the folk looked at them interestedly enough; then, as recognition dawned, the people tended to turn away quickly, to hurry off, to clap hand to mouth, some even to cross themselves. Children were hustled away, doors shut.

"We are scarcely welcome, it seems," Thomas commented.

Crossing the castle drawbridge through a salt curtain of spume, they rode in beneath the gatehouse pend under the watchful eyes of the guard, into the oddly-shaped courtyard, its area circumscribed by the cliff-top site, its floor naked rock. They were aware of eyes scrutinising them from window and wallhead, but no servitors nor grooms hastened to take their beasts' heads nor assist them to dismount.

Thomas lifted down the child and then went to help Bethoc. She was nibbling her lip tensely. He frowned and swung on the nearest guard, pointing peremptorily.

"Fools!" he cried. "Take these horses. Aid the Lady Bethoc. Send to inform my lord Earl that his daughter is here. Do not stand staring, dolts!"

"Let them stare! As I do!" a deep voice spoke, at their backs. They looked round, to find the Earl Patrick standing at a corner of the main keep. "So rare a sight!"

"Father . . .!" Bethoc exclaimed, and began to hurry forward, then restrained herself and halted. Young Tom William ran to her side and she took his hand.

It was more than just doubt at her reception which gave

Bethoc pause. It was the change in the appearance of the man before her. He had become almost old. Admittedly he would be in his sixtieth year, but it seemed scarcely possible that seven years could have made so great an alteration. He stooped where he had been straight, his face was lined, his hair grey and scanty. But still he had an imperious if distinctly fleering eye, and his voice certainly did not quaver.

"My lord," Thomas said, bowing. "It has been . . . long."

The Earl ignored him. His gaze was divided between his daughter and the child at her side. He moistened his lips and pointed.

"This . . . this is . . .?"

"Your grandson, Father. Thomas William," she got out in a choking voice. "He is . . . a fine boy."

They looked at each other, at a loss for words.

Thomas sought to fill the gap. "Now four years, my lord. He is like Johnnie, we think. We, we greet you. We hope that we find you well. The King's Grace sent for us. To come south. It has been long . . ." Thomas knew that he was all but gabbling.

He was stopped. "Quiet man! Speak when you are spoken to!" That was harsh. "Your turn will come." The Earl turned back to his daughter. "So — you dare come home, girl? You and your . . . brat! You bethink you of your father. Aye, and your mother. After seven years, you come to my door!"

"We came only because the King commanded us," Bethoc returned, bridling up. She and the child moved over to Thomas's side. "We came, in duty and, and affection. But we will go again, if it is to be the way. If you have no kindness for us . . ."

There was an interruption. The Countess Christian appeared in the keep doorway and came hastening out. Ignoring her husband, arms wide, she ran to her eldest child.

"Beth! Beth!" she cried. broken-voiced. "Oh Beth, my dear! God be praised — at last! At last!"

Mother and daughter fell into each other's arms.

"A plague, woman!" Earl Patrick protested. "What way is this to behave? Have done! This will serve nothing."

The women paid no heed, hugging each other and exclaiming incoherently.

The Earl turned on Thomas. "You! You . . . viper! You come here, after all that you have done? Stealing my daughter, dishonouring my house, making my name a thing for scorn, deceiving all . . .!"

"No, my lord — not that. None of that. We loved each other, could see no other way out of the tangle. Since Bethoc was not going to wed Duff MacDuff at any price, we had to go . . ."

"You broke faith with me, man. I trusted you, cherished you. Gave you a home. Trusted you with my children. And this is how you reward me!"

"I was torn, sir — torn between my duty to you and my devotion to your daughter. I had to choose — and chose Bethoc. You blame me? I blamed myself. But would, I swear, choose to do the same again. We have been happy, very happy — save for this sorrow between us." He gestured with his hands. "But it is seven long years, my lord. We had hoped that, in such time, you could have let it pass, put it some way behind you . . ."

The Countess halted him. She turned to him, and now she had the child in her arms, Bethoc smiling through tears behind.

"Thomas — here is a joy, at least!" she asserted. "A delight. Our first grandchild. He is an angel, this one!" She kissed the boy on one cheek, then the other. "Bless you, my dear! Patrick — see here. *Your* grandson, as well as mine!"

Unlike her husband, the Lady Christian had changed little in appearance, a little more plump perhaps, hair slightly more grey, but that was all. She looked as though she was going to come and kiss Thomas also, but apparently thought better of it, in the circumstances, contenting herself with smiles.

"My lady — I thank you! I much esteem . . . am greatly beholden . . ." Thomas shook his head. "It is good to see you, Countess . . ."

Thomas William wriggled his way to the ground, old enough to object to being cuddled in arms by strangers, like any baby. He edged away and over a little doubtfully to the fourth member of the party and stood, short legs wide, to stare up at the Earl.

"Beth looks well and bonny," her mother declared. "Does she not, Patrick? Marriage and motherhood does her no disservice, I think. And Thomas — you seem none so ill. Even handsome, after your fashion!" She was trying very hard, obviously.

The Earl growled something less than confirmatory.

Bethoc did her bit. "It is so good. So good to see you. To see you both again. We have been counting the days. The King said that we must come. I think that he must seek Thomas's services. In some other matter. We went to Ercildoune . . ." It was her turn to gabble.

"Yes, my dear," her mother nodded. "But — why stand out here, in this cold, salty wind? I do not know where the others are. Pate is wed, and at Whittinghame. Gelis is visiting her cousin, my brother's son, Robert Bruce, new back from the Crusade. He has married Marjory of Carrick. The others . . ."

They turned to go indoors, women leading. Thomas hung back, wary eye on his father-in-law. That man, muttering, followed on; and the small boy went approximately with him. But, considering the rather menacing-looking doorway, with its twin doors, one iron-grilled, the other nail-studded, the defensive arrow-slit-windows and the armed and helmeted sentry who had emerged from the porter's lodge to stand guard there, Tom William faltered a little and then reached up to hold the Earl's hand. He was used to elderly men, of course, most of his monkish friends at Monymusk having been of that age. If Patrick was surprised, at least he did not reject the small fist, and the pair went up and past the fierce-looking guard hand-in-hand. Thomas limped behind, marvelling.

From the vaulted basement vestibule-chamber of the main keep, they took a curious stone corridor, which was in fact a bridge over the swirling tide, to another all but free-standing tower built on a further rock-stack; and beyond this, over water again, to a third, which rose from a somewhat wider-topped bluff, with sufficient level area around the masonry to provide a narrow and unevenly-shaped grassy terrace garden on three sides, a place of delight on a summer's day. In this tower was the favourite private living-room of the household, not too large, commanding fine vistas yet snug in winter, with two fireplaces, rich hangings and shutters to seal off whichever window-embrasures took the prevailing wind and spray.

Here a girl, almost a young woman, sat stitching at a colourful tapestry. It took moments for the newcomers to realise that this was Eala, only nine when they had last seen her, now sixteen and scarcely to be recognised. She was slender instead of plump, tall, graceful, sweet-looking rather than beautiful. Although recognition was delayed on their part, there was none such on hers. She gasped out Bethoc's name, and dropping her needlework, rushed to embrace her sister.

The Earl Patrick and Tom William had had enough of all this feminine hugging and emotion. The boy saw the foot of a narrow winding turnpike stair in a corner, the door of which stood slightly ajar. Intrigued, especially as a tabby cat was peering round it, alarmed by the influx, he pointed to it. He was still clutching his grandfather's hand; and, shrugging, that man allowed himself to be pulled to the stairway and up, after the bolting cat.

Freed of the Earl's presence, the three women were able to indulge in a flood of excited chatter and exclamation, of breathless question and half-formed answer, of laughter and clutchings. Thomas, standing well back, found it good to watch; what his Bethoc had been starved of for so long.

When at length the master of the house returned, he brought with him his two younger sons, as well as his grandson and the cat. Johnnie was now eighteen, a cheerful, laughing young man, with a strong resemblance to his nephew. Alex was nearly fifteen, beginning to grow to arms and legs and angles. They were a deal less demonstrative than were their sisters, but seemed glad to see the prodigals, even though somewhat embarrassed by all the fuss. Their father disappeared again, talking about food.

When Bethoc and Thomas got to bed that night, they agreed that the homecoming, after a bad start, had been as good as they could reasonably have hoped for. The Earl's attitude was still restrained, to say the least; but Bethoc thought that her mother would work on him to good effect — she usually could do so, without seeming to. And he was clearly much taken with his grandson, who had largely saved the day, an enormous blessing in small bulk. The Countess was wholly in their favour — perhaps had been, to some extent, all along. And the others presented no difficulty. Eala was a dear, and her brothers seemed to bear no grudge. Pate and Gelis, of course, being older, might see things differently; but there was no reason to look for trouble there. It seemed as though the long chapter might end favourably enough.

Next forenoon, however, Johnnie came to inform Thomas that the Earl wanted to see him in his own room, and alone. Less than confidently, he obeyed the summons.

His father-in-law, standing before a fire, eyed him levelly. "It is time that we understood each other, Thomas," he said. "You have injured me and mine deeply — and I have heard scant regrets on your part. Were I to reward you according to your deserts, I would take my daughter and her child and confine you in the deepest pit of my sorriest castle!" That this was no empty flourish Thomas knew well. In every one of his many baronies the Earl held, amongst other privileges, the right of pit and gallows — that is, full baronial authority to imprison or to hang without reference to any higher courts. The King might protest, in the case of one of his own knights, but every baron in the land would vigorously uphold the Earl's rights.

"You could, yes. And earn your daughter's and grandson's undying hatred and contempt, my lord! And your liege-lord's displeasure. Since he it was who commanded our return. When I could have remained safe enough and content enough beyond the Mounth."

"Safe! Man, do you think that I could not have plucked you out of that Monymusk any day in these past years, had I so chosen? Are you so innocent as to believe that I did not know of your going there? I knew within months. Earl William of Mar is my distant kin, I'd remind you. He sent me word."

Thomas swallowed and said nothing.

"I need not even have come for you. Mar offered to have you out of that monastery and delivered to me whenever I wished. Think you that you could dwell in Mar and the Earl of Mar not know of it — King's steward in especial?"

"Perhaps I was foolish, my lord. I did not know. That *you* knew. But — you *did not* come or send for me. All these years. Why? I think that either you are less hard than you would make out. Or feared the King's displeasure. Since clearly it could be only the King who sent me to Monymusk."

"I *feared* nothing, man. I but held my hand. For Beth's sake."

"Then for that I thank you, sir. And hope that your love for your daughter will not die now that she is near you again."

"That you, you may hide behind her skirts?"

"It seems that I have been doing that for six years, my lord! Unknowing. Or else was hiding in the King's shadow."

"You make too much of the King's favour, Thomas. Kings are kittle cattle to rely upon, I'd warn you. What are your hopes from Alexander?" That last was asked in a totally different tone.

"I do not know. Only that he said that we were to come south. And that you, my lord, were likely to look less hardly on us."

"Humph!" was the older man's comment. But he went on, after a moment's pause. "Is it to be more stewarding, think you?"

"I know not. I suppose that it could be, since now I have learned the way of it."

"Aye, Mar tells me that you did none so ill up there. Made the royal lands yield two-fold and more."

"I am flattered that my lord of Mar took so much interest in my poor doings . . .!"

"Tush, man — do not sound so fine. You cost Mar siller!

Which will make any man take heed. As you did Durward and le Chien and others we could name. No doubt they were all milking the royal lands and purse! And you stopped it. I wonder that you survived those years! Mar is sick, to be sure, Durward old, dying they say. But le Chien — he is an ill man to cross, they say?"

Thomas pursed his lips and kept silent.

His father-in-law stroked his grey pointed beard. "You are an ingrate, Thomas, and presumptuous. But I do not think that you are a fool. You will see that there is little profit for you in working for the King, as steward of this barony or that. What have you gained from this of Monymusk? Save a hiding place. Now — if you worked for *me*, it would be different, would it not?"

"*You* . . .? You mean, as land-steward? Myself?"

"Just that. I have thought on this, at some length. Mind you, not for *your* sake! But for Beth and the child. You have to keep my daughter, to her fair comfort, somehow — and you will not live idle on my charity, I promise you! But I am no longer young. I have much more to do with my time than stewarding lands. I have stewards in each barony, to be sure — but they are all small men and none above other. There is no steward for all the earldom, two earldoms. I had hoped that Pate would take it in hand. But he is become far too high a man since wedding Buchan's daughter. He sees himself as destined for great things, does Pate, not seeing to rents and multures and farms and the like. We dwell here at Dunbar now, and the March earldom in especial is little cared for, Ercildoune standing empty. I want you to go there, Thomas, and steward it from there. See to all the two earldoms' lands, as chief steward. Do this — and I will seek to forget your past fault."

Thomas had been drawing a long breath as it began to dawn on him what the Earl was proposing, a breath which all but caught in his throat as the other finished. He could, in fact, scarcely believe his ears. Here he was being offered what was perhaps of all things what he could have wished for himself and Bethoc, something really far beyond their hopes — and all in the name of a penance and retribution. Chief steward of the earldoms of Dunbar and March would be a position of much authority and opportunity, as well as security. And at Ercildoune, his own home. He could find no words.

"Well, man? Will you do it? Alexander's service will advantage you no better, I swear."

The younger man swallowed. "Yes, my lord — I thank you. Yes, I will do it. I, I ask nothing better. Save your goodwill . . ."

"My goodwill you will have to work for, Sir Thomas Learmonth!" The other frowned. "But, see you — there is more goodwill than mine, to consider, in this. The folk — you will have to watch your step with them. At your stewarding and all else. They will look askance at you, mind, flinch from you at first, maybe."

"You mean . . .?"

"I mean that the simple folk believe you to have gone off to Elfland, man! With its queen, God help us! Foolishness but real enough to them. You were seen riding off Eildon with a fair woman in green. It was Bethoc but it seems that these woodmen did not know her. Yet knew you. Then you disappeared from mortal ken. For long, none able to find you. The tale spread and grew. Now you are back, after seven years. And seven is an unchancy number — the seven deadly sins, the seven dolours of the Virgin, the seven sleepers, the seven wise masters of the other world! I misdoubt if all men will welcome you!"

"But — this is the folly of ignorance! Madness. I heard something of it from, from . . . but could scarce credit it. You do not say that men truly believe this nonsense? It is but a tale, the start of my *Sir Tristrem*."

"Why not? You have the name for strange doings. Your rhymes and foretellings have seen to that. Folk believe in these things, elves, fairies, the small people, spells and the like. You have only yourself to blame."

"And you, my lord, did not deny these tales?"

"Would I have been believed had I done so? But, see you — there could be some good in this. If wisely used. Men may mislike the look of you, keep their distance. But they will think twice before crossing you! None will wish the evil eye put upon them or the powers of the little folk used against them! So your work should be the less difficult, the earldoms' interests aided. So long as you do not seem to behave to their hurt!"

"That I should not do, sir — even in the interests of your earldoms!"

"No. To be sure. But — I will expect my interests to be well cared for, Thomas. Now — be off. Enough of all this talk . . ."

Despite his lame leg, Thomas all but skipped down the turnpike stair, to go tell Bethoc.

Part Three

15

The small fortalice of Ercildoune stood in the level haugh of
the river fully half-a-mile west of the Earl's great castle, a
single square tower of modest dimensions within a stockaded
enclosure or pale, such as some called a pele- or peel-tower. It
was a fairly humble dwelling, consisting of a vaulted basement chamber containing the kitchen, a hall or living-room
on the floor above, no larger than twenty feet by fifteen, and
a bedchamber on each of the two upper floors, plus a garret
within the gabled roof which was surrounded by its narrow
parapet wall-walk, all reached by a narrow winding turnpike-
stair in an angle of the thick walling. Within the pale — the
space too restricted to be called a courtyard — were lean-to
erections of timber plastered with clay, containing the stable,
byre and storehouses, with a deep draw-well. The place had
its defensive features, arrow-slits in the walls — and which
also served to give light to the stair — a machicolation at
parapet-level above the basement doorway from which hot
water or other unpleasantness could be dropped down on the
heads of unwelcome visitors, and the stone-vaulted ground-
floor itself which would prevent the tower from being set on
fire even if intruders got so far and inside; the narrow,
twisting stair, of course constituting a major hazard for any
attackers seeking to go higher, easily defendable. For outer
defences there was only the moat, formed out of a channel
from the Ercildoune Burn's confluence with the River Leader,
so that the tower rose on what amounted to a tiny island in
the waterside meadows. Owing to the danger of floods,
the small pleasance, herb-garden and orchard, grievously
neglected over these last score of years, had had to be
established on slightly higher ground about one hundred

yards to the east, with its own little drawbridge across the moat. This was the inheritance, with only a modest acreage of land, which Thomas had heired from his far from well-doing father, a younger son of Learmonth of Balcomie in the East Neuk of Fife, who had married its heiress — if that term could be used for so unimportant a lairdship. It made a very humble home to which to bring his earl's daughter — although he did point out that it had been there in fact before the Cospatricks ever built their large castle and so was the original Ercildoune.

Not that Bethoc found any fault. Indeed she had been entirely in agreement that they would presently come here from the said castle, to set up house.

Pate had been the trouble. They had seen nothing of that young man for some time after their return, for he spent his time either at Court or in the company of the Comyns, into which great family he had married. Then one day he turned up at Ercildoune Castle, unannounced, with a party of young bloods, to hunt — and from the start made it clear that he at least was no welcomer of prodigals. He was stiff and unforthcoming with his sister and deliberately rude and overbearing towards Thomas. He had grown into a darkly handsome man, in a flashy way, with fierce down-turning moustaches and a black beard, the competitive spirit of his boyhood developed into a sort of ruthless, arrogant driving-force. He made it clear that he considered Thomas to be a low-born scoundrel who had humiliated them all by taking advantage of his sister — and incidentally made a fool of himself by arranging that false rendezvous on the Eildon Hills so long ago, when they had decamped. He declared that he did not approve of his father's weak acceptance of the return of the offender, and particularly of his appointment as chief steward of the earldoms. Moreover he much resented the pair of them lording and ladying it in Ercildoune Castle. Since his father was now domiciled at Dunbar, Ercildoune, the seat of the March earldom, should be his, as heir, not the little tower of Whittinghame in Lothian which he had inherited from his recently-dead grandmother. To find his wretched and despised brother-in-law in charge of his old home was not to be borne — and he would assure the Earl of it without delay. Meanwhile he treated Thomas like any servant, to attend to the needs of himself and his guests.

Fortunately he did not stay long. But before he had gone, the Learmonths had decided that they must move down to Thomas's own tower just as soon as it could be made reasonably habitable after its years in the hands of cottar caretakers.

In fact, they came to enjoy living in that little fortalice by the riverside, after the first uncomfortable weeks, developing quite an affection for its modest but easily run and convenient accommodation. It was much more snug in winter than the large and empty, echoing castle, and in summer conditions the Leader-haugh was a joy, with the sparkling, murmuring water, mallard quacking and flighting all around, the darting sandmartins nesting in the river-bank burrows, and salmon and trout to be fished for almost from the tower-windows. Young Tom William loved it.

As time passed it began to seem as though Pate was not the only one who was less than pleased with the returned couple. The King made no move, sent no messages, issued no summons to appear at Court. More than once the royal cavalcade passed up or down Lauderdale to or from Roxburgh, and did not pause at Ercildoune. It was certainly not for Thomas to thrust himself unbidden upon his liege-lord. He did send a letter to the secretary, Reginald, informing of his present state and conveying his leal service and duty. But it produced no reply. He had always felt that the chaplain disliked him, of course, and it was possible that he had not passed on the message to the King. And, to be sure, Pate was apt to be about Court and could well have Alexander's ear — which might not help. But it was a sadness for Thomas Learmonth, who had a gratitude and fondness towards his monarch as well as due respect and loyalty.

At least Gelis proved to be happy that they were back. She arrived to see them, in Johnnie's company, soon after they settled in, and thereafter was a fairly constant visitor. She had grown into a laughing, hearty, uninhibited young woman, opinionated and apt to nudge people in the ribs with her elbow to emphasise such opinions — which tended to be catholic and vehement — good company for an hour or two but somewhat wearing for longer. She was sonsy rather than good-looking, with a large bosom which she used at times to reinforce her elbow for added accentuation. She held no grudge against Thomas, indeed seemed rather to admire their elopement and initiative, only reproachful that they had not taken her into their confidence in the first instance. It seemed remarkable that so lusty a young woman — for she was now twenty-three — had remained unmarried; but perhaps it was that no really suitable suitor of her own standing had so far been prepared to take on what almost inevitably would prove to be a handful.

Gelis, surprisingly, was the indirect agent productive of the next of Thomas's prophecies. He had been deliberately shunning all such manifestations, seeking to put away from his mind any visions and urges, as occasioning mainly discomforts, gloom and resentments. But this one was compulsive and sounded a different note from usual. As her mother had mentioned, Gelis had been visiting the Countess of Carrick at her castle of Turnberry on the Ayrshire coast, at the time of the return to Dunbar; and when she came back she was full of the strange and romantic story. Her mother's nephew, Sir Robert Bruce, he who had been knighted on the same day as Thomas, son and heir of the Lord of Annandale, had been one of those who had gone off on the Crusade which had caused so much trouble — as indeed had the Countess Marjory's husband, Lord Adam MacDuff of Kilconquhar, a brother of the late Earl of Fife and uncle of Colban and Duff. In his wife's right MacDuff had called himself Earl of Carrick. Like so many another he had fallen victim to fever — no suggestion of leprosy in this case, but unfortunately fatal nevertheless. Robert Bruce, his friend, had sickened also, but recovered; and having had quite enough of crusading, had returned home. He had felt it to be his duty to come and give the bereaved Marjory an account of her husband's death, for which the widow was duly grateful. So grateful indeed that in the course of only two or three days, she whisked the less than dominant Robert off before a priest and married him. She was, to be sure, a headstrong, impulsive and sensual woman, as Thomas had perceived before the Battle of Largs when she had played hostess to the King. At any rate, she had found Bruce to her taste apparently, whatever his reactions. But she had not made him Earl of Carrick in her right, although she had only two daughters by her previous husband. Or, at least, if she had had any intention of doing so, the King had stepped in, when he heard, and stopped it, much incensed; for of course, apart from any injury to his pride, relative to his own dallyings with the lady, no marriages which affected earldoms should be contracted without express royal permission. So when Gelis had gone to visit her cousin at Turnberry, to hear about his various adventures, she had found him just a little doubtful as to his bargain, but the Countess Marjory in fine fettle, claiming already to be pregnant but not allowing this to interfere with her comprehensive enjoyment of life.

It was after hearing this account that Thomas found himself compelled to pen a rhyme, strange indeed. He saw the child in that woman's arms, saw the features develop before his eyes, clear, vivid and no child's features. Reading what he had dashed off, he tore it up, frowning. But the thing kept coming back to him, refusing to be banished. Yet, though it did not seem to make sense, any more than others which he had written, however significant, something assured him that this one was important. The child he saw was always the same, certain, clearly defined, and above its head a bloody crown. Eventually he set it down again, in what he decided was its final form, and then put the paper away in the kist in which he kept his *Sir Tristrem* papers, only Bethoc having seen it, and as mystified as he. The rhyme went thus:

> *Of Bruce's side a son shall come,*
> *   From Carrick's bower to Scotland's throne:*
> *The Red Lion beareth he.*
> *   The foe shall tread the Lion down*
> *A score of years but three:*
> *   Till red of English blood shall run*
> *Burn of Bannock to the sea.*

As to his stewarding, Thomas was well content. After the handicaps of neglected and unproductive land, opposition and suspicion and lack of authority, with which he had had to contend beyond the Mounth, dealing with the rich soils and pastures of Lothian and the Merse, the finest in all Scotland, and tilled heedfully for generations, was comparatively straightforward and satisfying. It had its problems and challenges admittedly; but these were mainly concerned with personalities and human nature rather than productivity and improvement — and always he had the Earl's potent presence behind him, near-at-hand and concerned, not a vague, distant and unlikely threat like a king whom none had ever seen. He found that his father-in-law had been right about the effects of his peculiar reputation. Very evidently he had become an object of disquiet and some awe, almost of alarm if not fear. Women and children generally made themselves scarce at his appearance and men were apt to stand their ground only warily. Yet there was an element of respect in the attitude of most, certainly no consequent opposition to his policies and authority. For his part, he was careful to show himself to be reasonable, moderate, friendly, and so far as he was able, normal. Gradually the suspicion and reserve lessened although it never disappeared entirely. Thomas grew used to being treated as someone apart — as he put it, like a tamed wild animal, not actually dangerous unless roused. He would have been more than human had he not rather relished the advantages of this as well as the drawbacks and sense of isolation.

Although grudging about admitting it, the Earl Patrick had reason to be pleased with the outcome of his appointment. As ever, it was a slow process, but Thomas obtained results and revenues grew. Even in these fertile and rich lowlands there was scope for much improvement, drainage in especial, scrub-clearance and the utilisation of waste ground. Manuring and liming had long been extensively practised, but he was able to introduce the idea of spreading seaweed and wrack on the riggs, as was done in Buchan, especially near the Lothian and Berwick coasts, even sand and crushed shell from the beaches. Upland Lammermuir offered scope for considerable further development, as some of the best sheep-country in the land. The earldom itself had never run sheep there, leaving such to tenants, particularly the church-men, but retaining vast areas as empty hunting chase. Thomas persuaded his father-in-law to invest in large num-bers of sheep, divided into hirsels, in a comparatively short time trebling the productivity of that territory and bringing new life and population to the green upland valleys and cleuchs. Unfortunately this had the effect of widening the rift with Pate who, from his house at Whittinghame in the Lammermuir foothills, looked upon the entire range as his own hunting preserve.

Active and fulfilled in large degree, then, Thomas and Bethoc too had few serious complaints with their life — although they both could have wished for the second child which continued to be denied them. At least the brain-child *Sir Tristrem* was now finished, all its hundreds of fyttes — if only partly to the author's satisfaction; and there followed, of course, the distinctly wearisome and enormous task of copy-ing out the epic in its entirety in legible script, not once but many times, in order that folk might have the privilege of being enthralled thereby. This was a task for winter evenings innumerable, at which Bethoc co-operated. She was indeed much better at it and quicker than was Thomas, who all the time found himself seeking to rephrase and improve.

If those were years of well-being and fulfilment for the Learmonths, they were no less so for the realm of Scotland itself. For once peace reigned within and without her borders. A series of good summers and moderate winters ensured good crops and stock reproduction, with plenty in the land. Alexander ruled well, on the whole, dispensing justice and keeping his nobles in order, shrewd at choosing able officers of state. Gamelin, Bishop of St. Andrews and Primate, died, after prolonged bed-lying, and the King appointed his clever but unscrupulous Chancellor, William Wishart, in his place — and, with a new Pope, Gregory the Tenth, got him confirmed by Rome without the anticipated difficulty. But concerned not to permit too much power in church and state to get into any one pair of hands, especially such acquisitive hands, Alexander removed Wishart from the chancellorship and appointed William Fraser, Dean of Glasgow, a very different type of character. Thomas was surprised to learn that Sir Reginald le Chien had resigned — or been dismissed — as High Chamberlain, the King presumably having got all he required from that quick-silver individual, and replaced him by Sir Thomas Randolph of Nithsdale, Sheriff of Dumfries, elderly but recently married to the child-bride daughter of Marjory of Carrick and the late Adam of Kilconquhar, less colourful but more reliable. Le Chien was given the sheriffdom of Nairn and the keepership of its royal castle, in compensation — which ought to keep him fairly consistently north of the Mounth. Buchan remained both High Constable and High Justiciar, and between him and MacWilliam of Moray they kept the North — and Fergus Comyn — quiet. Colban MacDuff, only recently succeeded as Earl of Fife, died suddenly, as did the older Malise of Strathearn; both these left only infants to heir their earldoms, which meant that the King could take them into his own hands to administer, an excellent way of avoiding the troubles to be caused by over-great magnates. And, of course, many of the other potential trouble-makers were still away on the Crusade — those who had survived. So the land experienced a most unusual period of calm and prosperity — for which Alexander naturally took the main credit. He was entitled to be pleased with life, with the Crown secure, his son Alexander growing stronger after a weakly start, a second son, David, recently born, and their sister, now twelve, betrothed to the heir of Norway — which should ensure freedom from future Norse raiding — and Edward Longshanks safely thousands of miles away in Palestine. The Queen, after this third birth, was in a more weakly state than ever, but that was not allowed to cramp her husband's style, nor ever had done. Henry of England, her father, was said to be now as sick in his body as he was in his mind — but, as such, he constituted no threat to Scotland. So, for the first time in two centuries, the Scots knew what it was to be able to look around them, and over their shoulders, and to perceive no dark clouds on the horizon.

That Thomas Learmonth might be afflicted with occasional forebodings was, in the circumstances, unfortunate; but no more than was to be expected of a prophet of sorts. All knew that such always foretold woe.

It was into this happy scene of well-being and near content that the first faint whisper of change sounded in the November of 1273 — although by no means all perceived any hint of danger therein. Henry Plantagenet, King of England, died, the man who had been little more than a cipher for long. Little loss, most said, carelessly. That it meant that Edward Plantagenet, the First Knight of Christendom, became King of England in his stead, should have worried more folk than it did.

*   *   *

It was a sultry day of late July, the following summer, that Thomas had his first encounter with his monarch since their return from the North. He was in fact engaged in the important business of transferring a swarm of bees to a new hive when the King arrived at Ercildoune Tower, an activity which anyone in the least knowledgeable will assure you is not to be interrupted lightly, even on account of royalty. So His Grace met with a less than rapturous reception when six-year-old Tom Williams had routed his father out of the orchard, to find Bethoc entertaining their liege-lord in the yard whilst a grinning and supercilious company stood around with the horses.

"Ha, Thomas — what a God's name have you been up to?" Alexander greeted. "The Lady Bethoc has done her best for you — but I vow you make a sorry sight! Can you not find some likely churl to look to your bees for you?"

"No, Sire. Bees are not to be farmed out to the uncaring, like, like . . ." Thomas let that go. He was suffering from two stings and was not at his most affable, his bow perfunctory. "If Your Grace had but sent word of your coming, I would have been able to receive you more suitably. At this my humble house."

"Still the same craggy Thomas, I see! The years scarcely mellow you, I perceive."

"Long years, Sire. I wonder that you recollect my . . . poor failings!"

"So — that is the way, is it? I recollect sufficient. But *you* — it seems that forgot your gratitude, Sir Thomas. A sad failure. I was disappointed in you."

"If I disappoint Your Grace I am sorry. For I have always sought to serve you to the best of my ability."

"You chose to serve another, however."

"The Earl Patrick? He sought my services. As my goodsire, could I refuse him?"

"You were in *my* service, man!"

"Had been, Your Grace. That task finished, you said nothing of any other. Sent me no word . . ."

"A plague on it, Thomas . . .!" Alexander seemed to remember the gallery of interested courtiers, and reined back his temper. "But enough of this," he went on, schooling his voice. "I did not come here to chaffer with a land-steward, in whosoever service!"

"My lord King," Bethoc intervened, hurriedly. "Will you not come within? Have some small refreshment? Here is no place to discuss affairs . . ."

"I thank you, no, lady. I am not here to discuss affairs, see you. Only to tell this awkward husband of yours that I require him to ride in my train in eight days' time. To London. To be at Roxburgh eight days from this."

"London . . .!" Thomas exclaimed.

"London, yes."

"But . . ."

"No buts, man. Your goodsire must needs spare you. Besides, he will be coming himself. And your lady here, I swear, will manage very well lacking you for a week or two. If you are as sour with her as with your sovereign lord, she will enjoy your absence!"

"If it is your command, Sire."

"It is. I go to attend Edward's coronation. He has left off his crusading and hurried home to mount his throne. And he is . . . pressing in his invitation!"

"But — why me, Sire? Why one so humble as myself? What has a land-steward to do with coronations?"

"Nothing. It is as seer and rhymer that I want you — True Thomas. Edward writes that he has taken Sir Michael Scott to his Court — Michael the Wizard. Claims that he foretells great things. For him — Edward Longshanks. It is not to be borne! So you shall come south with me and put the Wizard in his place. Two can play at that game!"

"Sire — this is — is impossible! Not to be considered. I cannot go to London to engage in a contest with Sir Michael Scott. In foretelling, or anything else. He is a man most learned. And that is not how these seeings and rhymings come about . . ."

"I am not asking you to consider it, sirrah! I am *telling* you. Commanding. You will come south with me and do as you are told."

"I have told you before, my lord King, that I cannot foretell to order."

"Then you will invent, Thomas — invent! I will not have Edward to crow over me with this Wizard. Who should be *my* subject. He was the Emperor's astrologer — now Edward seeks to be as great as any emperor. But not with *my* aid! So — be at Roxburgh within eight days. Lady Bethoc — my thanks." And the King beckoned to an esquire to bring forward his horse.

"I do not like it, Your Grace . . ." Thomas protested — but was ignored. Without further leave-taking the royal party clattered off over the drawbridge, to take the road towards Tweed.

"What am I to do?" the unfortunate visionary demanded of his wife. "What in the name of all saints am I to do? Is he out of his wits . . .?"

"You must do as he says, Thomas my love. You cannot disobey the King. You must go. And invent, if need be. Take some of your rhymes with you, to read. It should not be too difficult for you to make up some more. Suitable. For the English."

"That would be deceit, lies. To make a mountebank of myself."

"You could be . . . discreet. Careful in what you foretell. You would have to be, with Sir Michael there! Speak it as poetry, rather than seeing. Indeed, Thomas — why not take your *Sir Tristrem*? To read to them. Some of it. It is splendid. I vow they would forget all about soothsaying and Sir Michael's astrology if they were to hear your *Tristrem*! It would be an opportunity, my dear, would it not? A great opportunity . . .?"

He shook his head.

* * *

They made a most leisurely journey of it. They had to, for the Queen was little better than an invalid these days, although she had found spirit enough to insist that she did not miss her brother's coronation — and the cavalcade could proceed no faster than her litter could travel and no further than her strength would permit, however impatient her royal spouse. Anyway, this was to be no hard-riding company but a large and splendid retinue, a Court on the move. Its splendour was deliberate, indeed all but contrived. Alexander was at pains to proclaim to England in general and Edward Longshanks in particular the power and status of the King of Scots.

So they took two whole weeks to it, and sought to make as much of a holiday of it as was possible, in the high summer weather — although many of the younger men found the pace wearisome, Thomas not the least.

They were by no means alone on the road. Half of England seemed to be heading for London on the same errand, and the further they went south the more choked were the roads — and unfortunately the English nobility tending to occupy the available accommodation in abbeys, monasteries and hospices. Since, of course, monarchs could not be expected to go begging for a bed where lesser men slept comfortably, Alexander had to institute a sort of flying column of young lordlings who rode on ahead to pre-empt suitable premises, if necessary turning out inconvenient occupants already in possession. This worked fairly well for the loftier ranks — without endearing the Scots to other travellers — but the more lowly, such as Thomas, had to make do with some very indifferent resting-places and some bad-tempered fellow-guests.

Despite its high-handed methods and splendid state, the royal cavalcade did not have it all its own way, some of the English companies being even more large and still more magnificent — and quite as autocratic; de Clare, Earl of Gloucester, and de Warenne, Earl of Surrey, in especial outdoing the Scots and proving irritating associate-wayfarers, princely in their ostentation. Few were not thankful to reach London.

That great, crowded city always gave the impression of being packed to suffocation, with its seemingly limitless mixture of magnificence and squalor, its palaces and filth, its churches, monasteries and warehouses and tumbledown hoveldom, its riches and its stench. But on this occasion it was so crammed as to be almost beyond belief, with all the nobility and magnates of England present, with their over-grown trains, the senior churchmen likewise, great numbers of illustrious guests from overseas, especially from the Plantagenet lands of Anjou, Gascony and Normandy, envoys and ambassadors from all Christendom, large companies of Crusaders and members of the knightly orders, as well as the common folk flocking in from near and far — all to add to the already teeming population.

It took literally hours for the Scots to battle their way through the narrow, twisting, tunnel-like streets to the Tower area, even with the help of the flats of their swords, with the Queen swooning in the August heat and stink and noise. There they found that, although there was no room for them in the great fortress by the river itself, at least accommodation had been set aside for them at the Maison Dieu of the Whitefriars, or Carmelites, not far away along Thames-side, which, although grievously inadequate for their numbers and style, nevertheless turned out to be the envy of many of the great English lords and even bishops. Thomas found himself sharing a damp, riverside wine-cellar, as sleeping quarters, with a grumbling group of Scots lordlings including, unfortunately, his brother-in-law the Lord Pate, whom he had succeeded in avoiding all the way down.

Fairly soon after their arrival, and whilst the company was refreshing itself in the friary's large refectory, a resplendent herald arrived from the Tower of London with a summons for Alexander to attend upon King Edward. The way in which the message was delivered made it no invitation but a command, brief, peremptory — and all near enough to hear, knowing their sovereign-lord, held their breaths.

The King's good-looking and distinctly rugged features tightened and became set. Then he inclined his head, and relaxed. "Tell my good-brother Edward, sir, that I thank him for his welcome and will visit him on the morrow, when rested from our long journeying. Bid him a good night."

Appalled, the herald stared. "But, my lord . . . His Grace's summons! He, he expects your presence. Forthwith."

"Then His Grace must call upon his patience. As I am doing, sirrah! We are weary, all. The Queen in especial. Had your master sent to clear a way for us through this damnable city, we could have been here hours ago, and I might have been able to accept this invitation."

"My lord, I regret if you have been delayed. But, I pray you, answer the King's royal summons . . ."

"I have answered it, man! Do you chaffer and dispute with Edward when he instructs you? No — then do not do so with me. Off with you, fellow . . ."

The Scots company resounded with satisfaction, almost glee, as the herald departed, although there were some who looked thoughtful, even alarmed.

It was perhaps an hour later, with the eating over and the wine and ale flowing, that a commotion drew all eyes towards the doorway. Two trumpeters appeared, to blow a hurried and ragged fanfare, and as the same herald began to command all present to be upstanding for the high, mighty and illustrious King of England, Edward Plantagenet strode in, tall, impressive, formidable.

As all who could do so rose to their feet, not a few were, in fact, relieved to see that Longshanks was smiling.

"Alexander, my brother — I greet you!" he cried. He had a powerful, resonant voice. "I grieve that you are weary with your travel. Feeling your years, perhaps? You do not ail, I hope? See — I have brought you some especial wine, which I collected from Burgundy. It will rally your drooping spirits, I swear. Where is my dear sister? I had to hasten to see her."

Alexander inclined his head in something carefully less than a bow. "The Queen has gone to her own chamber, Edward. She tires readily. I thank you for your good wishes. And the flagon of wine. My own weariness is of the mind rather than the body — which bears up passing well despite my years! Three fewer than your own, if I mind aright! So your Burgundian wine may help dispel the ill-humours afflicting my wits."

"Your wits, my friend? I grieve the more if they are . . . clouded. Pray God it will pass!"

"No doubt. Probably it is but the stinks of this London affecting me. We are used to clearer airs in Scotland. And more mannerly folk."

"Ah! For stinks, Alexander, you should smell the Holy Land! As for manners, who offends my sister's husband shall suffer my wrath, I promise you." Edward shrugged. "As to my sister, since she has retired, I shall see her tomorrow. Convey my devotion." He turned. "Piers — the moneys."

The herald stepped forward and, bowing, set down on the table beside Alexander a leather bag. It clinked with the sound of coins and was obviously heavy.

"What is this?"

"Suitable reimbursement, Alexander. For your expenses in answering my summons to attend my coronation. With your train — which I hear is large. One hundred and sixty-five pounds, I think. If you require more, inform me. This in addition to the one hundred shillings each day for you and yours whilst you remain in London."

Alexander stared, as though unable to believe his ears and eyes. "Money!" he gasped. "You would pay me moneys? God save us — me!"

"To be sure. I would not have my summons to discommode you, my friend."

"Summons! I mislike that word. The King of Scots answers no summons, Edward. I came of my own choice at your invitation — that only. And require no payment."

"Nevertheless you have brought many a long way. And spread largesse as you came, I hear. As well as . . . other things! Take it, man — and be not so prickly. Piers will obtain an acceptance-note in due course, for my treasurer."

"No. Keep your gold, Edward. I neither want it nor require it. I have brought you gifts — as have many of my lords. For your coronation. But that is different . . ."

"Then consider this a gift, Alexander, if it suits you better. Now I will go back — I have much to see to. Tomorrow we shall talk. I shall send you word when to come."

And with an airy wave of his left hand — for his right arm was stiff from a stab-wound by a Saracen assassin — the Plantagenet turned and strolled off, his trumpeters prompt to blow a valedictory flourish.

Alexander sat down heavily — and in almost the same movement swept the money-bag from the table to the floor, where it lay.

"Curse the man!" he burst out. "Curse, plague and damn him . . .!"

*　　*　　*

The great and noble abbey-church of Westminster, rebuilt by Henry the Third and not yet completed, was as packed to overflowing as was the rest of London — but with the creamed-off quality, naturally. Distinguished visitors, clergy, nobles, magnates, knights, officers, filled every inch of the vast nave, standing so close-ranked that if one had fainted — and the heat was such as to make that not unlikely — he would have been apt to remain upright by the press of his fellows. Thomas, indeed, like other more prominent Scots, was forced to climb to one of the lofty, narrow clerestorey galleries not far from the crossing — but at least from there they got an excellent view of the proceedings up in the chancel.

Even this seemed to be crowded with richly clad and vested figures, almost right up to the high altar. A large choir, chanting melodiously, was partly responsible; but the high clergy took up most of the space, a full score of gorgeously robed bishops alone, with mitred abbots and Papal representatives, in addition. Only six seats were provided. The Archbishops of Canterbury and York sat opposite each other at either side of the altar, with two empty thrones between them. The Abbot of Westminster, whose church this was, sat beside Robert of Canterbury, and Queen Margaret of Scotland sat next to Walter of York. Alexander stood at her side — and even at Thomas's distance his frown could be seen to be black.

There had been trouble. Edward had planned it for Alexander to take all too prominent a part in the proceedings, in fact to lead in the royal procession by bearing ahead of it the Sword of State. This the King of Scots had flatly refused to do, since its symbolism would have been apparent to all — that he was one of the vassals of the English monarch, even if the most important one. So, at the last moment, the thing had had to be rearranged, and Alexander went to stand beside his wife in the chancel, there to await the royal entry, amidst general bad feeling.

They had to wait a considerable time and Alexander was pacing the chancel floor before at last trumpeting silenced the choir and from the chapter-house the royal procession entered the minster by the north transept. Heading it, after the guard, it was to be seen that Edmund Crouchback, Earl of Lancaster, Edward's brother, was bearing the Sword of State, who had formerly been given the crown to carry; so there had been some rearrangement of the magnates bearing the other symbols of kingship, the orb and sceptre, the cloak and spurs. The carriers of these paced in behind Lancaster, followed by Edward himself, all in cloth-of-gold, with his wife Eleanor of Castile on his arm. He strode with a sort of controlled impatience, almost cramped by the stately pace of those in front but clearly too slow for his long legs, whilst she seemed actually to hold back. That no doubt would be the role of any woman wed to that man.

Thomas eyed the Queen with interest. Although she had been married, as a mere child, for no less than a score of years, she still had an air of immaturity, almost youthful diffidence. But perhaps her looks belied her, for she was known to have a quiet courage and determination; indeed she had insisted on joining her husband on the late Crusade, sharing at least some of the hazards and discomforts of the campaign, even allegedly saving Edward's life when he was attacked by the intending assassin with the poisoned dagger, with her own lips sucking the venom from the wounded arm.

Edward led her to her throne beside the high altar, and without pause signed peremptorily for the ceremony to begin.

Thomas gained the impression that despite the multitude and magnificence of the clergy, the religious part of the rite was hurried over, probably at the King's command. The air of impatience was evident in the man — as it was indeed in his fellow-monarch. It was almost as though, for these two at least, this was not a church but an arena, a tourney-ground, with aims to be achieved, points to be won and all the ceremonial mere tiresome delay.

When at last the coronation mass was completed and Robert of Canterbury rose to administer the oath, Edward had stepped over to his place in front of the altar before him. Hardly allowing the Archbishop to finish each phrase, in forceful tones he repeated the words just uttered, undertaking to rule justly, to uphold the laws of the kingdom and to maintain and sustain Holy Church, this with his left hand raised and the stiff right hand laid on a book of illuminated gospels held out by the Abbot of Westminster. Then, quickly, he returned to his throne, sat, and gestured. An acolyte came forward with a golden vessel containing the holy oil, and with this the Archbishop anointed his brow in the name of the Father, Son and Holy Ghost. The intonings were barely over before Edward, leaving no doubts as to who was in charge of this ritual, was beckoning forward Gilbert de Clare, Earl of Gloucester, who bore the Crown of England on its red velvet cushion. This the Archbishop took, raised high, and then bowing, placed it carefully on the royal head.

"God save the King!" he said, and at once the cry was taken up by all around. "God save the King! God save the King!" rang out, full-throated, much more acclaim than prayer, till the very roof-timbers of the minster seemed to quiver, dust dislodged. On and on the shouting maintained, and this time the central figure appeared to be in less hurry to proceed.

The Queen leant over to touch his arm, but Edward stared straight ahead of him, almost grim-featured.

When at length the rhythmic clamour died away, the King took charge again. He pointed at his brother, Edmund of Lancaster, whose hump-back was very noticeable as he teetered forward with the great sword, clearly too heavy for his weakly wrists. Scornfully Edward snatched it from him, to hold it upright, firm, even with his left hand only — and at the same time he cast a glance across the chancel to where Alexander stood, a glance as eloquent as it was swift, naked.

Then the sceptre and the orb were brought, by two more earls, and laying the sword across his thighs, Edward took the former with his left hand, the other in his right held close against his side. Two more earls brought the golden spurs and, kneeling, buckled them on to the monarch's feet. Finally, a purple cloak was draped around his shoulders by the Bishop of London, and this stage of the proceedings was complete. Seated in full majesty the King of England waited while the shouted refrain rang out once more.

This time Edward stopped it short with an emphatic wave of the sceptre, which he then pointed at his queen. The Archbishop of York came over with a lesser crown, which he placed about Eleanor's attractive brow over the gold-net and pearled coif, and thereafter led a very modest God save the Queen.

Now Edward was brisk again. He thrust the sceptre, orb and sword at their former bearers, who still stood by, and who, with these symbols of regal authority, moved to stand behind the throne. Then leaning forward, as though saying 'at last!', he jabbed out his left hand to point directly at Alexander, in the most evident and imperious summons.

That man waited long moments, the target for every eye. It was not hesitation. There could be no question of hanging back to allow any other to go before him, even in this difficult business. But he was not going to hurry to that command. Eventually he paced over slowly in front of his brother-in-law and inclined his head.

Edward, eyeing him equally deliberately, spoke for the first time in this ceremony. "Fealty!" he snapped. "You will do your fealty, Alexander. Homage. To *me*!"

Seeming to savour that, the other nodded. "To be sure, Edward. Insofar as I may!"

"May? Fealty is fealty."

"True. But, like kinship, there are steps, degrees, in it. A man can be son or brother . . . or merely good-brother! There is fealty . . . and fealty!"

Frowning, Edward turned to another prelate who had moved closer. "My lord of Norwich — proceed!" he ordered.

That Bishop bowed low, a portly, purse-mouthed cleric. He held a paper in his beringed hand. "My lord of Scotland," he intoned. "Pray repeat the due oath of fealty after me in these words. "I, Alexander, become your man for the lands which I hold of you, Edward, King of England."

After a distinct pause, came the words, "I, Alexander, King of Scots, become your man, Edward, King of England, for the lands which I hold of you . . . in the kingdom of England, and for which I must owe you homage. Saving my kingdom."

The Bishop drew a quick breath and glanced at the seated Edward. Narrow-eyed, that man stared at his brother-in-law. He flicked a finger at the prelate to continue.

"And, and saving to the King of England, if . . . if he right have, to your homage for that kingdom of Scotland." That last came out in something of a rush.

Alexander looked from one to the other and spoke loudly enough for his words to ring around the crowded minster. "To homage for my kingdom of Scotland no one has any right but God alone. Nor do I hold it of any but of God."

Out of his depth, the Bishop gulped, shook his head and turned to his liege-lord.

Edward had half-risen in his throne, his florid features working. For long moments there was complete silence throughout the great company. He could refuse to accept Alexander's limited homage, but, to reject any fealty at all would serve no purpose, unless he was prepared to forfeit Alexander's earldom of Huntingdon and risk reprisals on Northumbria and Cumbria.

Edward sank back without raising his hand for the homage-receiving gesture.

The King of Scots briefly inclined his head and turning, paced back to his wife's side. In effect, despite the words he had uttered, he had not done homage for his English lands. The situation remained in limbo.

Thereafter, the vital process of homage-giving and receiving went ahead without hitch or delay, however long it took, with every major baron, that is holder of lands directly from the Crown, starting with the earls, coming up to kneel before their sovereign lord and the source of their power and authority, each to take his hand between their two palms and to swear to be his man, with all that implied. Since the baronage numbered hundreds, this made a protracted business indeed. Although Alexander was soon showing his impatience, Edward himself now did not — for this, after all, was what it was all about, this was power and might. Each of these barons, through his homage and land-holding, owed the King so many knight's fees, that is the services of a given number of mounted knights and so many scores or hundreds of armed men. On this the feudal strength was founded, the army of England built up. This was a weapon being forged, here in Westminster Abbey, or at least renewed and sharpened. And once tempered, Edward Plantagenet was not the man to let that weapon rust in its scabbard.

Later that day, in the great banqueting-hall of the Tower of London, the newly-crowned monarch entertained his guests and supporters, and in lavish style. Hundreds were present and no expense was spared in catering for their provision and pleasure. Never had the Scots seen such plenitude and variety of dishes and wines, never even heard of some of the rarities and confections. As for the entertainments, some were such as to raise gasps of admiration, wonder, even disbelief and embarrassment, with exotic acts performed by flame-swallowers, snake-charmers, pain-sufferers, knife-throwers and belly-dancers to add to the more usual acrobats, wrestlers, gypsies and performing animals. Clearly Edward had made use of his sojourn in the Middle East for more than crusading.

Precedence in seating being so awkward a problem in such a huge gathering, the device had been resorted to of having a number of smaller tables up on the dais, in a crescent flanking Edward's own, obviating much heart-burning amongst the illustrious. So there was the King of Scots' table, the Archbishops', the Papal Legate's, the foreign envoys', the Earl Marshal's, and so on. As for the rest, the vast majority, all could sit where they would in the body of the hall, fighting it out amongst themselves. Undoubtedly Alexander for one was well content with this arrangement, sparing him the necessity to converse with his host, or to object in principle at being mis-seated.

Thomas, for his part, looking for a suitably lowly place, perceived the severe person of Sir Michael Scott sitting alone in a corner well down the hall and eyed slightly askance by most of the company. He went to greet him and found himself welcomed almost warmly by that strange man, and so sat down beside the Mathematician.

Sir Michael was scathing in his reaction to almost all that he saw about him, as to the generality of his fellow-guests. He disapproved of vast banquets, it appeared, but had been specifically commanded to be present by King Edward, for some reason. He sincerely hoped that no royal foolishness was planned.

Thomas was in no position to reassure him.

Scott was full of himself and his doings and only marginally interested in Thomas's situation. He had, it appeared, written new books on alchemy and the transmutation of metals — and had a shrewd idea that Edward's eagerness to have him a member of his Court, as Medical Astrologer, was as much in the hope that he would discover him the secret of making gold as anything to do with his health. He explained how he had been in Rome studying chiromancy when Edward had arrived there on his way home from the Holy Land on King Henry's death, and had prevailed on him to follow him to London — a proceeding of which Scott now seemed to be doubting the wisdom. Evidently his astrology did not guide his own personal activities. Indeed, he proceeded to display a rather astonishing disbelief in his own prophecies by confiding that he had recently divined that he himself would die of a blow on the head by a stone weighing no more than two ounces. So now he made a point of wearing an iron-lined hat or helmet when he went outdoors — an extraordinary piece of mixed-thinking, in Thomas's opinion, for so superior a character, although he did not say so. What he did say was to thank the older man for the assurances, conveyed to him by King Alexander, that he calculated that there might be some worth in his little rhymes and predictions; and the good advice that he should apply himself to the study of astrology and allied sciences. Unfortunately, the difficulty was that there was nobody that he had heard of in Scotland sufficiently knowledgeable on these subjects to be able to instruct him. If, of course, Sir Michael himself was to return to his own country, he would rejoice to sit at his feet and prove himself an attentive pupil.

The other rather brushed this off, indicating that he had more to do with his time than teach the uninformed. But he did concede that if Learmonth was carefully to study certain writings of his own, which he might recommend, he might indeed develop one day into a quite useful member of the Scots community.

Thomas sought to sound duly appreciative. He wondered whether he should ask if Scott thought that King Edward in truth intended to issue any sort of challenge as to things of the unseen, as Alexander had suggested, but decided against it as injudicious.

The evening was well advanced before his unspoken question was answered. With the high standard of entertainment beginning to tail off and the wine having its effect on many heads, noise grew in the hall, shouts and remarks and dares. Not a few involved the Scots. Perhaps Edward himself was affected by this, or may have been partly responsible for instigating it, for his voice became louder, he shoutingly toasted sundry guests, adding comments not all flattering, and laughing resoundingly. He was not drunk but not unaffected. Inevitably some of his sallies were directed towards the King of Scots' table.

Alexander too enjoyed his wine, but tonight had himself under careful control, necessarily. Some of his lords were less discreet, notably the Earls of Dunbar and Buchan. From his lowly position Thomas watched and feared trouble.

Edward was no fool and it may have been that he perceived that matters might get out-of-hand, and chose to guide them his way; or he may have been intending such a move all along. At any rate, presently he smashed down his fist on his table, making the flagons jump and obtaining approximate quiet, and shouted over to his brother-in-law.

"Alexander — you have tasted my entertainment. Let us now taste of yours. You Scots boast much. Prove now for us your worth."

Alexander looked wary. "We left our entertainers at home, Edward," he said, mildly enough. "But find us fiddles and we shall dance you and yours off your feet!"

"The time for dancing was when the ladies were still with us. Besides, it was entertainment I said — not Erse cantrips! Spare us that! Better — I am told that you did bring one of your jesters with you — the lame rhymster. Let us hear what he can do, to add to our cheer on this my coronation day."

"Thomas might foretell to less than your cheer, Edward!"

"You think so? Would he dare? When the most celebrated diviner and astrologer in all Christendom is present — and has been sufficiently kind to presage for me only fair fortune and good cheer? Let us hear what your lamester has to say in front of Sir Michael the Mathematician!"

Scott, at Thomas's side, looked outraged. "This is un-suitable, intolerable!" he said.

"Do not threaten us with Sir Michael Scott." Alexander gave back. "I would remind you that he is a subject of my own. It was I who knighted him, indeed. As I did Sir Thomas Learmonth. I would advise you not to play the one against the other, my friend."

"I am not afraid of false prophets. Sir Michael has consulted the stars, which cannot lie. Let us hear your man — if so be that he dares to open his mouth!"

"Sir Thomas — come you!" Alexander commanded loudly.

Unhappily Thomas rose. "This is wrong, all wrong," he said, low-voiced, to Scott. "To be made sport for kings. But — what can I do?"

The other nodded. "Say your say, young man. All men can be foolish, crowned heads not excepted. Speak honestly what is in you. I for one shall not mock you."

Thomas limped up the hall to the dais, amidst stares and titters.

"So — the halt but not the blind!" Edward commented. "Pray not dumb, also! I have seen you before, have I not, Sir Thomas?"

"Yes, Sire. In this hall, a dozen years ago. I was esquire to my lord of Dunbar."

"And were you prophesying then, man?"

"I . . . contrived a rhyme or two now and again, Your Grace."

From the Scots high-table the Earl Patrick hooted. "To be sure he did! I mind it well. He penned a rhyme in this hall, by God! At the dancing. About the Lion, the Lion of Scotland. And jackals — English jackals!" His father-in-law sounded distinctly drunk. "How did it go, Thomas?"

Appalled, the younger man shook his head. "You, you misremember, my lord, I think . . ."

"Not I!" Patrick turned to Alexander. "You, Cousin — you saw it, read it. You mind? Lion and jackals, and, and . . ."

"Pleasure," Alexander nodded. "Pleasure and measure, was it not? And the jackals to watch their step. Something of the sort, if I recall."

Edward frowned blackly. "If such was the style of him then, let us hope that he has improved not a little! Abuse is not the province of a prophet."

"Ah, but Thomas was but a bairn then," Alexander asserted. "He has come far, since. Give us the one that foretold the Largs fight. About Hakon."

"Sire — these rhymes, jingles, are of little worth. Not for such occasions as this. They are mere scratchings of the pen. His Grace of England has the rights of it, in this. Any true worth in me is otherwise. In true verse, poetry. I have completed the long poem of *Sir Tristrem*. After years of work. This is of more worth . . ."

"Here is no time for long poems, man. The rhyme you penned before Largs, I say."

"That was ten years ago," Edward scoffed. "Are all his prophecies of like age?"

"He foretold Hakon's death, when none looked for it. Out with it, Thomas." Shrugging, Thomas repeated the lines he had so unwillingly written that day in Turnberry Castle in the autumn of 1263.

> *"The Norsemen sailed from the Orcades, to grasp at Alba's land;*
> *But a greater Lord than Hakon held Alba in His hand.*
> *He covered the sun that day at noon as sign of wrath and skaith;*
> *And the Norse were wrecked on Scotland, and the price was*
> *Hakon's death."*

"Hakon did not die at Largs," Edward objected. "He died, not in battle, but of a sickness at Orkney. A chance, a mere chance."

"He foretold the victory also, did he not?" Alexander insisted.

"One side had to win. An even wager! And all would have been gone if you had lost, to be sure. Give us something better than that, I say!"

Nettled, Thomas bit his lip. He thrust hand into his doublet-pocket and drew out some folded papers. Picking out one, he held it up.

"This none have heard — save only my wife. I wrote it before the other, before the Largs battle. It meant little to me then, scarce made sense. So I showed it to none. But now . . ." He read:

> *"The Norse shall fleet on the salt sea strand,*
> *And lie upon the foam;*
> *A score of thousand without stroke of hand*
> *Shall lose their lives each one.*
> *Their ships shall stand up in the sea,*
> *For seven long years at least;*
> *Till crows build nests in the masts of them,*
> *At the end of their bloody feast."*

There was a moment's silence. Then Alexander slapped his knee.

"God — it is true!" he cried. "I never heard this one. Why did not you tell it me, Thomas? But it is true. I was at Turnberry only months ago. And passed by Largs. The Norse longships still stand there, in the tide's shallows. Skeletons now, wooden ribs only, but upright in the sands. I was scarce close enough to see crows! But the fleet still stands on the strand."

"No doubt Sir Thomas also has been back to Largs since — and made his rhyme accordingly!" Edward suggested. "*My* notion of prophecy is for the future, not the past! Have you nothing nearer hand than ten years ago, Sir Rhymster? And of more concern to us here?"

There was a growl of agreement from the hall in general, with some more particular advice.

Stung more deeply, Thomas replaced the Largs paper by another. "Hear this, then," he exclaimed.

> *"Though England's lord of stature tall,*
> *Seeks Alba's pride to put in thrall;*
> *A Westland wight of humble name,*
> *Puts Southron might to woe and shame.*
> *In truth before he be betrayed,*
> *Thousands shall their end have made;*
> *Scotland thrice to the pass he'll bring,*
> *And Lion, not Leopard shall be the King."*

Now he had silence indeed, as men stared from the speaker to the two monarchs and at each other. Whatever that might mean in full, there was no more doubting the theme than the outcome.

"Insolent!" Edward declared, at last. "Insolent gibberish! The babblings of a malicious dizzard! Meaning nothing."

There was a ground-swell of angry support for that from the company at large, a menacing sound.

"*I* see meaning in it," Alexander asserted, when he could make himself heard. "In part, at least. This of the humble Westland wight I do not know. But for the rest it is sufficiently clear, to be sure. You cannot complain, Edward — since you asked for it!"

"I asked for soothsaying, truth in foretelling — if this man is indeed capable of it, as you claim. Not for contumely and barefaced abuse. At my own table!" He further raised his voice. "Sir Michael Scott — you sit down there, silent. Have you naught to say, to refute this, this impudent imposter? Come up here, man — and let us hear true divination. What the stars in their eternal courses foretell. Not the spleen of this crippled guisard! Come!"

Slowly the Mathematician rose and moved forward, disapproval in every rigid line of him. When he stood beside Thomas, he bowed, but far from deeply.

"My lord King," he said, in his curiously high-pitched voice. "I sat silent because there was nothing for me to say, in this. Divination and prophetic utterance are not subjects for an evening's sport! They come either from the inner eye and voice, sudden as lightning's strike. Or else out of long and careful measurement and calculation. Myself, I prefer the latter. But neither may be summoned at will for entertainment. By the seer himself any more than by an earthly power."

"Of that I am well aware, sir," Edward returned stiffly. "But this is not something new. These, these rhymes were made before. *You* prophesied good for me, a long reign, many triumphs and conquests. You heard what this lame man said? Have you nothing to say in return? Do you, with all your knowledge and learning, not rebuke this mountebank?"

"No, Sire. It is not for me to rebuke a man I believe to be honest in such matters. He may be mistaken. His divinings are not mine. But far be it from me to declare him of false intent."

"You cannot both be right, man! If your careful calculations are true, then this Thomas's must be false. Since the one makes a mockery of the other."

"False, Your Graces, I do not say. Mistaken — I know not. False means otherwise. Of intent to deceive. Sir Thomas Learmonth I believe to be no deceiver, even if he be mistaken."

"If not a deceiver, then still insolent and scurrilous. Abusing me to my face."

"You sought it, Edward. Commanded him to speak his

foretellings," Alexander said, almost gleefully. "You cannot condemn when he obeys. If Thomas is mistaken, time will tell. Let it be."

"Aye, Sires — let it be," Michael Scott agreed. "Better that this had never been started. Divinations and prognostications are no sport for a banquet."

"So say I," Thomas added.

"Silence! *You* have said sufficient!"

"Then have I Your Graces' permission to retire?"

"By the Mass, you have! Away with you!"

"You have my leave to retire, Sir Thomas. We shall not be long behind you," Alexander said graciously.

"I, too, Sires, would retire," the Mathematician requested.

Edward flapped a dismissive hand, but added no words.

His brother-in-law smiled kindly. "Sir Michael — retire, by all means. It is good to have seen you again. When you are of a mind, come back to Scotland. I would gladly find a place for you, and suitable employment."

Bowing, the two seers moved side-by-side down through the crowded hall and out — and both thankful to be so.

Later that night, humble though Thomas's quarters were, Alexander came to visit him in his wine-cellar.

"That was a foolish business, tonight," he said. "But you taught Edward a lesson. I have never seen him so put out. You did entirely well, Thomas. The old Warlock was good, forby. Scotland came out of it passing well."

"Nevertheless, Sire, I had rather that we had never been brought into it! It was all ill done . . ."

"Nonsense, man! Not on your part, at the least. I am glad that I brought you with me. It gave Edward pause — and that he needed, by the Mass! You had him out of countenance with that of woe and shame to England's tall lord! The Lion, not the Leopard, to win. But, Thomas — what meant you by this of a Westland wight? What is this? Who? If any puts the Southron to shame, should it not be myself? What is this of a humble man from the West?"

"I know not, Sire. That is but the way it came to me. I do not claim to understand all, or much, that I see and hear. It comes to me. This man I saw. He was no great lord. But he

319

was of mighty stature. And he it is who will stand in England's way."

"Why not myself? Where was I, the King, in what you saw?"

"I do not know, Your Grace. I can only speak of what I saw. What it may mean, who can tell?"

His satisfaction somewhat dimmed, Alexander turned to leave. "We return to Scotland just so soon as Her Grace is able for the journey," he said, in the doorway. "She is tired — she ever tires easily. A couple of days — no more, I hope. But, see you — it might be wise for you to keep out of Edward's way meantime, my friend. Keep your distance from his friends, likewise. You have scarcely made him love you, have you, True Thomas?"

Speechless, he stared after his liege-lord's handsome back.

16

Thomas was back in favour, and doubtful about it. Pleasant as it was to be appreciated and smiled upon again, both by Alexander and the Earl Patrick, with conditions consequently much more agreeable for Bethoc as well as for himself, nevertheless there were drawbacks too, demands, disturbances of his days' routine, hold-ups in his work — and these days he found himself to be very busy, managing the affairs of two earldoms a major task, at least to do it as he conceived it should be done, although it certainly had not been done that way previously. There had been not so much neglect as little attempt made to exploit. His experience in the North, even though conditions were so different, had opened his eyes to the possibilities and potentialities of the vast areas now under his effective supervision, a challenge to his capabilities. It was indeed small wonder that the Earl approved — even if Pate did not — with his wealth ever increasing and his many baronies blossoming and even co-operating in productivity, something never before contemplated, however far short of Thomas's aspirations. Even a higher fate seemed to be appreciative, for once; for this year, 1275, there developed a great sheep plague in England, with stock dying by the million, and as a result forcing high the price of both wool and mutton. Thomas's investment in stock for the vast Lammermuir sheep-walks, therefore, paid off with unexpected speed and profit, to Patrick's satisfaction — although if the plague spread to Scotland, Thomas warned, it would prove a different story. So far it was reported no nearer than Yorkshire.

The favour of his betters, however, seemed inevitably to produce new calls upon his time and abilities — not, God be praised, in respect of divination and suchlike but in more normal and everyday matters. As this present mission, for instance, a charge he could well have done without, however flattering it might feel superficially to be a royal representative of a sort.

Alexander, since the previous autumn's London trip, seldom failed to call in at Ercildoune Tower on his way up and down Lauderdale for visits to his favourite seat of Roxburgh. Out of these calls developed errands and injunctions, mainly of a secretarial or commercial nature. The carrying out of these held its own complications, for the Earl Patrick was concerned lest the King try to steal his profitable chief steward from him, and ready to be suspicious. But Thomas could not refuse his liege-lord's commands. Today, he was on his way to the port of Berwick-upon-Tweed, there to meet and greet, of all things, another Papal Legate.

Or perhaps Legate was not quite right. Legates were usually cardinals or at least archbishops. This man, Master Baiamundo de Vicci, whose unpronounceable name had already been converted to Bagimond by the English, was no more than a canon, chaplain to Cardinal Ubertus of St. Eustace, reputedly. Yet he was sent direct from Pope Innocent to England and Scotland as special nuncio, so presumably he was a man of some distinction at Rome.

Innocent, for better or for worse, had proclaimed yet another Crusade, with orders that it was to be preached from every church in Christendom. But as well as being preached, of course, it had to be paid for; and remembering the fiasco of Cardinal Ottobone's visitation, Innocent now required this Bagimond to draw up a careful valuation roll of all ecclesiastical benefices, in Scotland as in England, with the present-day actual and accurate annual values, not the old and outdated ones foisted upon Ottobone. He was thereafter to impose a tithe on all, and oversee collection. However, on this occasion, more realistically, the tax was only on ecclesiastical revenues, not on the baronies and lands of the laity. So the Papal demand to Alexander, that he provide all help and co-operation, met with a less fierce reaction than heretofore. Let the churchmen look after their own, he said; but, not to have any bad report go back to Rome this time, with possible retaliation via England and Edward, as after Ottobone's visit, he was prepared to give the nuncio at least the appearance of assistance. Hence Thomas's assignment. He was to greet this Bagimond, bring him to Roxburgh, and from there guide and advise him as to his visitations to the various religious establishments of this part of the kingdom.

Berwick's thriving port at the mouth of the Tweed, the largest in Scotland, was thronged with shipping from many lands. It usually was busy, but presently, thanks to the sheep-plague in the South, was particularly active, for England's great trade in wool and cloths fell to be supplied from elsewhere inevitably, and Scotland was reaping the benefit. Indeed not a little of the baled wool and salted mutton being exported from here came from Lammermuir and the Merse, for Dunbar harbour was tidal and could not accommodate the larger ships at low water.

The bustle of Berwick's teeming streets and wynds was confusing, and Thomas was at something of a loss as to how to discover if the Papal envoy had yet arrived — he was due to come north by sea from Teesside. No one that he asked knew or cared anything about such a visitor, and there were half-a-dozen ships from England tied up at the quays. Eventually he presented himself at the Greyfriars Monastery in the Seagait, thinking that the friars might be more helpful — and there found the nuncio already installed and the Prior fussing around him like a hen with a single chick.

Thomas had a surprise with Bagimond. He proved to be unlike any cleric or priest that he had ever come across, a bustling, chuckling, rubicund little man, round of face and person, bald and chubby, eyes almost lost in folds of pink flesh — but shrewd eyes and giving no impression of the lenity, if not lethargy, which might go with the plumpness and beaming smiles. A fluent linguist, he brushed aside Thomas's apologies for not having been present to greet him on arrival, on King Alexander's behalf, declaring that his passage had been swifter by a full day than expected and that he had been entirely comfortable with the good friars here, whose prosperity rejoiced his simple heart. Indeed he pointed out that he had been able straightway to commence his great task of listing and assessing the many churches and religious houses of the seaport, with the help of the Prior, and had been duly impressed. His clerks ought to be finished with their setting down of the details on paper within an hour or two. There were some small disagreements anent current valuations, he conceded, laughingly cheerful, but that would soon be smoothed out.

Clearly this Pope's envoy was of a very different character from the last; but Thomas got no impression, however easy he might be to work with, that he would be any more readily hoodwinked or put off.

By the time that they were riding westwards up Tweed on the twenty-five-mile return to Roxburgh, with the two monkish clerks behind, Thomas had already learned to respect the little man as well as to find him excellent company — which he perceived might have its dangers as far as Scotland's interests were concerned. Alexander, of course, while asserting that the churchmen could look after themselves, was determined that no large sums of money should leave his realm, for crusading or any other purposes. Holy Church, thanks to the generosity of Queen Margaret the Saint and her son King David, as well as to the industry and commercial acumen of the generality of clerics, controlled a large portion of the wealth of the kingdom; and no country could afford to export its substance in heavy taxation, whatever the Curia in Rome might ordain.

Along fair Tweedside, Thomas had further indication of his new charge's intelligence and acuteness of mind — and of sight. For those humorous little eyes missed nothing, the richness of the country, the frequency of tilled riggs, the plentiful flocks and herds, the many villages, hamlets and farm-towns, the parish kirks and the rich granges or church-farms. Bagimond all but smacked his lips — so that Thomas was moved to point out that all this was by no means typical of Scotland as a whole. When the nuncio saw the noble abbey of Kelso rising before him, where Teviot met Tweed, all towers and spires and buttresses, and learned that there were three others as fine within a few miles, Jedburgh, Dryburgh and Melrose, his satisfaction was joyous — although his guide suspected, not all to the glory of God only.

Alexander, who himself kept well out of the way, hunting at Kincardine of the Mearns, one hundred miles off even as the crow flew, had left instructions for Bagimond's entertainment and care at Roxburgh Castle rather than at Kelso Abbey across the river, presumably as a not-too-costly gesture Romewards. So Thomas's services were required only to help plan routes and destinations for the visitants and to provide guides. After two days with the Italians, he was able to return to Ercildoune and Bethoc, and thereafter to make only intermittent calls at Roxburgh to ensure that all was well.

Bagimond's task was, of course, a huge one, since every independent or semi-independent Church establishment had to be visited and inspected. He did not have to call on every parish church, thankfully, for the system established by King David attached most of these to an abbey, priory or other monastic house, which collected its offerings and revenues and paid the incumbent as vicar. So the valuations of each could be obtained from the various abbots and priors. But the nuncio liked to see for himself, clearly — although in the kindest possible way — not trusting his brethren in Christ not to under-value. He also made a point of having a look at many of the granges, which produced the principal incomes of the monasteries, most of which were productive and well-run. The Tweed, Teviot and tributary valleys were particularly rich in these, so that much could be done from Roxburgh. But gradually the circle had to widen and it became necessary to stay away for nights at a time, with Thomas feeling in duty bound to accompany the visitants, to ensure that all went well, at least as regards their travel and accommodation. The actual success or otherwise of their mission was no concern of his.

As that summer progressed, he came to develop quite an affection for the little Piedmontese, so different from most other higher clergy, even their own Scots bishops, abbots and priors. Obviously of humble birth, he adopted no haughty manners nor autocratic attitudes, remaining consistently modest, moderate and cheerful in all circumstances — and many of the circumstances were testing, to say the least, with long journeying frequently ending in less than friendly and co-operative welcomes, tax assessors seldom being popular. Yet the man had an innate authority, quite irrespective of his Papal credentials, as well as an eye and an ear for the truth and a quiet efficiency. His valuation-roll was likely to be a deal more accurate than any compiled previously. Thomas wished only that it was being done in a better, or at least more sympathetic, cause. The Crusades aroused little enthusiasm in Scotland, especially in view of the toll of sickness and death from fevers resulting. Dying in battle for a worthwhile objective was one thing; perishing miserably of disease quite another.

One of the visitations gave Thomas considerable satisfaction — that to the Trinitarian monastery of Faill, in Kyle, where he had not been since his marriage ten years before. Prior Nicholas welcomed him, at least, most warmly. He had changed but little, one of those unageing men who would look much the same as now, probably, for the next ten years also and longer, until some sudden assault would fell him. He was eager to hear of Thomas and Bethoc's doings, delighted to learn that they had a son. He had had occasional and garbled reports as to True Thomas in the interim, but nothing that carried conviction. Although on this occasion, inevitably, his time was taken up with his dealings with Bagimond, and their call a comparatively brief one, he urged that Thomas should bring his wife and son to visit him one day; did they not owe him that, who had married them? He confessed that though the life of the monastery was good, a challenge and presumably acceptable in God's eyes, there were times when, shamefully, he found himself looking longingly at the world outside and the company of other than monks.

It was on their return from Kyle, through the great Forest of Ettrick, that Thomas gained word of another acquaintance. Proceeding down Ettrick to the abbey-grange of Selkirk, formerly itself an abbey, at the remote hospice of Kirkhope they learned that the Auld Warlock Michael himself had come to dwell at Oakwood Tower, nearby — to the considerable alarm of the admittedly few local people. The travellers made a call thereafter at Oakwood, within its fine bend of the rushing river, below the hillock where the Romans had once established a marching-fort, and found a simple stone tower not much larger than Ercildoune — but no Mathematician, only a large number of cats. Foresters at the nearby little township assured them, with dire head-shaking, that the mannie did live there, right enough, with the cats, but was meantime away to France or some such place on an errand for the King. Thomas, for one, learned not a little as to how unchancy reputations grew, from the added details of Sir Michael's departure on his overseas embassage, for they were assured that the Wizard had in fact ridden off southwards on a great black horse, through the air and high above the Annandale Hills. It was also recounted how an offending farmer somewhere up Megget Water had irritated Sir Michael, who thereupon inflated and enlarged the wretched man's bonnet so that it rose in the air, spinning at great speed, and becoming a mighty wind carried off farmer, wife, family and house in the direction of Moffat. It became very apparent how Thomas's own unexplained disappearance for seven years had developed into an interlude with the Queen of Elfland.

When Bagimond had finished as much as could conveniently be achieved from Roxburgh, and moved off to cover Galloway and the South-West, Thomas drew up an itinerary for him but felt that this was as far as duty called; he could scarcely expect to be shepherded all over Scotland. They parted quite good friends, and Thomas would even miss the little man's cheerful company. But his own work and responsibilities had inevitably got considerably behindhand, and harvest was upon them. Also, latterly he had had to be away from home more and more, seeing less and less of Bethoc and Tom William — and he was a man who much enjoyed his home-life.

But it was not to be. On St. Michael's Eve in late September the King came riding down Lauderdale again, and this time with an army behind him. There was trouble in Man. Ivar Godfreysson, who had succeeded the late Magnus, son of Olaf Morsel, and had proved a sufficiently satisfactory sub-king, as far as Alexander was concerned, himself died and an illegitimate brother named Godfrey grasped the Manx throne in place of the child heir. He promptly declared himself to be an independent monarch and called upon Edward of England, Magnus Hakonsson of Norway and his kin the Norse-Irish of Dublin, to support him. This, of course, could readily develop into a serious situation, of which Edward, for one, might feel disposed to take advantage. So Alexander was moving in at once, and in person. The moment was awkward, for he had left his queen lying dangerously ill at the Abbey of Coupar in Strathmore. Margaret had been unwell ever since the return from London; indeed she had never fully recovered from the difficult birth of their third child, David, two years before. Alexander was scarcely a doting husband, but he was not a hard-hearted man and was unhappy at leaving his rather sad wife for any indefinite period.

Thomas, it appeared, was expected to take part in the expedition. His prowess as a captain of light cavalry, at Largs, was remembered and possibly exaggerated — and after all these years of peace, and the crusading deaths of her most adventurous spirits, Scotland was very short of experienced and war-tried commanders. He could either accompany the King or stay and help Pate of the Black Beard to muster and bring on the Dunbar and March levies — for the Earl Patrick was getting too old for active campaigning. Thomas had no hesitation in choosing the former.

So it was goodbye to Bethoc again, great two-handed sword out and sharpened, and on the march.

They were heading for Galloway, collecting men as they went. It was already quite an impressive host as far as numbers went, some six thousand strong. But, looking at the leadership, Thomas for one could scarcely feel confident, and recognised why the King had been urgent to enroll even such frail support as his own. It was a dozen years since Largs — and even there the generalship had been less than brilliant. No real warfare had taken place since — something almost unheard of in Scotland. There had been local affrays and feuding, of course; but such was poor training for full-scale armed conflict. The success of Alexander's policies had this reverse side. Buchan the High Constable was present, a veteran but now but a shadow of his former self. The High Steward was there, but he had never been much of a warrior. Durward, a fighter although past his best, had just recently died. There were new and untried earls of Fife, Atholl, Strathearn, Lennox and the Mearns, and no Earl of Carrick. In the lesser ranks of the nobility it was the same story. Sir Reginald le Chien was an unknown quantity in battle however vigorous in other ways; as was the new High Chamberlain, Sir Thomas Randolph. Admittedly the Isle of Man was no major power, but its people were warlike, of mainly Norse descent, and any assault by sea apt to be difficult — as Largs had proved.

When the King delayed at Roxburgh for two whole days, there were murmurings when it was realised that he was in fact waiting for one man — and that an Englishman. Sir John de Vesci, Lord of Alnwick in Northumberland, had heired the barony of Sprouston in the Merse from his Scots mother, and for it had done the necessary fealty to Alexander. Now he must make good his oath. Many, to be sure, were doing that; but de Vesci was rather special. He had been one of Edward's best lieutenants in the late Crusade, distinguishing himself in a number of engagements and, most importantly, leading two successful sea-borne assaults on Saracen-held forts. When he arrived at length, short, bull-necked and scowling, with no graces, he by no means further endeared himself to the Scots nobles; but Thomas, like his liege-lord, was relieved to see him.

An adherent more welcome to most, and with a large following, joined them at Lockerbie in mid-Annandale. Sir Robert Bruce the Younger, heir to the old Lord of Annandale and now husband of Marjory, Countess of Carrick. He brought with him her Carrick levies as well of those of his father's, amounting altogether to some twelve hundred men, a notable accession of strength. Alexander had reason to forgive him his offence in marrying a countess in her own right without royal permission. Although handsome and personable, Thomas adjudged him something of a weakling, however; and he wondered the more at the rhyme which had come to him that time on hearing of the marriage:

> *Of Bruce's side a son shall come,*
> *From Carrick's bower to Scotland's throne:*
> *The Red Lion beareth he . . .*

He had kept this one to himself, and still did so.

At Kirk Cuthbert's Town on the Galloway Dee estuary, the army halted and set up camp. This was the most convenient point on the Scots mainland near to Man; and here they must wait whilst Alexander sought to assemble shipping and boats from all the Galloway coasts. This was a major problem, there being no Scots fighting fleet, and nearly all their many trading vessels being based on the east coast ports. While they tarried, Alexander decided to use the interval to send envoys to Man, to try to convince Godfrey that resistance was pointless and stupid, that the King of Scots was prepared to be magnanimous and overlook this error of judgment, and to assure him that he could be entirely comfortable as sub-King of Man, as had been his predecessor, until the child-heir came of age. For this embassage the King chose the pair who had operated together on a previous occasion, Sir Reginald le Chien of Inverugie and Sir Thomas Learmonth of Ercildoune.

So Thomas, less than delightedly, found himself cooped up with le Chien in a fishing-boat and making the choppy crossing of some thirty miles of the Irish Sea. Part oar-work, part tacking into a south-westerly breeze, it took them seven hours, for most of which the older man was direly sick and moaningly cursing Alexander, Godfrey and all concerned. Thomas, used to fishing out from Dunbar in stormier seas than this, was smugly unaffected.

Man proved to be much larger than Thomas at least had imagined — and they had occasion to learn something of its size, for putting in at the first sizeable haven they saw, Ramsey, they learned that King Godfrey Godfreysson had his seat at Rushen Castle at the far south end of the island, some twenty miles further down the coast. Their further sail, parallel with the shore, past the Maughold, Laxey, Clay and Douglas headlands, although time-consuming, was calmer, in protected waters, and enabled them to discern something of the character of the island, which at this east side showed some quite dramatic scenery, with cliffs and bays and sandy strands, the land rising fairly consistently inland to quite high and rugged hills. It all reminded Thomas of Arran, which he had viewed so admiringly from Cumbrae, although it seemed to be perhaps half as large again.

Despite their early start, it was dusk before they reached the bay of Ronaldsway, under the shelter of the offshore island of St. Michael, which their boatmen said was the disembarking place for Rushen. They had decided that it was too late in the day to seek out the castle and an interview with Godfrey, and that they must look for accommodation for the night, poor as such was likely to be. But as they came round the last headland, they could see all the narrow coastal plain here to be aglow with the lights of innumerable fires. Clearly an army was encamped. In the circumstances they changed their minds, deciding to make an approach right away to the army commanders.

The Ronaldsway haven was busy, half-dark or not, with

much coming and going of boats, supplies being landed for the camp. The newcomers were ignored. Unchallenged they made their way inland to and through the noisy camp area.

They did not have to go looking for Rushen Castle, for on enquiry for the camp commander, although eyed strangely, they were told that King Godfrey himself was in command, and feasting with his leaders. They were directed to the small church of Ronaldsway, in typical Viking fashion taken over for this purpose.

Godfrey Godfreysson proved to be a heavily-built, hot-eyed young man, all shaggy fair hair and beard, loud-voiced with wine. There was no sort of ceremony about the envoys' introduction — quite the reverse. They merely had to push their way through the roystering, sprawling crew in the church to where what was presumably the leadership group were using the altar as a table. Even le Chien looked shocked. Standing before this, it took some time for any attention to be paid to them. At length le Chien obtained some notice by the simple expedient of stepping forward and banging his fist on the altar-top.

"We come in the name of the High King of Scots!" he exclaimed. "Which is Godfrey Godfreysson?"

The youngest-looking man there, leaning back, drinking-horn in hand, gestured with it, and belched. "I am Godfrey," he said, slack-mouthed and blurred of speech. "As you, and all, will find out, by God! You — how came you here?"

"On King Alexander's command. From Galloway. I am Sir Reginald le Chien of Inverugie, Thane of Formartine, Sheriff of Nairn and lately Lord High Chamberlain of Scotland. This is Sir Thomas Learmonth. Can we speak with you alone, sir?"

"Alone? You? No! Fiend seize you — I desire no speech with such as you! Or any lackey of Alexander. Off with you!"

"You would be wise to hear us, nevertheless, Godfrey Godfreysson!"

There was a growl from others at the altar-table, and one or two rose unsteadily to their feet.

"King Godfrey," Thomas put in. "Of your patience, hear us, who have come to your island bringing King Alexander's goodwill. He does not desire conflict with you. He is a man of peace — has proved himself to be so . . ."

"Yet he brings a great army to Galloway, lame man! Gathers ships. Think you that we do not know what is done? Is that not for conflict? Alexander but seeks to gain time, sending you here."

"No, sir. He sent us offering peace. He has no wish to embark his army. Would prefer to disperse it. He says that he is bound to support King Ivar's son, your nephew. His claim to his father's throne. For the future. But that meantime, until the lad grows to manhood, he will accept yourself as King of Man, subject to himself as High King . . ."

"I, Godfrey, am subject to none!"

"With respect, my lord, from King Olaf's time and Godfrey Crovan's and Ivar's, Man has been by signed treaty subject to the Scottish throne . . ."

"Then, fool, it is no longer! Tell your Alexander so."

"You cannot withstand the might of Scotland, man!" le Chien declared forcefully. "Which might defeated Hakon, with ten times your strength."

"Hakon had to land first, on a protected shore, fellow — as Alexander must do here. He will not find it easy, fiend seize him! I too have a great host gathered — not only here but throughout Man. And not only these. More to come. From Dublin and Orkney. And from Edward Longshanks . . ."

"You would rather be subject to the tyrant Edward, who slew ten thousand for a whim, in the Holy Land, than to Alexander, a man of peace? For it will be one or the other, I promise you! Man cannot stand alone . . ."

Le Chien's voice was drowned in angry shouts from all around.

"Enough!" Godfrey cried, slamming his drinking-horn on the altar-top. "Enough, I say! Be off with you both. Before I have your tongues torn out, to send back to Alexander as a warning!"

"We return to the High King, then, to tell him that Godfrey Godfreysson refuses to desist from his presumptuous rebellion . . ."

"Christ God!" The drinking-horn came hurtling through

the air, splattering wine, although the aim was erratic.

The envoys retired somewhat hurriedly.

Making their way back through the camp, their first anger subsiding, they endeavoured to cull some benefit from the journey by trying to assess the quality and numbers of the force assembled. In the firelit dark it was not easy, but they came to the conclusion that there were between four and five thousand men, some obviously Irish-Norse; and there would be little doubt as to their fighting-qualities. If Godfrey was not merely boasting, there would be further forces strategically-placed, none so far away.

As they neared the haven, Thomas put it to his companion that they would find little joy in passing the night here. Better, safer, in the boat. And if in the boat they might as well be asail. Their boatmen were fishers and therefore used to night sailing. It was breezy but not wild; and the wind would now be directly behind them, so that no tacking would be necessary and the length of their voyage halved, speed much bettered. And the sooner they could get back to Alexander, the better.

"Why the haste?" le Chien, no sailor, demanded. "We bring him but ill tidings. And he will not have assembled all the shipping he requires in the meantime."

"Nevertheless, I say that we should urge him to immediate attack," Thomas insisted. "You heard — Godfrey looks for further men, from Dublin and Orkney, if not England. Leave him and he will gather strength. He knows that Alexander is gathering ships — always slow work. So he will not expect any swift assault. I say take him by surprise. Attack at once. By night, if possible. At least cross in the darkness. If we could land here at Ronaldsway unexpected, we might well win ashore all but unopposed. Better a smaller number of men and ships, with surprise, than a large host awaited and countered."

"Perhaps, perhaps not."

"It is worth the trial."

"Alexander may not think so . . ."

* * *

Sir John de Vesci stamped to and fro on the poop of the

largest of the invasion fleet, cursing steadily. He cursed the shipmaster and helmsman, he cursed the Manxmen, he cursed Alexander for putting him in charge of this crazy expedition, he cursed le Chien and Thomas for urging it, above all he cursed the darkness, the fact that he could not see more than two or three of the other vessels, could not see land, could see nothing that he required to know, could not tell where they were and whether they could still hope to reach the Ronaldsway area before daybreak — and if so how many were likely to reach it. The notion of a night-time voyage and assault was madness from start to finish, and only a dizzard king would have agreed with the dizzards who suggested it. To all of which Thomas forbore answer and comment, le Chien remaining conveniently out-of-sight below. Such other of the Scots leadership as were aboard this leading vessel tended to agree with de Vesci, however much they deplored him and resented his having been placed in command.

Using all the shipping assembled, Alexander had been able to embark less than half of his army at Kirk Cuthbert's Town for this venture. He had been somewhat doubtful, admittedly, as to the wisdom of it all, but had recognised the enormous advantage which would accrue if a surprise landing could be achieved. He himself would wait behind and bring on the main body when transport became available — and when he could perceive how matters were going and where the major thrust should be made. They had sailed, therefore, as the dusk deepened and it would be too late for any possible spies to get word of it across to Man — and a confused and protracted business it had been getting between three and four thousand men on to a motley and heterogeneous collection of craft, large and small, in the darkness. That had been some eight hours before. Now they were somewhere in the Irish Sea, in thin rain and a fitful northerly wind, with less than two hours till dawn — and the fleet almost certainly scattered over many miles of sea, although so little of it could be seen. Thomas himself was feeling distinctly dubious about it all — but did not admit it, especially as his brother-in-law Pate was one of the most vocal critics in the matter.

334

The shipmaster of the vessel, oddly, seemed the least concerned — of course, he would not have to do any of the fighting. But he asserted that he knew where they were, and would have them at the south end of Man within two hours, God willing. He could not speak for the other ships but would be surprised if most were not there soon after. It was only thirty-odd miles, after all, and lacking mist or storm, should not tax any seaman too greatly. He announced that if it was sufficiently light they would see the coast of Man no more than a couple of miles on the starboard bow.

If de Vesci scarcely believed him then, he and the others were still more incredulous when, just under an hour later, their Dumbarton skipper declared that he dared go no closer inshore in this state of the tide and that he was going to let go the anchor. Although his hearers stared from him to the direction in which he pointed, they gained no enlightenment from one nor the other. Then they were roughly told to listen instead of exclaiming — and assured that what they heard was seas breaking on the shores of St. Michael's Isle and Ronaldsway Bay.

Whether it was due to a pre-dawn lessening of the darkness or to their own heightened perceptions or imagination, presently most believed that they could just make out the loom of land in the gloom to their right. Equally encouraging was the fact that small craft, crowded with men, began to appear around them — and presumably there would be others that they could not see. These, shallower in draught, could and did move closer inshore. This had the effect of making de Vesci and his lieutenants the more agitated and impatient, lest the landing-attempt went off prematurely. So calling one of the fishing-boats still closer, he clambered down a rope-ladder into it, with his closest associates, commanding to be taken shorewards — but still cursing comprehensively. Others followed his example, in other boats, Thomas, lame leg notwithstanding, finding himself in a fishing-coble, high-prowed and smelly, already occupied by about a score of Carrick men.

Feeling that everything was getting out-of-hand and that this was not how it ought to be, he was rowed onwards, westwards. There was another fishing-boat just in front and two more astern. The noise of breakers grew even louder.

Suddenly there were shouts ahead, and their boat had to swing aside to avoid a collision with the one in front, at the same time beginning to toss violently in wavy shallows. Thomas was astonished to see men jumping out into the water, which came up only to their middles. Their own craft surged on a further few yards and then shuddered as its stem grounded. Its Carrickers went over the side without delay, Thomas following them into the cold foaming waves, to stagger onwards, using his great sword as staff, over a sandy base.

In perhaps seventy yards of breaking shoal-water he was on to the dry, shelving beach. Men were standing and stamping about, at a loss, shouting to each other — but that was all. No fighting was going on. Pulling himself together, Thomas — who had had little or no sleep in the last forty hours — sent up an unspoken prayer of thankfulness that some of them at least should thus have achieved a landing on Man without loss or even opposition — and then set about doing something practical.

Taking charge, he rallied all the men on this section of beach, with others coming ashore all the time, and telling them to follow him, went northwards along the strand, peering into the gloom. He had gained the impression that de Vesci's boat, and most others, had headed slightly more in that direction. There were men, in small groups and large, all along that benighted shore, uncertain what to do. All were glad to adhere to someone who at least appeared to know what he was at.

He found de Vesci and the others, at length, conferring on a sand hill of marram-grass. All were as surprised as he was at this extraordinary situation, at having been able to land on Man without a blow struck. Presumably Godfrey's army just had not considered the possibility of so early an attack, or a night-assault, and saw no need to keep a shore-watch.

"If this is the style of him, we should not find Godfrey Godfreysson too hard a nut to shell," de Vesci declared — almost the first non-condemnatory word they had had from him that night.

"He will be surprised when he wakes, to find us drawn up and ready for him, on his precious island!" the High Steward asserted.

"Would to God I knew the lie of the land, here, to choose the best battle-ground." The Englishman turned to Thomas. "You, Learmonth, were here in daylight. Can you remember how it lies? How best to place our force here until we have gathered our full strength?"

It was the Steward rather than de Vesci whom Thomas chose to answer. "Godfrey would be still more surprised if *we* were to awake him! At his church-door. Why wait to find a battle-ground? If he is so little concerned with keeping watch as not to have discovered us yet, likely his camp will be little better guarded. Attack forthwith, I say."

"Assail sleeping men, Sir Thomas?"

"Why not? This is war, not a tourney, my lord. Godfrey has usurped this throne and challenged his liege-lord, and ours. He should be more heedful."

"Where is this camp, man?" de Vesci demanded.

"On level ground, yonder, south by west. Less than a half-mile."

"Unprotected? No ramparts, ditches, fortifications?"

"None. It is but open machar grassland."

"Then it is worth a venture. Even if we only scatter him meantime, it will give us time to muster our strength and choose the best field for battle. Let us teach this rebel a lesson in watch-keeping!"

So, wasting no time — for even with the belated dawn of a damp and cloudy morning it would be getting light within the hour — they gathered all the men they could find on the beaches, amounting now they reckoned to some twelve hundred. It was a small enough number to attempt to over-run a camp four or five times that number, but de Vesci chose to strike while it was still fairly dark rather than wait for reinforcements from the rest of the fleet and possibly find the enemy waking. Marshalling their mixed bag of men in some sort of order, and enjoining strict silence, they crept inland, Thomas leading the way. Of le Chien there was no sign.

When they came, without arousing any evident alarm, to a

spur of higher ground from which they could overlook the camp area, it was to gain no impression of stirring. The only features visible in the three-quarters dark were the ruddy glowings of a number of dying fires, which clearly had not been replenished for hours. So at least there was no move yet to start the day. There would be sentries, almost certainly, but these would be at their least alert just before dawn.

De Vesci passed back the whispered orders — spread out in line of advance in groups of a score or so, to move in slowly, steadily, without rush or shout, and so to beat their way through the camp from east to west, keeping line as far as possible. No chasing, no turning aside, just steady advance, steady killing. It would grow more difficult as they went on, with the camp aroused. There would be panic — but not to let the enemy's panic affect their own discipline. Leaders were set at intervals along the line. The signal to advance would be the trill of a curlew, thrice.

Thomas Learmonth it was, knowledgeable about birds, who wheepled that call, presently.

To try to describe what followed with any coherence or realism would be profitless. If there were any sentries awake, they failed to arouse their sleeping comrades — and it was left to the screams and yells of the wounded and dying to do that. And even these took a surprising length of time fully to bring the majority of the sleepers to wakefulness. Until then it was controlled and systematic horror, slaughter, massacre, unsparing, unrelenting. There could be precious little attempt to fight back, although some few individuals awoke sufficiently alert to try it — and took a little longer to die in consequence.

It was when, at length, the noise had wakened all but the completely drunken, that the panic started. Darkness, screaming, shock and lack of leadership, added to the effect of the rude awakening, could scarcely have had any other result. And panic is most highly infectious. The primary instinct was flight, to get away from this horror. Few indeed felt it incumbent upon them to attempt any counter-attack, and no real pockets of resistance developed. The terror came from the east and south, therefore the west and north beckoned and lay open. Waking, bemused and appalled men sensed this, at least, in their alarm, and turned to flee in those directions, singly, in groups and dozens. Quickly it became a flood.

The Rout of Ronaldsway was accomplished in only a few terrible minutes.

Once the Scots leadership saw that little further direction of their forces was going to be necessary meantime, they sought Godfrey Godfreysson, Thomas pointing the way to the church. But there they found all abandoned, with every sign of a most hasty departure, clothing, armour, weapons as well as blankets and sheepskins strewn everywhere. Man's young usurper had not waited to seek rally his people.

The invaders could scarcely credit their success, the speed and ease of it. De Vesci allowed some time for his men to chase the fleeing enemy and to make sure that they did not rally at some inland position; then he had the horns blown for a recall. The light was now sufficient to see some distance, and strengthening.

Whilst they waited for all to reassemble, the enemy dead were laid out, 537 of them, and such wounded as could drag themselves off allowed to do so. Thomas joined a group endeavouring to aid the more seriously injured, although there was not much that they were able to do.

Eating the Manxmen's breakfast, de Vesci held a council-of-war in the church. They had, thus cheaply, dispersed Godfrey's main army; but there were other forces, reputedly, and this large island would give ample scope for a prolonged resistance and possible counter-strokes. Scouting-parties must be sent out all over, while the main Scots host rested, reformed and was reinforced with stragglers from the fleet. It was no part of de Vesci's remit to conquer and occupy Man itself, merely making a landing and try to engage Godfrey and hold him until Alexander could come up with his main strength.

By midday, however, sufficient reports had come in from the scouts to convince all concerned that there was unlikely to be any co-ordinated resistance throughout the island. In every area groups and small forces were melting away.

Godfrey, it seemed, was by no means popular with the majority of Manxmen, there being much latent loyalty to the child-heir, his nephew. When, finally, assured word arrived that Godfrey had in fact sailed away for Dublin from Fleshwick Bay, on the west coast, all were prepared to believe it of so brash and incompetent a usurper. De Vesci decided to return to Galloway forthwith, although leaving most of his force to keep an eye on Man meantime, until Alexander's further requirements were known.

Thomas thought it best to accompany him.

So, after surely the briefest successful invasion campaign ever, leaving the High Steward in charge, much of the Scots leadership sailed back across the Irish Sea to Kirk Cuthbert's Town. There they found Alexander in a curious frame of mind, impatient for their news, thankful enough to hear it, but with only part of his mind and attention it seemed. For he had just had news of a different sort. The Queen had died at Coupar Abbey, and their youngest child, David, was sick. Clearly the King's present preoccupation was to get back northwards at the earliest possible moment. Their tidings from Man permitted it.

Next morning early Alexander was on his way, riding fast with a small escort, Thomas accompanying him as far as Lauderdale.

17

"My very good friend," Bagimond said, little eyes twinkling, "I have heard much of you, since last I saw you, all over your land of Scotland. Why did you not tell me that you were a celebrated soothsayer? I learned of your fame wherever I went. In especial in the North, in Mar and Buchan and Moray, where men speak much of you."

"You have been so far? Beyond the Mounth? Did you go to Monymusk? And Fyvie? And Deer?"

"All these, yes — and many more. To Pluscarden and Urquhart and Rossmarkyn." The little Italian made odd pronunciation of those. "Why did you say nothing of this your gift when I was with you?"

"He esteems his gift but little — if gift it is," Bethoc said. "It brings him little pleasure or content."

"Yet men speak much of it, declare him seer. Tell of strange, deep matters foretold."

"I would not have thought that *you* would have approved," Thomas said. "Does not Holy Church frown on such things?"

"There are fools in Holy Church as elsewhere, my friend. For myself, I do not frown on anything merely because I do not understand it — so be it that it is not clearly the work of the Devil. As I cannot believe could be so with your good self. God's gifts are infinitely various and should be made the most of, practised, employed."

"So say I," Bethoc agreed. "Thomas values only his poetry. Not the ryhmes he makes, foretelling the future, but his true poetry. This of *Sir Tristrem* and such-like."

"You must tell me of this also. Poets are to be cherished . . ."

Bagimond had arrived at Ercildoune on his way southwards to England. He had completed the first part of his great task, the making up of the assessment roll, and was now going to render due account of it to the Papal Legate in England, at that individual's apparently peremptory request. In the past two years there had been major upheavals at Rome. Pope Innocent, who had proclaimed the new Crusade and had sent Bagimond to Scotland, with a six-year tax-assessment and collection assignment, had died. He had been succeeded by the imperious Ottobone, of unhappy memory, as Pope Adrian the Fifth. However, he too had died, after a mere few months as Pontiff, and had been followed by John the Twenty-first. Remarkably, he was dead within the year; and now there was still another Pope, Nicholas the Third, an Orsini, who was apparently acting the new broom and questioning all his immediate predecessors' actions and appointments. Head ashake, Bagimond wondered whether all these sudden deaths were from entirely natural causes.

At any rate, he must go and render account to Nicholas's new Legate in London. Whether it would be well received by the present regime, whether even he would be permitted to return to Scotland to continue with his further four years of tithe-collecting, remained to be seen.

Thomas at least had no doubts as to that, declaring that his friend's industry and effectiveness in the matter could not be bettered. Especially when he learned that Bagimond's total assessment of tithe added up to the enormous sum of £7195, 6 florins and 6 pence sterling, a figure hardly conceivable even to the chief steward of the earldoms of Dunbar and March.

Bagimond had more intelligence for them than this. The Franciscan friar sent up by the Legate to summon him to London had brought other, more secular news. Edward of England, when he learned that Ottobone had achieved the papacy, and knowing his violently anti-Scottish sentiments, had written him a letter urging him to issue a formal edict declaring Alexander of Scotland to be a sub-king only, subject to himself, Edward, as Lord Paramount. He had asserted, in support of this, that the said Alexander had in the past done fealty to himself and also to his gracious father Henry the Third of pious memory — although he was refusing fealty now. It so happened, of course, that Ottobone was dead by the time that the King of England's envoy reached Rome; and indeed his successor, John, had likewise passed away before he had come to any conclusions on the matter. So that now the request lay before Nicholas Orsini, who was known to be a bird of a very different plumage, tough, aggressive and by no means pro-English — the Church Militant indeed. It all showed, however, how determined Edward was over this paramountcy issue and how alert the Scots had to be. With Queen Margaret dead, her brother might well have shed any remaining inhibitions about perhaps seeking to force his case by main strength. He was at present campaigning in Wales, engaged in hammering that unfortunate principality to his will, with a steel fist, ravaging and massacring on an unprecedented scale. But when he had finished with Wales, who could tell but that he might well turn his full and savage attention upon Scotland? Thomas pointed out that Scotland would be a much harder nut to crack than Wales — but at the same time he remembered, with some sinking of the heart, how militarily inexperienced they were, as demonstrated by the Manx business — and in any trouble with the veteran Edward, they would not have any support from such as de Vesci.

Bagimond said that talk amongst the knowledgeable was that Alexander was worried. The complicating feature of it all was, of course, the Huntingdon revenues, the greatest single source of wealth for Alexander. Comprising valuable manors and lands in no fewer than eleven English counties, the rich honour and earldom was something he was evidently by no means prepared to give up. But without paying fealty to Edward for it, this income was denied him. Alexander, not so much extravagant as careless with money, had never really concerned himself with raising maximum revenue from Scotland, by taxation. His great-great grandfather, King David of saintly memory, had impoverished the Crown grievously by his vast programme of abbey-building and endowment; it was only fair that the Huntingdon wealth his wife had brought him should help to redress the balance for his successors. Alexander did not want to lose it all. So somehow the fealty business had to be got round. Going to war with Edward would entail forfeiture of Huntingdon once and for all, nothing surer. But what could be done, to good effect, was not apparent.

Bagimond was off again next day, to cross the Border, promising to call again should he be permitted to return to Scotland.

That was in April 1278. It was June before Thomas heard more of the King's affairs — and this time he heard it from the monarch's own lips. Alexander came riding down Lauderdale with a gay and colourful train, not on this occasion equipped for war. Thomas should perhaps have felt flattered that his liege-lord should thus honour his humble tower of Ercildoune most times that he rode this way — and it was his usual route to Roxburgh, Galloway or further south — but he recognised that the King usually had some errand or service for him to accomplish on these occasions. This time however, after hearty greetings, reference to Bethoc's fair looks and Tom William's notable growth, plus the customary enquiry as to whether Thomas had any new rhymes and predictions for him, it was to ask him if he would fancy a jaunt down to Wales.

Thomas blinked and looked doubtful. "Wales, Sire? No — no, Your Grace, I have no notion to ride to Wales. I have more to do here. It is hay-harvest. And hogg-clipping . . ."

"Tush, man — do not play the farmer with me! It would serve you excellently well in this June sunshine. Get you away from Patrick's wool and mutton, for a while. Good company and new places. You have never been to Wales?"

"No, Sire. Is this . . . a royal command?"

"Save us, no! I can survive, I think, without your services! I but believed that it might cheer you."

"Then I thank Your Grace for your kind thought. But see my duties here as more pressing."

"You ever were a stubborn churl, Thomas! Why did I knight you?"

"I have often wondered, Sire. But, I pray — not churlish. Never that. I much esteem your royal favour."

"M'mm," the King said.

"You go to Wales, Highness? King Edward is in Wales, they say."

"Aye. Edward! I go to see Edward. Once more."

"This of the fealty, Sire?"

"God plague him — yes! He has me by the ears! But — see you, I cannot stand talking here, and all these looking on. Come ride with me as far as Tweed. You have wits in that stubborn head of yours, I know. Perhaps you may think of something that I and the others have missed . . ."

So Thomas rode at the King's side for a few miles southwards, and heard again Alexander's predicament — which indeed needed no retelling. Anxious for those Huntingdon revenues, the King had finally written to Edward, declaring himself prepared to pay fealty for them — but only them — and offering to come south to some suitable meeting-

344

place to do so. Edward had replied favourably enough, sending a safe-conduct and suggesting a meeting somewhere on the Welsh Marches. Which meant, of course, that Longshanks was not going to move a step out of his way, leaving all the travel to Alexander — although to be sure the man was engaged in warfare of a sort.

"You think that he will be any more willing to listen to reason, Sire? In his shameful claim to overlordship? Than he was in London. I heard tell of his letter to the Pope."

"The good Lord knows! But I wrote, offering fealty for my lands in his kingdom. He must know that I will go no further. Somehow I must convince him."

"Would it not be better, easier, to give up the Honour of Huntingdon?"

"No! That I will never do. It is mine. As it was my forefathers'. My inheritance. I will not yield it to Edward."

"If not give up, at least do not seek to draw the moneys. He cannot *make* you take any oath of allegiance if you do nothing."

"He could forfeit the earldom. Earldoms there, as here, are subject to Crown approval."

"He has not done so, yet."

"I need the moneys, man."

Out of a lengthy silence, Thomas spoke again. "Is there nothing which you might offer King Edward, Sire? Which he might wish to have? Which you value less than Huntingdon?"

"Have I anything such?"

"I was thinking of Man, Your Grace. The overlordship of Man. It brings you little profit or joy, I think."

"Man, in Edward's hands, would be a threat always to my west coasts. Surely you can see that, Thomas."

"More threat than at present? He has all the Cumbrian coast. If he wished to attack you by sea, he does not require Man, Sire."

"Nevertheless, I will not give him Man. That one is like a beast of prey. The more blood he tastes, the more he will want. I will not appease him with territories."

"Then, if you have nothing to offer him which he may want, there remains only what he will *not* want. Threats."

"How may I threaten England? He can place ten men in the field for every one of mine. And he is no mean fighter, however savage."

"I did not mean battle, Highness. But there are threats to which princes are subject, other than war, are there not? Treaties. Alliances."

"Ah. You would have me married off again, man? As would Wishart. My wily Primate suggests that I wed some French princess. But I can think of none of suitable years. And, God knows, I have had enough of required marriage!"

"I am less bold than that, Sire. I was thinking of a betrothal, rather. Where it might best serve. Your daughter, perhaps? The Princess Margaret is now in her eighteenth year is she not? Alliance with a kingdom which might pose a threat to England. France, meantime, is scarcely that. The Empire is in decay and Rudolf of Hapsburg's sons already wed. Who else could endanger England? Only the Norsemen. King Magnus Hakonsson has a son, Eric. The Norse, with their kin in Orkney, Iceland, the Hebrides and Ireland, are always a danger. To Scotland as well as to England. With their great fleets of longships. An alliance with Norway, through marriage, might serve you well. And give King Edward pause."

"Think you I have not considered that? The boy Eric is but in his twelfth year. And less than robust, I am told."

"Old enough for a betrothal. You were *wed* younger, were you not?"

"Aye — and would not wish that on any child!"

"A betrothal need not be followed by marriage, for years. But it would serve warning on the English. Any attack on Scotland could bring in the Norsemen."

"Such would take time to arrange. I need aid now."

"The threat of it might serve its turn. Tell King Edward of your intention. It could cause him to consider."

"I need more than that. Something more . . . immediate."

Thomas shook his head. "I do not know . . . but a thought came to me when Bagimond of Vicci told me of Edward's letter to the Pope. The thought that two could write to the Pope."

"Write and tell him that the King of Scots is not Edward's vassal? I have already done so."

"More than that. Suppose that you wrote to this new Pope asking him to appoint Edward to lead his new Crusade? He glories in the title of First Knight of Christendom. He makes much of his former crusading successes — he did so much more killing that Louis of France! If the Pope would name him to lead it, he might refuse. But it would much occupy his mind. He would be much tempted, I think. And there would be so much to do first. He might well forget Scotland for a time. Were not the best years we have had for long those when Edward was away on the last Crusade?"

Alexander turned in his saddle. "Save us, Thomas — I believe you have something, there! Dear God, I do! He might not go, might refuse, yes. But he would resent any other, thereafter, being given the leadership. As you say, it would much occupy his mind. If I told him that I had written to this Nicholas suggesting it, he might be flattered, even think better of me for it! Who knows? I could make much of Christendom's indebtedness. Aye, I believe that there could be some profit in this, at least. For the other, we shall see . . ."

Thomas turned back where Leader joined Tweed, wishing his monarch well. Whether he had been wise to proffer his suggestions, he did not know. But he was glad that he had not agreed to go on with Alexander, to see them put to the test.

*   *   *

As it transpired, it was from Bagimond, not Alexander himself, that Thomas heard of the outcome of that royal mission. The Italian had apparently had an awkward interview with the new Legate in London, and thereafter had to hold many exhaustive sessions with the Cardinal's clerks, who went into his Scottish findings and assessments item by item, criticising, comparing them with each other and similar establishments in England, comparing them with previous records. The result had been no thanks but a grudging acceptance and being sent back to Scotland to turn these assessments into solid money.

Bagimond had been kept almost three months in London, awaiting the Legate's permission to return; and during the last week the two monarchs had arrived at the Tower there, from Wales. In Alexander's train was Bishop Robert of Dunblane, with whom Bagimond had previously established good relations. He it was who gave the interested Piedmontese some indications of the state of affairs prevailing now between the kings.

It seemed that Alexander had eventually run Edward to earth, not on the Welsh Marches but at Tewkesbury in Gloucestershire, already on his way back to London — which had been an inauspicious start. There had been no open quarrel but the coolness between the royal pair was not to be hidden. Edward had pooh-poohed any idea of a fealty ceremony, for one so important as the King of Scots, taking place anywhere save at Westminster; and though Alexander would have been glad to get the wretched business over as quickly and briefly as possible, he had been forced to accompany Longshanks back to London. Relations had improved a little on the journey after Alexander had announced that he had written to the Pope urging the appointment of Edward as leader of the new Crusade, claiming him to be the finest and most experienced soldier in Christendom, even though the latter showed that he recognised this gesture for what it was. At the actual allegiance-ceremony in Westminster Abbey, although Alexander had made it clear from the first that his fealty would only apply to lands held in England, there had been another battle of wills and embarrassing interlude with the Bishop of Norwich — presently Edward's favourite cleric, for he was having trouble with Canterbury — seeking to insert a clause which could bear the interpretation that Scotland was in some sort of vassalage to England. There developed an unseemly scene and for a while it looked as though once again the entire ceremony would have to be abandoned and come to nothing. But eventually a compromise was reached by incorporating in Alexander's oath that he accepted his brother-in-law as Principal Counsellor to himself as King of Scots, a title which had been accepted on his behalf once before by his Regent during his minority, referring to Henry the Third. With that Edward had had to be content, and the fealty oath for

Huntingdon was given and accepted. The Bishop of Dunblane had indicated that he looked upon it all, on the whole, as a minor triumph for the Scots, since Alexander had achieved his objective in regaining the right to collect the Huntingdon revenues without conceding Edward's overlordship of Scotland. But others in the Scots party were less happy, according to Bagimond, seeing Edward's position as further strengthened, if only slightly. Principal Counsellor to the King of Scots might have represented a mere empty title where Henry had been concerned; but his son might make it otherwise.

Thomas asked if Bagimond had heard anything of a proposed Scots-Norse marriage and was told that the Bishop had mentioned something of the sort, but without special emphasis. There was however talk of another proposed marriage — proposed by Edward, presumably in his new role of Adviser — that the Scots heir-to-the-throne, Prince Alexander, should wed Margaret, daughter of Guy, Count of Flanders. Guy de Dampierre was kin and ally of Edward and much under his influence; and since Edward could scarcely suggest any of his own surviving daughters — he had had eleven of them so far — for the match, Holy Church's ban being automatic, they being full cousins of the prince — this was probably as near as he could get to being in a position to influence Scotland's future monarch.

Few could fail to see Edward Plantagenet as something in the nature of a great dark cloud looming up ever larger in Scotland's sky.

18

Roxburgh Castle rang with music, laughter, merriment, with no inhibitions as to dark clouds looming. The King had seldom seemed in better spirits, and most took their tune from him. Anyway it was an occasion for celebration. Not only was it the Prince Alexander's birthday, the eighteenth, when he entered officially into man's estate even though not yet of full age; but also the Norwegian envoys were present to sign the marriage-contract between the Princess Margaret and Prince Eric Magnusson. Not only that, it was the Earl Patrick and Countess Christian of Dunbar's fortieth wedding-anniversary, and to mark the occasion all three sons were to be knighted. Pate should have been given the accolade years before, as heir to two of the realm's great earldoms as well as son-in-law of Buchan the High Constable; but it was common knowledge that Alexander did not like him; and his father, estranged from him also, had not pressed the matter. But now, with his brothers to be honoured, he could scarcely be omitted.

In the circumstances a special table had been provided on the dais for the Dunbar family, at right-angles to the King's. As a notable treat, young Tom William, now in his thirteenth year, had been permitted to be present, and certainly entered into the spirit of the occasion.

Of all there, it could be that Tom's father was the least in tune with the general cheer. He had his reasons. The previous night he had had a recurrence of a dream which had come to him frequently of late, only this time it was much more vivid and circumstantial, grievously so, and he had been driven to write it down in the morning, in his usual rhyming form — although he had more or less promised himself to abjure all such for the future. And it made something of a nonsense of these present celebrations, unfortunately. The second reason was that he was filled with impatience. Tonight had been chosen to be the first public reading of *Sir Tristrem* — or at least some part of it — and he was all nerves about it. Moreover, Alexander was leaving it too late. It should have been done immediately after the eating was over and before the wine began to make men noisy. Already that was happening. Soon it would be impossible, with much of the company not in any state to listen properly, much less to appreciate. He had tried to catch the King's eye, but placed as he was at the Dunbar

350

table, this was difficult. He could hardly rise to go over and remind Alexander. He just wished that he had never agreed to do it. The idea had been Bethoc's and she had persuaded her father to put it to Alexander — who had been enthusiastic enough. Now it all looked like being ruined, made a fool of.

Bethoc sought to soothe him at the same time as trying to quieten down their son.

At length the King signed for a trumpeter to blow for quiet. Then calling all to heed him, he announced the principal event of the evening. It had been his great joy and satisfaction, earlier, to proclaim the betrothal of his dear and only daughter, Margaret, to the Prince Eric Magnusson, heir to the King of Norway, Magnus the Good. He rose and bowed to his daughter, sitting on his left. She stood also — as must all others. She was a tall, pale and rather colourless young woman, very much her mother's daughter. Now she hung her head during the applause. All knew that she was much against the projected marriage to a youth six years her junior.

Alexander went on, signing for the company to be seated again. "It is my pleasure that two of His Grace of Norway's envoys have come across the Norse Sea to sign the marriage-contract — the Bishop Narfi of Bergen and the Lord Thori Hakonsson, Chancellor. These we most warmly welcome." He gestured to his right where the ambassadors sat.

The two Norwegians rose, bowed and sat down again.

"The terms of this marriage-contract state that I will provide, as dower for my daughter, the sum of seven thousand merks in silver, to be paid at Berwick. Also the yearly rental of seven hundred merks, from the lands of Bathgate, Ratho, Rothiemay and Belhelvie. Likewise the King of Norway will grant lands of similar value within his realm. Lawful offspring of this marriage will have due precedence as heirs to the crown and realm of Norway. I now call upon my lord Chancellor Charteris to bring the two copies of the contract here for signature, and thereafter to call the names of the lords selected to come forward as witness."

From further down the table the new Chancellor, Thomas

de Charteris, who had succeeded Fraser, now Bishop of St. Andrews, brought up the parchment rolls, with quill and ink-horn, and space was cleared on the board for them to be unrolled and signed, first by Alexander then by the Norse envoys. The impressive roll of witnesses was then called, Patrick, Earl of Dunbar and March and his heir the Lord Patrick of Dunglass, high on the list. There was much rising and movement and pushing back of forms.

Thomas fretted.

This over at length, the King made another announcement, flat of voice this time. "Thanks to the good offices of the puissant Lord Edward, King of England and Duke of Normandy, a betrothal is hereby declared between my dear elder son and heir Alexander, Prince of Scotland, on this the eighteenth year of his age, and the Lady Margaret of Flanders, daughter of the Lord Guy de Dampierre, Count of Flanders. The terms of this contract are yet to be settled between the parties, but I pledge that the lawful issue of such union will have due precedence in heiring the kingdom and realm of Scotland."

There was an indeterminate murmur at this, with little of positive acclaim. None there was likely to consider that this was in any way a noteworthy or prestigious match for their heir-to-the-throne. The Prince Alexander, on the right of the Norwegians, a delicate-seeming youth, almost beautiful of feature in contrast to his lack-lustre sister, looked uncertain as to whether to rise to acknowledge this brief mention, but contented himself with faint smiles right and left.

As though relieved to have this done with, the King spoke again, more heartily. "Now — we also celebrate this day still another marriage, one of long standing, which has been greatly blessed and borne much fruit. In the year of our Lord 1241, full forty years ago, Patrick of Dunbar and Christian Bruce of Annandale were wed, both kin of my own. It has proved a happy, productive and most excellent union — as witness here tonight my lord Earl and his Countess with the six proofs of their felicity! And he waved an arm towards the Dunbar table.

Now there was something which the company could

applaud, more than merely formally, and loud was the acclaim.

The younger members of the happy family all looked much embarrassed.

"As mark of my esteem and congratulation," Alexander went on, "I would wish to improve on this happy occasion. I cannot, I fear, enhance the felicity and venerable years of my cousins Patrick and Christian. Nor can I enhance the grace and beauty of their three daughters, to whom I pay admiring tribute. But their sons, now, since they lack both venerable years and beauty likewise, if not grace — perhaps I may do something for these, at least. Patrick, Younger of Dunbar and March; John of Birkensyde; and Alexander of Whitwood — I command that you come forward."

The three brothers, now all so different in appearance, Pate tall, pale, black-bearded and intense; Johnnie burly, ruddy, cheerful; Alec slight, boyish, fair, rose and moved over the dais to behind the King's table, shuffling somewhat awkwardly, to line up, looking as though they wished that the floor would open and swallow them.

Their monarch ordered them to kneel, and taking a sword produced by one of his heralds, tapped each of them on his two shoulders, commanding them to make their due vows hereafter, to serve Almighty God, to protect himself and his successors on the throne of Scotland, to support justice and the right, to cherish women, the weak and the helpless, and to remain good and true knights until their lives' end, so help them God.

So arose Sir Patrick, Sir John and Sir Alexander, to resounding cheers. They bowed to the King, looked at each other doubtfully and were waved back to their seats and to the congratulations of men and the kisses of their womenfolk.

Thomas who had been remembering these three racing each other over the Eildon Hills, sought to offer his felicitations, which were gladly received by Johnnie and Alec but curtly rebuffed by Pate — who indeed seemed less than pleased over the entire episode. Gelis whispered not to heed him, asserting that he resented being knighted along with his

353

younger brothers and being made a carpet-knight at that —
that is, given the accolade indoors at a mere ceremony
instead of on the field of battle or on campaign, in more
gallant fashion, as he had apparently looked for after the
Rout of Ronaldsway on Man.

Thomas was considering this, reckoning that nothing
could have been less chivalrous and knightly than that
massacre in the darkness, when he realised that his name was
being mentioned. The King at last had come to the crux of
the evening.

". . . all know the Earl Patrick's goodson as True Thomas,
whose divinations and foretellings are renowned,"
Alexander was saying. "But not all are aware that he is also a
poet of much worth. Indeed it is as a poet, it seems, that he
would wish to be known, rather than a prophet. Tonight, to
celebrate this happy conjuncture, he is going to declare to us
the first part of a great new poem he has written. On the
theme of Tristrem and Isolde. The first time this will have
been heard by any company. I, for one, am eager to hear it.
Sir Thomas — we await your pleasure."

With Bethoc squeezing his arm and Tom William grinning
hugely, Thomas picked up his lute and, bowing, limped to a
corner of the dais where a herald had placed a stool. There
was much stir and comment throughout the hall.

He waited for quiet. When it was not forthcoming,
Alexander flicked a finger at his trumpeter, who blew a blast
which had the desired effect. Noticeably, Pate's voice, talking
loudly to his wife, was the last to fall silent.

"In this land we are largely of the Celtic race," Thomas
declared, a little more forcefully than was necessary. "We are
of the Cruithne or Picts, of the Scots or Irish, of the
Strathclyde and Galloway Cymric. All Celts. There are other
Celtic folk, of Wales and Cornwall and Brittany. This tale is
of these, our Celtic cousins, of an age that is past. Telling of
one of the knights of the celebrated Arthur. I call it *Sir
Tristrem*. It is a tale of great but guilty love, of war and strife
and sacrifice, of hatred and folly. It is joy and sorrow, love
and pain. It is a story of living."

He took up the lute and plucked a few notes to prove its

harmony. Then he picked out thereon a sad but lovely melody such as in the past he had entertained them with in the private hall of Ercildoune Castle. He paused, then still holding the instrument, he recited with strongly vibrant voice:

> Listen lords and ladies well,
> > And take good heed of what I say;
> I shall you tell as stark a tale
> > As e'er was heard in ode or lay.

> I sing of passion and of pain,
> > Of love and hate and death;
> Of pledge wherein there was no gain,
> > And cost of dear bought faith.

Between each verse he twanged two notes on the lute.

> Sir Tristrem's name and fame I praise,
> > Sir Tristrem's ardour bright;
> And fair Isolde's lovely grace,
> > Isolde's beauteous sight.

> These their troth pledged under God's heaven
> > Their hearts true trust between;
> Yet Isolde for King Mark was given
> > > To be his chosen Queen.

> Mark fair Cornwall's lord was he,
> > Uncle to Tristrem knight.
> Daughter of Dublin's king was she,
> > Her marriage her father's right.

Thomas need not have feared lack of attention. This of a king's daughter and her marriage arrangement could not fail to strike the hearers' sense of the dramatic, in the circumstances of that evening. Not a sound disturbed the hall.

> King Mark was harsh and stern and strong,
> > Isolde gentle as fair.
> Sir Tristrem swore the match was wrong,
> > To spoil it he would dare.

> *To Dublin town Tristrem was sent,*
> *To Cornwall to bring the maid.*
> *Heart sore within him so he went*
> *His vow made him afraid.*
>
> *In Isolde's bower in Dublin Tower*
> *They each renewed their troth.*
> *If she must yield to King Mark's power,*
> *He'd free her, on his oath.*
>
> *So south they sailed for Cornwall's land,*
> *Across the salt wave sea;*
> *But long ere they touched on Cornwall's strand,*
> *No longer maid was she.*

It was a stir of movement, not words, which rippled through the hall as the lute twanged, folk eyeing each other, the King and Princess Margaret, wondering.

> *King Mark perceived nothing amiss*
> *With his young bride so rare;*
> *And if her queenly nights lacked bliss,*
> *Her days did them repair.*
>
> *At Mark's castle a garden ground*
> *Was hidden in boskage green;*
> *Where daily Isolde her Tristrem found*
> *From mortal eyes unseen.*
>
> *Their love they shared, their bodies paired,*
> *Of Mark their hatred burnished;*
> *And little cared as passion flared,*
> *If cost their coupling furnished.*

At this, the end of the first of so many parts, Thomas paused for more than the note or two on the lute. Oddly it had not really occurred to him previously how apt, or perhaps the reverse, this might all sound in the present situation. He looked at Alexander. The King's normally frank and open countenance was, for once, less than clear and cheerful, a study in conflicting emotions, as he glanced from his daughter to the Norwegian envoys. These last might not fully understand all the nuances and implications of the poem; but to be sure Margaret did, as her flushed face and bitten lip indicated. On the other hand, Alexander was no ascetic, a lusty man with a strong sense of the dramatic, and was probably as keenly exercised by the tale unfolding as anyone present. If the issue was touch-and-go for a moment or two, diplomacy combined with good sense and natural disposition to win the day. He beat on the table-top with his wine-flagon in loud applause and shouted for Thomas to continue. All around similar sentiments were voiced, although not noticeably by the princess.

Somewhat more doubtfully now the poet acceded. First he explained that the entire epic was very long, running indeed to over three hundred fyttes or verses. It had taken him years to write. Needless to say they could hear only a very small part of it all tonight. Tristrem, they should know, was the son of King Mark's sister, the Lady Blanche Fleur, and Rowland Rees, Lord of Ermonie, and was one of the famed Knights of the Round Table. The tale had come down the three centuries in various forms, told in the Cornish, Welsh and Breton tongues, then rendered into German by generations of mistrels and minnesingers, and so had become altered into many different versions. Translating these, he had sought to winnow from them the original story and so had made up his poem.

He resumed his recital, relating how in time the guilty lovers had been discovered and the King told; how grievous had been Mark's wrath; how Tristrem had been banished to Wales; how his knightly prowess caused his uncle to desire him to return and to forgive him; how the guilty intercourse with the Queen had resumed; how again he was banished, this time to Brittany where he distinguished himself in deeds of chivalry, daring and courage beyond compare — but always his heart remained with Isolde.

Thomas ended there, with some of the company beginning to become restive, including his own son. Alexander, reassured distinctly by the way the thing was developing, was generous in his appreciation, and declared that he, and they all, would look forward to hearing more on another occasion. Perhaps, however, it was with just a shade of relief that he called for acrobats and wrestlers to come and continue with the entertainment.

As he had been reciting, Thomas had noticed Sir Michael Scott seated some distance down the hall. In the movement and general commotion which followed, receiving many congratulations on his performance, he found his way to the older man's side.

"I had heard that you were abroad, sir," he greeted. "On the King's business. I felicitate you on your safe return."

"I was gone, yes — on this of the Flanders match. Thereafter I was in France. On another mission for His Grace. Less . . . manifest."

"Ah. You were in France before, were you not? Two years or so back? I called at your house of Oakwood in Ettrick, learning that you had come to dwell there. I was assured that you had flown to France on a great black horse!"

"Fools! Our fellow-countrymen, my friend, prefer to believe fables than simple truth. As *you* have discovered. I fear that my journeying was more prosaic. But — this of tonight. I listened to your rendering of that ancient tale with some admiration — if not without question. Notable both in the composition and the delivery, Learmonth. In the memorising also, since you read from no notes."

"I have written and re-written these verses so often, over the years, that I can remember every word. But I thank you for your praise, sir. From yourself, that is worth much."

"I am no poet, see you. But I find your epic to sound well enough on the ear, your tale to occupy the idle mind — however ridiculous a fable. If you would but devote your undoubted abilities to more solid and profitable sciences — astrology, alchemy, philosophy, mathematics and such-like — who knows to what you might usefully aspire. His Grace has need of men of learning and truth, surrounded as he is by all these lordly buffoons and sly churchmen!"

"H'rmm." Thomas cleared his throat. "I do not aspire to any such heights, Sir Michael." He had lowered his voice a little, glancing around him. "I think that you over-rate my poor capabilities."

"Perhaps. I certainly do not over-rate your judgment tonight, young man. That tale of kings being controverted and cuckolded, made fools of in their marriage arrangements, was scarcely one to endear you to your liege. Nor to the Norsemen."

"I had not thought of it in that light. After all, most of it I wrote ten years ago and more. But the King did not appear to be offended or put out."

"No. He is sufficiently sure of himself, that one. I hope with good reason."

Thomas looked at the other quickly. "You . . . you think that he should not be? That there could be reason to . . . beware?"

"Shall we say that I am not convinced that the stars are so confident of the future as is our Lord Alexander? For himself, his house and his realm."

Lips tight, the younger man nodded. "I feared that," he said.

"You did? You have been seeing more visions, my friend?"

"I . . . yes." He came closer, speaking urgently, unhappily, still more quietly. "I have told none. But I have been plagued with evil dreams, of late. All to the same end. Last night the worst, most dire and particular. As to the King. I see a great and dark bird to hover above him and his, and he heedless. I see this bird, vulture rather than eagle, coming lower and lower. It swoops, and takes away in its talons a son. Then comes back for another son. Then a daughter. Alexander seeks to fight it off. He seems to gain on it, for a little. Then it grows still larger and more fierce. It takes the King himself. And thereafter his land lies helpless, below this evil fowl, with none left to defend it. And the creature settles where the King had been, and spreads its black wings over all. And all is darkness. It is . . . horrible."

Scott eyed him, plucking at his lower lip. "It could be but that your belly was incongenial."

"I have dreamed it many times. Your stars — do they paint any similar picture?"

"The heavens do not paint pictures, man. Do not play the poet or the minstrel. They move and measure and mark. They point and portend. They reflect and register, to all eternity. Man can calculate and consult, that is all. Seek guidance, humbly, not paint pictures and dream dreams."

"Nevertheless, sir, did you not by your stars, foretell the time and place and manner of the Emperor Frederick's death?"

"I made calculations, yes. Of the heavenly conjunctions. That is all."

"And the heavens — do they smile on Alexander?"

"They did, Learmonth, they did. Now . . . less so."

Thomas nodded. "I thank you," he said. Before he moved back for the dais, he added. "I did not tell you, I think — the evil bird wore the features of Edward Plantagenet."

19

The catalogue of disasters commenced almost at once. Within a month of the Norse envoys' departure, word came from Norway that King Magnus the Good had died. This, of course, affected Scotland, since now instead of being merely the betrothed of a fourteen-year-old prince, Alexander's daughter was contracted to marry the King of Norway; and the Norwegians wanted their queen-to-be married and crowned and if possible child-bearing, just as soon as possible, since nothing was more unfortunate for any realm than to have an under-age monarch and no lawful succession in sight. So arrangements had to be put in hand forthwith for the princess to be shipped to Bergen, however much she might protest.

Alexander chose Sir David de Wemyss and Sir Michael Scott to escort Margaret — the latter having become a favourite ambassador, thanks to his fame throughout Christendom and his phenomenal knowledge of languages.

But even before their ship sailed, the second blow fell. Without warning, as it were out of the blue, the Prince David, now aged nine, fell sick, and died within a few days. Never a robust child — none of Margaret Plantagenet's offspring were that — he had nevertheless given no indication of any fatal weakness.

The King was shattered. He had not been perhaps the most devoted husband, but he was a good father and much attached to his children. Almost certainly he was somewhat guiltily distressed at having to send away his reluctant daughter to a foreign land where, as queen, he would be unlikely to see much of her hereafter. And his elder son was delicate of health.

For the same reason that Eric of Norway's wedding was expedited — to seek to ensure the succession — now the match with Margaret of Flanders was hurried on. The custom, where thrones were concerned, was for the incoming partner to be brought to the country concerned for the nuptials; so envoys were sent to Flanders to urge that the bride be sent at the soonest. She was in her eighteenth year, so there should be little objection.

Scarcely had the ambassadors sailed for the Low Countries when Prince Alexander fell ill. It was another sudden and strange affliction which none of the physicians were able to put a name to, producing much vomiting and looseness of the bowels, with a curious breathlessness. The King, naturally, was desperately anxious, and brought blood-letters and monks versed in specifics and herbal remedies and the like from all over Scotland and the North of England, to Roxburgh. In time Edward even sent his own physician — the prince was his nephew, after all, as well as something of an investment. The invalid rallied but little, and all were at a loss — but at least the sickness did not seem to be fatal. The King even consulted Thomas, demanding whether he had any aid or comfort to offer? Could he foretell nothing? Needless to say, Thomas kept his dreams and forebodings to himself.

In the midst of all this distress and worry, a new difficulty loomed up. The new Legate in London decided that he was dissatisfied with Bagimond, and sent up another nuncio to Scotland, one Geoffrey de Vecano, to take over the collection of what he called Peter's Pence, the tithes for the Crusade. Bagimond was accused of not only being dilatory and weak about this collection, and onward transmission of the moneys, but even of peculation, of actually diverting some of the cash to his own use and making private bargains with Scots ecclesiastics, and lending out money, already collected, on usury. In vain Bagimond pointed out that whatever his assessments, King Alexander flatly refused to allow large sums in gold and silver to pass out of Scotland, as an impoverishment of his realm. Vecano insisted that the failure was Bagimond's, that all arrangements had been made for the moneys to be paid through certain Florentine wine-merchants trading with Scotland, so there was no need for the King to be involved at all. Bagimond, on his way back to Rome in disgrace, came to Ercildoune and told Thomas, who duly informed Alexander at Roxburgh. The King, who had so much else on his mind, ordered Thomas to attach himself forthwith to Canon de Vecano's entourage and not to leave it, to ensure that no gold or silver specie was exported from Scotland in Florentine or any other ships. The Italians could buy certain goods with their Peter's Pence, wool and hides, salt and dried fish and the like, as arranged, and these could be sent wherever they wished; but no actual money was to leave the country.

So Thomas found himself saddled with this thoroughly unpleasant and thankless task — for this Vecano was a very different type of man from Bagimond, much more like the late Ottobone, haughty, dominant and apt to broadcast excommunications. Fortunately he used the same monkish clerks as Bagimond had done, and with these Thomas had established a reasonably friendly relationship; otherwise his assignment would have become all but intolerable, since he was at cross-purposes with the nuncio all the time. The latter had established himself at Berwick-upon-Tweed, the princi-pal port, which was not too inconvenient for Ercildoune; and

Thomas did not have to go traipsing all over the country with the clerks, so long as he could see that no money was smuggled aboard shipping in the various harbours. He used some of Earl Patrick's men as aides in this surveillance, but was uncertain as to whether they were entirely successful. Vecano, when he found his efforts frustrated, brought in the threat of King Edward's intervention into the business, declaring that since the moneys were for the prosecution of the Crusade, and it was hoped that Edward would be leading that Crusade, this holding up of finance was actively injuring the King of England as well as damaging God's holy work. Thomas took this less than seriously, especially when he gathered from the clerks that the charges against Bagimond for peculation and usury were purely trumped up to serve as pretext for sending him back to Rome.

So that summer passed, with the prince little improved and an air of anxiety in the land. On the Eve of the Exaltation of the Cross, Margaret of Flanders arrived. And since she came to the port of Berwick, where the Flemings formed a strong trading community, Thomas was one of the first to greet her. She proved to be a large, hearty, uncomplicated creature of no beauty or grace but of good spirits — in notable contrast to her bridegroom. The prince had been unable to make the journey to welcome her, but his father came. Thomas accompanied the royal party back to Roxburgh, for at the prince's special request he was to continue with his rendering of *Sir Tristrem* after the wedding-feast. Anyway, since Vecano, as Papal Nuncio, was to be a guest at the wedding, the watch at Berwick could be relaxed.

Thomas had not seen the prince for some time, and when he reached Roxburgh he was shocked at the change in the young man's appearance, so pale and drawn and thin was he. But he was clearly making a major effort for the occasion. What bride and groom thought of each other was not to be known, but they both put up a brave front.

Advisedly the wedding was not to be long postponed; but a day or two had to be allowed for Bishop Fraser of St. Andrews, who was to officiate, and other important guests to arrive. Thomas had opportunity to return to Ercildoune for a couple of nights. Before he went, he was able to inform the King as to the Peter's Pence situation and the indications that it looked as though the Vatican at least was expecting King Edward to lead the new Crusade.

The nuptials were held at Kelso Abbey across the river from Roxburgh Castle, a splendid pile built by the good King David the previous century. Despite its splendour, however, Thomas on this occasion entered it with trepidation, for, just as he reached the great west doorway, he had a sudden and shocking vision of the entire magnificent roof collapsing upon a large congregation of worshippers, with screaming, terror-stricken folk fleeing and falling in all directions. It took him a little while to banish the picture from his mind and attend to the day's impressive though less distracting proceedings.

There was a second distraction for Thomas, when he perceived that of the two mitred clerics assisting the primate, one was none other than Henry le Chien, formerly mere Precentor of Aberdeen Cathedral. Enquiring from a neighbour, he learned that the old Bishop of Aberdeen had died, had indeed been assassinated, and that le Chien had somehow got himself appointed bishop in his place. Sir Reginald's hand was to be seen behind this, undoubtedly.

The actual wedding ceremony had been cut down to a minimum to conserve the bridegroom's strength; and fine as he looked in all his cloth-of-gold magnificence, the young man was obviously very weary before the end of it. Margaret, to be sure, had strength enough for both. Nothing would make her good-looking, but today she wore a bloom not to be denied. The King could be seen to be on edge throughout, his eyes never off his son, seeming to count every moment.

At the banquet thereafter the bridal couple were long in appearing; but there were few of the usual knowing comments and winks. When the King eventually ushered them in, to loud cheering, it was apparent that the prince was in a state of exhaustion.

On this occasion there was no special table for the Dunbar family, so Thomas and Bethoc occupied quite a lowly place down-hall. But even so they could see that, while Margaret did ample justice to the splendid repast, her husband merely toyed with his food and drank little or nothing. That he was merely getting through the evening as best he could was patently evident. His favourite physician, the Prior Adam of Kirk Cuthbert's, provided with a seat on his left, watched over him attentively.

In the circumstances it was something of a low-key celebration.

Thomas had been quite prepared to be told that his poetry-reciting must be postponed. When no such instruction reached him he went so far as to go up to the dais to ask the Chamberlain whether his services were still required. The King himself leaned over to ask his son whether he was in a mind for poetry, to be assured that he was, had been waiting for it. The prince had poetic, even slightly visionary, leanings himself, and apparently was enthralled by the Tristrem story. He was eager to hear more. The Prior Adam however advised that the reading should start as soon as was possible and should not go on for too long. He would signal when he thought that Thomas should begin to wind up.

So, accompanying himself on his lute, as before, the poet gave a brief résumé of the epic as far as he had reached previously, and then went on to recite Sir Tristrem's further adventures. How in Brittany he had made himself so useful, indeed all but indispensable, to the Duke thereof, by his knightly prowess and military successes, that he was pressed and persuaded to wed the Duke's daughter, Yseult of the Fair Hand. His passion for the lovely Queen Isolde was as strong as ever; but it was clearly a hopeless attachment, and he had been promised death if he ever returned to Cornwall. Moreover he considered that he could still love the Queen from a distance, wed as she was. The fact that the Duke's daughter was also beautiful, doted on him and had the same name as Isolde although spelled differently, added piquancy to the situation.

The narration had reached the stage of Tristrem receiving the grievous wound in battle which brought about the last dramatic episode of the story, when the Prior Adam held up a hand, and Thomas sought to bring the recital to a close not too abruptly. He had in fact got further than he had feared. The applause which greeted his finishing merged with a different sort of acclaim as the Prince and Princess of Scotland rose to leave the hall, so hurried was their departure, their bows perfunctory. The King went after them, signing that he would be back.

When Alexander returned, he beckoned Thomas up. "My son regrets. That he could not stay and hear more," he said. "He is weary. After his much sickness. This day has . . . taxed him, I fear. But he thanks you greatly. He much enjoys your poem. As do we all. But Alex in especial. He is eager to hear more. He hopes that you will favour him with the rest of your tale, Thomas, another day?"

"To be sure, Sire. When he so wishes. Did I go on for too long?"

"No, no. He would have desired to listen longer. Had his strength held." The King shook his head. "It is scarcely auspicious . . . for a wedding-night!"

"There will be other nights, Sire."

"Yes, God willing. But — it is a grievous thing! So young, all before him, a kingdom to inherit. Yet ailing, failing. Is there a curse on me, man? What have I done? For what is God punishing me?"

"I cannot think that it is that, Your Grace. But who am I to know? You must ask that of your priests."

"But, you — you foresee, foretell. What is to be, Thomas? What a God's good name is to be?"

Thomas swallowed. "I, I cannot tell you, Highness. I can only say what comes to me. We are all in the hands of God . . ."

"A plague on you, man! *You* sound like any priest, now! If that is the best that you can do for me, back to your wine!"

Bowing, Thomas Learmonth turned and limped off, and thankfully.

*   *   *

In fact, Prince Alexander never did hear the end of *Sir Tristrem*. Fairly soon thereafter the King and Court moved northwards for a Council meeting at Scone, and, with some

366

slight betterment in his son's condition, took the prince and princess with him. Yuletide was passed at the Blackfriars' Monastery at Perth; and in January the prince was well enough to travel to Cupar in Fife, where his personal confessor and mentor had been given the living. There it was that he received the desperate tidings that his sister Margaret, Queen of Norway, had given birth to a premature child, a daughter, and thereafter expired. Stricken, the heir to the throne fell into a sort of torpor from which nothing would rouse him. Fearing for him, his confessor decided to take him back, by litter, to his father and wife at Perth. They got only so far back as the Abbey of Lindores, above Tay, where the prince collapsed and could go no further. The next day would be his twentieth birthday. In a lucid interval he told the priest that night that he would live only to see the morning light. He had had a vision, he declared; when the sun rose next morning Scotland's sun would set. He died an hour after cockcrow, babbling of his uncle Edward. Edward, he cried, was the instrument of cruellest fate. He would conquer twice but the third time would himself be conquered.

In that year of 1284, therefore, Scotland had a distracted monarch but no heir. Unless, unless the uncomplicated Margaret of Flanders proved to be pregnant, which did not seem likely in the circumstances.

20

Urgently the royal couriers rode out from St. John's Town of Perth to summon the Council, so lately prorogued, to re-assemble at Scone Abbey in six days' time. And not only the Council but the entire Estates of the Realm. The command was peremptory; all must attend, only extreme sickness acceptable as excuse; this was to be an especial occasion, a gathering to decide upon the succession to the Crown, no less.

One courier came to Ercildoune, en route for the Abbots of Melrose, Dryburgh, Kelso and Jedburgh. It would be Thomas's first Estates Convention.

There was no room for any large proportion of those attending at Scone Abbey itself, and Thomas had to make do with very poor quarters in Perth town three miles off, which he shared with Prior Nicholas of Faill, who, as now Principal of the Trinitarian Order in Scotland, held a seat in the Estates. The friends were happy to be together.

The assembly was held in the Abbey-church, the only building large enough to contain the numbers involved. The desperately important nature of the business had not had to be underlined for anyone, and the turn-out was greater than on any occasion in living memory. It was reported that present were thirteen earls, eleven bishops and twenty-five great lords, not to mention the mass of the lesser lords and chiefs, the abbots and priors, the knights and officers and representatives of the burghs.

Thomas found a place on a form in the packed nave beside Sir Michael Scott — to whom others were prudently giving a wide berth — and who greeted him grimly. Prior Nicholas, as a churchman, had to sit elsewhere.

"Your evil bird has been busy, Learmonth! Are you satisfied?"

"Sir — I am desolated, rather! Would God my dreams had been proved utterly false . . ."

"Yes, yes — I but made untimely jest, man. Your bird was to take the three bairns. But, if I mind aright, the King also, thereafter. Do you still hold to that?"

"I hold to nothing, Sir Michael. I but repeated to you what I had dreamed — and to you only. I told none other — save my wife."

"Wise, my friend — wise."

"And you, sir? What of your own calculations and observations? How do you now see the future?"

"I see a small good facing a large evil. But then, any dolt could foretell that, today."

"But surely the heavens give some indication? Of the outcome?"

"Not yet, they do not. The stars move at their own pace. Slowly but inexorably. None may rush them, least of all myself."

"Slowly? Then . . . there is time? Time ahead of us? For the King?"

The other shrugged. "Alexander is a lusty man. In the prime of his life. But forty-three years. The outcome could surprise us all."

It was on the tip of Thomas's tongue to protest at Scott's very obvious lack of frankness, reluctance to commit himself, when the trumpets sounded for the royal entry, and all must stand.

Alexander strode in from the chapter-house entry to the south transept, his entourage having almost to run to keep up with him. Set-faced, his usual open and cheerful countenance strangely closed, he at least reassured all as a picture of robust good health. With the minimum of ceremony he marched to his throne-like chair in front of the high altar and beside the Chancellor's table. He waved a hand for all to be seated and for the Chancellor to begin. No more than that. Nothing could have made it more plain that this meeting was concerned only with business, and stern business at that.

Although the monarch presided at such sessions, the assembly was actually conducted by the Chancellor. When William Fraser became Primate, he was succeeded in the chancellorship by Master Thomas Charteris, an able and scholarly priest, whose dry, pedantic manner certainly did nothing to dissipate the atmosphere of gravity.

He bowed to the King. "My lords," he said, without pre-amble, "His Grace has called you together to advise him and his Council on the vital issue of the royal succession. All know that Almighty God has seen fit to take to Himself each and all of His Grace's children, Alexander, Prince of Scotland, the Prince David and the Princess Margaret, Queen of Norway. His Grace has no brothers, sisters or other close kin. There is therefore no evident heir to the throne save the new-born grand-daughter, the Maid of Norway. None can deny the gravity of this situation. Scotland needs an heir, acceptable to the realm. His Grace would have your counsel."

There was silence in the church. No one appeared to wish to be the first to speak. The earls, of course, had that right by long-standing tradition.

The King, recognising this, raised his voice. "Any or all may speak. So be it they have anything of worth to say. My Council seek your guidance. They would hear rather than speak, at this juncture."

Despite that, it was a member of the Council who did make the first contribution. It was Sir Reginald le Chien, former Chamberlain. "My lord King, a female infant, however royally born, can be no monarch for Scotland. *Ard Righ,* the High King of Scots, can never be a woman. It is scarcely to be considered. Never has this realm had a queen-regnant. We need a man, and a strong man, I say. This, for a start."

As men digested that, Sir Pate of the Black Beard, spoke. "Sire — how far back do we go in considering those of kin to the royal house? I myself have royal blood on both mother's and father's sides. My father's grandmother was Ada, daughter of William the Lyon. And my mother's Bruce line descends from William's brother, David, Earl of Huntingdon."

There was a stir at this bald first staking of a claim, not least from Earl Patrick who frowned darkly, whether at his son's general presumption or because any such claim should have come from himself, was not to be known. He coughed but did not speak.

Robert Bruce, Lord of Annandale and the Countess Christian's brother, hardly gave him time, anyway. "Any claim for Bruce, *I* make!" he declared strongly. "As chief of that house." He was a short, stocky, greying man, of tough reputation. "Forby, my nephew's claim fails, since King William omitted to marry the lady who produced the daughter Ada! My claim is by lawful descent. My mother was the Lady Isabel, daughter to David, Earl of Huntingdon, younger brother of Malcolm the Fourth and William the Lyon. Moreover your royal father, Sire, before his second marriage to your lady-mother, when childless, accepted myself as heir. There are those here present who can swear to it."

Expressionless, the King nodded.

"Highness, my lord of Annandale may have some small claim." That was John de Baliol of Penston. "But I must remind all that the Lady Isabel his mother was only second daughter of the Earl David. He had an elder daughter, Margaret, who married Alan, Lord of Galloway. Their daughter Devorgilla is my father's mother. Therefore my father, John Baliol, Lord of Barnard Castle, has the prior claim, as in the senior line."

"Baliol — an Englishman!" Bruce burst out. "God's mercy, man — we do not seek Englishmen for king! Although Edward might! Besides, there is no law of primogeniture for women."

"Address His Grace or myself only, my lord," the Chancellor reproved.

"Master Chancellor — if there is no primogeniture amongst women, then the offspring of the third daughter of the Earl David is also to be considered." That was John Hastings, Earl of Atholl. "My kinsman, John Hastings, Lord of Abergavenny, is the grandson of the Lady Ada . . ."

"Another Englishman!" Bruce scoffed.

Before the Chancellor could again reprove, Bruce's son, who had married Marjory of Carrick, spoke up. "I speak for the Earl of Carrick," he announced. It must have been a bitter draught for him to swallow that he could not rightly call *himself* the earl, not in front of the King, at least — although he was said to do so, as it were, unofficially — and had to speak in the name of his child son. "We are considering the succession to the throne, not some mere manor or estate. The rule and governance of this realm is at stake. Therefore, whatever the precedence and descent, what is required is a man of good strength and substance, accustomed to command and to war. Forby with a good line of succession to him, sons and grandsons. So that, God willing, there is not this trouble again after. No Englishmen, no men lacking great estate and power."

Thomas murmured to Michael Scott. "Special pleading for the house of Bruce, indeed!" He saw again, in his mind's eye, the vision of the Countess Marjory with the child in her arms, the Bruce child, and the rhyme he had dashed off:

> *Of Bruce's side a son shall come,*
>   *From Carrick's bower to Scotland's throne,*
> *The Red Lion beareth he . . .*

"Bruce may hold the key. How say you?"

The other shrugged, non-committal.

The Earl Patrick raised hand. "Sire — is all this vaunting talk of any worth or value? Your Grace is not old. You should have many years to reign over us. See Bruce and myself and many another into our graves! Time enough to talk of succession when Your Grace is my age!"

"By then it would be too late, Dunbar," Bruce asserted.

Alexander nodded. "There is much in my lord of Dunbar's contention," he agreed. "I shall have something to say on the matter in due course. But first, I wish to hear the advice of members of the Estates. So far, it has been, in the main, the lords of my Council who have spoken, men who are them-selves concerned in the matter."

But because the issue was delicate and so personal to the King, and to these great lords of royal connection, lesser men were loth to raise voice. A bishop or two uttered pious platitudes about praying God that the King's Highness would reign over them for many years, and no succession be required; Sir Malcolm Wallace of Elderslie declared that since whoever reigned in Scotland, in the unhappy event of the King's demise, would assuredly have to fight to retain the realm's freedom from English hegemony, it would be as well if he was a warrior, as Bruce the Younger had said, certainly not a girl-child; Lindsay contended that while it was no doubt beneficial if the wearer of the crown was able to lead his armies in the field, it was not absolutely essential — his own predecessor, Sir David, had been Regent when His Grace was a child, and as such had successfully led the royal arms — and a warrior for *Regent* would serve.

"Nevertheless, a child would serve Scotland but poorly, Master Chancellor," le Chien insisted. "A female child of foreign blood more poorly still."

"I would remind the Lord of Inverugie that the said child, the Maid of Norway, *is* direct and undoubted heir," a strong voice declared. This was Magnus Magnusson, Earl of Orkney, a voice which never before had spoken in any Scots assembly. Orkney, of course, belonged to Norway, not Scotland; but he was here as Earl of Caithness, which earldom, the most northerly in Scotland, had been incorporated with Orkney for two centuries, since Thorfinn Raven Feeder had been made Earl by his grandfather Malcolm the Second. It was an interesting commentary on the situation that Earl Magnus had chosen to attend this meeting, and at such short notice, brought down fast in a Viking longship. He had a concern for the Norwegian aspect of the succession, of course.

"Is my lord of Caithness right in this, Master Chancellor?" Sir Patrick Graham of Mugdock, Sheriff of Stirling, asked. "Inverugie contends that a woman cannot be *Ard Righ*. This, the King's grand-daughter, is heir-of-line, yes. But *can* she be Queen?"

Even the austere Thomas Charteris looked uncomfortable over this bald question. "This is difficult of answer, my lord. Perhaps it is for His Grace to decide. His Grace in Council. In most realms of Christendom there would be no question; the heir-of-line succeeds, if no male, then a female. Lacking some grave impediment. But this Scots kingdom has grown out of the ancient Celtic realm, which held differently. Therein the royal *house* was the succession. The most able and worthy member of it was chosen by the *ri*, mormaors and earls, to be High King. They always chose a man to lead, never a woman. So Sir Reginald is right in that. But it could be claimed that this is no longer a Celtic realm, since King MacBeth's time. Sir Reginald himself is no Celt, I think . . .!"

The first hint of laughter of the day greeted that.

"Nevertheless King Alexander himself was crowned on the Celtic Stone of Destiny, here at Scone, and had the Celtic High Sennachie recount his lineage back to the earliest Celtic times. I was there and heard it," le Chien objected. "So he commenced his reign as a Celtic monarch."

All men now looked at the King. Guidance surely must now come from him.

Alexander recognised it well enough. "My friends," he said, "this is a hard matter to declare upon. I *am* a Celtic monarch, crowned on the Stone — and I am proud of it. Yet to call Scotland a Celtic realm today would be untruthful, next to folly. How many here are of pure Celtic blood? Norman, Anglian, Saxon, Norse — all these strains are in us, in myself. The Celtic Church has all but gone. The old Celtic laws have been superseded by others. The mormaors are now earls — and these earls have chosen none but the heir-of-line to succeed in three centuries. Although usurpers may have gained the crown for a while by force of arms. I say that we cannot here tie ourselves to the ancient Celtic law of succession."

There were murmurs both of agreement and disagreement.

"Furthermore, it is my undoubted duty to support the right of my only present close kin, my grand-daughter. I can do no other. Her claim comes before any other, in all save the old Celtic polity. And I would remind you all, moreover, that the child's claim to the succession is written into our treaty with Norway, at my daughter's wedding. Any issue of the marriage with Eric of Norway was to be in line for the throne. That is signed and sealed."

"The child, Sire — will she not become Queen of Norway?" Graham asked. "Do we wish to see her Queen of Scots also? The realms united under one monarch? Hakon sought to conquer our land. We do not want his grandson's daughter to succeed where he failed!"

That drew some applause.

"King Eric is a bare sixteen years, Sir Patrick. Nothing is more sure than that he will wed again. Have more children. Only this one could be Queen of Scots. So your fears, I say, are groundless." Alexander paused. "But, while on this subject, my friends, I may remind you of another aspect of this matter of succession. I myself am not yet a man of great age. Forty-three years. I may marry again."

374

That brought everyone up short, as was intended.

"I have indeed been making enquiries, in some fashion. We shall see. I might yet produce sons."

"Then, then Highness, all this is but a beating of the air!" Orkney protested. "I . . . we need never have come."

"Not so, my lord. Such considerations are but possibilities, not facts. Only possible sons, possible marriage. The succession to the crown must depend at any time on better than possibilities. Hence this assembly. At best I could not have lawful offspring in under two years. And much might happen in two years."

"With Edward Longshanks on England's throne, Your Highness utters the truth!" old Bruce commented grimly. "I hold lands in England, and know the style of him. Any last weakness in our governance and he will move. So what do we do now, Sire?"

"Do, my lord? We make a declaration. And sign and witness it. I and my Council. We have heard such advice as members of the Estates in colloquium have seen fit to give us. All have had the opportunity to say their say. So I put it to all my lords of Council. That all acknowledge that my granddaughter is first in succession to my throne, meantime. Until such time as I may have further lawful issue. But that, should she not live, and I father no more children, then the succession shall devolve upon the senior Scottish-domiciled descendant of my great-uncle of Huntingdon. Is it agreed?"

Out of considerable whisperings and shufflings it appeared to be so, more or less. Clearly the Bruces were as well-placed as they could hope to be, at this stage.

Alexander signed to the Chancellor to continue.

Charteris had further business to get over, but it seemed dull stuff after the foregoing, and to be hurried through — the claim of William Comyn to the earldom of Menteith, presently held by Walter, brother of the High Steward, in right of his wife; the proposal by certain Lombard bankers to set up completely new towns and ports in Scotland in return for exclusive trading privileges — highly unpopular with all, and promptly rejected; the three-yearly survey of the state of the royal castles; collection of dues from the port of Berwick-on-Tweed, in arrears; and so on. Few present, including the monarch himself, failed to display a certain lack of concentration. The Chancellor consequently got his way in most of these matters, with minimum debate — although the King adjudged that the Menteith lands should be divided between the contestants but the title of earl to remain with Stewart.

Alexander rose and the momentous assembly was over, the decision made, for better or for worse.

Riding back to Perth, by the sparkling Tay, with Sir Michael — whose steed on this occasion proved to be a very ordinary and plodding roan and no great black stallion with the ability to fly — Thomas expressed his own doubts as to whether the infant Maid of Norway was a wise choice for a throne and kingdom which, whatever else, had always demanded a strong hand.

Scott shook his grey head. "It will not come to that, I think. Alexander was but keeping the Bruces in their place. He desires no uppish clamourers for his crown, awaiting his death — yet must keep his most powerful lords assured in his support. I may tell you now, Learmonth, since the King himself has revealed something of it, that it has been in search for a suitable new wife for him that I have made my secret visits to France."

"Ha — it has gone so far as that! And you have found one? To Alexander's satisfaction?"

"I believe so, yes. A most difficult and delicate task, you will understand. It is not every woman who might suitably wed the King of Scots. She has to be high-born. And of good looks. Alexander was most particular on that. And not only of child-bearing age but *capable* of bearing children — since that is the essence of it. Not easy, you will admit, and all to be kept most privy."

"Who, Sir Michael — who?"

The older man tutted at such impatience. "Who is reputed the most beautiful lady in all Christendom?"

"Lord — I do not know! At Ercildoune, I accord that to my wife Bethoc!"

The other frowned at such levity. "It is the Lady Yolande de Dreux, Duchess of Brittany. Who else?"

"Indeed? But — is there not a Duke of Brittany? One Arthur . . .?"

"He died. Two years past. This is the widow."

"A widow! Is that . . . does Alexander approve ∴ . .?"

"Learmonth — use your wits! It had to be a widow — since no whore would serve! I said she had to be *capable* of bearing children — and proven so. There can be no room for mistake in this. A barren wife is of no use to Alexander, however beautiful. I told you that my task was difficult, restricted and most private, demanding much wile and artifice. There are none so many young widows of beauty fit to marry a king. Yolande de Dreux is of twenty-four years and has borne two children, one the four-year-old present Duke."

"Save us — here is a tale indeed!"

"No tale, sir, but sober fact. I am not given to telling tales — leaving that to soothsayers and poets and the like!"

"Yes, yes — I did not mean that I doubted any of it, Sir Michael. Only that it is a most strange account, a delicate quest indeed."

"That is why His Grace sent *me*," Scott declared, with what in a lesser man might have suggested smugness. "I believe that I have provided the future Queen of Scotland."

"And the lady? She is willing?"

"I made it my business to persuade her. She is high-spirited as well as handsome. And she accepted from me that the King of Scots is likewise. Forby her brother John, the present Count de Dreux, is eager for it."

"He is? Why?"

"To be allied to the King of Scots will serve him well. Dreux, as you will know, is near to Chartres, on the Eure. On the Normandy border. For some of his lands, the Count is vassal to Edward of England, as Duke of Normandy. With such for superior it is an excellent precaution to have a powerful ally who also has reason to beware of Edward. This will suit Alexander also. I think that I have shown that his confidence in me was not misplaced, Learmonth."

Thomas glanced sidelong at his companion as they rode. That he should sound so pleased with himself was perhaps not to be wondered at, since this all would appear to add up

to a most suitable piece of diplomacy. And yet, and yet . . .
Thomas could not banish from his mind's eye the picture of a
dark and evil bird preying on Alexander and his house and
kingdom. In that grim prospect he had perceived no beauteous duchess, no belated offspring. But, to be sure, it might
have been only a nightmare . . .

21

Laughter, good cheer, relief, filled the land — or at least such
part of it as might be concerned with rule, governance and
future prosperity — and Yolande de Dreux was responsible.
From the moment that she arrived, on the Eve of St. Luke,
with her brother, at Berwick, the gloom began to lift. From
Alexander and all who met her, from all who saw her,
presently from all who heard of her. She was like that, a
delight to behold, lovely indeed but so much more than
merely beautiful — laughing, outgoing, unselfconsciously
happy, and infectiously so. The King could scarcely believe
his good fortune — and gave urgent orders to hurry on the
wedding arrangements.

The nuncio, Geoffrey de Vecano, had temporarily departed to London, in high dudgeon, the Crusade little better off
for his efforts, so that Thomas was not at Berwick when the de
Dreux party arrived, escorted by the Chancellor, Graham
and other of Alexander's magnates. But he saw her a few
nights later at a banquet which the Earl Patrick gave in her
honour at Ercildoune Castle — by which time all the Merse
and Lauderdale rang with the lady's praises. He was duly
impressed, and prepared to congratulate Sir Michael Scott,
also present. Even the women tended to signify approval,
Bethoc most generously so — which amounted to praise
indeed. The brother, Count John de Dreux, seemed amiable
but lacked much of what Yolande so animatedly possessed.

Alexander was obviously headlong in love from the first, like a young man again, showing off his new acquisition. Throughout the evening he could scarcely keep his hands off the Duchess, and all present agreed that the auspices for the succession could hardly have been better.

This was the Eve of Saints Simon and Jude, the 27th of October, and the wedding was set for All Hallows four days hence. Clearly the King would be finding the wait an eternity. Whether he would indeed have to wait, of course, was a matter for some speculation. Bethoc was confident that he would, without elaborating on her reasons.

Thomas and Bethoc were presented to Yolande by Alexander himself, in hearty fashion. "Here is True Thomas, of whom I have told you — a man of parts indeed — the parts sometimes testing of my poor patience! Eh, Thomas? And the Lady Bethoc his wife — who must need more patience even than myself! She is eldest daughter to our host, and so kin of my own. Sir Michael Scott you have cause to know. Sir Thomas, here, is another who looks into the future — but a mite differently! Thomas — have you any cheer for us to add to our present happiness?"

"I would say, Sire, that was scarcely possible. With so enchanting a lady!"

"Ah, sir — gallant!" the Duchess smiled. "I have heard of your fame. The poet, is it not? The tale of Tristrem and Isolde, I am told? This I must hear. Lady . . .? I fear that I did not hear the name aright. Forgive me."

"Bethoc, Duchess — a Scots name, allied to your Elizabeth. I hope that you will like our Scotland." Bethoc, at thirty-eight, was a little more plump but still exceedingly good-looking. The two women made a handsome if contrasting pair.

"I like it already, Lady Beth. Everyone so kind. In especial, my lord King. But I have much to learn. Perhaps you will teach me . . .?"

"You will give us more of *Sir Tristrem* at the marriage-feast?" Alexander asked Thomas. "I would hear the end of it all."

"If you wish, Sire." He glanced at the two women,

chatting animatedly, and lowered his voice. "The wedding, Your Grace? Where is it to be celebrated?"

"Why, in the Abbey, to be sure. Kelso Abbey. Where else?"

"Must it be there, Sire?"

"Why not, man?"

"I . . . I had ill apparition. The last time. At the prince's wedding. As I entered the church. I saw the roof fall, the entire roof. On all the folk, the worshippers. A grievous sight . . ."

"God be good! The roof . . .?"

"Yes. Men and women fleeing, falling, crushed. The church full. But — I do not know. It could be but some foolish notion, some disorder of the mind. These visions that come to me, they are not always true. Many, many have not come to pass . . ."

"It was at the wedding, you say? This evil thing?"

"No — I do not know when it might be. If at all. But it was at your son's wedding that I saw it."

"And *that* was a sorry celebration, to be sure! Dead within months! And now, this! A warning? No — we shall have no more of Kelso, then. I will change it. Marry elsewhere. At Jedburgh — aye, at the Abbey of Jedburgh. Better there. Abbot Richard will be much put out. But Abbot Morel at Jedburgh will be the more pleased. Yes — we shall have it there. Besides, too much of sorrow has come from Kelso."

There was dancing after the banquet. The King danced with Yolande for the first few sets, teaching her the Scots steps and reels with typical vigour and enthusiasm, to her much laughter. Then he came to offer his arm to his hostess; but the Countess Christian, now an elderly lady and growing heavy and stiff, smilingly declined. He led Bethoc out instead. Some competition then developed to partner the Duchess; but Pate stalked up, pushing aside the others, and took her as of right. He was the host's heir, of course — but that did not prevent some resentment at his unmannerly attitude, especially from his own cousin, Bruce the Younger, who had been first in the queue and who, as now officially included in the succession sequence, as well as acting earl for his son of Carrick, had an enhanced opinion of himself.

The Countess Christian sighed. "Pate makes enemies for himself, always," she said to Thomas, standing at her side, dancing being incompatible with his lameness. "I fear for him. Only trouble can come from his behaviour."

"He always was the competitor. Always strove for the mastery. Being first is important to him."

"Too important. But, even so, there is no need for arrogance. He turns all against him. His own father will scarcely speak with him now. I much blame the woman he married. The Comyns are all hard, ambitious, sour. A house I have never loved. We were against the match."

Thomas said nothing. They had been against *his* match, even more so.

The Countess touched his arm lightly. "I know that we were less than kind to you, Thomas — you and Bethoc. No doubt we erred. It was . . . difficult. But that is all long past. We are happy now with you as goodson. Rejoice for you and Bethoc and the boy."

"I thank you . . ."

"All our children we are happy about. Save only Pate. It is a sorrow."

"He will, perhaps, grow kinder with time."

"We have not so much of time left, his father and myself!"

When the King brought back a panting Bethoc, he retrieved his Yolande from Pate with a brusqueness not much better than Pate's own. Deliberately he made much of the Countess, Bethoc and Thomas, while turning his shoulder on Pate. Thomas did not fail to catch his brother-in-law's venomous glance before he strode off.

*   *   *

Jedburgh lay nine miles west of Roxburgh where the Jed Water joined Teviot, a pleasant little town climbing between the lovely abbey above the riverside haughs and the royal castle on its high spur of the Dunion Hill. Because of its comparative proximity to Roxburgh, this castle was little used, save as a hunting-house; but on Hallowmass of 1285 it came into its own. With the wedding being celebrated in Jedburgh Abbey, Roxburgh was too far away for convenience; so the festivities were held here.

Comparisons with the last royal wedding, only three years before, were inevitable. Then there had been tension, anxiety over the bridegroom's health, gloom over Prince David's death, the King distracted, even how Margaret of Flanders would serve as Scotland's future queen. Now all was confidence, enthusiasm, good spirits, bride and groom both emanating satisfaction. If Alexander had any misgivings about falling roofs or other disasters, he showed no sign of it.

Jedburgh Abbey was slightly smaller but more beautiful than Kelso, more graceful and less massive. One of the finest buildings in the land, indeed, it made no second-rate choice for royal nuptials. Remarkable were the three tiers of arcading soaring on clustered pillars on either side of the lengthy, lofty nave, the topmost clerestorey gallery lit by no fewer than thirty-six arched windows on each side. King David, in typical lavish fashion, had spared no expense at its erection. It was a source of satisfaction to not a few present and admiring that day that most of the moneys therefor had come from David's rich English earldom of Huntingdon whose heiress Matilda he had married. Small wonder indeed that Alexander had been so determined to cling on to its wealth, despite the required fealty-oath to Edward.

The Primate, Bishop Fraser of St. Andrews, conducted the service, assisted by Abbot John Morel; also his rival, Abbot Richard of Kelso, who was being placated, less than successfully, for the switch in the venue; the King was unlikely to have told him of Thomas's vision. Bride and groom looked magnificent, gave their responses in ringing tones, and radiated good health and gratification both. It was the most joyful and splendid occasion Thomas for one had ever attended. Even the procession from the abbey up to the castle, through Jedburgh's thronged and decorated streets, turned itself into a dance and frolic, with musicians playing, choristers skipping and capering as well as singing, and Alexander and his new queen stepping it out as gaily if with more of dignity.

The feasting which followed was no less heartening, unstinted, lavish. Much thought, indeed imagination, had been devoted to the provisioning, both in food and drink, that Yolande's brother and other foreign guests should not leave with any notion that Scotland was a poor and backward country, lacking any refinements which others might enjoy. The land had been scoured for delicacies and kickshaws, the castle's rough walls hung with tapestries and arras from Roxburgh, evergreens decorating all, great fires ablaze, lanterns, torches and candles turning early winter evening into day.

Concerned lest the abundance of wines and ale should produce any drunken debauch as the night wore on, so often the case, the King had not only issued strict orders but, instead of the usual noisy if hearty entertainers, so apt to evoke wagering and argument, had devised something new for Scotland, a pageant, which it was hoped would not only grace the occasion but hold the attention and restrain the bibulous. A number of themes had been debated, until Thomas himself had suggested that, since he was to recite the final episodes of his *Sir Tristrem* later, it might be acceptable to stage a brief summary of the highlights of the earlier parts, to remind all of what had gone before and to inform those who had missed it. This had been enthusiastically agreed. So Thomas had been much involved, selecting set pieces which might serve to recall the essence of the tale, to advise on costumes and the like and the painting of scenery. He and Bethoc had been given places at the end of the dais-table, where he was to act more or less as master-of-ceremonies.

Since only some four scenes of pageantry were practical, it had been difficult to choose incidents in the long epic which would be both dramatic to watch and informative as to the story. The first was comparatively simple, the Court of King Mark at Tintagel, with Tristrem being sent off to Ireland to fetch the fair Isolde. This went down well, even if the acting was somewhat wooden. Tristrem was played by Johnnie of Birkensyde, looking very colourful if self-conscious; and his Uncle Mark by Alec wearing a handsome white beard of lamb's-wool. Thomas declaimed a brief commentary. The applause was generous. Whilst the scenery was being changed for the next episode, a troupe of a dozen dancers, masked, came on in front, suitably garbed in old-fashioned style, to keep the company entertained.

The second scene was at the Court of the High King of Ireland, with Isolde none other than Eala, now Lady Douglas, and turned into a strikingly good-looking woman. The amatory by-play between herself and her brother Johnnie, while the King and Queen of Ireland — Peter Haig, Younger of Bemersyde and Gelis, now married to the heir of the Swintons — carefully looked the other way, was much appreciated.

The dancers came on again, now more skittish in their performance.

The third scene portrayed the arbour in the orchard at Tintagel, with the two principals indulging their guilty passion, the fact of them being brother and sister adding spice for the audience. King Mark's discovery of them thereafter was suitably dramatic.

It was at the third dance sequence, as the scenery was being changed to the Breton Court, with special elaboration contrived in honour of the recent Duchess thereof, when it happened. Thomas, as before, was filling in the gap in events with a short summary — which had to be almost shouted to overcome the music of the dance — when suddenly his voice choked and died away. He rose slowly to his feet, to point a trembling finger. As everyone turned to stare, he sat down again heavily and leaned forward over the table, hands covering his face, body shuddering.

The dancers, unaware that anything was amiss, went on with their skipping and posturing.

Bethoc was bent over Thomas anxiously demanding to know what was wrong, clutching his heaving shoulders.

"Death!" he gasped. "Death! Dancing there. With the others. God help us — Death!"

She gazed from him to the dancers and back. "Thomas — I see nothing. Nothing, my dear . . ."

"It was there — I saw it, I tell you." He spread his fingers wider, to peer through them, and groaned. "Saints of mercy — he is there still! See — in the midst. A skeleton — a white skeleton. And grinning, a grinning skull!" He hid his face again.

"But . . . I see nothing, my heart! Naught but the dancers. As before . . ."

"Then you are blind, blind! Look — there he has come to the front, staring at us. Horrible! Horrible!"

Others nearby on the dais had heard Thomas's words and were gazing, exclaiming, questioning each other. Clearly none saw anything untoward. But Thomas's reputation was sufficient to ensure that what was being seen by him was not to be laughed off or ignored.

The King was on his feet, shouting for the dancers to be removed. Frowning, he came stalking across to the Learmonths.

"What a God's good name is this?" he cried. "Thomas — what are you at? What folly is this?"

Thomas shook his bowed head wordless, not even looking up.

"Save us, man — take hold on yourself! What is to do? This talk of death . . .?"

Thomas clenched his fists so that the knuckles showed white, and straightened up. He peered towards the now empty space before the half-erected scenery, then rose to his feet beside Alexander.

"I saw it, Sire. An evil sight. Dancing amongst the others. A gleaming skeleton. White. Pointing, capering, vile . . ."

"*I* saw nothing, man. Save these mummers. Nor did any. You dream, Thomas — you are overwrought."

"I *saw* it, Your Grace. As clear as I see you. It was a sight most terrible."

The King stared at him, biting his lip. "What does it mean, then? What does this mean?"

"It cannot mean . . . anything but ill." Yolande had come to stand beside them, lovely features drawn with concern. Seeing her, Thomas shook his head. "The ill — it may not be for you, Sire. You and the Queen. It could be . . . anyone."

"It is *my* wedding, *my* banquet — spoiled!"

"I am sorry, Sire — sorry!"

"Too late to be sorry! What to do, now? We cannot continue with this . . ."

"No, Sire — no! I could not . . ."

"The rest of it? The poem? The reciting . . .?"

"No, Your Grace — not now. I could not do it now. Not after . . ."

385

Alexander looked upset, almost angry. But Yolande laid a hand on his arm.

"It matters not, my good lord," she said. "Another evening, perhaps? Let us not spoil this especial one. I would . . . retire early, moreover!"

"Ah, yes — yes, to be sure!"

"And Sir Thomas also should retire, I think. Lady Beth — do you not think so? He is not himself . . ."

Thankfully Bethoc agreed.

Alexander, with the night's delights ahead of him, allowed himself to be more gracious, to put the unfortunate matter behind him. He told Thomas and Bethoc to be off; and sent word for the rest of the pageant to be cancelled.

The hall was buzzing with excitement, comment, question and conjecture as the Learmonths left and the marriage-feast was brought to a premature close.

It was strange how the events of that evening affected folk — and soon the thing was noised abroad all over the land, in varying versions. Some scoffed and mocked. Others were impressed and anxious. Some even asserted that they too had seen the skeletal figure of Death dancing. Many were the fears and forebodings expressed, the reasons therefor canvassed. Alexander was inconsistent. Interested and concerned over Thomas's previous visions, he refused to take this one seriously — presumably because he had been present in person and had seen nothing. But he blamed Thomas for ruining his wedding-feast, even though jocularly.

22

That winter of 1285/6 was one of the wildest and most stormy in the memory of men. Week after week the gales and rain persisted, while the country lay beaten and waterlogged, cowering. In December, thunder and lightning and hail were an almost daily occurrence, a phenomenon never before recorded. For months little or no work could be done on the land, stock was drowned in raging rivers and fishing-boats could not put to sea. Men huddled indoors, idle — and, as idle men will, drank too much, plagued their womenfolk, told tales, and wagged their heads over present and future. God's wrath was obviously involved, the figure of Death at the King's feast spoken of more and more, as presaging calamity, and some would-be prophet — not Thomas nor Sir Michael Scott — actually announced that the Day of Judgment was at hand, various dates being offered.

Thomas himself was prophesying nothing. After the Jedburgh business, he was determined not to be implicated in any more embarrassments and offence-giving. The prophet's was an unprofitable profession, most evidently. He cursed the weather like everybody else, however, and vehemently; for it sorely affected his work as land-steward and his ability to travel over the widespread domains of the two earldoms.

At least Bethoc was able to see much of her ageing parents, for Dunbar Castle was all but untenable in such prolonged storm conditions, on its exposed sea-girt rocks, hidden in spray for days on end and with great waves frequently breaking right over its towers. So the Earl and Countess were spending this deplorable winter at Ercildoune which, tucked into the Border hills, was at least sheltered, even though distinctly cut-off because of flooded valley-floors and impassable fords. Actually, in one respect, it developed into a quite sociable and happy winter for the Dunbar family, for Johnnie at Birkensyde was only a few miles up Lauderdale, Gelis and Alec, respectively at Swinton and Swinwood in the Merse, were able to reach Ercildoune without great difficulty. Pate however kept his distance, most of his time spent with his wife's Comyn kin.

They did not see much of the King. He left Jedburgh and Roxburgh soon after the wedding, to take his queen on a tour of her new realm, to visit most of his twenty-three castles. The weather soon made this impracticable and they were forced to remain in the Central Scotland area. The little castle of Kinghorn, in the Fothrif area of Fife, seemed much to appeal to Yolande, reminding her of her childhood home; and in his open-handed way, with nothing too good for his love, Alexander presented the place to her outright. They seemed to be spending much of their time there — although being on the coast also, if less exposed than Dunbar, it must have been a wild roosting-place frequently that winter. Perhaps it suited their lovers' mood.

In March, the Earl Patrick was summoned to a Council-meeting at Edinburgh to deal with some demand of Baliol of Barnard Castle regarding a kinsman long imprisoned in Scotland for rebellion, a claim which it seemed King Edward was supporting. But in view of the difficulty the royal courier had met in reaching Ercildoune, he decided not to attend. He was, after all, in his seventy-third year, and traipsing round the country in such conditions was for younger men. Besides, was not the date, St. Donan's Day, 18th March, one of those listed for the Day of Judgment? If the world was going to come to an end then, Patrick would prefer to await it in comfort before his own fireside. Alexander should have more sense than to call Council-meetings in these conditions.

That day, the 18th, in fact turned out to be one of the best for months, with the wind dropping, the sun shining and the chill lifting. Thomas, with so much outdoor work crying for attention, would have been off and busy, but the Earl sent for him to come up to the castle.

There he found Peter Haig closeted with Patrick. This was the brother of Hodierna Haig, the Countess Christian's long-serving lady-in-attendance and companion. Their father, old Haig of Bemersyde, a few miles to the south, one of the Earl's chief vassals, had just died at an advanced age, and Peter was the new laird. The system of land-tenure required much adjustment on such occasions, with new valuations to be negotiated, charges listed, tenancies extended or terminated and so on, in all of which the steward was concerned. Thomas knew Peter well, of course; indeed they were quite good friends, Haig an amiable large man. So, with the Earl accommodating, there were no major difficulties and the business was concluded expeditiously enough despite the large extent of land involved.

There remained only the important matter of the signing of the necessary charter by the Earl, with Thomas as witness. Reading it over first, in reasonable Latin, Patrick grinned rather apologetically when he came to the part about the said Peter Haig and the male heirs of his body, in lawful succession. For this was something of a sore point with poor Haig. Although now married for almost twenty years, he had produced five daughters but no son. Moreover, he had no brothers, cousins or near male kin. Inevitably, it was a matter which preyed much on the man's mind, his flock of plain daughters long a source of some merriment in the Border area.

Now he shook his head gloomily, declaring that however fine-sounding the Latin, this part was no more than belly-wind since it seemed certain that he would be the last Haig of Bemersyde.

His lord pooh-poohed. "Tush, man — never give up! You are not so old, yet. And your good lady not past child-bearing, I think! Play the man, Peter — play the man!"

"Playing the man has earned me only daughters, my lord. I have had enough of them! It seems that we can produce none other. I dare not risk any more!"

"M'mm." The Earl cocked an eyebrow at Thomas. "How says our soothsayer? Is Peter to be the last of his line? Or shall he yet produce a son?"

"That I cannot tell, my lord."

"Tut — be not so stiff! Not with a friend. Surely you can give him some word? A blink of hope? You have given others in plenty — although not always hope!"

"Not for long. I have given up making forecasts."

"Aye, so you have said. But this is different. A friend in need!"

"*Is* there any hope, Thomas? Any hope at all?" Haig asked, almost pleaded.

Thomas pursed his lips, frowned and then shrugged.

> *Time and tide, what e'er betide,*
> *Haig will be Haig of Bemersyde.*

He jerked out the jingle, and then turned away.

The others stared at him and at each other.

"God save us — you hear that?" Patrick exclaimed. "That was quick."

"Thomas!" Haig cried. "Man — I thank you! I thank you! This is a wonder! Praises be!"

"I but said . . ." Thomas stopped. Why spoil it for him? Why point out that what he had said could mean much or nothing, that he had not stated that there *would* always be Haigs at Bemersyde.

"There you are, then, Peter! Back home with you and deal with your wife in suitable fashion!" The Earl clapped his vassal on the shoulder, reached for the quill and ink-horn, and signed the charter with a flourish. "There — Bemersyde for generations of Haigs! Thomas — come, witness. Then we shall drink to it . . ."

At the wine, Thomas was further provoked. The Earl, now in excellent spirits, demanded additional display of his son-in-law's talents.

"Now that you have broken your silence, tell us more," he urged. "What do you see for the future, Thomas? For us all? Tell us."

"No, my lord. That is not for me to tell."

"Something, man. Some morsel. You are always so accursedly close, constrained!"

"I cannot. You do not understand. None ever understands. I cannot foretell to order . . ."

"You have just done so! I understand very well — you fear to prophesy lest you be proved wrong!"

"No doubt you are right in *that*, my lord!"

"You are stubborn, Thomas. Can you swear to me that you have had no least foreseeings of the future of our liege-lord and his realm?"

Thomas frowned and hesitated. "I have no sure vision, nothing that I can vouch for."

"That is not what I asked, man! You *have* foreseen something — that *I* swear! Do not put us off. Out with it."

"If I do, you will not like it, my lord. Any more than I do."

"Ha — so you admit to it! Try us — we are not bairns. What do you see?"

"I see storms, storms before us."

"Storms, man? We have been having storms for months. *I* could have prophesied that! Because it is quieter today, we would be fools to think that the storms are overpast. Come — you must do better than that!"

"The storms I speak of will not be such as these, my lord. Much greater, more dire. Such as this land has not suffered before." Thomas spoke slowly, deliberately, now. "It will carry much away."

"Storms do. When is this great storm to be?"

His son-in-law raised hand to brow for a moment, eyes shut. "Before tomorrow at noon. Tomorrow — a day of calamity and misery. Before the twelfth hour . . . a blast so vehement as shall exceed every former period . . . a blast that shall strike the nation with amazement, that shall humble the proud — the sorest wind and tempest that ever was heard in Scotland . . ." His voice tailed away.

The Earl wagged his grey head. "I am disappointed in you, Thomas! You have been listening to this Day of Judgment nonsense, I think. This of storms and wind. You will have Peter doubting his Haig rhyme, if this is the best that you can do!"

"This tempest, Thomas — can we do anything to guard against its hurt?" Haig demanded.

"Tie down your thatching at Bemersyde, man — if it has not already been blown away!" his lord advised. "And be thankful that you have stone roofing to your tower. Eh, Thomas?"

"I must leave, my lord — I have much work awaiting me. In your interests."

"Very well — as you will. We are finished here. But see you, Thomas — I want you back here tomorrow. I have sent for George Gordon and his brother. I have a bone or two to pick with them, as you know. So be here betimes. That is, if your tempest allows!"

Nodding, tight-lipped, he left them.

That evening, with the wind rising once more and the rain blattering, Thomas all but quarrelled with Bethoc over her father.

*   *   *

Strangely, the morning dawned bright and clear, with only a modest breeze remaining. Thomas Learmonth was neither bright nor clear, however, after a bad night, more depressed than his wife had ever seen him. Silent and with no appetite, he admitted that his head ached vilely. Bethoc, concerned, would have had him not to go up to the castle. But when he insisted, she went with him.

With the sun shining and the larks trilling, their reception by the Earl Patrick was predictable. Thomas suffered it in silence, with his wife and mother-in-law seeking to tone down the old man. The Gordons of Gordon, Huntlywood and Legerwood were there, probably the most unruly of the Merse vassals, with whom Thomas had had many tussles; and they were only too happy to join in the fun. Hurrying to windows to peer out and see if the tempest was approaching kept these bonny fighters cheerfully amused — especially as it helped to dilute their lord's ire over the discussion of failures to pay their feudal dues and other delinquencies.

All they got out of their victim was a curt reminder that it was not yet noon.

When midday passed without incident, however, and the afternoon advanced, the joke became somewhat stale, and the discredited if reluctant prophet was left in peace to act land-steward — whereupon he was able to get something of his own back.

Then, with the business completed and the Gordons preparing to depart, only moderately chastened, there was a commotion in the courtyard. A courier from Chancellor Charteris in Edinburgh had arrived, in a sorry state, having all but drowned in the flooded Leader, his horse swept away at a ford and himself rescued by cottagers. But sympathy for the man was forgotten as, brought before the Earl, he gasped out the Chancellor's message. The King, good King Alexander, was dead. The King was dead. And the Council was recalled. The Earl of Dunbar must attend . . .

Appalled, they stared at the dishevelled courier — all except Thomas, who went over to a window and gazed out, shoulders bowed. There Bethoc came to him, to put an arm around him.

"You knew?" she said.

He took his time to answer. "I . . . feared. Knew that something most dire would befall. It has hung over me, like an evil bird. And yesterday, yesterday the creature came close. But it was Alexander that the foul bird had come for."

"Oh, Thomas, Thomas! You could have told *me*. Alexander — poor Alexander! And poor Yolande!"

"Aye."

They turned back to the others.

"So this, this was your tempest, Thomas?" the Earl said, visibly shaken. "The storm that was to shake Scotland."

"Yes, this. Just what was to befall I did not know."

"And I scoffed — God forgive me!"

They questioned the courier as to what had happened. He told them all that he knew, all that the Chancellor had passed on to him and others. The Council was in the castle of Edinburgh, the King having come from Kinghorn in Fife. They finished their business with the darkening and then ate in haste, for Alexander had announced that he was going back to the Queen at Kinghorn that night — nothing would keep him from her delectable side. All sought to dissuade him, for the wind had arisen with the dusk once more and it promised to be another wild night. But the King would not hear of it and, with only three attendants, he set off for Queen Margaret's Ferry across the Scotwater. There, they learned, the ferrymaster had been much against sailing, declaring wind and sea too rough; but the King did not heed him. They had won across the Firth to Inverkeithing in safety and there took refreshment, despite the night hour, at the house of the master of the royal salt-works — who also did his best to keep the monarch from proceeding further in the stormy night. But to no avail; Alexander was determined to press on the remaining nine miles. In the Aberdour area it seemed that he had become separated from his companions in the darkness and rain-squalls — why was not yet fully established. But when these three finally reached Kinghorn Castle thereafter, the King was not there. With daylight they found Alexander only half-a-mile away, on the sands at the foot of a cliff, he and his horse both with broken necks.

In silence they listened to that grim recital.

The Council would meet two days hence, again at Edinburgh, to decide what to do, presumably to proclaim the infant Norwegian princess to be Scotland's monarch — unless, God willing, Queen Yolande proved to be already with child. Either way, there would be Guardians of the Realm to appoint and no doubt a Convention of the Estates to be called. The Earl Partick was urgently requested to be present, riding conditions notwithstanding.

23

Wise Council decisions or none, it did not take long for chaos to set in, almost anarchy. It had been Alexander's own decision, almost entirely, that the Maid of Norway should be next in succession; and while this was accepted in a half-hearted and tentative fashion, it was not popular and many held that it was not proper or binding. There had never been a High Queen of Scots — the thing was a contradiction. Scotland's monarch was traditionally the *Ard Righ*; there was no female equivalent. Old Bruce held this view strongly, needless to say, and gathered a strong party round him to support the contention in general and his own claim to the throne in particular. The Baliol supporters rallied similarly. But the hands of both groupings, like those of the official legitimists, were tied over the Yolande situation. If she was pregnant and produced a son, he would be undoubted heir to the throne. She had been wed for five months and none doubted her fertility any more than her late husband's lustiness. Unfortunately, the bereaved Queen-Consort gave no indication as to her state. After Alexander's funeral at Dunfermline Abbey she hid herself away in her castle at Kinghorn, seeing nobody. Messages remained unanswered, callers were turned away. Rumours grew, naturally — that she was indeed with child, that she was not but claimed to be, that she had miscarried, even that she was consoling herself with a lover and would pass any resultant offspring as the King's. Pro and anti-Yolande parties developed likewise.

Unfortunately there were other fingers probing into this pie also, from south of the Border. It was surprising how many descendants seemed to have sprung from the Earl David of Huntingdon, brother of Malcolm the Fourth and William the Lyon, both of whom were so frugal of progeny; and most of these now found it politic to put in at least a tentative claim to the Scottish throne — it was suggested, at King Edward's instigation. That he intended to fish in such troubled waters went almost without saying. Just what his line would be was a matter for much speculation.

Inevitably a waiting game had to be played over Yolande, since months had to elapse after the King's death before it could be established beyond all doubt that she was not going to have a child — which would take them up to the turn of the year. Meanwhile the other interests jockeyed for position in their various ways — to the realm's disadvantage and confusion. Bruce, for instance, tightened his supporters' adherence by getting them all to sign a Bond of Association promising more than mere token aid in his claim — his brother-in-law, the Earl Patrick, was one of the signatories — and reinforced this by assembling the nucleus of a large armed force in Annandale, cadres which could be transformed into a major army at short notice. He took over the royal castle of Dumfries and the Red Comyn's house of Buittle. John Baliol of Barnard Castle, for his part, sent in an official claim to the Scots Crown, asserting that as senior descendant of the eldest daughter of the Earl David, his was the undoubted right; and if the Crown could go outside Scotland to a Norwegian princess, how could there be any lawful objection to an Englishman? Moreover he added that King Edward supported him. Whether Longshanks did or not was a matter for question, when it became known that he had written to young King Eric of Norway proposing a marriage between his son and heir, Edward of Caernarvon, being called Prince of Wales, and the child Margaret. Also he had requested the Pope for the necessary dispensation as to blood relationship, the Maid being in cousinship to the young prince. This news set Scotland by the ears indeed and did Bruce's cause considerable good. Envoys were hurriedly sent to the Court of Norway.

So the land was in a turmoil, with ordinary folk not knowing where to turn and fearing for the future. This last was true of Thomas Learmonth, whose forebodings were by no means ended by the King's death. He grieved for Alexander, whom he had come to look upon almost as a friend. The fact that he had feared for him for long did not lessen the sense of loss, the sorrow that so vehement and lively a character had been snatched from the earthly scene in the prime of life, and by so foolhardy an accident. For Yolande too he was greatly concerned; and though like so many others he hoped and prayed for a child from her, a son in especial, he could not shut his eyes to the fact that there had been no hint in any of his dreams of any last-moment offspring of the King appearing to frustrate the menace of that evil bird which hovered over the kingdom. Indeed any indications which had come to him suggested that it was from the Bruce line that they must look for future rule. Yet he was far from happy about Bruce's attitude and behaviour, and concerned that the Earl Patrick was supporting him in it, this bound to lead to trouble. The fact that Pate was also against Bruce and his father was scant consolation; that difficult character seemed to be concerned not so much with his own very doubtful claim as with that of John Baliol, to whom the Comyns were related. Perhaps he felt that he had more to gain from that source, if it had Edward's backing. Whatever the reasons, in all this there could be the seeds of civil war and fratricidal strife.

The infant Margaret of Norway was formally proclaimed Queen on July 2nd, there being no word of any pregnancy from Kinghorn. The Council as formally requested that King Eric would send over their Queen to Scotland as soon as possible and before the winter storms. Eric however sent a refusal. With the dispensation received from Rome, there was nothing to prevent the betrothal to Edward's heir. Canute's dream, the uniting of England, Scotland and Norway, looked to be a possibility at last. Most Scots grew the more alarmed, for none had any doubts, in that event, as to who would rule that roost and how he would rule it.

The Guardians decided to send a deputation to Edward, to make clear their attitude, and under guise of seeking his aid in the realm's problems, to try to discover his intentions. The Bishop of Brechin, Abbot Morel of Jedburgh and Sir Geoffrey Moubray had to go all the way to Gascony to run Longshanks to earth, where he was presently making his will felt with sword and fire. There they gained only general assurances that he had Scotland's best interest at heart, and would inform the Guardians as he went along.

At least the weather had improved.

After various trials, humiliations, accusations, even demands for physical examinations, Yolande at length left Scotland for good, with it crystal-clear that there was no heir for Alexander with her. So ended a mere year's interlude, which had started with such joy and high hopes. Many were sad to see her go.

Royal patronage gone and Earl Patrick no longer taking any active part in affairs of state, Thomas's life became much more localised and circumscribed. He was busy enough, his steward's activities fully employing his time; but he had to confess that he missed the occasional excitements and excursions which Alexander and his Court had provided. His prophesyings, too, were in less demand   for which he was thankful — with the worst of the dreaded happenings fulfilled and past. Only Edward's shadow remained.

Two echoes of less dire and older foretellings reached him at this time, when he encountered Sir Reginald le Chien at Dunbar Castle, where he had come to try to persuade Earl Patrick to switch allegiance over the succession issue from the Bruce to the Baliol/Comyn faction. He was unsuccessful in this, but was able to inform Thomas, firstly that the Lord Fergus Comyn had died whilst hunting, at Aikey Brae in Buchan, being swept from the saddle by the branch of a tree; and secondly that in the terrible winter of gales, extraordinary sand-storms had quite overwhelmed the Forvie area, further south, covering that entire fertile barony in yellow sand, so that now only the tip of the church-tower projected above the smothering desolation. When asked, levelly, about the three sisters whose malisons were to invoke this disaster, le Chien admitted that they were no longer at Forvie, having been dispossessed, unwed. Where they were now, he had no idea. He did not add that the dispossessors were Comyns. Although he tried not to allow himself to sound impressed by these fulfilments, le Chien clearly was so.

Thomas felt strangely unmoved, as though it all had little to do with him. But Bethoc was excited and perturbed.

*   *   *

Perhaps the Learmonths, in the circumstances, should have foreseen, without any supernatural help, the major change in their state when, at the age of seventy-six, the Earl Patrick suffered a heart attack, recovered but refused to take his physician's advice, tried to continue to live as before, took another and died. Sorrow and a sense of loss were enough, especially as the Countess Christian herself was ailing; but what followed was in a different degree of upset. Pate Black Beard was now eighth Earl of Dunbar and March, and was not slow in letting all know it. In the confused circumstances of the period it might take some time for him to make his mark on national affairs, although he could, and did, switch the support of the two earldoms from the Bruce to the Baliol cause. But on the more personal level he could act right away. One of his first moves was to dismiss Thomas from being steward of the joint earldoms.

So, abruptly, the Learmonths' entire situation was altered. Instead of having great responsibilities and some hundreds of thousands of acres to oversee, Thomas reverted to being merely a small laird, renowned and knighted but impoverished. Fortunately the Earl Patrick had made belated provision for his eldest daughter at his death, so that she inherited the neighbouring small Lauderdale property of Huntshaw, no great esate but considerably larger than that of Ercildoune Tower; and since this likewise marched with

Birkensyde where Johnnie was no farmer or land-manager, he gladly retained Thomas's services in running this property also. Nevertheless, at almost fifty, Thomas found himself leading a much restricted life compared with the past many years, especially as he had trained up their son Tom in land-management, and he was now able and eager to take over much from his father. So he was given the day-to-day runnng of Bethoc's inheritance — which, of course, would one day be his own.

Until he might adjust himself, time hung rather heavily for Thomas Learmonth.

It was in these circumstances that he almost came to welcome a sudden stir on the inconclusive and faction-torn national scene. The most prestigious of the Guardians, the High Constable, Alexander Comyn, Earl of Buchan, died — he was an elderly man and never robust after his crusading fever; and shortly thereafter, another Guardian, Duncan, Earl of Fife, Colban's son, was assassinated — allegedly by some of his own people, aged only twenty-six. Since these two were the most prominent of the Baliol supporters, there was inevitably talk of sinister motivation. Warlike sounds emanated from many — and none louder than from the Earl Pate of Dunbar — and armed forces began to assemble in various parts of the land. Bruce and his ally the High Steward moved quickly. In addition to Dumfries they took over the royal castle of Wigtown, occupied Kirk Cuthbert's Town and so more or less immobilised the great Baliol bastion of Galloway. Since Annan controlled the Solway crossings from England — the only effective route for armies from the south on this west side, on the firm tidal sands — de Soulis of Liddesdale was a supporter, and the warlike westland clans of Johnstone, Herries, Maxwell, Jardine, Kirkpatrick and the rest were all Bruce vassals; and Bruce's son controlled Carrick and Ayr whilst the Steward held Kyle, Cunninghame and Renfrew, the entire South-West of Scotland was firmly in Bruce hands. With Dunbar and March controlling the South-East in the Baliol favour, and the rest of the Lowlands jockeying for position and choosing sides, the scene was set for bloody conflict, major civil war.

This was promptly contested by the Primate, Bishop Fraser of St. Andrews, who declared that in the absence of a monarch there must be a supreme authority in the realm, otherwise there could only be anarchy. That authority meantime was the guardianship, duly appointed by the Council, with the high officers of state. These must have the right to summon a due and proper Convention of the Estates, otherwise the voice of the realm could not be heard. Bishop Wishart of Glasgow agreed, although a Bruce supporter, and pointed out that no higher authority than the Guardians existed at present; therefore their decision on such a matter could not be countermanded save by an express decision of the said Estates. Accordingly, if nobody could call a Convention, save a non-existent monarch, the Guardians' powers became unlimited — which he scarcely thought would commend itself to his friend the Lord of Annandale. He appealed to the Chancellor for a ruling.

Master Charteris announced that it was his considered opinion that this was a lawful and proper Convention of the Estates, its decisions binding. It was evident that the great majority of those present agreed.

Bruce, quite unabashed, declared that he would accept that. But he asserted that it was evident that such confusion and doubts must continue to arise so long as there was no recognised head of state. He therefore proposed that a Regent be appointed forthwith — a proposal promptly seconded by James the High Steward, one of the Guardians.

This drastic and unanticipated move set the gathering in a dither. Talk, argument, conjecture, broke out everywhere.

Pate caught Charteris's eye. "Master Chancellor," he called, "is it competent for this gathering to appoint a Regent? Is it not a matter for the Council?"

The Chancellor hesitated. "This is something on which I am uncertain," he admitted. "Regents, in the past, have been appointed by the Council rather than the Estates of parliament. Yet all the Council is here present. My ruling would be that this Convention would have the right to decide whether there should *be* a Regent. And, if so, the councillors only should decide who is to be so."

That did not please everybody, by any means. There was much private debate and counting of heads and allegiances. It was fairly obvious from James Stewart's quick seconding that this was a planned move of the Bruce faction. Probable also that the old warrior saw *himself* as the Regent. This would not suit the Baliol/Comyn party, needless to say. It looked as though, thus early, there would be a lining-up of sides and hardening of attitudes, which could affect the entire proceedings.

Sir Michael Scott created a diversion, waving his hand. He was still wearing his steel-lined hat which was to protect him from the two-ounce stone which he had prophesied would eventually kill him — it was even suggested that he wore it in bed, although that was hard to believe.

"Chancellor — I would speak," he said — and such was his renown that he obtained an immediate hearing, even from the arrogant lords. "I say that a Regent cannot here be appointed. There cannot be a Regent without a monarch to derive from. Regency is but an extension of the Crown, appointed to rule in the monarch's name. But we have no monarch at this present. The Princess Margaret of Norway has been proclaimed queen by the Council. But this is only a proclamation. She has not yet been enthroned nor seated on the Stone of Destiny. Until that is done, she cannot be monarch, Queen of Scots. Therefore until then, she can have no Regent. That is all."

There was silence. So utterly authoritative did the old man sound that there was no argument. Even Bruce, bull-like in his stocky, massive-shoulder stance, glowered but did not raise voice.

Thankfully the Chancellor drew a deep breath. "If that matter is disposed of, then we can move to the principal business before this session." He picked up a paper. "It is the attitude we are to take with regard to the King of England's proposal to wed his son and heir, the Prince Edward of Caernarvon, to the Princess Margaret of Norway to be our sovereign lady. This is . . ."

"Master Chancellor," John Comyn the Red, Lord of Badenoch and head of that great house, interrupted. "Before we move on to such heavy matter, I would raise the position of my nephew John Comyn, son of my late and noble half-brother, Alexander, Earl of Buchan and High Constable of this realm. He, John, is undoubted heir to the earldom and office of High Constable, and would have been confirmed therein by the King's Grace long ere this had it been possible. I therefore request that, lacking the *Ard Righ* or High King, the other *ri* or earls confirm the said John as Earl of Buchan and High Constable of Scotland, as only they can do."

"I support that," Walter Stewart, Earl of Menteith said. He was a brother of the High Steward but held his earldom in right of his Comyn wife.

"Does any contest it?" the Chancellor asked. "This is a matter only for the earls."

"I say otherwise," Bruce declared. "The earldom of Buchan may be a matter for the earls, and John Comyn is the evident heir. But the High Constableship is one of the great offices of state and carries command on the field of battle, lacking the King's presence. Appointment thereto is surely the Council's business."

"The Constableship has descended hereditarily for six generations, ever since its appointment," the Red Comyn asserted. "Bruce cannot deny that."

"But it is in the Crown's gift. Lacking the monarch, it must be the Council's decision."

"I accept that the Constableship must be a matter for the Council," the Chancellor said. "Have any councillors other nomination?"

"I nominate *my* nephew, Patrick, Earl of Dunbar and March," Bruce cried. "He descends from the royal house and is wed to the late Constable's daughter."

That set the church in a stir. Thomas, this time beside his brothers-in-law Johnnie and Alec, eyed them.

"Here's a to-do! Who would have thought of this?"

"The old devil!" Johnnie exlaimed. "He hates Pate!"

"What does it mean?" Alex wondered — like many another.

"It could be a shrewd move," Thomas said thoughtfully. "To drive a wedge between Pate and the Comyns. That is what it is. He seeks to weaken the Comyn and Baliol faction. It can only be that."

Charteris banged on his table. "Does any other councillor support this nomination for the Constableship?"

"I do." Bruce the Younger, acting Earl of Carrick, called dutifully. Today he had beside him his son Robert, now fifteen years, the true Earl of Carrick, a youth of stronger features than his father, not tall but slenderly well-built.

"Are there other nominations? No? Then I call a vote. Only earls and councillors may vote on this. Those voting for the new Earl of Buchan raise hands." He paused. "Now, those who say the Earl of Dunbar and March."

There was no need to count. The Comyn had it by a large majority. Pate was unpopular, making enemies as his mother had said.

"I declare John Comyn, Earl of Buchan and High Constable of Scotland," the Chancellor said. "Competent to speak and vote as such."

"Bruce ought to have guessed that he would be defeated," Johnnie declared. "He has lost the round."

"Lost? Be not so sure. Pate is not Constable, no. I would think that your uncle never expected or intended him to be. But if I know Pate, there will be bad blood now between him and the new Buchan, his good-brother. Bruce will divide the Comyns if he can."

While others were arguing to similar conclusions, the Chancellor brought forward again the vital matter of the King of England. He called on the Bishop of Brechin, senior of the three envoys who had gone to Gascony seeking Edward, to summarise the results of that mission.

The Bishop conceded that they had been well enough received but that they had gained little value. Edward had made it clear that he was determined to marry his five-year-old son to the Princess Margaret; that he was even building a great ship at Yarmouth to fetch her; and that King Eric agreed. He asserted that he had Scotland's well-being at heart, that he would seek to take the Scots Council with him in all that he did — but reminded them that he was Principal Councillor to the northern kingdom. Finally he had demanded that the overlordship of the sub-kingdom of Man be handed over to him forthwith.

From the outcry which greeted this last, old Bruce's powerful voice prevailed.

". . . not to be borne. God damn him! God damn him, I say! Edward — he seeks only to devour this realm. Give him opportunity and he will swallow us piece by piece! We must withstand the Plantagenet."

This time he had practically all present with him.

"My lords," the Chancellor said, when he could make himself heard. "To withstand is good advice, all will agree. But *how* to withstand? King Edward's position is very strong. He is indeed the Principal Councillor. He is the Princess's great-uncle, her only close kin on her mother's side. He has great influence with the young King of Norway, who is known to owe him large moneys. He has some favour with the Pope, who seeks to have him to lead the new Crusade. He is accepted as the First Knight of Christendom and is respected and feared by other princes. And he is a notable soldier and controls the greatest army in existence. When we talk of withstanding, let us consider what we have to set against all this."

Even Bruce was silenced by this catalogue.

Out of the hush it was the Primate who spoke. "Clearly my lords we cannot hope to prevail against King Edward in power and might. If indeed we have to work against him. Better if we could be seen to work *with* him. Whilst preserving our position and due rights and interest."

How, how, was demanded from all around.

"Accept this marriage — since I fear that we cannot stop it. But hedge our acceptance about with conditions. And strive to see that these conditions are kept by requiring that they be incorporated in a solemn treaty. We are a sovereign realm and can so require. No mere understanding, but a signed and sealed treaty . . ."

"Edward would break any treaty!" somebody shouted. "Remember what he did to the Welsh."

"I think not," Bishop Fraser demurred. "Not if we use our wits. We could make it difficult for him to renege. Bring the

405

Pope into it. We are a wholly separate province of Holy Church. A clause incorporating that, under Papal authority, must give Edward pause."

"It is the realm he wants, not the Church," the Red Comyn asserted.

"The Church is part of the realm, a part Edward cannot grasp for himself. Use it. Other clauses we could insert, which he would find awkward to break, if carefully worded."

Sir Michael Scott again sought the Chancellor's attention. "This bishop talks good sense," he declared. "This of the Crusade also could be used. The princes of Christendom recently agreed that no subject of one could be brought for trial for offence before another. This because of the crusading army of many nationalities. There has been much trouble over this in the past. Edward assented, at the Pope's instigation. The principle is established, therefore, for more than crusading. So — a clause that no Scot is to have to answer for any offence committed, in Scotland, save by a Scottish court. That will stay Edward's hand also."

There was some murmur of agreement, especially from the greater nobles, many of whom held lands in England and who were very much aware of Edward's hold over them in consequence.

"Then this of Man," the Wizard went on. "We cannot save Man, if Edward is determined to have it — for his great fleet could take it at any time. But we could use his demand for it. Give us reason to include another clause in the treaty. That this realm, being separate and distinct, all existing marches and borders shall remain unaltered and inviolate. This, in case he nibbles further, at the Honour of Tynedale or the Liberty of Penrith. Or even across Solway."

There was general agreement on this also. But Sir Reginald le Chien demurred.

"This of a treaty is all very well," he said. "But it all could be of no avail. If Eric of Norway agrees to let his daughter be married to Edward's son, there is nothing that we can do, or say, to stop it. Edward need conclude no treaty with Scotland if he has our Queen safely wed and in his hands."

"The more reason why she should not *be* our Queen!"

Bruce shouted, and gained some support.

Thomas raised hand to the Chancellor. If le Chien could intervene, so could he. "My lords — as a sovereign realm we are most surely entitled to insist on certain conditions, for our Queen. King Eric is the weaker vessel, a mere youth. Write to him, the Guardians or the Council, requiring him that he send our liege lady to *us*, not to Edward. As is surely our right. And free of any marriage-contract."

"Aye! Aye — good for True Thomas"

"The lame man is right!"

"But would he do it?" le Chien questioned. "This mere boy. When he is in Edward's pocket."

"I say that he would. If we make it seem a condition of gaining our Crown. He, or his advisers, will know well that there are, are difficulties here. Over this succession. They will not wish to risk offending. A throne is at stake."

"Learmonth has a point," Scott decided judicially. "Send such a letter."

The Wizard's so positive pronouncement seemed to dispose of the matter; perhaps none there, even le Chien, sought to take on two soothsayers at once.

The Chancellor asked if there were any other clauses suggested for the proposed treaty.

As High Justiciar, John Comyn the Red was concerned with the administration of justice and the laws of the land. "We must leave Edward with no doubts that our laws are different from his — and must remain so," he declared. "No English judgments here. Should this Edward of Caernarvon become husband of the Queen of Scots and then one day succeed to the English throne. So — a further clause that no law be imposed on Scotland which has not been passed by the Estates. No Englishman appointed as Justiciar or sheriff. Forby, no vassal of the Scottish Crown be required to go beyond our own borders to do homage."

In that gathering, this last was obviously of prime importance.

"If all agree, these terms shall also be incorporated," Charteris said. "We thank the Lord of Badenoch. Any other?"

But John Comyn had not finished. "I have another matter to raise. Concerned with things nearer home. I refer to the unlawful assembling of large numbers of men, armies indeed, by certain lords here present, against the peace and weal of this realm. I demand that this meeting of the Estates condemn all such and require such forces to disperse forthwith."

Shouts arose throughout the church.

The Chancellor looked unhappy. "My lord — perhaps later? Can we finish first with this of King Edward and the royal match?"

"No! This is of greater immediacy. The peace and security of the realm. It should have been taken first. Let us have it out now."

"Your complaint is in general terms, my lord. Would it not be better to speak with such lords privily, lest such dispute mar the harmony of our proceedings?" If Charteris sounded dispirited, he was scarcely to be blamed. This issue would almost certainly end the usefulness of the day.

"This is no private matter, man. It concrns all. And all know who is concerned! The Lord of Annandale, the Lord of Liddesdale, the High Steward and others."

So there it was, the gauntlet thrown down.

Bruce picked it up almost with relish. "What cause for complaint has the Lord of Badenoch? Since when has it been an offence to muster men? Does he himself not have sufficient? Comyn, I say, can count more men than any other in the land. What ails him?"

"*You* do, Bruce! We all know why you have assembled this host. You would use it to uphold and support your claims. To make up for what you lack in right and truth, with armed force."

"Not so. It is quite otherwise. They are mustered to go to the aid of my lord Earl of Ulster. He is having trouble with the Irish rebels. I have lands in Ulster and must see to their protection. So I support Richard de Burgh, the Earl."

"A likely tale! Why did you take my town of Dumfries? And my castles of Buittle and Wigtown . . .?"

"*Your* town of Dumfries! God in Heaven, man — Dumfries is all but in Annandale . . ."

"I am seated there, as in Wigtown, as Justiciar of Galloway and governor."

"My lords, my lords!" Charteris cried. "Spare us! This is a Convention of the Estates. Any differences you must settle between yourselves, not here. And all debate must be conducted through myself as Chancellor."

"I told you — this is a matter for all. The peace of the realm . . ."

"The peace of the realm is safe from me, Comyn!" Bruce asserted. "You should watch your own kin . . ."

"Damn you, Bruce . . .!"

The Chancellor banged on his table, but to no avail. Uproar developed. Without a monarch's presence to instil respect, and Charteris himself, although an able man, no bishop or great cleric, there was no restraining these powerful lords and their supporters. Fraser the Primate came over to the Chancellor's table to advise him to bring the session to a close, saying that nothing more could be achieved now. Nodding, Charteris raised hand and voice.

"This Convention has done what it was called to do," he announced. "We have decided on our moves towards the Kings of England and Norway. The Council will demand a treaty in the terms specified, with Edward. And desire Eric to send his daughter forthwith, at this stage without any contract of marriage, if he wishes her to wear the Scottish Crown. More we cannot do meantime. Accordingly I declare this Convention adjourned and thank all for attendance."

Only a few could actually hear his words in the noise; but his rising, bowing and hurrying out made the situation sufficiently clear.

With the church emptying, Thomas made his way to Michael Scott's side, where Prior Nicholas also came limping to them.

"A sorry affair," he commented. "If Scotland's great ones cannot do better than this, what chance have we against Edward and his might and cunning?"

"Edward will have his fools also! But it is bad, yes. Unseemly."

"Unity we need, not this three-way strife. I fear, I much fear . . ."

"Your ring-tailed gled on the watershed and one king ruling kingdoms three! You are remembering that — and making it Edward?"

"It could be. Could it not? Or Edward's son. I never conceived of Norway."

"Nor need you. Norway will never rule Scotland. This I know."

"But England? England ruling both?" Nicholas demanded.

"England's destiny is less clear. I see confusion there. Scotland's and England's fates are in conjunction, yes. But not Norway. The heavens are clear on that. But — did you not speak to me of *Bruce* succeeding, Learmonth? Some other prediction?"

"Yes, that too. I do not understand. It is all a mystery. It was at *young* Bruce's birth that I had this dream or vision — the boy Earl of Carrick. Not his father nor grandsire. Nothing is assured in my mind."

"Of only one thing you may be assured with *old* Bruce, Learmonth — trouble! Especially with Comyn. I should not wonder if they come to blows here and now, outside this church. They and their tails! Come, we will leave by the priest's door and leave them to it . . ."

24

Thomas often asked himself thereafter, why — why, when he had foretold so much, when he had given so many others warning, why he could not have given himself some warning, some foreknowledge that the year that followed was to be the worst of his life. It seemed strange that he should have received no least hint, nothing to prepare him. But then, he had never dreamed nor foretold on his own affairs.

It made a bad year for Scotland too — and surely the land had had more than its share of such, of late. Admittedly Edward Longshanks agreed their treaty, almost out-of-hand — which perhaps should have warned all that he cared little or nothing for its terms and had as little intention of keeping them. Within three months, in July, he had sent his envoys up to the same Birgham-on-Tweed, to sign in his name — but before doing so, in June, he moved into Man and took over that island as English territory. Not only that, but his principal envoy at Birgham was one of the most feared and hated men in England, Anthony Beck, Bishop of Durham, the least likely cleric England had produced since William the Conqueror's savage half-brother Odo. He represented the Church Militant with a vengeance and with a mailed fist, a fighting soldier rather than a priest, and a veteran campaigning crony of Edward's. Having signed the treaty, he baldly announced that the King had ordered him to remain in Scotland as his lieutenant and mouthpiece. He would transmit to the Scots the Lord Paramount's will and commands. From the first it was clear that he looked upon himself as more or less the governor of Scotland.

Not content with this, Edward demanded the delivery to Bishop Beck of all Scottish royal castles, all twenty-three of them 'in order that no disaffected persons might take and make use of them against their lawful liege lady and princess'. When the Guardians refused, he sent off his new ship to Norway to collect the princess.

There was a brief upsurge of hope thereafter, in Scotland, when it became known that King Eric and his advisers had, in fact, refused to agree and had sent back the Yarmouth vessel empty, announcing that they would despatch the young princess in a Norse ship, under the care of the Bishop of Bergen, to the Norwegian territory of Orkney, *en route* for her realm of Scotland. Envoys from the Scottish Guardians and from Edward, if so he elected, should meet her there. Clearly the letter from the Scots Council had had its effect.

Bishop Beck, making angry noises, left to consult his master in the South.

Then, in September, the dire news came to stun them. The six-year-old Maid of Norway, the last of Alexander's line, had reached Orkney sick and weak after a stormy voyage and there died in the arms of the Bishop. The little body was now on its way back to Bergen for burial.

Scotland was staggered by this final catastrophe — although there were some, to be sure, who saw it as for the best. Reactions were immediate. The great assembly called for Scone for the enthronement of the young Queen on the Stone of Destiny was hurriedly changed to be a meeting of the Three Estates, for the grim but urgent purpose of deciding on the succession now and the course the nation was to take — and old Bruce made his way thither with an army behind him. The Comyns promptly began their muster; and John Baliol of Barnard Castle, now by the recent death of his mother, the Lady Devorgilla, calling himself Lord of Galloway, made a proclamation naming himself Heir of the Kingdom of Scotland — and, to demonstrate that he had his priorities aright, promptly made a grant of all the Scottish Crown lands in Northumberland and Cumberland, including Tynedale and Penrith, to Bishop Anthony Beck of Durham. As for Edward himself, he was sufficiently exercised by these developments to leave whatever he was doing and set off northwards forthwith, sending fast couriers ahead of him to summon the Guardians and magnates of Scotland to appear before him, with the various claimants to the Scots throne, at Bishop Beck's Norham Castle on the Northumbrian side of Tweed, for his decision as to who should gain the said Crown. He also ordered his armed forces to march northwards, just to emphasise realities.

All this, needless to say, had the Guardians at their wits' end, scarcely knowing which way to turn — for, after all, they were anything but a united group anyway. The avoidance of a Bruce–Comyn armed clash was of immediate urgency — but fortunately the Red Comyn, Guardian, was sufficiently influential with his own clan to order that there was to be no head-on collision with Bruce's forces for the moment; and it might well be that King Edward's decision would put *their* nominee, Baliol, on the throne anyway. So the question of meeting Edward became paramount. That they would have to see him was evident; but this of being summoned over the Border to appear before him in England, as suzerain, was anathema, even to Comyn. They therefore sent a reply to the King of England, Scotland's Principal Councillor, in more courteous terms than they would have wished, to the effect that they would be glad to meet and consult with him on the situation; but that since the discussion was to be concerned with the independent kingdom of Scotland, they held that it should rightfully take place on Scottish, not English, soil. They would be at Birgham on the Tweed to meet His Grace in due course.

The Scone assembly was postponed, with Bruce and his army somewhere south of Perth.

In all this, Thomas of course had no part to play. He was summoned to the Estates meeting, but would not have gone in any case. For that summer his own troubles had struck. In July the Countess Christian died, greatly mourned but full of years, all but bed-ridden and glad enough to go rejoin her husband. At the funeral at Dunbar, Bethoc suddenly collapsed. It was a physical rather than an emotional failure, although no doubt the distress of the graveside brought it to a head. For a while she had been a little less than her usual serene and equable self, more silent, less forthcoming, less patient; but she — and therefore her husband — had put it down to her change-of-life, for she was now in her forty-third year. But this collapse was clearly much more than that. In great abdominal pain and weakness, they took her to the castle, and bed; and a few days later back to Ercildoune.

From then on, gradually but consistently, she weakened and wilted before Thomas's anxious eyes. The pain was only intermittent, sometimes fierce but often scarcely felt; but the dwindling, failing process went on inexorably. Physicians and clerics shook their heads, prescribed simples, potions, purges, blood-lettings and the like, but to no avail.

Thomas, eaten up with apprehension and helpless love, alternated between cursing and praying. At least he was able to be with Bethoc much of the time, thankful enough now that he had not the duties and demands of two earldoms to manage, and with Tom William able to take over much of the remaining local responsibilities.

In these circumstances the dilemma and drama facing the nation took very much second place in Thomas's thoughts. He remained concerned, of course, but the sense of involvement was no longer so strong.

Edward at Norham and the Guardians at Birgham faced each other across Tweed, no more than ten miles apart, neither willing to compromise. Bruce came hurrying south, minus his army meantime, prepared to argue his claim before Edward or anyone else. Baliol joined Edward at Norham — and unit after unit of the English host arrived in the vicinity. All hovered on the brink, but climax delayed.

On the face of it, Edward made the first conciliatory gesture. He sent Bishop Beck across Tweed to assure the Guardians that, while it was not possible for the King of England to come to *them*, the Scots representatives would in no way compromise their position by crossing over into England, all rights being expressly reserved. Moreover, he would relax his condition meantime that the Guardians must recognise him as Lord Suzerain and Paramount, requiring only that the various claimants to the throne, coming before him as arbiter, should do so, this being entirely necessary if they, and all, were to accept his findings as binding.

This was a cunning move, to be sure, all but irresistible for the claimants in their need for a decision. Baliol, it appeared, accepted this suzerainty issue already — which could have the effect of putting Bruce in a very prejudiced position. There were many other claimants, of course — fourteen in all — but only two or three had any real basis for consideration, the rest going in for it merely for the pickings they might glean thereafter from the winning candidate. Most of these were English-domiciled, in fact, and the majority were fully in favour of accepting Edward's overlordship. Bruce saw himself being squeezed out; and the Comyns were already committed by their cousin Baliol's acceptance. So the claimants all would accept the King of England as Lord

Suzerain of Scotland, even if the Guardians did not. Bruce and others may have had their reservations about disclaiming such allegiance afterwards, but if so they did not broadcast it.

Graciously Edward conceded a point, having gained all that he required — he would hold the actual Court of Claims, the Great Cause as he named it, on Scots soil, at Berwick-on-Tweed. Since a town would be necessary for housing it all, and the large numbers attending, and Berwick was the only large town in the area, this was perhaps less of a concession than it might appear. The date was set for the hearings to commence, on the second day of Lammas, in August, three weeks hence. Meantime, Edward would make a brief tour through Lowland Scotland, receiving token submissions of at least some of the royal castles — as was only suitable. He would leave his army on his own side of Tweed, however.

So Edward Plantagenet entered Scotland for the second time, and now almost as a conqueror. He rode to Edinburgh — passing up Lauderdale within bowshot of Ercildoune Tower, where Thomas, for one, looked in the other direction — on to Stirling, Perth, St. Andrews and Dunfermline, before returning to Berwick by Dunbar. Some of the keepers of the royal castles made, for their part, a token refusal of handing over the keys of their strongholds until an order to do so was signed by one of the Guardians accompanying the English party, the Red Comyn and Bishop Fraser — the other two, the Steward and Bishop Wishart of Glasgow, refusing to partake — but this was as far as individuals could go. The people of Scotland as a whole looked on aghast, bewildered, betrayed.

On the second day of August 1291 the so-called Great Cause was convened at Berwick Castle towering above the Tweed estuary and crowded harbour. Edward was at pains, now, to put on a splendid show, since all built up the image of his own power and majesty. There were no fewer than one hundred and four auditors appointed, allegedly to assist the Supreme Arbiter to a right decision; forty each nominated by Bruce and Baliol — who would, to be sure, cancel each other

415

out; and twenty-four of Edward's own English Council, twelve lords temporal and twelve spiritual, in theory there to ensure that the other twelve claimants got fair play. At the opening ceremony, of course, all the Competitors had to take a public oath of fealty to the King of England. Their agreement to abide by his eventual decision was taken for granted.

There was no least hurry, for this was as good as a campaign, and all must be done with almost military precision. Although only four of the candidates' pretensions were to be taken seriously, the other ten's claims, submissions and genealogies were also heard in full and at great length. Edward himself, of course, was not present throughout, filling in the time with hunting, hawking and visiting sites of strategic importance in the Border area — but he heard all the summaries.

As day succeeded day, the competition was whittled down to the four main contenders, Baliol, Bruce, Hastings of Abergavenny and Count Florence the Fifth of Holland; the first three descending from daughters of Earl David of Huntingdon, the fourth from Ada, a sister of the same David. This automatically would have relegated the Hollander to fourth place had he not claimed a special factor. He declared that, in return for a grant of the Garioch lordship in Aberdeenshire, the aforesaid Earl David had resigned to the said sister Ada all claims for himself and his heirs to the throne of Scotland, for all time; and that there was documentary proof of this — but unfortunately he had not been able to lay hands on the original papers, only copies. Whether or not, in fact, Edward was impressed by this story — which most others pooh-poohed — he found it convenient excuse to adjourn the proceedings. Inevitably there were pressing calls developing for the King's presence elsewhere in his farflung dominions, and the Crusade question was coming to a head. So Count Florence was given ten months, no less, to find his papers, Edward departed, taking his army, and Scotland's monarchial situation was left in limbo until Edward's return next June.

Few had any doubts, however, as to what the outcome

would be. Every indication was, despite this interlude, that the King would declare in favour of John Baliol. So generally was this accepted that even old Bruce, now eighty, came to the conclusion that he personally was unlikely ever to sit on the Scots throne, thanks to Edward; he therefore executed a transfer of his claim to his son Robert, acting Earl of Carrick, and thereafter to his grandson, Robert, true Earl of Carrick, all his supporters and auditors concurring. Few failed to see this as anything less than an admission that they were almost certainly going to have an Englishman to reign over them, even if it was not Edward himself, only his puppet. Perhaps, however, the most ominous feature of all to arise out of this first stage of the Great Cause, for thinking men, was the manner in which the Scots magnates, from the Guardians down, councillors, prelates and nobility, had become conditioned to accept Edward's will as supreme, his word as law — and none more notably than Patrick, Earl of Dunbar and March. To all intents and purposes the King of England was already ruling Scotland. Alexander might well have turned in his Dunfermline grave, and his neighbouring royal corpses with him.

That winter came to lie heavily on the land. On Thomas Learmonth, to be sure, more heavily than on most, with private anxiety overlaying national as he watched Bethoc's state deteriorate.

*   *   *

The winter passed, even for Bethoc, although she was only a pale shadow of her former self when spring came. Thomas was at least slightly enheartened that she had got that behind her and could look hopefully to the more clement weather to come to her aid. The lengthening days and strengthening sun did indeed bring some rise in her spirits. Nevertheless Thomas was surprised, not to say disquieted, when, one fine morning in May, she besought him to take her to the Eildon Hills.

"Lord, lass — the Eildons!" he exclaimed. "You cannot mean that, my dear?"

"I do, Thomas — I do. With all my heart. It is May and

the cuckoos will be calling. As I love to hear. *Our* place. It will be the last time. Take me, Thomas."

He bit his lip, wordless.

"It will be good, good," she insisted. "We shall sit under our tree. And plight our troth again, for . . . hereafter. As we did twenty-seven years ago. When we knew so little, yet loved so much. Now we know so much — but love still more! Although I had not thought that possible. It will be good, Thomas dear. Take me."

"But, lass, lass! You are not sufficiently strong. How can you ride to the Eildons? You have ridden no distance for many months . . ."

"It is none so far — but five miles. You shall take me, bear me up. I shall do very well, in your arms, before you on your beast. We shall ride slowly. If I greatly tire, we shall turn back. But I *will* not — that I know, Thomas."

There was no dissuading her — and the man did not truly wish to do so. Tom William would have gone with them, but Bethoc gently told him no, that this was to be a day for his father and herself only.

So, the next morning, being bright, they set out, Bethoc wrapped in a travelling-cloak, sitting across Thomas's thighs, alean against his chest. He rode his oldest, staidest bay mare and kept her to a steady walk, no more. So that it took them an hour-and-a-half to reach the skirts of the Eildons, at Newstead's Roman ruins — but, after all, there was no least hurry. Bethoc made no complaints.

Slowly, heedfully, they rode up over the foothill slopes, amongst the golden-flowering whins and broom, to their hawthorn-tree, its blossom not yet out. Bethoc gripped his wrist as the unfailing, measured calling of the cuckoos came to them from near and far. Carefully lifting her down from the saddle, he held her close.

"So long ago," he said. "And yet . . ."

"And yet, but as yesterday. What is time, Thomas? Tell me."

"Time? Time, I think, is experience, Beth," he said, after a long moment. "Little to do with hours and days, with months and years. We can experience what is almost infinity in mere seconds, in some sudden happening or awareness. Or years can pass with scarce a notable memory to mark them. Yet a weariness can seem an eternity; and joy, the joy which will endure and measure true time, can pass like the flash of a kingfisher's wing, vivid, vital, never to be lost or forgotten. No, time has little to do with sundials, hour-glasses and clocks, lass. Why do you ask?"

"Because . . . because here we are, back where we started, Thomas. Almost. You and I beneath this tree. Listening to the same sounds. Almost as though there had been no interval. Loving only the more. If twenty-seven years can pass so, what does it mean? What of the next twenty-seven? I will not be here — not in this poor body. *You* may. But our love, the enduring part of us, what we have nurtured together between us — will it be here? With the cuckoos and this wind-blown thorn? You, Thomas, with whom past and present and future are more one than with most of us — tell me."

"I am no wiser than you, my dear. Less so, I often think. My dreams and visions and jingles are flashes, not forethought nor wisdom nor knowledge — Auld Michael is right in that. But I do believe that love is eternal — true love, not passion or desire or mere fondness. It comes direct from God, for true love is against all man's lower nature, is part of God, and is therefore indestructible, eternal. It has nothing to do with time. Nor, nor death. Order and beauty are of a like creation. But because love must be of the person, the persons of men and women and of God, it is the very crown of God's handiwork. So — our love, that is so much greater than ourselves, will be alive twenty-seven years hence, two hundred years hence, on, on. And why not here, where first it blossomed into flower? Elsewhere too, to be sure — but here, yes."

She nodded, satisfied, and he spread the cloak for her to sit.

For long, hand-in-hand, they listened wordless to the haunting, soothing echo of the cuckoos, hearts full. When at last she spoke, Bethoc was back to the subject of time, which seemed to be much on her mind.

"How long will I have to wait for you, Thomas?" she asked suddenly, factually.

He swallowed. "Wait . . .? You mean . . .? My dear — do not speak so."

"Why not, Thomas? In our life together we have never deceived each other. Why do so now? I shall not live much longer. I know that — as I think do you. That is why we are here. On Eildonside, surely, is an excellent place to speak of the future, is it not? These strange hills which the ancient ones made their own, where the other world is close — aye, and where *you* once rode off with the Queen of Elfland for seven years! So — I will have to wait for you . . . yonder. I think that I dread the waiting rather than the dying."

He shook his head, with difficulty finding words. "What am I to say, lass? If time is as we believe, in truth immaterial, with eternity the reality, then . . . then yonder there will be no time to count, no weary waiting. This measuring of time is an invention of man, not a dimension of God, I say. Therefore beyond the grave, where experience and true awareness and *being* will be all, man's dull and heavy-footed time will be left behind. It will not be you, but *me* left behind, my love, who will have the weary waiting."

"Poor Thomas! Dear Thomas! Then . . . I am sorry. Will I be able to help you in your waiting, think you?"

"That I cannot tell. But I think that the knowledge that you will meantime be happy, fulfilled, and loving me still, not waiting but *preparing* for me — that will help me await my time."

"You have thought much on this, my dear?"

"Yes. Or not so much thought as left my mind open."

"Not to visions or foretellings?"

"No. Those I do not trust, however many may have come to pass, after a fashion. This is different. This I believe."

"As do I. And am glad . . ."

Presently, well aware of her flagging strength, she proposed that they should be on their way home — but not in any sad nor depressed, final fashion. Bethoc's serenity had come back.

Weary, aching, limp as she was when at length he carried her up the turnpike stair to their bedchamber at Ercildoune, there was the old gleam in her eye. She even laughed a little as he undressed her shrunken person.

Bethoc died only ten days later, unafraid, scarcely content to go, but assured. Thomas, grieving, desolate, accepted that the ride to Eildon and back might well have expedited her passing, by weeks perhaps — but could not find it in his heart to regret it. Tom William was more critical.

25

Thomas Learmonth stood in front of the high table in the great hall of Ercildoune Castle like a prisoner before a judge; indeed the Earl Pate *was* justiciar now, Justiciar of Lothian, appointed by the new King John Baliol; even if Thomas was no prisoner. Pate lounged at the other side of the table, drinking-horn in hand, amongst his friends and chief vassals. Drink-taken, he was not actually drunk; in fact he drank less than his father had done, but did not hold his liquor well.

"I did not ask for excuses, Learmonth," he declared loudly, his words slurring a little. "I asked by what right you think to interfere in the affairs of my carldoms, now that you are no longer steward?"

"No right — but no interference, my lord," Thomas answered briefly.

"Do not use that tone to me, sirrah! I'd remind you that my foolish sister, whom you abducted and seduced, is now dead. I, and mine, owe you nothing, nothing! You would be wise to remember it, I say!"

Inclining his head slightly, the other did not speak.

"Well, man? Your answer? To what I asked. This of Lammermuir. How dared you to interfere?"

"I said no interference, my lord. These farmers, graziers, your good tenants, who run sheep on Lammermuir, they came to see me. As they had every right to do, since I it was who, with your father's support, first led them to run the sheep there . . ."

"You need not tell us that, fool!" he was interrupted. "We all know well that it was you who ruined the best hunting-chase south of the Scotwater! Covered it with plaguey, stinking sheep, fouling the ground, driving the deer away."

"To your very great profit, my lord."

"Profit! I am not a chapman, Learmonth! Some merchanting huckster with his nose in his purse! Lammermuir deserves better than sheep and graziers. And will have it, by God! Every sheep is to go — you hear? I have commanded it. Yet you, you upstart, dismissed, told them otherwise. Told them to keep their sheep. Even how to better their accursed flocks . . ."

"They sought my counsel — and I gave it. How to make up for the land which you were taking from them. How to reclaim waste land, drain and dyke bogland over which you could never hunt. Land along the shore, where the seaweed gives fair feeding — as they do north of the Mounth. Rent the commonty lands of the burgh of Dunbar. Seek new pastures, rather than kill their flocks . . ."

"But on *my* land, man — all my land! And against my commands."

"You had not commanded that they should not do this. And it is still to your profit, my lord. You but gain in the land. Why complain?"

"Curse you, Thomas Learmonth — how dare you speak to me so! You are still my vassal — have you forgot? I hold you in the palm of this my hand!" The hand which did not hold the drinking-horn gripped tight into a shaken clenched fist, entirely eloquent as to what its owner would like to do. "You, and all, do as I say on my lands — and respectfully. You hear? My father you made fool of — but not me! You will keep your insolent tongue between your teeth in my presence! You will have no dealings with my tenants and servants. You will keep away from my brothers and sisters — you hear me?" Pate's voice rose, almost cracked in his curious, all but hysterical and self-feeding rage — to the considerable embarrassment of most of his companions,

422

Swinton of that Ilk, Gelis's husband, the Gordon brothers, Peter Haig of Bemersyde, Pepdie of Dunglass, Landals of that Ilk, even Sir Reginald le Chien, visiting, and now a great man in the realm also, for supporting Baliol, Justiciar of Moray and hoping even for its earldom now that Gillespic had died. All these, and others, looked away, at their wine, at the stone-vaulted ceiling, but not at their host nor his lame brother-in-law.

"I hear, yes," Thomas said levelly, coldly. "And where you have the right to command me, I will obey. Where you have no right, my lord, I will follow my own judgment. As to your brothers and sisters, my son's uncles and aunts, they are all my good friends — as once you were. I shall see them so long as they are pleased to see me . . ."

"Devil roast you — we shall see about that!" And the drinking-horn came flying through the air at Thomas. Fortunately Pate's aim was erratic, although the target was splattered by some of the spilling wine. "Boast you for the last time, wretch! I will silence your insolent tongue. I . . . I . . ." Half-rising from his seat, shaking in his rage, Pate all but choked.

Thomas spread hands helplessly, inclined his head towards the others, and turning, limped from the hall.

As he rode homewards down the Ercildoune Water to Leader, once his ire had abated somewhat, he cudgelled his wits to think why Pate should hate him so. It was strange, almost unaccountable. It certainly could not all stem from his being made to feel foolish over that deceit at Eildonside so long ago, at the elopement. None of the others had held it against him unduly. And it was not as though Pate had been so notably fond of his eldest sister, and so especially resented her unsuitable marriage. Perhaps he had always felt resentment at Thomas's privileged position in the Dunbar household? Almost certainly he had been grievously offended by his knighthood, when he himself had had to wait so long for his own. But none of this was sufficient to account for so intense a hostility. Could it be something to do with the visions and soothsaying? A fear, a revulsion to that? Some deep, almost uncontrollable reaction in a character of hot temper, jealousies and overweening pride?

Whatever it was, clearly it was something that he, Thomas, would have to take into consideration now, very seriously. Bethoc's death had removed any last constraints. And now Pate was riding high, close to the new King — and what was more important still, adhering tenaciously to Edward Plantagenet. Controlling the east and mid Border region as he did, he had his importance for Edward. His ancestor, the first Earl Cospatrick of Dunbar, had previously been Earl of Northumbria — and Pate, in his cups, had indicated more than once that he would like to recover that great and now English earldom. With Edward these days to all intents and purposes ruling Scotland through his weak puppet, John, whom he had so carefully chosen in the Great Cause, and with Englishmen flooding into high positions in the northern kingdom, the divisions between the two countries were being daily eroded. It was not inconceivable that the earl who controlled so much of the Scottish march might conveniently be given at least some part of neighbouring Northumberland to control also, in Edward's favour. So, as well as being Earl of Dunbar and March, Justiciary of Lothian and governor or warden of the marches, Pate might well become one of the most powerful men in two kingdoms, his royal blood nowise hindering. Certainly a bad man for a humble knight to have as enemy.

Thomas had got thus far when such thoughts were rudely driven from his mind. Two-thirds of the way down between castle and River Leader, the Ercildoune Water, constricted by a spur of the White Hill, cut through a brief and narrow defile, plunging over a series of shelves in rapids and small cataracts. The track wound down beside these between steep banks — and here it was that debatings abruptly ended. In the half-dark of the March evening, four men materialised out of the shadows, to launch themselves upon the horseman, two leaping down on him from the bank, one grabbing his beast's head, one grasping at his leg to pull him out of the saddle.

Totally unwarned, Thomas could do nothing to save himself. His mount rearing, two bodies landing heavily on top of him, his lame leg wrenched, he crashed to the ground. All but stunned by the fall, he was aware of blows rained on him, kicks, and then the gleam of a dirk's steel. He felt a burning, stouning agony in his chest, saw a red flood welling up before his eyes to drown him — then oblivion.

*   *   *

Tom William found his father in the early hours of the morning, after his horse had returned riderless to Ercildoune Tower, and he went searching with a torch on the road to the castle. Thomas was lying in the burn below the rapids, half out of the water, upper parts sprawled over a flat rock.

At first, the younger man thought him to be dead, so limp and cold was he. But, hoisting the soaking body, with difficulty, over the back of his own beast, Tom William heard his father groan. Thankfully he hastened home with his burden, bewildered. Thomas was a superb horseman; and he was no drunkard, to fall off his mount. It was not until, removing the sodden clothing to put him into his bed, with heated stones from the wood-ash of the hall fire, that he discovered the two stab-wounds in his father's chest, near but not at the heart.

It was some hours before Thomas recovered consciousness, very weak through loss of blood, in extreme pain and aching all over. But his mind was clear enough, after the first moments; and haltingly but firmly he stilled his son's anxious demands and queries.

"Wait!" he panted. "Wait you. This is . . . a close matter. We, we must go . . . warily. No, no — no use to . . . inform the Earl. Worse than useless. His doing! Yes — *his* men. Attacked me. I recognised . . . Dod Home, his chief falconer. And another . . . of his grooms. Four of them. I was to die. They would think me dead. Threw me . . . into the river. No use . . . in telling Pate!"

"God save us! You cannot mean it? You, you mistake, surely? He does not love us — but not that, not that!"

"Yes, that. We quarrelled. Or . . . he did. Cursed me . . . before all. Swore he would silence me. When he discovers . . . that I am not dead . . .!"

"Lord — then he shall pay for this, earl or no earl! By all

425

that is holy, he will! Has he run mad . . .?"

"Perhaps — after a fashion. But he has all the power. Now. Earl, Justiciar . . . and with the new King's ear. We cannot fight Pate. Not now. As we are."

"What, then? Will he, will he strike again, think you?"

"Strange if he does not. When he learns. I will have to think. Think what is to be done. But . . . not now. Later. My head . . . Meanwhile — no word of this. Outside this house . . ."

Thomas had ample time to think, as he lay there in slow recovery. He had time to review his life, to consider every aspect of his present situation, to decide what was important that remained to him, what he still sought from living as he waited to rejoin Bethoc. He was nearing his mid-fifties, and had no especial ambitions left to him, save to write more poetry, no achievements to which he should look forward. Almost certainly the high tide of his life was past — and he would not have it otherwise. Moreover, a man did not have to be a soothsayer to foresee that desperate times lay ahead for Scotland. John Baliol was making a weak and foolish monarch — as all could have foretold, including the man who chose him; and already, within only a few months of his coronation, there was widespread unrest, the first stirrings of revolt even, especially in the South-West, the Bruce country — which undoubtedly was all that Edward of England required as excuse to intervene and take over personal rule, with his minions already in all key positions and occupying the royal castles. Edward was, indeed, all but deliberately provoking revolt, revolt on all sides. He was appointing sheriffs and magistrates of his own in Scotland, directly contrary to the terms of the Treaty of Birgham, his officers bringing Scots before these. He was encouraging Scots nobles, with pleas, to come direct to him, through Bishop Beck, ignoring Baliol. He had even summoned that hapless individual to Westminster, to appear before him in court for having failed to pay a wine-bill of the late Alexander's to one of Edward's Gascony vassals. Eruption could not long be delayed. And then the mailed fist would smash down indeed, the Plantagenet in his element. And there was little doubt which side the Earl of Dunbar and March would choose to support.

So, one day, Thomas took paper and quill and ink-horn, to write at some length, not poetry or rhymes this time. When he had finished he called Tom William.

"Two matters, lad," he said. "One a letter, one a charter. The letter is to Prior Nicholas, Minister of Faill Monastery, in the sheriffdom of Ayr. Get one of the men to ride with it. And to bring back an answer. The charter is of this tower and lands — the only property of which I have any right to give charter, since your mother's lands of Huntshaw are now all yours. Ercildoune is hereby conveyed to yourself, every stick and stone of it. We shall find someone who can sign his name to witness it . . ."

"But — but, Father! What is this? What are you at?"

"It is simple enough, Tom. I am bowing to fate, that is all. Leaving here. I am going to join Holy Church . . . after a fashion! Going to my friend Nicholas at Faill — if he will have me. He who married us. To end my days in that good place . . ."

"Faill! A monastery! You . . . you, turn monk! Save us — not that . . .!"

"Scarce a monk, no. But a brother of sorts, perhaps. A lay-brother. They have wide lands at Faill — orchards, corn-rigs, sheep and cattle, as have most religious houses. There is much that I could contribute there. Use my skills. And in good company. And I have my poetry. I will be safe from Pate, your uncle. And . . . and from much else, I fear!"

Astonished, the young man stared at him. "You *mean* this? You really intend to go? You, Sir Thomas Learmonth, Knight . . .!"

"I do. I have made up my mind. It is for the best, lad. Better men than I am have done the like, lords, kings even. Never fear, it will be no hurt or trial for me. At Faill, as I know, they do themselves very well. It is only the leaving you that concerns me. But then, you too, I think, should go away for a while. From Pate's spleen. There are troubles coming, heavy troubles — none can doubt it. And this Borders area will be at the centre of it. You would be drawn in — nothing more sure. As a vassal of Dunbar, yet with Bruce blood and sympathies. There will be war, not honest battle against a foreign foe but brother against brother, the nation torn in pieces. So I urge that you go, lad. On your travels. Before the evil catches you up. You are a young man, only twenty-five years. With no ties, once I am safely at Faill. Your lands here will not run away. And there is some little siller for you. And you can come and see me now and again, if you will. Is it not best, Tom?"

Wordless, the other looked at his father and wagged his head.

Thomas had his way. In due course their man returned from Ayrshire with Prior Nicholas's reply. He would be delighted to welcome his old friend to his establishment, as resident, for so long as he cared to stay. Indeed nothing would make him more happy. He must come whenever he was ready.

He was ready soon enough, in that he was fit enough to travel if he rode quietly, Tom William accompanying him; and such few belongings as he felt were essential carried on a pack-horse. But it was not quite so simple as that. Just to pack up and leave openly, riding westwards, would not do. Whether Pate and his minions knew that Thomas had survived he could not tell — although it was probable that they did, by now. So long as he remained in Ercildoune Tower he was safe enough, for any further murderous attack would again be surreptitious; even Pate would not make open assault on a fortified tower-house of a law-abiding and well-known vassal. But once observed, on the long road to Faill . . .? Secrecy was essential, not only for the journey. The last thing Thomas would wish was to bring down his powerful enemy's wrath on Nicholas and the monastery. So it must not be known whither he was bound. The departure, therefore, must be secret, by night — as secret as the original journey to Faill. And it would be best if the local folk could be discouraged from trying to find out, in due course, where True Thomas had finally gone.

It was this secrecy similarity with that other time, which set Thomas's mind working along a parallel line. Myth, his

428

unchancy reputation, could surely aid him? He had disappeared before for seven years; another disappearance would probably be accepted without too much question, especially if he could contrive something strange and dramatic to presage it — or better, to follow once he was safely gone. Some sign . . .

In fact he had to contrive nothing; it was all done for him. There was the usual ale-house in the castleton village, where sorrows could be drowned and news and views embroidered. A few days after the message arrived from Faill, Tom William brought back a ridiculous story. Two of the ale-house regulars had been returning home in the dusk of the previous evening, undoubtedly in elevated state, when they claimed to have beheld an extraordinary sight, a stag and hind, no less, parading down the street between the cot-houses, bold and unafraid, the two visionaries less so. Admittedly there was forest-land nearby, but never before had such a thing been seen or reported. Sober folk, needless to say, ridiculed the whole thing, despite picturesque details submitted by the privileged pair — who had apparently made the rest of their way home more hurriedly than usual. Thomas, however, was far from ridicule. This would serve very well — a talking-point. He would be off to Faill that very night; and afterwards Tom William could let it be known that the hart and hind had in fact come for him, sent by his friend the Queen of Elfland to spirit him back to the Land of Faerie, as some had predicted! It would serve — and the common folk thereafter would not ask where Thomas had gone; as well as anything he could devise.

And so, that April night, with the darkening, Thomas Learmonth said goodbye to Ercildoune. Stiffly, carefully mounting his staid mare, the same which had carried the double burden to Eildonside eleven months earlier, he looked back from the saddle at his little stone tower.

"Aye," he sighed, heavily now. "Farewell!" He nodded, and altered his tone of voice:

> *The hare shall kittle on my hearth-stane,*
> *Ere there will be a Laird Learmonth again!*

Tom William eyed him questioningly. "I thought that *I* was to be Laird Learmonth now?"

"Laird, yes — but not of Ercildoune, lad. Of Huntshaw and other places, no doubt. But not, I think, of Ercildoune. We all have our day — and its days are done. But — enough of this. A new start. Come, you . . ."

They rode down to the Leader ford, to splash across and head westwards into the night, two mounted men and a pack-horse.

Postscript

Thomas was right in his last prophecy, at least. We read that in 1294, the following year, Thomas, son and heir of Thomas Rymour of Ercildoun, made over the lands of that place to the Trinitarian house of Soltra or Soutra, at the head of Lauderdale, of the same Order as Faill — no doubt for suitable recompense. Thereafter history reports no more of him. His father, however, we do read of still. In 1297, according to Blind Harry, quoting John Blair, Wallace's colleague and chaplain,

> *Thomas Rhymer into the Fail was then,*
> *With the Minister, which was a worthy man . . .*

and there he was instrumental in aiding the Westland hero, son of Sir Malcolm Wallace of Elderslie, wounded and in hiding from the English, in the early stages of his leadership in the Wars of Independence — whose mighty task the young Robert Bruce, Earl of Carrick, was to take up and at length bring to fruition. Thomas's later poetical works, notably that of *The Prophesy* and *The Eildon Tree*, were presumably written at Faill; but none ever achieved the eminence of *Sir Tristrem*. Of his predictions, many were fulfilled in one way or another, some belatedly — it took until 1771, for instance, for Kelso Abbey's roof to fall in, and on a godly and indeed Reformed congregation which was then using the place as parish church; and some are not yet fulfilled — although it must be remembered that many rhymes and foretellings were concocted by later propagandists to help their various causes and issued under the Rhymer's name to give them added authority. Even James the Sixth, it is alleged, was not beyond such activity. But then, he it was, after all, who was the son of a French wife who should rule all Britain to the sea, of Bruce's blood in the ninth degree.

As for other characters, Sir Reginald le Chien died the same year as Thomas retired, and although his two sons had their own prominence thereafter, as Lord of Duffus and Bishop of Aberdeen, the house of le Chien, or Cheyne, died away in remarkable obscurity, and Inverugie by the sea lairdless indeed its lands became, no trace of le Chien's castle now being visible although a later 15th- and 16th-century stronghold was established about a mile inland by the Keiths. As for Sir Michael Scott the Wizard, it is recorded that, about the same time, travelling in Italy, in church he was injudicious enough to respectfully raise his steel hat at the Elevation of the Host, whereupon a small stone fell from the roof on to his head and killed him. His body is said to have been brought back to Scotland for burial in Melrose Abbey.

Those who know anything of detail about the terrible wars in which, from 1296 to 1314 and Bannockburn, Scotland fought for her freedom from Plantagenet domination, will be aware of the treacherous and contorted part played therein by Patrick, 8th Earl of Dunbar and March, Black Pate. Readers who would wish to know more of that desperate struggle and what happened to King Edward, Hammer of the Scots, his puppet, John Baliol, and other principal actors in that drama, need only read the history-books — or the present writer's novels on Robert the Bruce and William Wallace.